The Man Who Saved Henry Morgan

A NOVEL

Robert Hough

ANANSI

This edition published in 2015 by
House of Anansi Press Inc.
110 Spadina Avenue, Suite 801
Toronto, ON, M5V 2K4
Tel. 416-363-4343
Fax 416-363-1017
www.houseofanansi.com

Distributed in Canada by
HarperCollins Canada Ltd.
1995 Markham Road
Scarborough, ON, M1B 5M8
Toll free tel. 1-800-387-0117

House of Anansi Press is committed to protecting our natural environment. As part of our efforts, the interior of this book is printed on paper that contains 100% post-consumer recycled fibres, is acid-free, and is processed chlorine-free.

19 18 17 16 15   1 2 3 4 5

Library and Archives Canada Cataloguing in Publication

Hough, Robert, 1963-, author
The man who saved Henry Morgan / Robert Hough.

Issued in print and electronic formats.
ISBN 978-1-77089-945-2 (pbk.).—ISBN 978-1-77089-946-9 (html)

1. Morgan, Henry, 1635?-1688—Fiction. I. Title.

PS8565.O7683M36 2015   C813'.6   C2014-907745-9
                                         C2014-907746-7

Book design: Alysia Shewchuk

Canada Council   Conseil des Arts
for the Arts   du Canada

ONTARIO ARTS COUNCIL
CONSEIL DES ARTS DE L'ONTARIO
an Ontario government agency
un organisme du gouvernement de l'Ontario

We acknowledge for their financial support of our publishing program the Canada Council for the Arts, the Ontario Arts Council, and the Government of Canada through the Canada Book Fund.

Printed and bound in Canada

MIX
Paper from
responsible sources
FSC
www.fsc.org   FSC® C004071

As always:
Suzie, Sally, Ella

The following is a work of fiction.

ONE

THE JUDGE WAS a drunk bastard, all right—swaying in his tall-backed chair, that gin-rosin smell wafting off him, his nose a mound of headcheese run through with purple thread. I wasn't surprised. The world was filled with people who couldn't bear to be in their own company, and it made no difference if you were rich or poor, loved or loathed. Sometimes, there was only one thing for it.

"I didn't do it!" I pleaded. "It was an honest game, Your Honour, no foolery or nothing, just a friendly match between men! I'm an upstanding sort, see..."

"I see nothing of the kind, Mr. Wand. As far as I can tell, you're as slick as an oiled weasel, and you've a choice to make. A dozen years in Newgate or deportation to the Isle of Jamaica. The choice is yours. You've ten seconds before I decide for you."

Ten seconds? I didn't need *three* seconds. No one survived twelve years in Newgate, not unless you belonged to someone, and even that was no protection against typhoid or madness. On the other hand, Jamaica's best-known town, a devil's warren called Port Royal, had a reputation I'd heard about in seamy rat-run taverns, and from the sounds of it I'd fit right in. There was another sorry fact to consider: my pitted face was known by constabulary types all over England, which was making it harder and harder to ply my ignoble trade.

"Jamaica," I said.

He slammed his gavel and was on to the next.

I was twenty years of age, and up for pretty much anything.

AFTER A SECOND night of jailing, I was shuffled down Dock Street with fifteen other poor blighters who'd taken the same deal as me. It was a chilly day, the sky a grey tarp. As always, it was raining, the sort of light spittle you felt more than saw. We were in leg irons, and told to not talk or stop or make sudden movements. As we trudged toward the Thames, people came out of their houses to jeer, lob pieces of fruit gone mouldy, and generally act like spiteful bastards.

After an eon, we reached an old wooden ship. The prisoners who could read started laughing—when they told us the boat was named the *Charity,* the rest of us chuckled grimly as well. Our legs irons came off and they marched us to a darkened hold with the smell of damp rugs. They fastened our ankles again, this time to a row of rusting clamps fit to the bottom of the hull, our choices sitting or lying flat or propping ourselves on our elbows. Either way it hurt like a bugger, for I'd had a fair roughing-up during my arrest and I ached no matter how or where I held myself.

At the far end of the hull was a mound of crates, destined for the New World.

The seas were high. We bounced about like kittens on hot coals. Seeing as we were city boys, without sea legs of any kind, our bums ran and our stomachs did rollovers and our lips turned cracked and flaky. I was next to last, the prisoner at the very end a red-haired giant whose ankles were so thick they barely fit in the shackles. His beard looked like a bushel of rusty wool, minus the bushel, of course.

Once a day, the hatch opened. We all moaned and shaded our eyes even though we were well pleased: it was our daily feed, a bowl of stiffened porridge with bread and warm water. On our third day at sea, as I lifted a mouthful to my lips, I noticed my spoon was wriggling. I dropped it and saw my rations were run through with some sort of bug, a repulsive beetle-like thing but with more legs and two sets of waving, oily antennae.

"Yours too?" said the big man beside me.

I gestured up with my chin. "It's a game they're playing."

Not one of us complained, for there's food gone off and there's food gone off for a reason, and we all knew this was our jailers' way of showing what they'd do if we failed to mind ourselves.

If I was in their shoes, I'd have probably done the same.

DURING THE DAY, shards of sunlight snuck through gaps in the hull, letting in just enough off-pink light you could eye the faces around you. At sundown this seeped away, like the light of a dying candle, and the only thing you could see were the squiggles and streaks a mind throws on the back of the eyelids.

"Eight days we been," someone said.

"Seven," said another.

"Bloody eight," said a third, and before you knew it, an argument broke out. Most thought eight and some thought seven and one or two put it at nine. The discussion fizzled when a mangled bully-for-hire smashed his head three times against the hull. "Shut yer gobs!" he yelled. "We'll have weevil stew if you keep up this bollocks!"

He was right. The guesswork stopped and this was a relief. As I learned on that voyage, time's a right twat, put on earth to make you question what you have and how you got it and whether any of it was worth it. Take time away and that awful wishing-for-things goes with it. My stomach righted itself, and I quit yearning for loosened feet. I stopped longing for whatever food might be in the crates piled at the far end of the hold, and I stopped wishing they'd give us more fresh water (for what good would it do, really?). I even stopped thinking about London and soot and all the mushroom-coated places I'd called home; if I missed any of it, I missed it the way you miss something you've known your whole life yet always resented, like a sixth toe or a forehead boil.

And then the hatch opened for good. Light flooded the hold, as well as time and place and hope and want and need. We groaned, not just because our eyes smarted but because life was rushing back hard. We covered our faces. Had our legs been free, we'd have scurried like rats to shadowy corners. Instead, we listened to pairs of boots trundle below deck. A long iron tube ran through our leg clamps, and when I heard it slide against metal I knew we were being freed. I opened my eyes to a squint. A trio of jailers stood above us. "Right," boomed one of them. "All hands on deck. The captain'll have a word, he will!"

My trousers drooped from my hip bones. Feeling dizzy and weak, I clambered up the strutted plank to the deck. As I moved, I was careful I didn't tumble into the man behind me, seeing as he didn't look like the type who'd put up with much. My skin felt warmed, sunlight being a thing you can step into, like water or mud.

Soon, we stood on the gently rocking deck, blinking like spastics. My eyes slowly bore the light and I took my first good look at Port Royal. From what I'd heard, the town sat on a chunk of land connected to the rest of Jamaica by a long causeway. Yet I couldn't see much more than a wall of grey warehouses, capped at either end by low stone forts. The rest of Port Royal must've been tucked in behind, and I reckoned this was where all the debauchery occurred.

A door near the ship's forecastle opened and the captain emerged; he wore a red jerkin, a three-point hat, and, slung across his chest, a cutlass fierce enough to quarter a hog. He walked up and down in front of us, neither smiling nor frowning, his high leather boots smacking the deck. As he passed, he gave each and every one of us a good long once-over, as if trying to decide which of us would make something of ourselves and which of us would squander the second chance granted by His Majesty the Bloody King.

"Gentlemen," he announced. "I'll not mince words. Your lives were not purposeful, nor given to productivity, in the Old World. See that you turn over a new leaf in Port Royal. For those of you without lodging, there's a camping settlement to the west of the town called Turtle Crawles. As soon as you've helped off-load this ship, you will be free to go. Good day to you."

He marched toward the same door he'd come out of two minutes earlier. The rest of us stood looking at one another, heads swivelling and shoulders shrugging, until a stocky fellow with a pong about him bellowed, "Well, you heard the captain! Those crates inn't gonna move themselves!"

Once more we went into that cursed hold. A little queue formed, and when my turn came, I bent over and picked up a small wooden box marked with letters I couldn't read. It was heavy as a boulder, and by the time I'd carried it up, I was breathing hard.

Thick-necked stevedores were waiting in rowboats, hands raised. I passed my crate off and went below and then I went below a third time. When the *Charity* was empty, we all climbed into the smaller boats, finding kneeling space amidst the crates. They dropped us on land before heading toward a warehouse along the way. We all stood around, saying little, hair whipping, waves soaking our boots. Soon, little groups of two or three began drifting away.

The red-haired man was standing next to me. He turned and fixed his narrowed eyes on mine. Blue as berries, they were.

"What you thinkin'?"

"Dunno," I lied. "You?"

His beard looked bright orange in the full sun. Already, his nose was sprouting freckles. "I reckon it'll be this Turtle Crawles for me."

I looked about, face all creasy, like I was having a ponder when I knew damn well what I was going to do. "Think

I'll have a wander into town," I said. "Think I'll see what's what and why."

"Good luck," he said, at which point he walked away.

Meanwhile, I got to bloody work.

Two

I WALKED EAST ALONG the front of the warehouses, practically rubbing my hands together I was so excited. My nose wrinkled at the smell of fish and salt and dried kelp, which had washed up in great tangled thickets. I'd never been on a beach before, and was surprised to find the sand wasn't so much like powder as finely ground pink shells. At the last storehouse I had a look around the corner and spied what was obviously the Port Royal jail, for above it was a gibbet, its noose rotating lazily in the air. I had a smirk, thinking the forces keeping a man down are always the same, no matter who you are or where you are or how far you've bloody travelled.

Just beyond that was the causeway leading to the rest of Jamaica; it was long and thin and sided with mounds of rock. On either side of the causeway, speckled fish about the size of a man's sock kept leaping in and out of the water, making little splashes that caught both the eyes and the ears. They were mostly silver, with flashes of yellow and green along the sides.

I found a little cove protected on each side by black coral rock. Here I stripped off my shirt, boots, breeches, and skivvies. Then I dove in, letting weeks of grime and sweat and general awfulness wash off my body. As much as I was able, I gave my clothes a wash as well, after which I wrung them out and draped them on sun-absorbing rocks. Then there was nothing for it but sitting stark naked and waiting, the sun beating down hot, the funny pink sand making a thousand pinprick impressions on my backside. When my clothes were dry—it didn't take long—I dressed and felt human. I walked back along the beach until I reached the opposite end, where a bleached lane pointed to the heart of the town. The streets were sided by two- and three-storey wood houses, the cobblestone covered with crunchy pink sand blown up from the beach.

That's when I stopped and noticed something troubling.

The town was quiet. I could hear dogs barking and the odd goat bleating, but that was it, none of the bustle and wantonness I'd been counting on. All my hope turned to unease, like it does when you figure out you've been lied to. I passed a grog shop, only to find it padlocked and dark. A few steps later was a tavern; it too was dark all over, as was the second and the third, each one looking as if the owners had left in a fright. This was nothing short of a catastrophe, for in my line of work I needed a lively pub with a certain type of clientele to get things done. I took to pounding my fists on locked doors and hollering, just in case anyone was about. At one rickety establishment, a jalousie swung open above me and out leaned an ancient woman with wrinkles so deep it looked like her face was marked with black creeks. Her skin was neither white nor black but a mixture of the two; later I learned such people were called Creoles and they made up the rank and file in Port Royal.

She wore a kerchief and smoked a cigar. The fourth and fifth fingers of her smoking hand were partly gone, and looked a little like sausage bits. It didn't help she held the cigar between stubby half fingers.

"What you want?" she called down.

"Where's everybody?" I called up.

"What everybody you be meanin'?"

"I mean *everybody* everybody."

She scrunched her ancient face and turned a little to one side, as if favouring a good eye. "Dem around, everybody still around, just takin' little bit vacation. Der's no money in town, not no more. Not since dem last sailor types go off. You should see the place when der's money. A some different Port Royal it is, my yes, a some different place. You wantin' company? A room? Supper?"

"That's it, yeah."

"You got money, den?"

"Not a farthing."

"Den it's Turtle Crawles for the like of you."

She withdrew her craggy face. I was hot and hungry and withered. Halfway along High Street, I came across an open-air marketplace. Some of the stalls were manned by crones selling carrots and fruit and slabs of meat turning green-grey in the hot sun. My stomach gurgled hard. I thought about having a chat with one of the sellers, nicking a bit of this or that when she was distracted by my running mouth, and was about to do so when my eyes were distracted by a pair of strange-looking beasts having it off near a stall selling bananas and some sort of bumpy star-shaped fruit. By the look of them, they were half rat and half weasel, with a flattened ugly nose like a piglet might have, though there was clearly no pig in them. The one was putting it to the other like his life depended on it, both of their long whiskered noses twitching madly and their eyes flashing like pools of fire. I couldn't take my eyes off, for it was a freakish sight and a reminder I was well away from home.

One of the crones started laughing. "Ha! Ha! Look at 'im! 'Im never seen a *wiggly* before! You *are* new 'ere, inn't ya Mister? Now don't you go near 'em. Just let 'em be. They can leave a nasty bite, dem ones can, a nasty bite indeed, nothin' the wigglies like better'n fresh meat, whoo hoo..."

On and on she went, pointing and making fun while I failed to see the fuckin' humour. I walked off, red-faced; I could still hear her croaky voice as I passed the jail and the gibbet, and soon I was moving along the face of the warehouses again. The *Charity* had gone off. Seabirds squawked like mad buggers. There was nothing but air and sand and sea. The wind whistled, though in a way it didn't back in London. It struck me it didn't matter if I liked it here or not; I was stuck, which was the way most of us live our lives anyway, so it didn't bother me particularly. All I needed was a little ingenuity, a little of the old *imagination*, and that's when I noticed a church, sitting in the shade of Port Royal's main fort, just minding its own business, waiting for a man like me to have at it.

Even I had to admit this church was a beauty, covered in angels and spires and leering evil-faced gargoyles, the high-arched windows stained with scenes from that barmy fiction called the Bible. The Spanish must've built it when they ran the island, and if the Spanish were known for anything, it was having a high style. The tall wooden door swung open with a loud grating complaint. Inside I stepped. The air was cool and clammy. I shivered and scratched at the salt still hardened on my skin. The altar was carved from stone, as were the statues of Christ standing before the first pew. There was an organ with huge brass pipes that anybody with a bit of spirit could've jimmied apart and sold for scrap metal, assuming there was someone on the island willing to pay for it. I gave a loud *whoop* and my voice echoed between cold walls, growing fainter and fainter until it melded with the thoughts spinning through my head.

That's when I noticed a rectangular box, attached to the side of the church — *well what do we have here?* was my snickering thought. It was made of heavy wood with a large slot cut into the lid, so there was no doubt what it was used for. The lid was held in place by a padlock. Now, over home I would've never been without some sort of wire or pick for just such a slippery purpose. But home was several thousand miles away, so I tried to dislodge the box. Fixed tight it was, probably with metal posts sunk into cold stone wall. Not to be bested, I went outside and found a chunk of rock that'd crumbled away from the church's foundation. Back inside, it took no more than two or three hard swats to shatter the lock and open up that thick wooden lid. Inside I found a single coin about the same size around as a hen's egg. It'd been cut rough from silver, and was jagged along the outer edge. Stamped on one side was some sort of Spanish slogan and on the other was a crowned head, both images so faint I had to squint to make them out. I put it in my teeth and bit down, happy no flecks of paint came off. Though I had no idea what the coin was called, or what it'd buy me, I was sure of one thing.

It was a start.

I WALKED AROUND a bit more, just getting my bearings. As far as I could tell, Port Royal was shaped like a square with rounded-off corners, most of it covered with buildings and houses and shops and pubs. The north and east sides both faced mainland Jamaica. The south side, with its wharf and warehouses, faced the sea. I spotted thin spires of smoke coiling into blue sky, so I scuffled along till I cleared a clump of buildings at the southwest tip. There, I spied a crowd of men sleeping rough on a long craggy beach, the western face of Port Royal staring out to sea as well.

My first surprise was their sheer number. I'd expected to see the others from the *Charity* and maybe a few more unfortunates. Instead, they were fifty or so in number, all sitting in clumps and gazing out over the water. As I walked, I kicked up little pink clouds, my neck starting to smart with the beginnings of a burn. I promised myself I'd get a bandana or find a Monmouth cap if any were to be had, for it wasn't hard to imagine the sun simmering the brain until the simplest thought was a grand effort. As I got closer, I started to note the difference between those who'd just arrived on the *Charity* and those who'd been on that beachfront awhile. It was the skin. Ours was sheet white though on the way to pink. Theirs was a settled-in mud colour, like worn leather or the wrap of a cheroot. Though we had few wrinkles to speak of, even the young among them had deep dark troughs caused by sun and sea spray and wind.

Whereas we had all of our bodily parts, a goodly number of them had eye patches or muscular arms ending at the elbow. One jumpy blighter had a length of whittled lumber for a right leg.

I spotted the red-haired bloke from the *Charity*, standing off in the distance. I walked up to him. Against burnt skin, the blue of his eyes looked polar.

"There're Frenchies here," he said. "And the odd Dutchman."

I perked up my ears and heard conversations in foreign tongues. I gazed up and down the beach, sizing things up. Every twenty feet or so was a low smouldering fire circled by stones. Over each one, strips of meat dangled from wooden frames, drying in woodsmoke. Some of the men were sitting on hollowed-out tortoiseshells, and some were drinking from cups made from the shells of baby tortoises. At the end of the beach was a pile of what looked like algae-coated rocks. With closer inspection, it turned out they were turtle corpses, mounded in the sun.

"Least I know how Turtle Crawles got its name," I said.

"The poor fuckers just wash up onshore, belly side up, flapping them little flippers like they was trying to fly. Hunting them's no harder than walking up and daggering open their bellies. Leastways, that's what they tell me."

We sat in sand with a group of men from the *Charity*. Like everyone else, we faced the ocean and watched sun glint off the water. A conversation would start, usually ending in some bawdy comment about so-and-so's ma or what so-and-so would do when he'd earned his riches, and then we'd all go quiet and look out over the water as though some great meaning was hanging in the ocean air. After a while I got bored; I lay back and felt pinpricky sand in my hair. I put my hands over my eyes, thinking I'd just rest my eyelids. Course, I nodded off right away, jerking awake a moment later. I shot my hand to my pocket, and was happy to find the coin where I'd left it.

All around us, raggedy-looking men fed the fires with brushwood. Others were taking hunks of tortoise and running them through with skewers fashioned from tree branches and bits of carved-up driftwood. Soon, these skewers were passed around by blokes who looked like they'd just as soon kill you as say hello. Another man had a gusher of ale made from manioc (manioc being some root I'd never heard of) and he offered measures to anyone who could get his hand on a cup or calabash. I poked around and someone offered up a tortoiseshell mug, which I dipped into the frothing beer. Now I won't say it was the finest ale I'd ever had, but after two weeks of skunky water it was a fine quaff indeed. Soon my mind started to feel heavy. I helped myself to another mug, thinking *sod me what's this all about then?* Someone started passing out strips of a smoked beeve he referred to as "boucan," offering that the hills around Jamaica were filled with cows waiting to give up their lives for just such a purpose.

All in all it was a grand feast, a man's meal without the bother of veg or fruit, and that suited me fine. I accepted another ladling of fizzy manioc beer, though I kept wondering why the others would share their drink and victuals with a stranger like myself; in the world *I* knew, this didn't happen. Or if it did, it came with a cost, usually a debt that'd need repaying at the worst possible time and with the worst possible people. Yet after my fifth or sixth ladling of brew,

I decided it was time to give my suspicions a rest. Slowly, the sun approached the ocean. When it reached a certain nearness, it accelerated toward the horizon, turning into an exploding orange fireball. No one had clocks or pocket watches, which was fine for no one gave a toss about the time or how fast it was or was not passing. More gushers of ale were dragged onto the beach and soon we were done for. The others were all talking boastful and laughing, and before long this laughter turned to song, the words of which were new to my ears:

> *Fifteen men on a dead man's chest*
> *Yo ho ho and a bottle of rum*
> *Drink and the devil be done for the rest*
> *Yo ho ho and a bottle of rum...*

A silly piffle it was, if only because it went on and on and on, one man adding a verse and then there was the chorus and then another man adding another verse. Each time, there was roaring laughter and hand clapping and back slapping and then the song went on, round after round after round, every singer sharing the gist of his life if not the sordid details. The funny thing was, a lot of those lives resembled my own, hard circumstance leading to harder choices. Maybe it was the grog talking, or maybe it was feeling like I'd escaped all of the things that can hold back a man forever, top among them being the country you were born in and the family that raised you and the neighbourhoods that knew you best. I only know the next time the chorus came around, I widened my gob and started singing as loudly, and as raucously, as anybody there.

THREE

I WENT TO BED all head-spinny and awoke in soft purple light. The dawn was like dusk, only in reverse: the sun sped through red and orange and yellow before settling low and bright white over the causeway leading to the rest of Jamaica. We were all suffering. Men groaned as they toddled toward the water, where they did their business. I was no different. My head ached and my stomach felt weak and I was all-over tender. I rose and wove my way to the waterline. From away I heard retching noises, men sicking up in the brush topping the beach, and I had a feeling I'd soon be joining them.

After having a piss, I looked around and saw that fires were already going and water was being boiled and men were walking along the beach, stabbing tortoises that had washed up during the night. I crouched and splashed water over my face. This helped a little with the cobwebs, though dampening myself with water I couldn't drink worsened my thirst tenfold. All around my feet were tortoiseshells, lumps of kelp, and pieces of driftwood. Someone offered me a calabash filled with bitter black tea. Breakfast was pretty much the same as the night before, turtle meat and boucan, though with little green bananas thrown in for good measure. I sat eating. The men who'd come in on the *Charity* no longer sat off by themselves, and instead were mixed in with men who'd been here awhile. Next to me, sitting on a turtle shell, was a seaman with long sinewy arms and an eye patch.

He was smoking a fag and when I asked *did he have another?* he shrugged and offered me one. I torched it off his and sucked in stale tobacco. My heart sped and the beach turned a little beneath me. Still, my sick feeling lessened, if only a little. After that we settled into the day's activity, which was the same as yesterday: sitting, mostly, and watching over the ocean.

Finally, I couldn't stand it. "What we watchin' for?" I asked.

A billow of smoke wrapped his whiskered face before turning to wisps in the breeze. When he spoke, his voice was ragged, like he'd been smoking harsh tobacco since the age of nine, which probably wasn't far from the truth. I thought of him as old even though he was probably no more than thirty.

"A privateer named Henry Morgan. Helped take Jamaica back when Penn and Venables was roamin' the seas. Rumour is he's got his own letter and ships, now. Should be launching a mission any day, and when he does he'll need men."

"Right," I said, as if I had the foggiest what he was on about. I *had* heard about Penn and Venables back home, for they were the ones who'd robbed Jamaica from the Spanish, leaving a few foreign noses out of joint I'm sure. Yet I'd never heard of this Morgan fellow, and was trying to form a question about who he was without revealing I was too stupid to know. This was a tough dance, what with my brain so foggy, and before I had the chance, my smoking companion rose on spindly legs and buggered off, eyes fixed downward like he was hunting for something.

I sat drinking burnt tea. With time my confusion lifted, leaving a hollowed-out feeling in its place. Meanwhile, the sun climbed high and blazing in the blue, blue sky. The wind dropped mid-morning and all was still and quiet. My hangover started to wear off, which meant my head kicked in again, propelling me to my feet.

A ropy blighter was carving his initials into the side of a calabash farther along the beach. I sashayed toward him. "Ahoy," I said, using a word I'd heard a hundred times last night.

He looked up, squinting.

"Use that blade when you're done?"

He had a flattened nose and a dirty white cotton shirt opened enough to reveal a chest covered with kelpy green anchors and schooners and the like. He looked hard at me, no sign of helpfulness or friendliness about him. Then he flipped the knife and caught it by the blade so the handle was toward me. "Wouldn't lose it," he croaked.

Still. A reason for *being* there. What my ol' granddad would've called a grand purpose. Feeling pleased, I walked up and down the beachfront looking for little pieces of washed-up wood. Though finding dark pieces wasn't a problem, finding pieces light in colour was. I kept at it, and after an hour or so I was sitting before a pile of wood and I started to whittle. After a bit this attracted some attention, a few men now standing over me, which was fine for they was throwing some well-needed shade.

"What you up to?" someone asked.

"You'll see," and I kept at it until my hands cramped and my shoulders ached. Thirty-two pieces I had, half of them white and half of them black, so roughly carved you could barely make them out as men on a chessboard. Standing over me was the owner of the knife, so I handed it back with a grateful nod. Then it was a matter of finding a stick and tracing a grid with sixty-four squares in the sand. If there was no money in town, at least I could see if some of these Turtle Crawles types were worth a coin or two or maybe even more.

"Right," I said. "Who'll 'ave at me?"

There were now a dozen men or more, all looking down, and for a few moments they just stood there blinking like dimwits.

"Well come on," I said again, "who'll 'ave a game?"

"I fuckin' will," came a voice. A scrawny fellow pushed to the front of the others, his face suffering from a scar that started at his hairline, leapfrogged over his eye socket, and ended in a veiny pink blossom at the corner of his mouth. He plunked himself into the sand. "What colour?" he asked, and when I told him I wasn't fussed, he said, "White for me, then."

For the first twenty moves we sort of jostled and parried, enough for me to reckon that scar-face was a fairly decent player. Not a good one, mind, but decent enough. I asked him where he'd learned to play.

"Where'd *you* learn to play?" was his snappish reply.

I shrugged, playing the dolt. The long and short of it

was: if you were after a man's money, which I most definitely was, you didn't charge at him, playing full force, humbling him first game. Do that and he'd bugger off. Instead, you threw a couple. You made it close, but at the last second you laid an inverse trap, so called because if he took it, he'd win sometime later. Acting the pride-damaged sucker, you then asked him for another game and when he said yes, you did it again. And if you did it right, if you made him work hard for his win, he'd get that gleam in his eye, a gleam saying he was just some git off the street and you were the alehouse player and yet *he* was putting the boots to bloody *you*. It worked even better if a crowd had gathered, and that crowd was egging him on, telling him he was a right talented bastard and about to be a rich one as well. Then, with any luck, *he'd* be the one to say, "Let's make things a little more interesting, yeah?" and that's when you crushed him. Or if you thought he was good for it, you strung him along and waited for the stakes to really get up there before you played your strongest.

So that was my plan. I'd lose a few and then my pilfered coin would come out. That coin would turn to startup money and hopefully I'd be back in business. Yet midway through that first game, just as I was planting the seeds of his oh so narrow victory, an awkward feeling welled up inside me. I felt nervous and jumpy all over, the way I got when I'd picked bad strategy. A sixth sense it was, and it honked like a stepped-on trumpet.

That's when I saw it. The men on that beach had shared everything with me, from libations to victuals to homemade cigarettes, and there was no way they'd have done it solely out of human kindness. There must've been a *reason*, some benefit gained from a bond amongst us laggards, strength in numbers or honour among thieves or some other such bollocks. If I emptied this man's pockets, I'd be excluded; it was as clear as snot on a baby's upper lip. So I made a snap decision, one that grated against my every impulse. I'd let him keep whatever money he might have for some future gain I didn't understand yet. It's called a gambit, like.

So I twinned my bishops and I reclaimed the centre board and I hammered at his pawns and like that he was toppled. He just stared at the board in the sand, not understanding how the game had turned against him so fast. It's a feeling I knew well, and trust me when I say that chess and life are one and the same, for you don't always know you're losing until you're *really* losing. The crowd was silent, at least until one flaky-skinned bugger with a flap for a left arm announced, "Jaysus bloody Christ, you see dat der?"

Then it was a matter of everyone wanting to play. Another bloke sat in the impression left by my first opponent; within ten moves he looked down at his board and he looked up at me, his eyes the definition of bamboozlement. Then he gave a great big belly laugh that reeked of manioc beer and turtle.

"I'm fucked, yeah?"

"Fucked proper."

Over the next hour or so, I must've played a dozen others, all of them wanting to know how I did it and where did I learn to do that and would I bloody well teach them. Finally I rose and another took my place, and as I walked along the beach I noticed a half-dozen other men, all carving out pieces of their own. Soon, a half-dozen games were going on at once.

I turned and noticed the red-haired giant was striding toward me, building up so much steam I wasn't sure he'd be able to stop in time.

"So," he said. "You're a boardsman."

"Looks that way."

"That's your talent, like?"

"If you can call it that."

"You don't look like a chess player."

"That's why it works."

"I figured you for cards."

"Just the board. Only thing I'm good at. Only thing I've *ever* been good at. Trust me. It's not an accomplishment. It's just the way it is."

"Where'd you set up?"

"Usual places. Alehouses. Knocking-shops. The odd public square, though you had to be on the lookout for constables, like."

"Yeah, but in what cities?"

"All over. London. Manchester. Birmingham. Small towns, big towns, towns in the middle. Got so's I was sick of 'em all. Got so's they were all sick of *me*."

He looked at me all puzzled, like he couldn't believe what he was seeing. Then the corners of his mouth turned up and everything about him changed. Suddenly he was a lad again, and I knew he was going to add my display to that list we all keep, the one made up of amazing things we've seen or heard or felt or touched. Sometimes, I think that list is the only reason any of us bother.

"What's your name?" he asked.

"I've had many."

"What you mean?"

"It's Benjamin Wand, though when I was little they called me Benny The Boy Wonder. Later on I was Benny 'The Magic' Wand, though these days I'd be happy if people just called me Benny. You?"

"Taylor Land," he said while reaching out a hand.

We shook. It was like slipping your fingers inside a turkey carcass.

Soon it was too dark to tell the black pieces from the white pieces. Bonfires were lit and turtle meat roasted and calabashes passed from mouth to thirsty mouth. Though I wouldn't have thought it possible, we were even more spirited than we'd been the night before, the talk all *Henry Morgan this* and *Henry Morgan that*, and how he was going to make us all rich bastards when he finally got here. Toast after toast was made in his honour, and even with all that drink in us, there weren't any of the arguments or punchups I was used to when hard men bibbed together. Again, I had no explanation for this, as it all ran so opposite to the world I knew at home, where it was dog eat snarling dog and no one gave a toss for no one but themselves. Like I say, there seemed to be an understanding we'd all have to pull together at some point and this pulling together all revolved around a man named Henry Morgan. After a bit, it made me feel like I was part of something, even if I didn't know what that something was, and to celebrate I poured so much ale into me I could only walk in a stumble, and when some tottery blighter pulled out a hogshead of rum, I confess I might've had a taste or two of that as well.

FOUR

A FTER A DAY or two, most lost interest in the board. The game was too slow, it was too boring, it made your bloody head ache, the pieces washed off at high tide. I wasn't surprised—the wonders of the game are lost on most people, and for this most people should be grateful.

There were a few, though. A stocky Welshman with an amply knockered mermaid inked onto his neck. A Londoner with one proper ear and a bud of mashed cauliflower for the other. A frothing Irishman who spoke with such a ferocious accent none of us could understand him so he made himself understood by jabbing a flattened thumb at whatever it was he wanted. There was also the first bloke I'd played, the one with the daggered face. He was the most serious of the lot, and often I'd see him sitting off by himself, muttering *if he does this . . . then I do this . . . and if he does this . . .* as if you could master the board with memory instead of vision. These four played day and night amongst each other. Mostly they came to me with questions, or they'd get me to show them openings or endgames or whatever, most of which I made up on the spot. If I played a serious game with any of them, I'd spot them a few pieces or I'd do it blindfolded. For a time these blinded games drew a crowd, but then everyone got tired of that as well.

One day turned to the next. The weather never changed. Always hot and sunny it was, except for the few minutes it rained each day, the skies darkening and then opening with a fury none of us used to British drizzle had ever seen. At such times, the others would dance around like nutters, faces tilted upward, soaking themselves to the skin, having a wash that didn't leave dried salt on the skin. Each night there was bibbing and face stuffing and general carrying-on, and then we'd awake thirsty and hurting in the head and stomach. Those of us who came in on the *Charity* turned the dull red-brown of everyone else. Another group of tattooed reprobates was dropped off by a boat called the *Flying Wren* and the sun rose ugly peeling blisters on their lily-white faces as well.

One morning I awoke and walked to the shoreline and splashed my face and took a quick look at the sun racing into the streaky red-orange dawn sky. I stretched and groaned and had a look around, the thought that something was different coming into my dewy head. I gave my eyes another rub and a few seconds later I realized what it was. The turtles that washed up every night (and all through the day) weren't there. The beach was clean as a baby's sponged backside, save for lumps of seaweed and bits of gnarly wet driftwood.

Some of the others had risen and they were all doing what I was doing, by which I mean walking up and down the beach with a worried look on their scarred, wrinkly faces. Over the next twenty minutes, everyone else woke up—it was hard not to with the sun being what it was. They crawled out of their lean-tos and flimsy half-built shacks, and pretty soon a hubbub arose. There were those who thought it was the end of the season, and the turtles had moved on to spawn somewhere else. Another lot believed the turtles were smarter than we thought, and had decided to bugger off to someplace where they weren't hunted with such enthusiasm. Another had it the little fish eaten by the turtles had wised up and taken their leave, the turtles flippering away after them. Yet another theory had it that God had grown tired of our drunken ways and had taken away the turtles to give us a piece of his mind. (Mind you, the bloke who voiced this notion was touched in the head and spent most of his days muttering to himself. I told him to keep that religious shite to himself, a request causing more than a few to have a good snigger, the love of God being in low commodity in a place like Turtle Crawles.)

The beach was clear the next morning and the morning after that and the morning after that as well. By the fifth day, it didn't matter *why* Turtle Crawles no longer lived up to its moniker; we only knew whatever boucan and smoked turtle meat we had left wasn't going to last for much longer. Some of the men collected lengths of rope, fallen from the decks of passing galleons and washed up on shore. They cut these so they looped around one foot, the outside of a palm tree, and the other foot. Then they scurried to the top and shook loose whatever coconuts happened to be there. Soon everyone was at it—there were more than a few falls—and for a while our stomachs rumbled with the change of diet. Yet there were only so many trees to pluck, and around the time the smoked meat finally petered to nothing, the palm trees lining Turtle Crawles were likewise bare.

We spent our days walking up and down not just Turtle Crawles but above and below it as well, where the sand turned to craggy stone filled with little pools and eddies. There we foraged for seaweed, which could be dried and turned into a passable soup. We'd lie awake at night listening for rain. When none came, we'd go wading for sea urchins, which surrendered a circle of sweet, oily meat when boiled and cut open. Others went into town, robbery in their souls, only to find the locals were a hard lot carrying muskets or machetes as big as yardsticks. We were on our bloody own, in other words.

Long hours were spent sitting still, eyes closed, preserving energy, wishing this Henry Morgan would show. At four o'clock each day, a breeze kicked up for twenty minutes or so; it cooled us just enough we could imagine sleeping at night, growling stomachs or no growling stomachs. We complained of dizziness and falling trousers and achy joints and the skin sores you get when food is anything but plentiful. Eventually, I figured enough was bloody enough. Seed money or no seed money, I needed to bloody *eat*, so I got up and slithered away, camaraderie be damned. I moved slow, so no one would notice and wonder *what's the bloody chess player up to?* When I'd put enough distance between them and me, I turned and trundled along a pathway leading to the town proper. I went up one street and came back down another, finding nothing beyond a barren marketplace and one locked-up tavern after another. I tried door after heavy wooden door, thinking with time and a little luck there had to be a publican willing to earn the coin wearing away the bottom of my pocket.

There was.

It was at the end of Port Royal's biggest thoroughfare — High Street, it was called — right where Port Royal funnelled into the causeway leading to the rest of the island. The tavern was big as a barn, with a sign swinging creakily in the breeze. Later on, I'd learn its name was the Bear Garden, or just the Garden for short.

I seized the door handle — it was the size of a rolling pin — and pulled. It swung open with a loud creak. As I said, the place was enormous, though without torches going it was gloomy, the only light coming through windows filthy with dust. There were tables and chairs and an upstairs where trollops no doubt earned a living, or leastways had done so when times were better. An earthen pit was in the middle of the tavern, where a scrawny black bear was leashed to a metal post. A big fellow with tattoos was giving the bear a bucket filled with fish. Hearing the door, he turned to look. The bear, too, pulled his noggin out of the bucket and peered, head tilted to one side, looking puzzled.

The man waved a hand. "We're closed. I'm just feeding Suzie."

"I've money."

"Real money, or money you got comin' in later?"

"Real money."

"In that case, I've just opened."

Along the far wall was a long cedar plank stretched across a row of puncheons. I took this to be the bar, for on one side of the plank was a row of stools. I sat, the publican taking his rightful place on the far side of the plank. Behind him was a bureau topped with ceramic jugs.

"Now then," I started. "I've recently come into a coin of unknown value, and I've no choice but to trust that you'll provide me with food and drink of a fair and equal value. Failure to do so will naturally result in a later visit by the aggrieved party, namely me, and some truly vicious Turtle Crawles types..."

The man grinned and held out his hand. I gave him the coin. "It's a piece of eight," he said. "Pure Spanish cob."

"Will it buy me lunch?"

He turned and uncorked a jug and poured me a measure of rumbullion. It went down hot and burning, and when I was done, he gave me another. We then introduced ourselves, the publican's name being David Walsh. His story was he'd privateered with Penn and Venables but had decided to settle down with his share of the swag.

"So you've heard of this Henry Morgan?" I asked him.

"He captained one of the other ships, but yeah. I knew him."

"What's all the fuss, then?"

Walsh cocked an eyebrow. "The savviest bastard you'll ever see. A real on-the-riser and a favourite of the King. A man's man and then some. I just wish he'd hurry up and get here. It's about time Port Royal came alive again."

The scraggly bear groaned. I looked over and watched Suzie rest her head on the back of her paws. She yawned, and I swore I could smell her fishy breath all the way over where I was sitting.

"I've some mutton and trimmings," said Walsh. "Will a sandwich of that do?"

"It will at that."

Walsh tossed the coin and caught it while having a

whistle. He walked off to make me my meal; taking advantage, I ducked under the cedar plank and refilled my cup before popping back up on the customer side. After a bit, the door to the kitchen opened and Walsh came out and put a pair of dark-bread sandwiches before me. I took a bite.

"Lovely," I said, through a mouthful of stringy meat.

FIVE

I TOOK THE LONG way back, figuring I'd trudge over the
north end of Port Royal and make my way back down
the beach toward Turtle Crawles. When I got to the top of
Port Royal, I stopped and gazed across the water toward the
mainland. I was looking at the capital of Jamaica, a town
called St. Jago. From what I'd heard, it was full of decent
people, if such a thing existed. In fact, the reason Port Royal
existed at all was to guard St. Jago from the Spanish; my new
town was like a castle wall, though built from scallywags
and reprobates instead of stone and mortar. I couldn't help
it—I was imagining the lives people had across the water.
I pictured Sunday dinners, bath time, and mothers being
helpful. Soon I felt bitter, all over. It was the same bitterness
I summoned whenever I cheated people out of their money,
though I sometimes wondered who the real victim was—
me or the ones I was swindling?

I walked past yet another Spanish-built fort at the northwest tip of Port Royal and headed back down toward Turtle
Crawles. That's when I heard a distant hollering. I shaded my

eyes and saw five ships well out in the harbour, three little ones with a single sail each, a medium-sized boat with two, and a big bastard with three. The water was full of splashing bodies, and it didn't take a genius to figure this Henry Morgan had finally come, which meant I had a decision to make. Given how furiously the men in the water were swimming, it was also one I'd have to make quick.

Now: I reckoned I could stay back, and somehow get some money together and somehow find myself a board with its pieces intact and somehow go back to the one profession I knew well and truly. Or, I could go off with this Morgan fellow, despite my knowing bugger all about boats and open water and sacking foreign cities. I thought for just a moment, a moment being all I had, and it came down to my first plan having one too many *somehow*s for my liking. There was also the real consideration that I'd just spent my pilfered seed money on a mutton-with-trimmings sandwich, the sad truth being you can't gamble if you've nothing to gamble *with*.

A second later, I was sprinting down that crushed-coral beach, pumping my arms, heels striking hard, trying my damnedest to catch up. I hit the water, more flopping than diving, boots and breeches filling. I came up sucking air and recalling that I, pit-faced urchin and a son of two scoundrels, couldn't swim worth shite. I sputtered and kicked and windmilled my soggy arms, the only consolation being that most of the bastards in the water were as pitiful as I was — at the very least, I had all my arms and legs to flail *with*. After a bit I stopped and could no longer touch my toes on the bottom, and it occurred to me if I didn't get on with it I'd sink and that'd be the end of Benny Wand. So I kept going.

My arms tired and I spewed up water and every time my head slipped under I kicked like a furious child, knowing full well if I drowned, not one person on this earth would give a toss. I kept flailing, using far more energy than I had at my disposal, if that's a thing that's possible. I believe my vision went black from lack of air, and the next thing I knew, a hand was reaching down from a gunwale and grabbing me by the collar.

The arm attached *to* that hand, meanwhile, was thick and pink and pasted with freckles.

"For fuck's sake," Taylor Land said. "Nothin' like leaving it till the last minute."

He hauled me up like I was a bag of laundry, even though I'm far from a small man myself. Once on deck, I doubled over and tossed up a bucket-worth of salt water. When I finished sputtering, I emptied my boots and held my wet face up to the sun. My heart struck against my ribs. The deck rotated beneath me. Everything looked sharp, the way it does when you've had a scare. At least I wasn't alone; there were dozens of others on their knees, heaving up sea water, everyone else pointing and laughing and making harsh comment.

"QUIET!"

I put my boots back on and stood. A mean-looking bastard with a pistol tucked into the waist of his breeches was moving along the deck, yelling we should shut our gobs and line ourselves up and for Christ's sake be quick about it. We did so and there we waited, facing back toward Jamaica, intense sun drying our slops. Curious as ever, I looked up and down the deck; at the same time, I tried to keep my head swivelling to a minimum, just in case being nosy was against some rule no one had yet told me about. Still, I couldn't help but notice how the ship had been altered. The forecastle and roundhouse had been sheared off and replaced with boards. A dozen cannons were mounted around the deck, each one poking through a hole in the gunwale. Even I could tell the ship had been fixed for two purposes and two purposes only, those being fighting and moving fast in open water.

As we all stood there dripping, I noticed rowboats were coming toward us from the other four ships, and that they were filled with men picked up in places other than Port Royal. When they reached us, the men climbed out grumbling. The boats went back and forth like that again. When they were done, we were about seventy-five in number, all standing on deck and wondering what it was all about. Off in the distance, it looked like Port Royal was bobbing up and down and not the boat we were planted on. After a time we grew fidgety and nervous. Soon this gave way to whispered asides and snickering comments, *maybe we're in the wrong place* or *maybe we got the date wrong* and the like. After a while these died down and we were quiet again, the only noise the squeak of a trap door opening near the front of the boat.

A man came out, tall more in bearing than in actual height. A lean build he had, with shoulder-length brown hair. He had a narrow forehead, a slender nose and cheekbones like market-day plums; as he got closer, I could see his eyes were a piercing grey. He was dressed in heavy breeches and worn black leather boots and a white cotton shirt that fluttered in the breeze. On his head he wore a plain old Monmouth cap, like a commoner might do, and his handsome face was neither bearded nor clean-shaven but somewhere in between. Despite his humble dress, you could've picked him out as someone who figured himself special. It was his way of taking up space. A lack of shame or apology, he had. Like he was born to be in charge and bloody well knew it.

"Gentlemen," he said. "Welcome to the Brethren of the Coast. My name is Henry Morgan, and you are aboard the *Pearle*, my flagship vessel. I am the captain of this ship and the head of this expedition."

His voice was kingly (surprise bloody surprise) and it rang out over wind and waves. He reached a slender hand into the right pocket of his breeches and pulled out a scroll of paper covered in writing. "*This*, gentlemen, is a Letter of Marque granted by none other than the King of England. It is dated the Fourth of April, 1668."

He held it up and let us admire it even though most of us couldn't have read the words written on it.

"As you all know, we are at war with the country of Spain, and the island of Jamaica is our only major possession in the New World. It is our job to protect it from foreign invasion, and we will do this by keeping the enemy busy in other parts of their empire. This *letter*, gentlemen, instructs me to harry the Spanish Main in any way I see fit, and in so doing we will give the New World its freedom. We will separate the Main from Spanish domination!"

There was loud cheering and men pumping fists into the air. Meanwhile I listened hard, for I'd had no idea it was a war I was getting myself into. The fact was, I put borders in the same category as religion; as far as I could tell, both were invented to keep men in their places, and if that was the case, I saw no reason to fight for whatever country those borders contained, be it England or Spain or France or what have you. Then again, what was I going to do? Jump overboard and swim back?

"It's no purchase no pay, gentlemen. Four shares for the captains, master's mate three, quartermaster two, barber-surgeon two, cabin boys and scrub boys a half. Six for your leader. Any objection?" There were none. Everyone was grinning and/or chortling, though I held back, looking for Morgan's angle. "As for bodily harm, it'll be 600 pieces for a right arm, 500 for a left unless you're left-handed and then it's the reverse. A leg's worth 500, a digit 100, an eye 100 unless you lose both and then it's a thousand. First man over a rampart or on board a Spanish vessel gets an extra 500. Any man shot, with either bullet or arrow, will be given 500 should he survive. Any man doused in oil—500. Torture—500. Imprisonment—500. Questions?"

A wizened old runt with an eye patch spoke up. "What if yoos only got one eye to start with? What you get for losing an eye then?"

"Then it would be a thousand," said Morgan.

"Whoo-hoo!" rang the old-timer, as if he was looking forward to a life of darkness.

Morgan smirked. "Any other questions?"

There were none.

"We sail tomorrow, gentlemen. In the meantime, please join me in a jigger of rumbullion!"

A few grisly deckhands came around, passing out calabashes filled with strong drink. I took one and downed it and no sooner had I finished than someone handed me another. It was just like on Turtle Crawles, with the men taken on at Port Royal keeping to themselves at first, and the men who were already with Morgan doing likewise. This distance melted as the grog went round, and soon we were all yammering like we'd known each other forever. It turns out the others weren't all "rehabilitating criminals" like the Turtle Crawles lot. Some were indentured servants, with stories of escape from Barbadian plantations. Some were old British navvies, so tired of boot licking and deck swabbing they'd jumped ship, shirt-backs lit by moonlight, swimming for hours through shark-infested waves in the name of freedom. Some were admitted heathens, who'd ditched Puritan settlements up north, many bearing scars and brandings that showed what sins they'd committed before running off. Sprinkled among these were brutes with skull tattoos and arms ending at the elbow and gold rings run through ears and noses. Some had even done their eyes with charcoal—something to do with repelling the sun—and one foul-smeller had his beard done up in little yellow bows that, on anyone not so murderous in appearance, would've looked right frilly.

Course there was boasting, mostly about women known or crimes committed and foreign lands reached. After listening to a couple of tales, Taylor Land pointed to me and said, "Hey! This man here's a real boardsman. The terror of every tavern from Bristol to Birmingham. You must have a story or three, yeah Benny?"

"Wha'?" I said. "You want a story from the likes of me?"

"We fuckin' do," said another.

"Right then," I said, plumbing my memory before a good one came. "So. Here it is, take it or leave it, believe or don't, what do I care? Either way, I was playing some chubby bastard in a rum hall in Devon, where I'd headed due to some,

er, entanglements I had back in London. I played the blubbery fucker for over an hour, making each game as close
as I could make it, when he finally made a bet worth betting, I think it was fifty or sixty quid. It was enough for me
to finish with him, so I hammered the futile bastard. Used
an opening of my granddad's called the Peaty Wench and
took him in all of twenty moves. He looked up at me, chin
fat wobbling, eyes wide with shock.

"'You were stringing me along,' he said.

"''Fraid that's the name of the game,' I told him.

"'Well it's highway robbery, and I won't honour my
wager.'

"'What you mean?' I said, all calm, though inside I was
starting to churn, the way you do when someone's puttin'
the screws to you.

"'I shan't pay you, sir. You were competing under false
pretences.'

"That's when I saw red. Was no other word for it.
Throwing game after game with men like him — with their
nice families and their thimblefuls of sherry and their boiled
ox-tongue body odour — is dull dismal work and I reckoned
I'd earned every penny. So I stood. Smiled at him all nice
while collecting my chessboard. 'Ah well, I suppose I *was* a
bit dodgy,' I told him. 'No hard feelings, then?'

"'None, sir, though in the future I'd ask that you...'" and
I hit him as hard as I could with the corner of the board,
which was a heavy wooden model I'd still be using if I hadn't
split it in two over his hairless scalp. The blow caught him
high on the cheekbone and when he fell onto his back I
clocked him one hard on the nose, the bastard spouting
blood while yelling, 'Mercy! Mercy!' in a fat nasal twang.

When I reached into his pocket, I found almost two hundred quid, all of which he was soon relieved of. After that I
left immediately for St. Austell, and kept my nose clean for
a week just in case men of his were out looking."

Everyone howled at my little tale, saying *good one!* and
a few even patting me on the back. There were a few more
stories, some better than mine and some not, and then
someone hauled out a gill of fiery awfulness they called
Kill Devil, so named because it was strong enough to drop
old Beelzebub himself. Soon I'd linked arms with the others,
and we were all singing shanties about bummery, rum
quaffing, and the lash. For supper we had platters of tortoise meat, boucan and hardtack, which we attacked like
wild animals, using our fingers to tear the meat into digest-
ible pieces, our chins running with molten fat, stomachs and
mouths calling for more more more, there being nothing
whets the appetite like abundance.

After a blazing red starboard sunset, darkness came on
in a heartbeat. Torches were lit and supported in the gun
ports. With time, the shanty singing dwindled and then
stopped altogether, the singers now showing off their guns
by firing them into the sky, the smell of gunpowder so
strong it roasted the inside of the nostrils. This was an awkward moment seeing as I was unarmed, though this went for
most of the Turtle Crawles lot, so at least I had company. The
night ended with some of the men losing their suppers in
black, star-flecked water. Others dropped where they stood,
curling up and looking like huge snoring babies. I found a
spot in the *Pearle*'s stern, where I lay flat on my back with a
foot up on the gunwale, my attempt to slow the sky's lazy
spinning. Taylor Land came over and did likewise. I could

hear him quietly singing an old Highland ditty to himself, something having to do with clover and sheep and the feeling of sea mist on a man's face.

After a bit he piped down. "Benny," he said. "Fuck of a story you told back then."

"It happened."

"Can I tell you one myself?"

"Course."

"Back in the orphanage, there was this older boy, an ugly bugger always nicking my things, pushing me about, making life miserable. In time he'd've bent me over a barrel, I was sure of it. Bigger 'n me, he was. By a fair sight."

"Bigger than *you*?"

"I was fifteen. He was sixteen, maybe seventeen."

"I hope you let him know what's for."

"I did. Walked up behind the bastard and spoke his name and when he turned I brained him with a churn stick I'd lifted from the kitchen. Gave it everything I had, and I was strong for my age. After that he was all drooly and shaky and gentle as a lamb. The nuns locked me in a closet for a week. No food, just a bit of water. Thought I'd die in there."

"I bet it was worth it."

"I'd no regrets. When a bastard's got it coming, a bastard's got it coming."

He stopped talking and went back to half humming and half singing under his low husky breath. We both lied there looking up and that's how I fell asleep, flat on my back on a slowly rotating deck, listening to a big man sing about things he wished he knew better.

SIX

THE ROWBOATS STARTED running as soon as we woke the next morning. Those men who'd been picked up from Turtle Crawles stayed to man the *Pearle* and the others went back to their own ships. Soon after, anchors were lifted and sails unfurled and we all buggered off. Those who knew how to make a boat go in the direction you wanted it to go in were running around, pulling on this rope and yanking on that rope and yelling directions. Those such as myself, by which I mean useless twats, were given a bucket and a piece of lye that ate at the skin and smelled like burning leaves. As for instructions, we asked for none and none were given, though we knew if we didn't find some part of the deck to clean, there'd be someone wanting to know why. We were scrub boys, lowest of the low. Leastways I knew my place.

"Some new life," said Taylor Land, whose right hand was moving in weak meaningless circles over the deck. I agreed, our optimism of the night before sorely dwindled. At least back home my hands wouldn't be stinging, my head wouldn't be reeling from the smell of detergent, and hard men with missing teeth wouldn't be jeering when they passed, saying we looked like fancy boys seeing as our backsides were pointing upward. As I scrubbed oil and powder off that deck, I gave an ear to any and all palaver near me. This way I found out the ship was heading west at a right clip.

At lunch we stood around for an hour, eating plantain and smoked turtle, and as we did, I inched toward conversations held by real seamen and not first-timers such as myself: the land off in the distance (but getting closer) was called the Yucatán, and once we rounded it we'd head toward some middling town in New Spain I'd never heard of called Villahermosa.

We travelled all night, no strong drink on offer, so it was a sober night for us all. I slept below deck in a hammock, amidst snores and the words called by men in their sleep. When I woke, I was given strong tea and hardened griddle cakes and then it was back on my hands and knees, working at invisible stains. By mid-morning I overheard another bit of useful information: we'd crossed spumes of brown muddy water and this meant we'd reached some river leading to our target. The *Pearle* came about and headed for shore, as did the smaller ships trailing along behind us. Myself, I stood and stretched, pulling at back muscles grown sore and weak. Taking the opportunity, I peered toward shore and could have sworn there was no river to be seen nor travelled upon: as far as I could tell, there was nothing but trees and ferns and plants grown together to create a dense wall of forest.

I went back to work, and when I next stood and helped myself to water, I had another gander. This time I could see we were nearing a part in the forest wall and the mouth of a small river. Soon after, we landed on a soft-pillow shoal, the bottom of the boat making a *shhhhhh* sound as we came to a rest. The other ships did likewise and we all jumped into calf-high water, careful to put a lid on any high spirits or loud noises, for who knew if any Spanish bastards were about. As I said, there were seventy or eighty of us, the jungle so dense we couldn't even step on land. Ahead of us, the skinny river poked into dense green. Gurgling and brown it was, and smelling of sulphur.

Four men stood conferring with Morgan, and I took them to be the captains of the other boats. They'd been talking for about five minutes when I began to slosh toward them, feigning interest in some bloody tree or vine that happened to be close to where they were grouped, the reality being I'm a curious bastard and always have been.

I needn't have bothered. When I was still a dozen paces from their little group, Morgan stepped toward the rest of us. With his chin tilted upward, and the glimmer caused by entitlement in his eye, he announced, "We have two choices, gentlemen. The first is we fill the small boats and row them up the river. We'd reach the target by nightfall, the problem being we'd be in plain sight the whole time."

He paused. Nothing on his face said he had feelings good or bad about the idea.

"Number two. We tromp through the jungle and in this way stay hidden until the last possible moment. The problem is we don't know what is *in* that forest. There could be snakes or dangerous insects or hostile natives, and there's always the chance of losing our way. Yet once we got there, surprise would be ours."

Again he paused. "All those in favour of taking the river say yea, all those in favour of forging a jungle path say..."

His voice petered out. There was a look of frozen surprise on his features. We turned, and saw what strange appearance had interrupted Morgan's train of thought.

There were eight of them, all standing still and mute. How they came upon us without crackling a branch or rustling a tree was one question, and what they *were* was the other. They looked like puny ghosts, not one of them standing over five feet high, though they all had wide shoulders and barrel chests and short stocky legs. Their bare feet were so caked with mud it looked like they'd been born that way.

They wore tall hats the shape of cylinders, and how these hats stayed on their heads was a mystery, for I could see no strap running under the chin nor over the ears. They also had blue woven gloves and long white robes that closed over the chest but then opened over their legs and midsection, revealing codpieces made from bunches of banana leaves. What really unnerved me was they wore wooden masks as white as their robes—stranger still was the *look* of these masks, for they had snubby pig noses coupled with the whiskers of a cat. Across their cheeks and forehead were painted bright red streaks like slashes of blood, and somehow when you put this all together they looked like something from another strange, fierce world.

The Indian standing more or less in the middle started talking in some strange language, his clucky words mixing with the sound of liquid rolling around in the back of his throat. When he finished his piece, Morgan said nothing; though he must've been as confounded as the rest of us, he didn't show it. The Indian pointed toward the wall of jungle and spoke again, the back-of-his-throat gurgling louder this time, like what he was saying was right important and needed hearing.

Just then, one of the captains stepped toward Morgan. I picked him out as the mean-looking bastard who'd yelled at us to be quiet that first day on board the *Pearle*; later I'd learn his name was John Morris and he was captain of a two-master as well as the expedition's second-in-command. He was also carrying a flintlock the size of a small dog. "Want me to give 'em a message, Henry?"

Morgan made a hold-your-horses gesture and said, "Let's figure out what they want, John."

The Indian spoke up a third time, his voice still sounding bothered. Morgan did the only thing he could do, which was stare at these strange jungle buggers while trying to guess what they were on about. Just then, a sailor from one of the other ships came sloshing through the ranks. He was bearded and grisly-looking, and had red peeling hands that marked him as a scrub boy. Some kind of scabby disease covered his face; in the world I knew back in England, he'd have been dismissed just for his gut-turning appearance. Here, no one seemed to care or notice.

"Captain Morgan, sir."

He was out of breath, from either nervousness or sudden exertion or maybe a bit of each.

"What is it?" asked Morgan.

"When I come to Jamaica, there was a storm and the ship I was on went down, sir. Most everyone drowned, though I washed up on these very shores. Lived with these native blokes for eight months. Not a bad lot, if I say so myself."

"So you speak their language?"

"Not well, but some."

"Well then, *talk* to them, man!"

The man turned to the Indian in charge and had a chat that went on forever, I think because he was asking the Indian to say his piece over and over so there'd be no blunders over meaning. Finally, he nodded his head and turned to Morgan. "Right," he said. "As far as I can tell, they're sayin' the river's crowded with bloody Spanish and taking the rowboats would be suicide, pure and simple. Yet if we walked through the jungle, we'd hit swamp and get sucked up to our chins an' that'd be the end of the likes of us. There's another way, though."

Morgan straightened. "Yes?"

"They'll guide us *round* the swamp. They say they'll find us food, get us there in one piece, and then fight with us. But they warn it's a long way, like."

"How long?"

There was another conversation with loads of grunting and clicks. The sailor turned to Morgan: "Five, six nights. Maybe more."

There were low groans and chatter. Morgan cogitated, jaw muscles gnashing. Morris and the other captains were looking at him, as were all the other hard men under his command. Meanwhile, the sun beat at our necks and there were bugs at my face and hands.

"Ask them why they'd help us."

"Don't need to. They bloody hate the Spanish for taking half of 'em slaves and practically killing the other half. And what they done to their women is another matter altogether. I seen it myself, and I can tell you they've far more reason to hate the Spanish than we do."

There was no emotion on Morgan's face. Just thinking, he was.

"Well then," he finally said. "We had best get a move on."

THE INDIANS ABOUT-FACED and walked toward a break in the jungle maybe twenty feet left of the river. It was no more than a part in the branches, so small none of us had noticed it before. Once they stepped inside, it was like they were swallowed whole: one by one they went into it and one by one they disappeared. Morgan looked at John Morris and said, "Keep ten armed men back to watch the boats."

Morris nodded and went down the line, tapping shoulders belonging to the first ten men with guns. Once chosen, they nodded and sloshed off back to the boats. Then we set off, Morgan the first to offer himself to the woods. The other captains followed — apart from Morris, their names were Freeman and Jackman, the fourth a Dutchman named Marteen. The rest of us lined up to follow the captains. I was about halfway along. The line moved slowly, seeing as we were bunched up and sloshing through water.

When I got to that tiny entrance — it was no more than a slit — I took a deep breath and stepped from hot-sun heat to wet dark heat. It was like stepping into a sponge, the jungle giving off a soppiness that seemed to come from every leaf and branch and gnarled mossy twisted tree trunk. Every bead of sweat on my skin stayed there, soaking my clothes and attracting winged creatures with its salt.

We trudged. Huge deep-green leaves, some the size of canoes, swatted against our sides. I can't say it was a feeling I enjoyed, for with men ahead of me and men behind me and thick jungle on either side of me I felt trapped, was no other word for it, and trapped is a feeling most men will do anything to avoid. We took step after squishing step. There was no bluster nor boasting nor friendly jibing: just the in-out in-out of hot chugging breath. The bugs were ferocious, and unlike any I'd seen back in England. Some were big fat buggers that hovered around the mouth and nose, getting in the way of taking a decent breath. Others were little and dark and made a high whining noise, forever building and fading in volume—some of the men rolled up leaves and stuffed them in their ears to block out the maddening sound. There were stinging bugs and nipping bugs and little biting red buggers that crawled up the ankles and left a ring of welts. I won't even mention the mosquitoes, except to say they were vicious black bastards and leave it at that.

As far as I could tell, we were walking more or less parallel to the shoreline though at the same time veering inland a little. After a bit we started to move to higher ground, the jungle floor drying somewhat, and then for a while we took a long slow turn to the left and I knew we were piercing the heart of the jungle. Every once in a while we'd hit a clearing, the canopy above us breaking, and hot sun would fall upon our shoulders and warm our damp clothes slightly. But then we'd be back into it, marching around a giant swamp somewhere off to our left. Occasionally we'd come to little streams, and word would come down the line if we so much as dampened our flaking lips we'd end up with a shivering fever or maybe even dead. Other times they'd be small rivers we *could* drink from, the whole company settling on the banks and dipping their faces into cool rushing water. One time, while having myself a drink, I looked down the stream and saw a huge grey-skinned monster, half in the water and half out, all teeth and leathery scales and demon-red unblinking eyes, looking so much like a dragon I figured maybe they existed after all. Heart pounding, I hissed, "Bloody 'ell, what's that then?"

The privateer slurping water next to me chuckled. "It's called a crocodile." He wiped his damp chin. "Fuck of a thing, inn't it?"

Other times, in the middle of dense jungle, the air alive with monkey howls and birdsong, we'd stop altogether. The first time this happened, I looked back at Taylor and Taylor looked at me, both of us shrugging. Slowly, news came down the line, from mouth to mouth to mouth, advice from the Indians pointing at this and that up ahead.

Do *not* touch the tip of such-and-such a plant leaf, its tip being sharp and filled with some demon poison that'll cause your forearm to swell to the size of a pumpkin.

Do *not* eat the mushrooms with the black underside, as they contain a magic elixir that'll open the skies and surround you with colour.

Do *not* relieve yourself in any of the jungle streams, as some small awful bug will travel up your stream and invade your body via the tip of your John Johnson.

Do be on the watch for a lizard with a garland of scaly purple skin around its neck. If it sank its teeth into your flesh, it wouldn't let go, even if you cut off its head.

Do be wary of a little black mouse racing around the jungle floor, searching for bits of food contained in wild turkey shite: it carries a fearsome disease that causes the skin to dry up and shrivel away from the body, leaving bloody big patches of exposed muscle and bone.

Do grow eyes in the back of your head, the jaguars less likely to pounce if they think they're being watched.

And so on and so on, each warning more courage-draining than the last. With my senses sharpened by fear, the jungle began to change. When we'd first stepped into it, all I could see were two walls of dark damp green. After a half day of hard marching, I began to see it for what it really was. It was more like a chessboard, with all of the pieces — half of which were buzzing, crawling, or slithering — fitting together with perfect sense. There was even a sort of rightness about it, the problem being it was a rightness not meant to be spied by the likes of us.

My legs tired and my stomach rumbled. We finally came to a clearing bigger than any we'd seen so far, half the size of a football pitch, though oval in shape. At one end was a stream making restful rushing noises and at the other there were fallen trees some of the men sat on. The rest was mossy and wet. Above us, the skies were turning lavender. We all pulled up and the Indians looked at Morgan. Their meaning was clear: we'd stop here for the night. Morgan nodded, and you could hear murmurs in the company — *thank Christ* and *about bloody time* and the like. Supper was hardtack and boucan, though some of the Indians tromped back into the trees and returned with armloads of a fist-sized orange and green fruit. These were passed around, everyone taking a bite. It tasted sour though refreshing and I wished there was more.

After eating, we all sat around resting, legs pulsing, skin itching, swatting frantically at bugs, when something curious did happen. The natives, instead of lolling like the rest of us, set to making little piles of fallen dried palm fronds

and twigs. Then they squatted, and began screwing sharpened sticks against logs they'd found dried in the sun. As
barmy as this looked, it wasn't long before a spark set ablaze
handfuls of dried moss, which they put to the little pyres
they'd made.

Pretty soon they had low fires, the smoke drifting up and
forming thin wispy clouds above us. A second later, one of
the Indians stood directly above his low flame, slowly gyr-
ating while the smoke drifted up and inside his long white
robe. Another Indian did the same and so on, and soon all
of the Indians had jigged in sweet choking smoke.

We all looked on, stunned, when something even more
astounding did occur. I looked over at Morgan. As I watched
him ponder, I could practically hear the thoughts thrum-
ming through his head—how he was a captain with the
Brethren of the Coast, and a proud representative of the
King's will in the New World, and was no bloody way he was
going to tolerate this native superstition on display before
him. I figured he'd stand and grumpily tell the Indians to
keep their pagan buffoonery to themselves.

I was wrong. He stood all right, but not to give them a
piece of his mind. He must've reckoned that these Indians
knew the jungle like the backs of their red-brown hands,
and if anyone had a reason for filling their skivvies with
mossy smoke, then they would be the ones. The next thing
I knew, Morgan was on his feet and striding toward one of
the little flames, where he let his breeches and shirt cuffs fill.
After a moment of confusion, Captains Morris, Freeman,
Jackman, and Marteen followed, and pretty soon we were
all waiting in line to bathe ourselves in smoke, though not
one of us had a clue why.

My turn came, and I turned and twisted above low flames. I can't say it was pleasant, for the heat produced by the fire was the last thing I needed in that broiling jungle, plus the smoke drifting up and into my face made it difficult to draw breath. After a minute or two I went and lied down on a mossy bed and looked up at the sky, which was beginning to streak with violet. As well as being coated with dirt and sweat, I now smelled like a brush fire, my every bodily nook doused with smoke.

Then I noticed something. The bugs had disappeared, or leastways it seemed like they had. I couldn't hear them, couldn't feel them, couldn't see them darting frantic in the sludgy air. It was a glorious feeling, like having a stomach ache all day and then noticing it's gone away. We were exhausted, the lot of us, and with the bugs leaving us alone and our stomachs filled, we all admired the darkening sky for a minute or two before falling dead away.

I CAME TO in creamy light, cursing for I wanted back into the mild bugless dream I'd been having. The smoke had worn off and the bugs were at me like flies on rotting meat. Around me I heard groaning and farting and other ugly noises men make when awakening with no women around. We all shat and drank simmered water and chewed on pulls of boucan. Within twenty minutes we followed the Indians out of the glade and back into dense jungle, the path as narrow and sweltering as it'd been the day before. Throughout the day we spread out, and after a few hours I found myself trudging in a group with Taylor Land and three others, nothing but empty narrow path ahead of and behind us.

"Benny," he said.

"Yeah?"

"We've neither pistol nor cutlass. What'll we fight with?"

In front was a scarpy-looking blackguard with a flint-lock to be envied. He stopped and turned and looked up at the sliver of white sky above. His voice was a pained croak, like he'd been punched more than once in the throat. "Hang back till a few of them Spanish cunts've fallen. Soon's we take their weapons, you boys'll be outfitted, yeah? You won't be the first mateys to start off unarmed and you won't be the last."

He turned and walked on and I have to say I felt a little better.

IT GOT SO the groups ahead of and behind us were so distant their conversations were swallowed up by jungle and we did feel well and truly on our own. Occasionally we heard monkeys howl and the squeal of pigs. Other times a strange ratcheting howl filled the woods; it sounded like it came from a large gut-shot bird, though we could never spot one in the canopy or lower branches. We kept on. Our feet grew sore. We didn't cross any rivers that endless day, and soon my lips were dry and the back of my throat burned fiercely. We camped that night in soggy lowland. This made the ground soft and good for sleeping, though the bugs were a torment and we all clamoured for another of those strange Indian smoke baths. After that we fell right asleep, curled into achy balls.

Shortly after breakfast the next day, a fine drizzle started. Though it cooled us a little at first, the bugs did worsen and our eyes filled with rainwater as well as the dripping sweat caused by hiking. It lasted for most of the morning and when it ended, a double rainbow arched through the sky. We kept going. That night's rest was had again in thick jungle, all of us keening for a clearing like we had the first night. A routine was starting: we'd stop, build fires, douse ourselves with smoke, choke back boucan, and sleep. There was little in the way of chatter or jibing, all of us miserable and just wanting to get the bloody march over with.

Sometime during the fourth day, in the middle of the afternoon, we skirted a large algae-coated pond. An enormous crocodile was sitting on the opposite bank, its jaws craned open, a lump in its gullet the size of a small pig; we could hear it, straining to breathe, making a noise like the creak of floorboards beneath a rocking chair. Later on that day, our little group was walking along when one of the men stopped and pointed a thick freckly forefinger into the air. "Look," he whispered, and sure enough there was a jungle cat, all spots and the size of a large dog, perched in the lower branches of a tree. It watched us pass, as curious of us as we were of it. Course we walked backwards as we passed it, one of us tripping and smashing his head so hard he was out cold. Someone slapped his face and he came awake groggy, saying, "Where am I?" which happened to be the same weighty question running through all our heads.

That night, we weren't allowed fires seeing that we were close, and there was no way we'd be mistaken for a small band of Indians out for a trek. We all groaned, for we'd all come to rely on a fire-bath to sleep, and that night we were kept up itching and swatting and digging forefingers into our ears and noses. We left, poorly rested and grumpy, at dawn. We trudged all day. That night we were told we should keep any conversation to a whisper. We all munched on boucan and turtle, again missing our smoke baths, heads roaring with unspoken thoughts.

The next morning, I awoke when one of the captains — Freeman, I think it was — tapped his boots against the bottom of my feet. It was still dark out, the sky above flickering. Within ten minutes we were all on our feet and then we followed the Indians into the jungle. Any starlight or glow of the moon was blocked by canopy and so we had to walk through pitch-black gloom, leafs popping out and scraping against our faces. How the Indians knew where they were was beyond me; without light I couldn't tell where the path was or even was it there, so I made sure I kept close to the hazy grey impression of the next man's back. After a half-hour or so the sky began to lighten, a blessed relief this was, the jungle looking golden in the early dawn. As the air began to heat, I chewed a twist of boucan, the captains saying we'd eat on the march that morning. We began to climb, tree roots serving as steps.

After an hour or so, I noticed the jungle was thinning. We could now see through the woods, columns of sunlight funnelling through gaps in the canopy. The trees too seemed to change, from huge gnarly ancient things to sorts I recognized from home. We pushed through a copse of pine trees. Beneath our feet was black earth mixed with rust needles. Up ahead the whole company had stopped near the edge of the grove. We waited for the rest to pull up, time I used to sneak up through the ranks and have a look through the last of the trees. Below was Villahermosa, all leafy and unaware, not a wall nor rampart nor watchtower in sight, just ripe for the pillaging it was, in a little bowl surrounded by tall green rustling trees.

Bloody hell, I thought.

Check and fuckin' mate.

SEVEN

I T WAS MORE town than city, just a square with narrow lanes winding from all four corners and a second, smaller square tucked behind. At the top of the main square was a church, the rest of the plaza sided with low wood-beam houses. In the middle of the square was a fountain of a small boy peeing, like some joke the whole town was in on. There were flowerpots in every window and street lamps posted on wrought iron poles. I could smell woodsmoke and cooking. All was silent save for birds and breezes. As I said, it was a pretty little place, with no way to fend off the unwashed likes of us. Still, every man amongst us believed the people living in that little Spanish town had it coming. We believed it because we were filthy and hungry and to a one we'd been born poor. We believed it because we'd braved their hot woods, because we'd survived their insects, because we overcame the tight-chested feeling that comes when thick jungle rubs against you. We believed it because we wanted to, morality being a thing dreamt up by men, and put to use when and only when it's convenient.

Those with pistols started powdering and loading, and those with cutlasses drew them, admiring the way they gleamed in the sun. The Indians parted their robes and surprised us by withdrawing long swords that, swung with relish, would've sheared a man's head off. Then we walked down. Practically sauntered, we did. There was no need for whooping nor hollering nor using energy we didn't need to use, so why bother? As we neared the main square, the townsfolk came out of their neat little homes, hands in the air, looking saddened and grave. We looked for gun barrels sticking out of second-floor windows, but no matter how hard we tried we saw nothing but worried faces, pressed against shutters and curtains and the like. Soon we were going through houses, ordering everybody out; they all emerged, hands held up, children clinging to skirt folds, the men stony. There wasn't a whiff of a fight in any of them.

We corralled them all onto the square. There were maybe four or five hundred, save for a few old or sick people we'd left lying in their beds. The captains lined them up so they all faced the same way and then Morgan paraded in front of them, just like he had the day he first addressed us on the deck of the *Pearle*. Unlike the rest of us, he looked neither glib nor triumphant nor proud of his daring. Instead, he wore the face of a man with a job to do and nothing but.

He turned to John Morris. It was that same carrying voice: "Lock them in the church, please."

"All of 'em?"

"Every one. If they do as they're told, they will not be harmed, am I understood?"

Morris shrugged and we trapped the Spaniards in their place of worship, something that struck me as fitting, for I figured anyone who swallowed that Good Book nonsense was already in a kind of cell, whether he knew it or not. At first it was easy work, but as the building began to fill we had to start pushing and shoving and ignoring the cries of fearful children, and this did slow our efforts. The job turned sweaty and when it came time to shut the massive wood doors I could hear them breathe out so they'd fit. Meanwhile, the Indians who'd guided us, seeing that the enemy was locked up and out of reach, buggered off.

We milled about the town square, awaiting orders, listening to the muffled whimpers coming from inside the church. The sun blazed hot overhead and if there was a breeze in the air, I couldn't feel it. Siding the front doors of the church were two high arched windows; pressed against those windows were dozens of flattened Spanish faces, eyes wide and staring out unblinking. Morgan turned and gave a single quick nod to his captains.

Then, we had at it.

I TOOK A lane away from the square. Taylor came after me, saying if anyone could figure a good place to start it'd be me. I picked the first house not full of raiders. It was a neat little home, both the roof and the kitchen table made of heavy dark timber. There was a big room downstairs and two smaller rooms upstairs and these three rooms managed to contain a decent amount of riches. Practically giggling, we took everything made of silver, meaning spoons, knives, forks, picture frames, candlesticks, jewellery, all of which we carried out and dumped in a pile growing in the middle of the square.

We went to the next house and oh, oh, the glee of it, the freedom of it, the utter bloody *justice* of it — as we dumped every drawer, as we snatched every keepsake, as we smashed apart each piggy, I could hear Taylor tittering and I knew why. Sheer glory this was. Every step through that steaming and fearsome jungle had been worth it, for with each pilfered necklace and pocketed earring I was getting even with all those who'd made my life miserable back in England. I'm talking about unforgiving landlords and brutal schoolteachers and truncheon-swinging police and priests with fat roaming hands. *Sod the world* was running through my head while we emptied one house after another, and it was intoxicating as Kill Devil. At the fourth house, we burst in and there was a trembling old bugger in one corner, blind by the looks of him and certainly feeble. He sat there, mouth trembling, hands shaking, voice a whisper. We ignored him and set to robbing, me running upstairs and Taylor staying down. That's when I opened a bedroom drawer and saw an old matchlock pistol with a dented wooden grip, nestled on a pile of bloomers.

"Blimey," I said out loud, and I heard big feet come pounding up the stairs. I held up my new plaything. "You lucky bastard," were Taylor's words even though anyone could tell it was a shite pistol at best. I didn't care. A gun was a gun was a gun, particularly if you didn't happen to own one. I was armed, now. A feeling of power surged through me, like I could do anything to anyone so long as I was a Brethren.

Which is pretty much when it hit me, a feeling of dread it was, creeping up my spine and filling my ears with angry noise. It was nothing I'd asked for or wanted, but there it

was, settling in the knees and shoulders and pit of the stomach, making me feel sick all over, and though I knew there
was a reason for feeling that way, I didn't know what that
reason might be. It was like playing the board, when the
other man hangs a queen and, though a part of the brain
screams for you to take it, another part of you knows it must
be a trap so you look and you look and when you still don't
see it you put yourself in your opponent's polished shoes
and you ask yourself what *you* would do were you the likes
of bloody him.

And that's when you see.

I rushed toward the door. "Jesus, Benny," called Taylor
Land. "Where you goin'?"

A few houses along, I found John Morris, who was stuffing Spanish cobs into a burlap sack. "Captain!"

He stopped. "This better be good."

"It's a set-up."

"What's a set-up?"

"This, all this, the Spaniards giving up so easy, like."

"They gave up, scrub boy, because they're cowards."

"Granted, captain, but..."

He took a step closer. His face was a coil. "They gave up
because they're in the middle of a jungle, in case you hadn't
noticed, and no one's ever had the stones to attack them.
They gave up because we got the drop on them, plain and
simple. Now bugger off."

I did as ordered and found Captain Freeman, another
two houses along, loading a pack with gold trinkets. He
looked up when I came charging in. "Make it quick," he
said, and so I told him what I suspected.

"What's your name, sailor?"

"Benny Wand, sir."

"Let me remind you of something, Mr. Wand. We are not the British navy. You are not a conscript. We are an equitable organization. You're free to leave at any point, though you'll quit your share of the purchase if you do. Now make your decision, matelot."

I fell into a brood. Though I kept looting, Taylor noticed the disgust about me and once or twice he asked me what had gotten up my snout. "Nothing," was my curt answer, and after a bit he accepted I was in a mood and there was bugger all he could do about it. Calm down, I kept saying to myself. You're new at privateering. The captains know more than you. Morgan knows more than you'll *ever* know. Stop thinking you're smarter than everyone. Stop thinking everything's a bloody chess match. Stop, stop, stop, stop, stop.

I couldn't, though.

It was like asking a cow to skip rope.

WE WORKED BY torchlight, too busy to sleep, taking anything and everything not nailed down. No one thought of sleeping. The next morning, we filled long thin canoes the townsfolk used to trade goods up and down the river. Our plunder included about forty negro slaves, who looked not at all fussed to be coming.

We launched with daybreak. The river flowed toward the ocean and this made the paddling easy, even with the canoes so weighted they barely cleared water. By now our captives would've figured we'd buggered off and despite the heresy of it they'd have punched out the church windows and freed themselves.

It was a glorious afternoon for everyone but me, full of high spirits and singing and grand talk. Meanwhile, I grew more gloomy and convinced. Along the way we drank from heavy red-clay bottles of Spanish wine, and whenever a bottle came to me I quaffed like a gutter drunk, enough they'd grab the bottle from me and tell me to mind my bloody share.

We kept paddling. Sometimes wine or spirits will focus your thoughts on the thing bothering you, and this was one of those times. There was a slight breeze and I tried telling myself nothing terrible could happen on such a nice day. It didn't work. I couldn't imagine it *not* happening: when you really gave it a thought, it was the only thing made any sense. After six hours of drunken paddling, we came around a shoal heavy with trees and vines and then entered the tiny bay connecting the river to the ocean. The singing stopped, the paddling stopped, bottles were dropped from loose grips.

Just like I'd reckoned, the bloody boats were gone.

EIGHT

I T ALL CAME in sickening flashes.

One guard's head was cleaved in two, the halves like coconut shells filled with pulp. My eyes squeezed shut and when they opened, a poor bastard was in half, torso and legs hanging like laundry from a tree limb. The eyes closed and then it was a body with its head buried in the sand, and if we'd pulled him out we'd have found not a cut nor bruise on him. Blink and a man with his privates stuffed in his mouth and blink and a man with his ears and eyes gone and blink and a man carved up like a dinner roast and blink and open and blink and open and blink and open, the images coming like bits of a hellish painting, all browns and reds and violet.

We beached and stepped out on shaking legs, each of us looking and not looking at the same time. Trembling, I was, all over. The wine in my stomach frothed into my mouth and it took deep sickening swallows to get it back down. We were next, that much I knew. Taylor sloshed over, lifting his knees high with each step. His breath had the same sour reek as mine, and he was pale as the day we'd landed in Port Royal.

"They knew we was comin'," I stammered. "Probably those smoke baths or maybe scouts in the woods. Instead of fighting, they stranded us. Now they're off to get reinforcements. They'll be back with the Spanish bloody army. It was their only move." I pointed at the massacre. "That's waiting for the likes of us."

So this is it, I couldn't stop thinking. So this is the end of *me*. It's what happens when death races toward you—all of your thoughts spiral inward, till you're the only person left on earth. It's a type of despair, feeling that alone.

Other canoes were pulling up and soon our entire force was standing in dank water, a goodly number of men losing the Spanish wine we'd taken on the way in. That's when I looked around for Morgan, thinking if nothing else I could watch his uppity rearing be put to the test. I spotted him among the captains. His mouth was a slit, his eyes narrowed. Lines spanned from the corners of his eyes. This went on for ugly long minutes, and then he was pointing. "You. And you, and you, and you ... get rid of those bodies."

The selected men looked at each other. Then they started dragging the bodies toward the waterline, kicking each cut-apart corpse with a boot heel. One by one the guards logged with pink water and slowly sank, and each time one of the bodies slipped beneath the sea, trapped air formed bubbles on the surface of the water. Then we were all quiet and standing there breathing rapidly, until John Morris piped up, his voice a snarl.

"Only one thing for it, Henry. We take the boats back to Villahermosa and claim the whole bloody city hostage.

Though not before we do to some of them what they done to us. We'll put on a little show of our own." Morris was breathing hard now. "When their army shows up, we accept nothing short of safe passage. In return, whatever townsfolk we haven't butchered get to live. It's the only way."

Instead of ordering the men into the canoes, Morgan turned to Captain Freeman. "What do you think?"

Freeman was a tall, considered fellow; when he spoke, it wasn't like listening to Morris, whose words were always charged with spite. "They've got us, I'm afraid. Santiago's a half day away. By morning tomorrow there'll be a thousand of them here. Maybe more. They'll have the rack with them. We'll be torn limb from limb and I'm not exaggerating when I say that."

Morgan then looked at Marteen, who said in his funny Dutchman accent, "It's the only vay I can see."

"You heard him!" blustered Morris. "It's the only bloody way. And the more we stand around on the beach feeling bad about that lot" —he pointed toward the spot where the bodies had sunk— "the less time we'll have to take back that cursed city."

Morgan looked at Jackman. "Do you agree with this?"

Jackman thought for a moment, chin against chest. Then he lifted his head and said, "I do."

Morgan eyed the rest of us. There was a stillness in those sharp grey eyes. Already, word was passing back down through the ranks, saying how we'd take back Villahermosa and make each and every one of those papist bastards sorry for what they done. It was a popular plan, even though there was no way the Spanish army was going to surrender to the pathetic likes of us, hostages or no hostages.

That's when Morgan surprised me again, just like he'd done when he stepped into that Indian smoke bath. Without another word, he turned and walked off and stood at the water's edge, his back to us all, hands clasped behind him, just looking out over the ocean and its popping pink bubbles. He wasn't moving nor doing nothing else, just standing there, peering. Though there was no time, and all around him was horror, he was choosing that moment to have himself a right think.

Already, some of the men were stepping back into the canoes, sure Morris's plan was the only one there was. Others were powdering their flintlocks and others were sharpening their cutlasses on rocks. Morgan didn't move. It was like he was enjoying the bloody view. John Morris paced and bitterly muttered *for fuck's sake* under his breath, and soon there were other such comments coming from the rank and file, *what the hell is Morgan doing?* being most common among them.

A minute passed and then another before Morgan turned and walked back to where we all stood on weak legs. Each man was silent and looking on with frantic flitting eyes. I prayed I was wrong about the man; since first laying eyes on him back in Port Royal harbour, strutting about like a rooster, I figured he'd gotten his post the way everyone did, through family and privilege and bugger all else.

"If we go back," Morgan said, "it'll be our deaths. A few prisoners will not stop the Spanish army from slaughtering us all. That much I know. Now. There's thick jungle on either side of us, so we could try walking out of here, but chances are we'd get lost and starve, or surface and be spotted."

"So we go back to Villahermosa!" said Morris, fists clenched at his sides. "At least we'll show 'em what's what. Give 'em a taste of their own medicine, like."

Morgan shook his head. "Our objective is to escape with the loot, not spill Spanish blood. I'd ask you to remember that, John."

"But there's no other way!"

"Oh no, John. I believe that there is."

WE GATHERED ALL the slaves we'd taken and lined them up along the shoreline. Morgan found someone who spoke Spanish, which only helped a little for the slaves seemed to speak some language unknown to anyone but themselves. Still, they knew a little of the enemy's babble and with a bit of hand language thrown in for good measure they soon understood what was on offer, their faces breaking into broad smiles. Then we roughed up their clothes and ripped their shirts and tore at their trousers and rubbed dirt on their faces, all so they'd look like a group of sorry escaped slaves overwhelmed by fear and hunger, their only hope rescue by passing ship. We stepped behind the jungle wall, the slaves staying on the beach and doing a good job looking frightened and weary.

The heat began to climb. Sweat gushed from my hairline and into my eyes. My shirt soaked through and the backs of my knees grew wet, causing my breeches to stick to me like muddy cloth. We waited, saying nothing, mouths shut, as if the slightest sound might scare away the entire nation of Spain. After twenty minutes or maybe more, I heard a murmuring come down the line. Sure enough, there was the distant outline of a ship; it was so far off it took a while before I reckoned it was heading in the direction of the Old World. A galleon it was, the size of an English village and so laden with goods it could barely move.

My thoughts were so loud I swore the others could hear me. Or maybe it was *their* thoughts, somehow gaining purchase inside my ears. Either way, we all had the same determined wish, *stop you bastard stop stop stop stop* and the galleon was so far away and moving at such a snail's pace that, for a while, it was easy to convince ourselves maybe it was slowing. But no. The bloody thing kept on going and then the sea was empty and still and tortoise green. We waited. After another half-hour another big ship appeared, this one almost as low in the water. When it was close enough to spot our beachhead, the slaves all jumped and waved and shouted and whistled and generally put on a show worthy of the Globe. Again I listened to the thoughts of other men as they listened to my thoughts, *stop stop stop you bastards stop*, and though I could see a ruddy Spaniard on deck, looking at the slaves through a telescope, the bastards kept on going, and whether it was because they were too wily or whether it was because they figured a bunch of slaves weren't worth the bother, I couldn't say. All I know is Morgan's trick failed again, and when I looked over to see how he was reacting, all I could see was he wasn't — he had that same look about him, like the world was incapable of pleasing him or disappointing him.

Like the world just *was*, and nothing more.

A third ship came about an hour later, and it too sailed on, nary a thought nor a notice sent our way, and this time the voices in our ears were desperate and losing hope, for above us the skies were starting to darken. All around us, men were hanging their heads, lost to their final thoughts.

"Benny," Taylor said while peering up at the weakening sky.

"I know."

"It gets dark, we're dead men."

"I know."

"I won't die like those poor bastards on the beach," he said. "If I have to go down, I'll go down fighting."

"Me too," I whispered, though I had no idea whether this was the truth. I'd seen a bit of death in my time, and I knew for some it comes peacefully and for some it comes with bitter anger and for some it comes with a blubbery despair. Already, I was starting to wish I'd made something of myself in this life. This startled me — it felt as if I'd been carrying this desire around for a good long time, not realizing it was inside me, when all of a sudden it popped up and all I could think was, *where'd you come from, then?*

I heard the men around me draw breath once more. A ship with three masts was approaching, smaller than a galleon but still decent-sized — a barque, I think it was, but like I say, I knew bugger all about boats. Once more the slaves all jumped to their feet and began shouting and waving and calling in that strange, strange language of theirs. Once again we told ourselves the boat was slowing, the only difference being that this time it was actually happening. My heart pounded, though not from dread but from hope. It was nearing. It just *was*. About twenty feet from shore, it dropped sails altogether and came to a rest against a sandbar, the slaves cheering and pumping their fists to the sky as a dozen or so Spaniards jumped overboard to have a look-see. They waded toward the slaves, and started pointing at muscled thighs and strong backs and one buck with particularly thick arms. Another Spaniard strode up toward the beach to inspect one slave's backside, a move taking him to within ten feet or so of the jungle wall. I looked over at the captains and wished only for carnage. I was not disappointed. As calmly as a man out for a Sunday stroll, John Morris took three long strides toward the Spaniard, his cutlass raised high. He hit him in that little space between the neck and the top of the shoulder. The blow carried through the man's body, shearing off his arm and much of his flank before coming to a rest at his lower ribs. Only then did the Spaniard turn and see Morris, and in the second before he fell there was an understanding in the dead man's eyes. He never even made a peep.

The other Spaniards — simple traders they were — turned and saw their error, eyes wide and jaws dropping and wet pools forming in the front of their breeches. Jackman was the next to stride out, his cutlass blow coming more horizontal and nearly lopping off his target's head. The other Spaniards all ran without hollering or yelling or carrying on, their only hope to reach their ship and somehow set sail before we could catch them. Meanwhile, the few men left on board were all scrambling for weapons they either didn't have or couldn't find. I watched the gutting from within the jungle, the water filling with arms and legs and lopped-apart torsos, and then Morgan's men were killing the men left behind and tossing them into bloodied salt water.

Overjoyed I was. My life was mine again, and if a few Spanish traders had to die, so be it: the New World was rancid with them as it was. But mostly I felt admiration for this man called Henry Morgan. I'd been wrong about him being a typical rich halfwit—we'd have been dead men without his calm thinking, and no one could say different.

Morgan walked up to the slaves. "You're free now," he said over the sound of our men whooping and hollering. "Go."

The slaves peered at each other. Given what they'd just seen, they were nervous about leaving. Morgan spoke louder. "You're free! Now go!"

Still they stood there.

"*Libre*! You're all *libre*! Now *vaya*, *vaya*, I beseech you."

The rise and fall of his voice, along with the gesture of his hands, finally convinced the slaves this slender light-skinned man had kept his promise. At first they couldn't believe it. Their mouths hung open and their eyes bulged. Smiles came over them and then they cheered and laughed and patted each other on well-muscled shoulders. A few of them even took to dancing in the shallow water. It didn't last. After a bit of rejoicing they had a look around and stopped laughing and cheering, their dark faces fallen. It was a sad sight, these sorry bastards all looking at one another, faces drooping with *what now?* expressions. For all I knew, they'd been born slaves and knew as much about jungle survival as we did. Instead of racing for homes that didn't exist, they all just stood there, except for the ones who sat on wet sand.

"Well done, everybody!" Morgan bellowed. "Let's get to it, men!"

A cheer went up—we had our health and our swag and the future those two things could buy us. Working by moonlight, we dumped the traders' load, crate after crate of fustic and plantain headed for one of the other islands.

As we did, the freed slaves waded into the water and picked up the bashed-up crates and hauled them back to the beach. When the barque was empty, we began filling it with swag, and when the ship proved too small, we lashed overflowing canoes to its stern. We tightened the sails and were off. The slaves waved from the beach. I had no doubt they'd stay until morning, when another Spanish ship would pull over and enslave them for real.

Having learned his lesson, Morgan wouldn't let us burn a lamp nor torch on board, his navigators travelling by memory and the stars. Being so laden, we could barely move, which made us easy prey for any Spanish warship. There was nothing for it but finding secluded bays to hide in by day, during which time we counted and divvied the loot. We set sail at night, hugging the shoreline for fear of being run over in open water. This meant being extra careful of rocks and reefs, but Morgan had men who were geniuses when it came to finding their way in the low glare of moonlight. It took us five full days to limp back to Port Royal, and anxious long days they were.

But I will say one thing.

When we finally got there, we were rich bastards, every last one of us.

NINE

ﾧ

O NE BY ONE, we jumped into shin-deep water, pockets
   spilling, grins wide, erupting with thirst and hunger
and lust and every other madness caused by glory. Ready for
a celebration, we were, and suddenly Port Royal was geared
to oblige. Every hawker, pitchman, and claims-maker in
town was waiting for us, like they'd risen from the dead,
and how they knew about our success in Villahermosa is
anybody's guess except to say good news must travel as fast
as bad. The moment we tromped onto the beach, they all
started selling, be it some item we'd perish without or some
delectable we'd be fools not to sample or some experience
we had to have or we'd go to our graves all the sorrier.

First off, there were victuals, and believe me when I
say these blighters knew what we craved, their little tables
blessedly free of boucan, hardtack, turtle, or seaweed tea.
They had mango and coconuts and raspberries the size of a
large man's knuckle; they had yams and carrots and squash
one vendor claimed was "of the same size and succulence
as your mistress's bosom"; they had jackfruit and guava

and pineapples so rich with sugar it caused a tingling in the teeth; they had pimento, cinnamon, and a ginger so potent your nose could pick it out from twenty paces, and that was with the breeze in the wrong direction; they had choco-late and sweet wine and a special tobacco that grew in the island's interior and was known for sharpening a fellow's understanding of the world's mysteries. Meanwhile, those infernal wigglies ran around everywhere, snorting at boot heels and shitting a pea-green stream and generally look-ing sinister, though everyone else just ignored them so I figured I would too.

A healthy number of Morgan's men must've kept women on the island, be they wives, girlfriends, mistresses, or some combination of the three. Those vendors selling anything of a frilly variety — lace, silk, velvet, damask — were doing a brisk trade amongst those who hadn't bathed in weeks. The same went for those hawking perfume, ambergris, and something called "oh day toy-let" — you name it and some fast talker was spraying the wrist of an unshaven galoot who may or may not have had a hand attached *to* that wrist. The customer would sniff, rumple his nose, and comment, "Smells like flowers, yeah?"

There were also men who clearly had children on the island, for those vendors with little dolls and toys and string-and-ball games were having a field day as well. I can still recall one ham-fisted buccaneer trying to choose between a bunch of wooden dolls, each with petticoats, ribbons, and gold slippers. He kept looking them over, picking them up, holding them close, and inspecting them until finally he broke into a smile and bought the lot.

A bunch of us strolled along, enjoying the thrill in the

air, the other matelots throwing around money like it'd have no value if it weren't shed that day—I saw one privateer buy himself a monkey, another a baby jaguar that mewled like a baby, another some sort of exotic bird with violet tail feathers and an ear-displeasing squawk about it. Course, you didn't ask what they'd do with their new pets for they didn't know themselves.

A shifty-looking piker, in a long buttoned doublet and tall boots, sidled up to Taylor and me. The others walked on. "Good afternoon, gents. I trust you both count yourselves among Captain Morgan's entourage?"

"What's it to you?" charged Taylor.

"Ah well," was the man's answer. "It won't do. It won't do at *all*."

"What's that, then?"

"If I'm not mistaken, you've no pistol in your belt and your friend here has nothing but an old Spanish matchlock, suitable for blowing the chin off his own face and not much more. What you fellows need are a pair of high-quality flintlocks."

All ears, I was. The man saw this and grinned like one of the crocodiles we'd seen on our way into Villahermosa. Knowing a thing or two about the art of persuasion, I had to applaud the way he was reeling us in.

"Now it means little to me, gentlemen. But it might mean something to *you* the moment you draw on a foe who isn't so disadvantaged, if you appreciate my meaning."

Taylor chuckled. He saw the game too and was equally impressed. "It's true," he said to me out the corner of his mouth. "I've bugger all and yours is pure shite."

The man heard. "Fortunately, that's a problem I just

might be able to remedy." He parted his doublet and revealed a pair of handguns. "Might you be interested?"

"We might," I admitted.

He took them out and handed them over. "Made by the great Galin of Nientes. Note the hand-carved hammers— this one's a breaching whale, this one is an enraptured mermaid. And the barrels! The right is carved with a sea god feasting upon grapes, while the other is adorned with all the moon and the stars in the sky."

We held them in trembling hands. Though I knew as much about guns as I did about boats, even I could tell they were works of art. "They fire true?"

"They do, sir. They do indeed."

"We'll find you if they don't," snarled Taylor.

"I'd expect nothing less," said the man before naming a price that could've bought a small house in Cornwall. We didn't care; with the booty settled, we both had enough to buy an entire Cornish village. Without bothering to haggle, we handed over enough silver cob to satisfy the man. He made a hat-tilting motion and walked on smiling, his eyes peeled for another customer. I kept the sea god, Taylor the moon and stars.

We both peered through the empty barrels. "Straight as a minister's prick, wha'?"

"Straighter," said Taylor.

Newly armed, we walked on, urchins running around everywhere, little salty-haired boys no older than ten and some a far sight younger, handing out scrawled-upon cards. By the time I'd flung my useless Spanish gun into the waves, we had quite a collection, all of them featuring the names of hotels and the ladies who plied their trade there, or leastways that's what Taylor, who knew how to read, told me. I'm talking about working women, with monikers like No-Conscience Nan or Mary "the Countess" Carleton or Salt Beef Peg or one particular harlot whose name and specialty were one and the same, the chubby-thighed Buttock-Clench Bertha. Course, I was no stranger to this world. When I was thirteen, my ma informed me she'd have no fancy boy as a son and the next thing I knew I was sitting in a chilled room in my skivvies, Ma saying if my dad was half a man he'd have taken me himself *but oh no, oh no, at home he is, in bed with a bottle, and who knows when he'll be good for anything?* A yellow-toothed hag came out, though when I say she was a hag, she was probably no more than thirty. She gave me the once-over and then joked to my loathsome ma, *well, if that's all there is, I need charge yoos half only!* Ma had a right cackle over this one, slapping her knee like there was a bug on it, though when she noticed I wasn't laughing she turned serious and asked what the hell I was waiting for, an invitation from the Queen? The woman took me away. I remember her breath was smoky and her hands were coarse. A baby was crying somewhere.

My point *being*, each establishment, now open and eager for business, offered specials to lure in the punters: ten percent off full suppers at the Black Dog, two ladlings of grog for the price of one at the Cat and Fiddle, rooms by the hour at the Green Dragon, Chinaman pipefuls at the Sign of Bacchus, or a soothing massage for any buccaneer willing to grapple with No-Conscience Nan, who was professionalizing at the King's Arms. Just wandering, we were, until I thought of the only Port Royal drinking establishment whose door I'd yet darkened, a business offering entertainment of both a two- *and* a four-legged variety.

"Fancy a drink?" I asked, and when Taylor said he would, we headed toward the Bear Garden. As we walked, I recalled how quiet and desolate the warehouses lining the wharf had been when we'd arrived on the *Charity*. Now they hummed like beehives. Men in navy slops were carrying out barrels of fustic, cochineal, indigo, sugar, tortoise-shell, cow leather, brazilwood, logwood, corn, pimento, coconuts — you name it and some bugger was lugging it dockside, where ships would soon come in and carry it off to points north, east, west, and south. Its customers would be anyone, even rogue Spaniards who'd grown tired of the prohibition against any trade not lining the pockets of the King of Spain. If you asked me, that was the reason we were going to win the war — even the Spanish weren't loyal to Spain.

We walked on and soon we were on a small street linking the beach to High Street.

An old biddy was lolling from an open window, calling out to passersby, "That's it, boys, just a few feet more!" We nodded and kept walking, flower girls with low-cut blouses stopping us every few feet and asking did we want to buy a carnation or rose or tulip for that special someone. We bought a few just because we could, and kept going, High Street more madhouse than passageway, the street so crowded with drunks and footpads and fallen women and rooting wigglies it was difficult to keep moving in a straight direction. Outside one public house, a fierce-looking brute with huge gold earrings and a nose partially lost to knife battling was standing next to a gusher of wine, its spigot open and releasing a tawny red sun-glinting arc. "Anyone don't take a drink 'll have me to answer to!" he yelled while waving about a cutlass. It was a needless threat. A queue had formed, man after man filling his gob with intoxicating syrup, the bugger laughing and yelling, "Right, you can pass... right, you can pass... right, you can pass!," his voice so hoarse it sounded like growling.

We each had a glug, wiped our faces, and kept moving. The street was thick with goats and pigs and sheep and even the odd lumbering cow, all being led to restaurant kitchens up and down High Street, half the sounds reaching our ears being bleats and whinnies and oinks. There was squealing too, though mainly this was from the flower girls, who kept getting their backsides pinched in return for their labours. Fights, too, were breaking out—an imagined slight, a judging glance—and so crowds were gathering, money passing from hand to hand as the combatants swung drunkenly at one another. At one such fisticuffs Taylor wanted to stop and spectate. "What's your hurry?" he called when I kept on the move.

We came to the Garden, its doors looming high and wooden and arched above us. With a grin, I shouldered them open.

INSIDE, IT WAS dark and noisy. Suzie the Bear was doing hind-leg walks and barrel rolls in return for lobbed sardines (the fishes provided at a premium cost by the barmen, no doubt). Every square inch of floor space was occupied with seamen, all of whom I recognized from the Villahermosa mission. Thick-armed wenches walked around with mugs of ale and jiggers of sweet Portuguese wine; when one passed, you dropped a coin into her trough skirt and helped your-self. Trollops, both black and white, circulated as well—you knew them for they wore satin corsets instead of chambray skirts, and they said things like, "Fancy a go, gov'nah?"

"What we doing?" Taylor yelled over the din.

"The bar!" I yelled back, so we pushed through the singing and yelling and fish-tossing and backside-pinching throngs. Progress was slow, barging out of the question. Finally we reached our goal, banging our fists on the cedar-wood planks and yelling for service just like everyone else. This caused the man beside us to turn in our direction, and when he did, I saw it was John Morris, Morgan's second-in-command. He gave me one of his harsh Morris glares, as if the very sight of me had put him off his drink.

"Well, look who it is." His voice was dripping with it. "What brings *you* 'ere?"

Without waiting for an answer, he turned away. I craned my neck around, thinking if Morris was here then maybe the other captains were here, and if the other captains were here then maybe Morgan himself was in attendance. No such luck; the only person I saw was Taylor, standing behind me holding jiggers of Kill Devil. "Look what I found! Cadged them off that lovely over there."

The ensuing swallow seared the roof of my mouth, the back of my throat, and the walls of my gullet before it dripped burning into my stomach. Still, it did its job, and over the next hour I sampled every manner of spirit, includ-ing a fermented honey you let ooze down the back of your throat. The Bear Garden was a din of roared song and merry spirit, and before long Suzie the Bear was taken out of her sandy pit and replaced by a half-dozen dark women.

They all started dancing to a fiddler. I don't know where they came from, but they were well fed and ample in all the places where ample looks fetching, their movements including buttock shaking and breast waggling and suggestive glancing. The customers cheered and whistled and howled like stuck dogs. Soon, customers were throwing pieces of eight into the ground-coral sand at the bottom of the pit. Every time this happened, a rouse went through the building, for it meant whoever tossed the pieces now had the privilege of taking the woman of his choice by the chub of her wrist, leading her outside, and having at her in the alley siding the building. A few minutes later she'd be back, resuming her dance, grinning like a jack-o'-lantern, until another punter tossed a bit of his purchase into the sand: she'd leave and come back and leave and come back and so on and so forth. I'd watched this pageant for about fifteen minutes when another blustery shout went up and then there was none other than my matey Taylor Land leading off a strumpet not half his size. He'd just taken to the street when a pistol went off.

The fiddler stopped playing and the bar went quiet and the scent of gunpowder wafted. John Morris was the culprit. He was sitting pit-side, half scowling and half smiling in that searing John Morris way of his. Everyone turned.

"Enough with the darkies," he grunted. "Time for some white meat, yeah?"

Morris re-powdered his flintlock, an action spurring a quick conference among the Bear Garden barmen, who all seemed to know who John Morris was and so decided it wise to hustle out the negresses. The pit was empty for a few minutes, an absence that frustrated the customers, who started pounding their fists against tabletops and chanting, "White whores! White whores! White whores!" This turned to cheering when a few doors opened upstairs and a score of curvy pale harlots, their skin tone consistent with sleeping through the daylight hours, flounced down the stairs. They all wore high-waisted frocks that belled at the waist, red satin shoes, and corsets that plumped their breasts into dollops of snow pudding.

The fiddler resumed his fiddling, and the girls started dancing, though compared with the dark ladies it was barely a dance they were doing, more like a sullen perambulation with the occasional hip gesture. The men roared their approval anyway, and the sallow-faced women kept at their little jig until some pasty bugger with a nose the size of a puppy's head roared they should be off with their clothes. The harlots pretended not to hear, a tactic in no way pleasing to their audience. The Bear Garden clientele went back to pounding whatever they could find to pound, and chanting, "Take it off! Take it off! Take it off!" in the same rhythm they'd employed not minutes ago.

The performers remained unmoved and stubborn, the noise in the bar so prominent the fiddler stopped bothering to fiddle. The comeliest of the strumpets called out: "What? Take off me Sunday suit? I've got me re-poo-tay-shun to think about, 'aven't I?"

A groan went up, along with dozens of sooty arms, until the giant-nosed bloke started a new chant, *who the fuck cares?! who the fuck cares?!* —the girls sticking out their tongues and continuing their silly little jig, the chant growing louder and louder and the men crowding closer and closer, *who the fuck cares!? who the fuck cares!?*, and just when it seemed the veil separating decency and degeneracy might tear to ribbons, John Morris stepped up.

A hush fell. The whores stopped jigging. Morris was that sort.

He nodded toward the girl with the Cockney tongue. "I've five hundred pieces of eight what says you'll dance naked right here and right now."

It was a laughable offer: a Spanish piece of eight was worth a British pound, more or less, and five hundred of them was sufficient to buy a home with a view of the Thames River and quarters for a servant. Yet we all understood his real intent. Back in London, our whole lives had been run not by people but by money. Enough and you're this class, not enough and you're that class. Enough and you talk one way, not enough and you talk another. Enough you have lessons, not enough and you come of age an ignorant bugger. Enough and it's lamb, not enough and it's mutton so tough you spend your night chewing. Enough and you can enter a shop with nice fresh goods, not enough and it's black and blotchy bananas for the likes of bloody *you*. On and on it went: the clothes you wore, the church you attended (if you were thick enough to do so), the single-sheet you read (if you could read the printed word). Most of all, it determined the way people looked at you, and it was this look that'd made me desperate to leave England. It withered you, was the truth. Made you tired and headachy and wondering what the point was. By offering up this fortune, Morris wasn't saying he was desperate to see a naked and skinny white woman. Far from it. He was saying he was axing a system that'd choked him since birth. He was telling the whole world he was fighting back.

"Wha'?" she exclaimed with a nervous laugh. "Five hundred pieces of eight? Just to see my precious?"

We all roared with laughter. Even Morris chuckled.

"Show me the bleedin' dosh," she said, and when Morris held out two hands spilling with silver, a smile came to her face.

"Bleedin' 'ell! Looks like I won't be needing these..."

She started unbuttoning her frock and soon she was prancing and naked, wiggling her pasty-white behind, laughing at the punters while they laughed right back, all of us sharing in this triumph, and that included Morris himself. It was an enjoyable moment, though the floor chose that moment to start tilting beneath my feet and I figured if I was going to have companionship that night it was going to have to be soon. I got up and headed toward the rough wooden staircase where the professional ladies stood between clients. Not choosy, I walked up to the first girl on the stairs; she was chubby and blond-haired and the furthest thing from the bony yellow-toothed hag I'd lost my childhood too.

"Twenty quid," she said. "That's your lodging too."

"In London you could buy a horse for twenty quid."

"Well, this ain't London, govnah, though if it's a little whinnying you want, I suppose I could manage some. Cost you a few shillings more, though."

"Another time, darling," was my answer, for I'd spotted another more to my liking, and if I was going to part with twenty quid, at least I was going to be happy with my selection. This one was olive-skinned and a feast to gaze at, her dark hair falling in thick bangs to her eyebrows. Since she was giving me the grin, I went up and said, "It'll be twenty, I suppose?"

She shook her head and grinned. "Twenty-five, handsome."

"Twenty-five? And knock off the handsome business. I know what I looks like."

"It's still twenty-five. If you're surprised, it's 'cause you're new to town and you know neither me nor me particulars."

"Well then, you'd best enlighten me, yeah?"

"They call me Two-Tongue Tessie," she said, and to demonstrate she flicked her tongue out of her mouth. Split up the middle it was, the tip like a serpent's. Whether she was born that way or had it done to her by someone with a demented sense of purpose I had no idea, nor did I care: she wiggled the twin tips, showing me how they moved free of one another, as if each had a dastardly mind of its own. Funny, it was a deformity made me think I knew her, or leastways how her life must've been.

"Right," I said, "you'll do," and I followed her upstairs and along a lamplit corridor to a room just wide enough for a bed and a small table supporting a wash bowl. I collapsed on the bed and watched the ceiling rotate above me. Her quarters smelled of incense and sea salt.

"No slaps nor pinches nor kisses," she said as she removed her corset. A pair of nice ones tumbled out. We chatted while she soaped me. "So. One of Morgan's men, are we?"

"We is."

"Heard you had a right go of it in Villahermosa."

"You heard well."

"Staring death in the face an' all."

"Eye to eye."

"Tell me. You care 'bout things more or less now?"

"What you mean?"

"Now you've come close to topping it, you care more 'bout things or less? It's a simple question, matelot."

"Dunno," I said. "Didn't care much before and if that's changed, I can't say I've noticed. What's with all the chit-chat, then?"

"Just trying to be friendly. Now. Have a lie-down, why don't we?"

I did, and then she was atop, tossing her black hair from side to side as though lost in the sheer pleasure of it all, grunting words a man could go his whole life not hearing (and not *wanting* to hear) from a wife or sweetheart.

And there I was, eyes closed, a rich man finally, the whole world at my beck and call, a delectable wench cantering above me, when a sick feeling came from nowhere. Bloody hell, I thought — before my inner eye was a colour-soaked memory of that awfulness back at the river head. Yet it wasn't the slaughter of our boat guards popping up in my head — it was the Spanish merchants we killed, that horrible mix of surprise and terror on their faces. It wasn't the gore or the moans or the pink bubbling waters — it was the way they were too scared to scream. It was their eyes gone wide with knowing they'd reached their end. Even my ears got in on the act, that sickening thud of English steel halving flesh, and why why why was this visiting me *now*? To banish the pictures in my head, I opened my eyes and looked up at Tessie. I watched her jiggling bosom and her nice-enough face and even this didn't help, oh no it didn't, and when Tessie felt it too, she bent over and swished her tongue over my neck, licking it like it was candy.

"It's the Kill Devil," was her read. "It'll take its toll, all right, but don't you worry. That's why you spent the extra fiver."

Then she was moving lower, dampening my chest and belly and what all else, her tongue a pair of salamanders intent on slaking their thirst, and it was this quenching—this shameless divining—that finally took my mind off Villahermosa and got the job done proper.

TEN

I AWOKE TO WHATEVER seaman was in the room one over, for he kept moaning, "Wha' 'ave I done? Wha' 'ave I fuckin' *done?*" through paper-thin walls before coughing and sputtering and grunting and scratching himself so loud it sounded like a rake on gravel.

The light outside was a limp blue. I hung my head out the window and the smell of that awful back alley, full of animal innards and chamber pot muck, did the trick. I pulled my head in, my right arm resting on the windowsill and my damp forehead making a red spot on top of my shaking arm. Here I stayed gasping for a minute or so. Then I wiped my gob, glugged all the water from the pitcher next to the peter bowl, and staggered back to bed.

I had no feeling of sleep after that. I only know I awoke to a hard rapping on my door. I was lying on my stomach, face buried in a lumpy and brown-stained pillow, wishing whoever it was would go away. There was more rapping, though this time the person outside was yelling in a Creole voice, "Time up! Out ya be gettin'!" and then it was another door pounding and the same voice yelling the same thing a little farther down the hall.

I dressed and found a public house where eggs and trotters were on offer, along with real coffee. This in itself felt like a miracle; before Villahermosa, the only coffee in town had been chicory, and even that'd been hard to find. After breakfasting, I located a bathhouse near the Merchant Exchange where I had myself a long hot soak, the bath filled and refilled by a warty old crone who called me luv. While soaking, I asked for a shave and, after a few minutes, was visited by an old codger who had to've been seventy if he was a day.

He stood before me, hands and lower lip shaking, as if he had some sort of palsy. In his left hand he held a razor that glinted in the light.

"Never mind," I told him. "Think I'll grow a beard."

"Ahhhh, don't gimme tha' bollocks, mate. There's nought to worry about. Strange thing is—the moment I touch a man's face, me hand goes firm as a tart's backside, yeah?"

He pulled up a little stool from nowhere and, sure enough, the moment that razor found my skin, his hands stopped shaking and his body stopped quivering and the shave he gave me was the best I'd had in the whole of my life. I paid him double and told him I'd see him again.

"Ta," he said before leaving. "Been doing this for sixty years and I 'aven't lost one yet!"

That afternoon, I rented a room in a boarding house on Lime Street, around the corner from the fish market. My room was in the back of the building, overlooking a pen holding a pair of butchery hogs named Katy and Mr. Pete.

Aside from the odd grunting caused by Mr. Pete having a go at Katy, who didn't seem to fancy him much, the room was as quiet as it got in Port Royal. Each morning, a breakfast of tea, porridge, eggs, and sometimes kippers was served in the basement by the owner, a bulbous-nosed Limey called Rodge. One day he sat across from me while I was spreading jam on my toast. He looked at me all sideways and I knew a question was coming.

"It true what I heard?"

"Depends what you heard."

"It was Morgan saved the day in Villahermosa."

"It was, yeah."

Rodge gave a big phlegmy laugh. "Jesus. If it'd been me, I'd've shite myself."

"You'd not've been alone," I told him. "There were more than a few skivvies fouled that day."

Rodge chewed this information over, and then gave me a broad toothy grin. "Well, in that case, make yourself at home, son. Any man of Morgan is welcome in my humble ah-bode."

SO THAT WAS it, then. There was bibbing and eating decent food and carousing with a double-tongued lovely named Tessie, and if that got boring, there were rooms you could go to, dank back-alley dens run by small yellow men who, grinning and bowing and pocketing your money, would bring you a skinny pipe as long as your arm. I tried it once and found it not for me — three puffs and I puked, the visions afterward a torment.

During this time I gave not a single thought to chess,

thinking those days were behind me and good riddance. As far as I was concerned, I'd found something better: in a single expedition with Morgan, I could make a hundred times what I made in a year of running a dodgy board. Yet some things are a part of you, and seem to follow you around like a hunting dog. Late one morning, I was sitting in my room, head as foggy as a London winter, when I heard a knocking at my door. It was Rodge, towel over his shoulder, wet spot on his shirt, hair plastered to his forehead, his nose the colour of a monkey's gums. "Someone downstairs to see ya, Benny. Outside, like."

"Who?"

"What I look like? A mind reader?"

I threw water on my face and tamped down my clothing before going down. Sure enough, there was a tall skinny man with a one-horse trap; he had one of those Adam's apples like a child's toy on a string, bobbing up and down whenever he swallowed. But that wasn't the oddest thing about him. His arms ended where the elbows should've been, and instead of elbows, he had funny little hands shaped like starfish. He kept them at his sides, where they trembled just enough so you'd notice.

"You Wand?"

"I am."

"Henry Morgan wants a word."

I laughed out loud, though he stayed sober. "Wha'?" I said. "You serious?"

"Get in the trap," and my palms went sweaty, like the underside of a fish. I must've been in trouble in some way. Probably my whining back at Villahermosa, telling the other captains it was all an ambush when I should've kept my big mouth clamped, though if that was the case, why would Morgan himself deal with it? Why not get one of his underlings to tell me I was through? Why be bothered with the puny likes of me?

"You sure you got the right Benny Wand?"

He rolled his eyes and told me he didn't have all day. My inclination was to run, the problem being that Port Royal was surrounded on all four sides by surf. With no other options, I climbed up, thinking *bloody hell when am I gonna learn?* The driver clicked his teeth and we were away, winding through the streets of Port Royal, the poor bastard having to lean forward to grasp the reins with those stunted little hands of his. We reached the thin causeway from Port Royal to the mainland, the causeway so narrow I could have leapt from my trap seat and landed in ocean. Beside us, those strange speckled fish kept leaping out of the water and dropping with a splash, as if excited we were leaving.

Though I'd been in Jamaica for almost five months, I'd never seen the rest of the island, Port Royal being for cutthroats and ne'er-do-wells while the mainland was for churchly families who woke with the sun and worked hard to settle Jamaica in the name of England. Yet here I was, passing tidy little homes, not an alehouse nor knocking-shop in sight, children playing nice in the streets, trays of scones left cooling on windowsills with no one caring someone might nick them. I rolled my eyes at it all and then we climbed into the mountains looming thick and green above the city of St. Jago, the trap making sighing noises in the soft sandy track. The road more or less hugged the coastline, with water to our right and sugar and tobacco plantations rising into the foothills on our left. We rode this way for twenty minutes or so, any attempt of mine to chat with the driver met with no more than a nod or a grunt or a puffing on his cigar. There was a brief time when the edge of the roadway and the edge of the mountain were one and the same, and seeing as the driver's hands were all but useless, or leastways seemed that way, I had a nice panic, thinking the fall would kill us both several times over. I breathed this away, telling myself he'd likely driven this route a thousand times and as usual I was inventing calamity where none was to be had. Sure enough, we reached a small black-earth track that wound up from the coastal lane. The driver clicked, and without the slightest tug or movement of the reins, his mare knew to turn.

As we rode into the island's interior, the breeze died and the air turned from hot to searing. Soon my shirt was sticking to my front and back. With each breath my lungs felt heated and I thought of the trek into Villahermosa, with the bugs and flies and what all else buzzing in our faces. We reached a break in the forest and a front gate bearing a single word with loads of letters in it, somewhere near thirty in fact, so I guessed it to be Welsh. Beyond that was a lane leading to a grand house.

"Mind yourself," said the driver, and when I climbed down, he made loud clicking sounds with his teeth and was gone.

The gate was low and wooden. For a moment I paused, thinking *what was I supposed to do?* With no insight or no one to answer the question, I thought the hell with it and pushed it open and walked toward the house, which looked like it'd been uprooted from back home and floated all the way to Jamaica. Unlike the houses in Port Royal and St. Jago, which were made of wood and propped on stilts, this home was granite. The front door was painted jet black, and there were shuttered windows and a pair of chimneys protruding from a sloping slate roof. All it needed was smoke curling from those chimneys and it would've looked like a proper English manor.

I reached the front door and found a knocker shaped like the King's head. I used it to club the door two or three times, not sure whether this was the mannerly thing to do or not. The door opened and I was looking at a tall beautiful woman, her eyes jade, her skin like fine white paper, her chestnut hair in a bonnet (and when I say she was beautiful, I mean she had real beauty and not the sort achieved through kohl and cheap plunging frocks and a quickness with cheap compliments). She smiled and offered her hand. I didn't know whether to kiss it or give it a friendly little shake. I chose the latter. Like everything else in the New World, it was warm to the touch.

"My name is Elizabeth Morgan," she said. "You must be Mr. Wand."

"Yeah. You got it."

"Please, please, come in, follow me."

We walked along a hallway, the floors made from light wood. There wasn't much in the way of furniture — a chair here, a sofa there, with crates scattered about — though I couldn't stop my head from whipping around, taking it all in, still not believing I was in a house so regal.

"You'll have to excuse the disarray," she said while looking over her shoulder. "As you can tell, we've just recently moved. We were lucky to find this place. It's starting to have a look of home about it, don't you think?"

We were at the end of the hallway, before a pair of tall glass doors. She pushed them open and walked into an enormous room anchored by an equally enormous stone fireplace. In front of the fireplace were a pair of winged chairs. Both were angled toward the mantel.

"We've more furniture coming from England," she said. "So right now we're having to make do. But please. Make yourself at home. I'll go find Henry. He must be around here somewhere. I know he's eager to speak with you."

She turned and walked from the room, leaving me alone. Though there were any number of things could've drawn my eye — the height of the ceiling, or the crystal chandelier hanging from it — I noticed that beneath one of the side windows was a small table, and on that table a chessboard. From where I stood, it looked like one worth putting to use.

I sat for another minute or maybe more, and just as I was about to go have a look at the board, I heard footfalls coming toward me. I looked up and it was *him*, Henry Morgan, the one and only, coming into the room, looking straight at me and even giving me a bit of a smile. He was dressed pretty much the same way he dressed on a ship, breeches and a clean white pressed linen shirt, though on top of it he wore a brocaded doublet that suited his position as a gentleman landowner.

"Mr. Wand, is it?" he asked. He thrust a hand forward and gave mine a hard squeeze.

"So good of you to come. Have a seat, please."

I took the chair closest to where I was standing. Morgan headed toward a little box on the fireplace mantel, and when he wasn't looking I took a deep breath to calm myself.

"Ah hah!" he said. "I've been looking forward to this all

day!" He picked up the box and opened it, pulling out a long narrow cheroot. He then held the box out to me. "Would you care to smoke, Mr. Wand?"

"Course, sure, I mean... if you're offering."

"I am indeed. Please, please, go ahead."

He sat across from me, lighting his with a wooden match. When he was done, he handed me the matchbox and I did the same, the draw tasting of almonds and fig and maybe even a little apple. It was right delicious, better than I'd ever had before, the tobacco for sale on the streets of Port Royal tasting like horse dung at best. My guess was he'd brought them in from one of the islands where tobacco grew surely as weeds.

"I've been curious to meet you, Mr. Wand."

"If I've done something to offend, I—"

"Of course not." He pointed a finger at me. "Now. Please tell me. How did you know?"

"Know, captain?"

"About Villahermosa. About the missing boats. I had a chat with Freeman."

So that was it. It was just like I thought, except he didn't seem put out, so I still couldn't figure what he wanted from my being there.

"Just a guess, I'd reckon."

Morgan leaned forward in his seat. "Oh no, Mr. Wand. You *will* tell me."

I swallowed. There was nothing for it but the truth, and that was a position I was unused to. "It was too easy, wasn't it? If we'd really surprised them, the moment they spotted us they'd have been rushing around like mad buggers, at least *trying* to hide their loot. But they didn't. That's what bothered me. They must've known we was coming, and if that was true, then being so accommodating was part of a plan, yeah? They was *too* accommodating, though. They was *too* obvious. That's how I knew."

Morgan nodded, and looked at the tip of his cheroot. "These are delicious, but it is true they don't hold a light well." He took a few hard puffs, bringing it back to life. Then he redirected his gaze at me. "We assumed they would assault us on the way out."

"How's that?"

"Come now, Mr. Wand. We're not stupid. Or at least we're not *that* stupid. We reached the same conclusion as you. We assumed they were planning an attack during our retreat."

"At first... I mean, speaking respectfully an' all, at first I thought that too. But then I asked myself: if they was going to fight, why not take us on the way in? Before we'd taken their loot? It would've been a lot easier, yeah?"

Morgan puffed. "Or maybe they wanted us burdened."

"Or maybe they didn't want to fight at all. Imagine you was them and saw the likes of us coming, savage mean bastards what meant business. You'd get help is what you'd do. Once I figured that, I knew they'd strand us while racing off to get the Spanish army in Santiago. If your move with the slaves hadn't worked, they'd have drawn and quartered each one of us, sure as you and I are sitting here."

Morgan raised an eyebrow. "We'd have been gutted, all right."

"I reckon they saw our fires."

Morgan shrugged. "Or they had scouts. It doesn't matter. What matters is that the taking of Villahermosa was a major victory for the British presence along the Spanish Main. That's one thing I hope you understand, Mr. Wand. With every successful mission, we weaken the oppressive Spanish governance of the New World."

Morgan's cheroot had gone out (as had mine), so he struck another match. When his cheroot was glowing red, he looked up at me and grinned.

"Tell me, Mr. Wand."

"Yeah?"

"Since we've been talking, you've had more than one glance over my shoulder. You've had several, in fact. As the only other thing in this room is my chessboard, I have to conclude that *it* is the thing you're glancing at. You don't happen to play, do you?"

Inside, I grinned. Course Morgan played. His type always did, for they figured it made them look smart. My livelihood back in England had depended on that fact.

"A little bit, yeah. Or leastways, I used to."

"Well then. I'm always looking for a friendly contest. Shall we see what you're made of?"

Morgan rose to his feet. He returned with the board and the little table, both of which he lowered between us so white was facing me. The cheroot, which he'd held between the second and third fingers of his right hand, had burned out again. "Blasted thing," he said before putting it aside.

Meanwhile, I admired the board. Beautiful, it was, the surface lacquered so it shone like a baby's tooth, each piece hand carved from ivory, with enough small differences to make each one worth admiring. One of the knights was smirking, and the pawns all had their own expressions, ranging from fierce to friendly.

"By the way," he said. "You've played more than a little. You're practically drooling."

"It's a right beauty, captain. Any fool could see that. It's nothing to do with my knowing the game or not."

"Please. Go ahead."

"What? Me go first?"

"I insist."

I used an opening called the Ruy Lopez, which'd just been invented by a Castilian monk so was also known as the Spanish Opening. Morgan chortled. "Good one," he said. "Fitting."

My opponent, I soon reckoned, was no Turtle Crawles piker. With each variation in the opening, he knew the counter, so it wasn't till the mid-game that our contest began to shift slightly, Morgan making a few ill-advised parries, and by defending them I was gaining slightly in territory if not material. For me the game was written already, there being an ebb in Morgan's position he'd not yet sussed.

Nor would he ever: I'd learned the hard way you don't embarrass your social betters, and it didn't matter if you were in London or Port Royal. Around the fortieth move, I left an opening that, if he took it, would guarantee his win. All he had to do was sacrifice a knight—the smirking one, as it happened—and when players sacrifice a piece, it never occurs to them it wasn't their idea. But first he had to fall for it. I watched him give it a think, considering whether the position gained would be worth the loss in material. In the end he smartly hung the horse, which I snatched up all grinning and merry-like. There the contest ended. My defence crumbled like rancid cheddar. After eight or nine more moves I toppled my king, admitting defeat, sighing like I meant it.

"Good game," I said. "That was a brilliant gambit, like."

Yet instead of turning all red and grinny, as if he'd just bedded an earl's daughter, Morgan studied the board. His chin was in his slender hand, the muscles in his face gone tight as wire. Those grey eyes, knifing through space — he couldn't take them off the board. He was calculating, thinking, drawing his conclusions. In fact, he looked just the way he had at Villahermosa, staring out over pink bubbling waters. Inside, I felt all wrong.

He looked up. "You ever throw a game with me again, Mr. Wand, I'll have you in the stocks for a fortnight. Do I make myself clear?"

I said nothing. Couldn't believe it. I'd never met a posh bugger who liked the game more than the idea of winning. It's the reason none of them are any good at it — it's just the win they want, their self-regard stoked.

But not Morgan. Not *him*.

"This time I'm white," he said as he reset the pieces. A moment later he moved a pawn to queen's fourth, again warning I'd better give him my best game. We played three more times. Like I said, he was a good player — better than good, even — though no match for someone born with an understanding that on every board there lies a glorious truth and it's your job to reveal it. Fact was, I heard music when I played chess. When I was getting at that truth, it was like birdsong. When I was crapping it, it was rusty pots clanging together. It was a hammer striking metal. It was a hippo blowing farts from a sackbut.

In two of the games, Morgan stayed with me, though

the last was a rout. He lost each game by growing restless and launching attacks that would've worked with the burghers he was used to playing but not with me.

"So," he said when we were done. "You're a professional."

"Used to be. Gave it up, though. Now I'm one of your Brethren."

"Where did you work?"

"Grog shops. Taverns. Gentlemen's clubs when they'd let me in—it gave the gents something to do waiting their turn. Leicester Square in a pinch, though the real punters prefer the indoors."

"I should have known."

"No. That's the whole point, captain." I pointed at the chop marks on my face. "I've the look of a blowser, of a blackguard. I'm a commoner just happens to play a posh game, and it has to be that way. If you could spot the player in me, I'd never make a penny."

"Well put."

"I could spot you a knight for the next…"

Morgan yawned, not really listening. He stood. I followed suit and he walked me out of the house toward the lane running along in front. He whistled, and then muttered, "That damnable chauffeur. He's got to be around here somewhere!"

We waited. Morgan was swivelling his head in every direction, and that's when it happened, those steel-grey eyes settling on yours truly. Yet his gaze wasn't saying *I've got you figured* or *you don't fool me, Wand*, which was a look I was well used to. It was something else altogether. It was like he was studying me, assessing what I was or was not, and I don't believe anybody had figured me worth the effort since

I was a young boy, my old granddad still puttering away in the kitchen.

I looked down, all self-conscious, and after a bit there was the clopping of hooves. When Morgan spoke, he sounded as if he'd come to a decision. "Mr. Wand. Is there any chance you'd come out and have a game with me again? I know I'm no match, but I've a feeling I might learn a thing or two from you."

"Course, captain. You know where to find me, yeah?"

Morgan chuckled, shook my hand, and wished me a good day. Then he turned and walked back toward his beautiful white house and his beautiful wife, and I felt a swelling of the same ambition that'd popped up and shocked me back in Villahermosa, when I figured my life was over and done with. The truth was: if I had a wish for anything, for anything at all, it was to have another game in a house like this, on an ivory board with hand-carved pieces, a cheroot tasting of figs and almond burning between my nicked-up fingers.

ELEVEN

I T WAS A bumpier ride on the way down; I hadn't visited a privy for hours and was feeling it on my kidneys. At my urging, the driver stopped behind a grove of old trees near the entrance to the causeway and I relieved myself before climbing back on. After traversing the causeway, he dropped me in front of Rodge's Lodges and with a quick nod left me. My excitement was the sort that leaves you feeling restless and tight-chested; in this world, it's who you know that counts, and knowing a man like Henry Morgan wasn't going to hurt me in the least. But there was more to it than that — it was that way he'd looked at me, like he was figuring out things about me I didn't know for myself.

I didn't feel like eating and I didn't feel like taking a walk along the wharf and I didn't feel like having a drink. Instead, I decided I'd go upstairs and try to figure out how I'd murder the rest of the day. After unlocking my door, I lied atop the bedcover and gazed at the ceiling, my head filling with insane wishfulness, when the room started to shake. The bed was jiggling beneath me, dust falling off the ceiling into my face and nose. My firearm, which I'd left on the bedside table, was rotating slightly in a counter-clockwise direction. I grabbed it, thinking it might go off on its own, and leapt to my feet. I made it to the middle of the stairs, which were rattling like a pair of wooden teeth in an old man's mouth, when it all stopped. I stood, listening for screams and yells and old ladies shrieking.

There was nothing.

In the common room, I found Rodge carefully putting back a few leather-bound books that'd fallen from shelves. "What the bloody hell happened?" I blurted.

"Wha'?" he answered. "*That*? We call 'em tremblers. We 'ave them all the time in Port Royal." He laughed; I looked a sight. "I remember the first time I felt one. Takes the breath away, don't it?"

"It does at that."

"Don't worry, you'll get used to it. Just a feature of life here. Every once in a while we get religious types, over from the mainland, saying tremblers are God's way of showing His displeasure for all we get up to over 'ere."

"So it's the Lord's punishment, is it?"

"Apparently."

"He'll have to come up with something better to top the likes of us."

"He will at that. By the way. You joining us for supper?"

"What's on the menu?"

"Tripe and mash."

"In that case, sure. Cheers. "

THAT NIGHT I ate a lonely dinner, my only company an old lodger who sat over in the corner, his back to me, shovelling his food with grunts of appreciation. I ate quickly and yearned for a decent smoke, thinking if there was any to be had, it wasn't in Port Royal. Instead, I went to the Garden, where I had a cider while watching Suzie the Bear catch kippers in mid-air. After settling up, I hit the Jamaican Arms and had a pint, thinking maybe I'd recognize some of the customers. I didn't, so I drank up and left, after which I tried the same at the Black Dog and the Blue Anchor and the Cat and Fiddle. Bored I was, and well and truly sodden by the time I spotted Taylor Land at a corner table in the Wind and the Willow, holding court with a bunch of muckety sailors.

When he saw me, he bellowed my name and waved me over. As I helped myself to a seat, he was loudly telling some story about a grave-digging job he'd had back in London.

"So there we was, after the service, about to put the bloody casket in the ground, when we hear a knocking. Johnny and me we looks around, searching for the door someone was knocking *on*." There were laughs and titters; it was one of those stories you knew the ending of, the fun seeing how the teller gets there. "This goes on, every few seconds *knock knock knock*, and I don't mind saying I was getting a case of the heeby-jeebies, when Johnny he looks at me, face wide with the understanding of it all. 'Jeezus Christ!' he blurts, and sure enough, we barred open the top of the casket and the poor bastard was alive, and who the idiot doctor was proclaimed him dead I don't know, but if tha' was me doing the knocking, I'd sure enough want to have a little word, if you catch my meaning!"

The others howled, so I did as well, though I wasn't really paying attention to the stories being told. Instead, I was still astounded that the one and only Henry Morgan had taken notice of me. It was all so unlikely I kept it to myself, just liking the way it felt inside, and with each drink that feeling grew, until I was more or less grinning at every fool thing said around me.

Course, it was a feeling didn't last. Over the next month, it began to sink in that Morgan had seen me just to satisfy some curiosity about the events of Villahermosa, and since then had forgotten all about me — he'd been a powerful man acting on a whim and nothing more. I should have known. In fact, I felt quite the fool, and was ashamed I'd seen myself in a better light than I deserved. I was drinking and drabbing and starting to feel a little bored when, one day, in the middle of the week, my view of the way things worked was thrown into question once again. It seems the stubby-armed driver was issued from on high and started going from alehouse to alehouse, asking if anyone had seen the chess player. He found me at the spot where I sometimes took my lunch. It was just shy of two and that day's offer was beans on toast.

Thrilled, I was.

FIVE MINUTES LATER, we were on the causeway leading from Port Royal to the mainland, roiling ocean water to our right and stiller lagoon water on our left, our eyes squinting against the sunlight reflecting off those strange leaping speckled grinning fish.

The driver puffed angrily on his cigar as we climbed into the hills above St. Jago, my fear about plunging into

the ocean coming back, though not as fiercely as the first
time. At Morgan's plantation I climbed down, the driver
wasting no time clicking his teeth and buggering off. This
time it was Morgan himself who greeted me. I have to say
he looked pleased.

"There you are! I've been looking forward to this all
day. You'd not believe how busy I've been. It's been weeks,
hasn't it? The board is waiting, Mr. Wand. Oh, it is most
assuredly waiting!"

We strode through the mansion's main hallway and
into the huge room where I'd met him weeks earlier. There
were fewer crates scattered about and more furniture: a
sofa, chairs, statues, all of them ornate and with the look of
the French about them. Morgan caught me noticing. "It's
Elizabeth. She fancies the finer things of life—you know
how women are. In fact she's in town right now, buying up
the whole city if I know her. Please, please. Sit."

The board was on the little table next to the fireplace.
Morgan was about to take his seat when something occurred
to him. Striding back to the room's entrance, he called out,
"Nelson!"

I heard footsteps. Morgan stepped outside the room and
had a conversation with someone I figured worked for him,
likely a butler or some such. He returned and sat. "You're
white, Mr. Wand. And remember: no quarter asked for and
none given."

"I get it," I said, grinning like a fool child. I wiped the
smile off my face and chose knight to bishop three, just to
show him my bag of tricks was a large one.

So we played. As I said before, he knew his openings and
his mid-game tactics and all kinds of things I barely knew

myself. I started hearing the music good chess makes, for like I said, Morgan was a strong player, and to beat him I had to try, which is the thing I've always liked most about the game — to play it proper, your mind can't be on all the things that bother you throughout the rest of the day. It can be a salve, in other words, when it isn't ruining your life in other respects.

A tall native in waist pants and doublet appeared with a tray. He placed two glasses of beer and a jar of pickled eggs on our table, gave a little nod, and walked off. Morgan was concentrating so hard he didn't seem to notice.

He was stuck on a move, so I took a nice long draft of bitter. Finally, he put me in check. I blocked him, advancing a piece while doing so. "Remember," I said, "to take is a mistake," and he looked at me with a smirk, as if to say *like fuck it is*. The game went on, Morgan falling after twenty minutes or so, and then he sat staring at the pieces, wondering how he could have made every move he was supposed to and still watch the life seep out of his side.

He took a good long swallow of his bitter. "Tell me, Mr. Wand. What's wrong with my game?"

"Nothing, captain, you're a strong—"

"Bloody hell! Aren't we past that?"

Again, there was nothing for it but the truth. Funny, the way it bubbled to the surface whenever I was around Morgan.

"If you ask, captain, I'll tell."

"I want you to."

"Develop your pieces. Bide your time. Don't launch any parries till you're sure. In this game, it don't pay to be reckless."

He chuckled. "So I've heard. Another?"

We played again. If he'd heard my advice, it was his choice not to heed it. This was a shame, for it was a close game and if he'd listened, it would've been closer still. When I offered to spot him a pawn for the fourth, he looked insulted and I knew not to offer again. The next was no contest.

"Sorry," I said.

"One of these games I'll beat you, Mr. Wand. I don't know how, but I promise you I will. I'm a competitive man and I do *not* like to lose. But I do appreciate it if you put up with me until then."

"Course."

He was still studying the remains of our last game. "If only chess was like real battle."

"I'm sorry?"

"Your game, Mr. Wand. Your chosen profession. It's easy, compared to the real thing. It's tactics and nothing but. No lives at stake. No morality to muddle your thinking. It's child's play, Mr. Wand, compared to the real thing."

Morgan saw the confusion on my face and went on: "When we pulled into Villahermosa, and the city just sat there all pretty, begging to be sacked, the captains and I knew something was afoot. The only question was what. You *do* know what John Morris wanted to do?"

I shrugged.

"Put a few feet to the fire. Make them talk. Woold a few of them."

"Woold?"

"It's a technique, Mr. Wand, and not a pretty one. You clamp a vise to a man's head and give it a few turns. If he doesn't become forthright soon, the eyes pop out. First one then the other. Jackman and Freeman were for it too. Even Marteen, and he's the noblest of the lot. Morris said he'd be happy to do it if I hadn't the stomach."

"But you didn't do it."

"We're privateers, Mr. Wand, not barbarians. We represent the British throne in the New World. We have standards to uphold — my orders make that clear. Yet when I saw what'd been done to those poor men guarding our boats, well..." Morgan shook his head. "We were lucky, Mr. Wand. Damn lucky. If that slave trick hadn't worked, a bit of principle would've caused the death of every man in the expedition, including my own. Do you follow?"

"I think so."

"No. You don't. But maybe one day you will. Now play."

We had one more go, though it was a game in name only. Something was occupying Morgan, and midway through he resigned. We left the house and found his driver already waiting, puffing away, arms over a sunken chest. I was about to say goodbye when Morgan asked me a question. "The mood down in Port Royal. How is it?"

"What you mean?"

"Are the men still contented?"

"You mean happy, like?"

"*Yes*, Mr. Wand. Is everyone still happy?"

"I'd say yeah, far as I know."

We were standing next to the trap. It seemed he was admiring his view of the mountains and the town and the blue water well beyond.

"That'll change," he said. "When the money runs out, that'll change. You mark my words, Mr. Wand."

THAT NIGHT, I went to see Tessie. Afterward, our bodies damp with sweat, I asked her something. "Tessie, how'd your tongue get that way? If it's not my business, don't tell me, but I'm a curious bugger I'm afraid."

"Now you're askin' me to reveal my secrets…"

"Suppose I am."

"I was born this way. It's called lingual bifurcation."

"A mouthful and a half, that is."

"Back home they all thought it the sign of the devil. It's why I came here. Couldn't get no peace. People whispering behind my back. Saying I had the mark of the serpent an' all. Never mind getting a real job. That's been out of the question since day one, it has."

"Well, you won't get any bother from me."

"And why's that?"

"No such thing as the devil. Nor God, for that matter."

"Wha'? You don't believe in God?!"

"You *do*?"

"Course."

"But why?"

"It's what you do to get by."

"Not for me."

"What's the point of it all, then?"

"There isn't one. My own ma started shilling me on the street when I was six, and since then I've spent my life cheating people over a chessboard. Not a lot of meaning in that, far as I can tell."

I turned my head and looked at her. I swore I could picture the way she must've looked when she was little, before life drove her to a place like Port Royal. If I wasn't mistaken, the same thought was running through her head.

"Benny? It true you're the best chess player in Jamaica?"

"Maybe Port Royal. The rest I can't say. Don't know what goes on in St. Jago, now, do I?"

"Could you teach me?"

"You want to learn?"

"'Well you see them playin', you know. In the bar or out on the main square. I always wondered how them pieces moved over that board and for what reason. Looks like it might be a way to pass the time. During the day, like, or on slow nights."

"I'll teach you. You might regret it, though."

"What you mean?"

"That game gets its hooks in you, it might not let go."

"I'll gift you a free go in return, so's long as you don't tell Agnes."

"In that case, I really will teach you."

She laughed. "Now," she said, "time you buggered off. Others are waitin', yeah?"

I told her I'd see her soon and then I went for a bit of a stroll. After a bit, my walk took me past Turtle Crawles, and I noticed there were eight or nine men out there, sleeping rough next to low wispy fires. The next day there were a few more out there and the next day a few more still. It wasn't just them — the turtles had come back, no one ever did figure out where they'd gone to, and the smell of roasted meat hung over the beach like a cloud. The next day there were more mateys still, all passing bottles and muttering how they wished Morgan would hurry up and pick another target. They'd run out of dosh, was the long and the short of it, having spent it all in Port Royal grog shops and brothels. I wasn't far behind them.

I cut down on the drink and the drab, and though I missed seeing Tessie, it was the way it had to be: every day more buggers were moving back to Turtle Crawles. Rodge's Lodges began to lose its renters, till only a few of us were left, and we were there only because Rodge had lowered the rent. Every morning, at breakfast, we'd ask for double rations of banger or egg or whatever else was on offer, a way of getting to dinner without spending money on lunch. Rodge would generally oblige, though not without complaining our stomachs would put him in the poorhouse and when was Henry Morgan going to launch another expedition?

The cost of things was dropping. A pint of English bitter, a full quid after Villahermosa, was down to a few shillings. You could have a full meal with sticky wine for not much more. That same strumpet who earned five hundred pounds for a naked dance two months earlier was now offering brutish acts for a tenner, and that included a night in a hot, bug-infested room. The number of stalls in the market dwindled, those hawking silks or perfume or imported sweets the first to go. Soon, only basics were left: meats, veg, day-old fish, yams. Stores were closing as well, shopkeepers offering the finer things in life being the first to padlock their doors.

By early fall, the first of the saloons shut down, the understanding being they'd open when there were fortunes in Port Royal needed wasting again. The restaurants began closing, and pretty soon I was taking all my meals at Rodge's though he was getting skimpy with the meat and heavy on the potatoes. The only other option was to join the turtle eaters on the beach, something I'd be doing soon enough. With all this, the mood in town changed. Every bastard was grumpy, every street-corner conversation about Henry Morgan and what the hell was he waiting for? Didn't the bloody Spanish need a tarring somewhere? Didn't those olive-skinned bastards have a city in line for sacking? As unfair as this might sound, there were even times I felt the same way myself, as if I was here to make my fortune and it was the sworn duty of one Henry Morgan to help me do it. Then I'd give my head a shake, and remind myself, if it weren't for Morgan, I'd still be playing the board for quid notes a go.

One afternoon I was having a pint with Taylor at the Bear Garden when it came time for the next round. It was mine to buy and I was complaining. "Don't know how much longer we'll be able to do this," I said. "The swag's running pretty low."

For some reason, Taylor grinned.

"What's with you, then?"

"This morning I heard a rumour," he told me. "Down at the market, like. Those Creole fish women seem to know everything. They're the ones really run this place, you know. They own half the leases in Port Royal and they save every copper."

"Well, don't keep me in suspense."

"Seems the governor of Jamaica, a pudgy joker named Bollingsworth, has got it in his head that the Spanish are dusting off their cannons and sharpening their cudgels, all with a mind to taking back the island of Jamaica. Because of this, he's got Morgan and his captains out stealing ships for another mission, the idea they'll hit the Spanish Main hard, if only to make the Spanish think twice about Jamaica, or anything else for that matter."

"Really?"

"Would I be sayin' so if it wasn't?"

As rumours went, it wasn't a tough one to swallow seeing as Morgan's captains hadn't been in town lately. Only a month earlier, John Morris had been out every night, slumping at his regular table, roughly shouting for rumbullion and a trollop in need of a spanking. Now he was nowhere to be seen, his absence a relief to many.

Morgan, too, had stopped sending his cigar-puffing driver, and as far as I saw it, there were two possible explanations. The first was he'd grown tired of the board, which I doubted: when certain men get a taste for the game, it doesn't go away easy, and I knew for a fact Morgan was one of them. The second was he was off the island with his captains, and it was this possibility I clung to, seeing as I was weeks away from joining the others on Turtle Crawles.

Days went by slowly. All anyone could talk about was Morgan this and Morgan that, and believe me when I say there's nothing for slowing time down like anticipation. One morning, Rodge placed a bowl of lukewarm cream of wheat before me, the days when he served rashers and/or kippers and/or eggs long behind us. I looked up and thanked him and was surprised. Instead of him looking all dour-like, he was wearing a bright smile.

"Swallowed a canary, have we?"

"Not as such."

"Then what's lightened your load, Rodge?"

"Went for a walk this morning, didn't I? Off to the market, spenders in pocket, mind the bloody wigglies, see what I could rustle up, same old story, yeah?"

"For fuck's sake, Rodge. What you sayin'?"

"They're out there, Benny. 'Ave a see for yourself."

After choking down the porridge—it tasted like mashed paper—I rushed to the wharf and, sure enough, saw five ships, sails dropped, not moving, out on the horizon. As I say, they were far off and I still didn't know bugger all about boats, except to say one looked huge, three or four sails minimum, while three had a pair of sails each, and finally there was a little sloop with a single mast only. I squinted, and if my eyes weren't playing tricks, they were all outfitted with cannons, which meant one thing and one thing only.

They were Morgan's, all right.

TWELVE

M ORE DAYS PASSED, time a maddening lurch. Why
Morgan didn't get right to it, like he'd done the
first time, was anyone's (and everybody's) guess. To kill the
hours, I'd wander down to Turtle Crawles and reunite with
some of the blackguards who'd come over on the *Charity*.
Their spirits weren't suffering too badly, for they'd figured
out how to make a sour frothy wine from simmered banana
peels. Though it seared the gullet and was as tasty as it
sounds, it did cause a man to see things through a certain
glow. Everyone talked about the next mission — where it'd
be, how much they'd take, what they'd do with their swag.
This helped. At night, I'd stagger back to Rodge's and lie in
my little bed as the room slowly swayed and rocked, and
I swore I could hear distant voices singing *blow, blow, blow
the man down* ...

It wasn't long before I had to tell Rodge I was well and
truly skint. He shook my hand and I said I'd be back soon,
for with Morgan on the horizon riches were on their way.

"I'll keep your room for you, Benny," and it surprised me for I really think he meant it.

Then I was on the beach with the rest, eating turtle and passing calabashes, scaling trees for coconuts, watching Morgan's fleet for a sign the day had come. I missed a real bed and visits with Tessie and decent food, though on the plus side there was this thing between us men, meaning we'd lived through Villahermosa and had regard for one another and laughed easily in each other's company.

There was one bloke known for a sharpness of vision — we all called him Eagle Eye Eddie, or Eagle for short — and one afternoon he stood and walked to the water's edge. He shielded his beady little eyes and peered out.

"Look," he said.

A bunch of us walked as close as we could to the sea without being in it. I squinted and could see nothing but those five boats bobbing and swaying out on the horizon.

"Wha'?" someone said.

"Can't see bugger all," said another.

"He's having us on," said another, though not a one of us sat back down on the beach. In fact the opposite occurred. As we stood there, hands shielding our eyes, others noticed and joined us while asking, "What you see? What you bloody *see*?" until finally we all did see it, a little black dot which didn't seem in motion unless you turned your head for a count of ten and then looked back at it again and saw it was a tiny bit bigger.

Though the sun reflecting off the water left spots on our eyes, we kept watching and sure enough the black dot grew bigger and bigger until it became a small boat rowed by a pair of strong-backed men. There was a third man in the boat, doing sod all but stare back at us, and after another ten minutes or so we could all see the man was John Morris.

It came to a rest on the shoreline. Morris climbed out, boots splashing in water. He walked toward us, knees lifting high with each step. Those of us gathered all perked our ears.

"We leave tomorrow," he barked. "Eight a.m. sharp. There'll be transport waiting. And be in good form. I'll not have any pukers."

A cheer came and then questions.

"How long'll we be at sea?"

"What's our target?"

"What'll the swag be like?"

His response was to glare, as if we were all something to be tolerated instead of counted on. He sloshed back. There were those who watched the little rowboat turn back into a bobbing black dot, but I wasn't one of them.

THE NEXT MORNING was the madness of boarding and then we sailed east. Our progress was swift until we cleared Jamaica's eastern tip and turned north in open water. Here we were hit with a head-on gale, our progress a slow zigzag into strong winds. I was on a sloop named *La Concepción* with Jackman my captain. Though I would've preferred Morgan, I could've drawn Morris, so I supposed I couldn't complain.

Taylor was on the same ship. Jackman's first mate gave us both scrub brushes but told us we could use that day to get our sea legs back. Mostly we stood around, leaning on gunwales, watching the island of Cuba bob in the distance. The wind blew angrily, so we tied on bandanas to stop our hair whipping in our eyes. Some complained of feeling queasy, though I was let off easy. Toward the end of that day we reached a small string of islands along the southern shore of Cuba. Here we anchored in the shelter of a cove that hid all five ships from passing traffic. Night fell. As we feasted on mutton, a rumour passed we were still waiting for a few ships from the tiny French island of Tortuga, on the north shore of Hispaniola and a day away. We all pegged them for coming the next day seeing as Jackman limited us to just two jiggers of sticky wine with our suppers, keeping us fresh and ready for travel in the morning.

Dawn came orange and calm, not a wave on the cove nor a whisper in the palms above, though this was bound to change when the winds gathered. We had real coffee and rashers, which we enjoyed all the more knowing after a day or two the perishables would run out and it'd be boucan and salted turtle unless we managed to scavenge a bit of fruit or fish. After we ate, I noticed a rowboat depart from the head ship, which was anchored at the very end of the bay. I watched as it stopped before the next ship down, a double-master that'd been fitted with cannons like the rest. The man rowing the boat called out something, and though I couldn't make out what it was, I could see the lads on board all shrugging their shoulders. The boatman moved on to the third ship in line, where he again yelled something met with looks of confusion. This happened at the fourth boat as well, and though we still couldn't hear his question, we could see the boatman was a huge bastard dressed in naval slops and an old Monmouth cap. Again he didn't get the answer he wanted, and he moved to the last boat in the line, which was ours.

He cupped his mouth and hollered, "Oi! Any you lot called Wand?"

There were a dozen or so on board who knew me from Turtle Crawles. To a one, they all pointed.

"You're gettin' moved, like. To Morgan's boat."

Yes! I thought, and I was about to get a move on when I noticed Taylor, standing there, glumly watching, eyes squinty. Bloody hell, was my thought.

"I'll be bringin' my mate," I hollered.

"What you mean?"

"I'm bringin' my mate's what I mean."

"My orders were for one only."

"Then I won't be bloody goin'."

We had ourselves a little standoff, the boatman and I: narrowed eyes, tightened jaws, nobody blinking, Taylor saying *don't be fussed, Benny.*

"All right," the boatman finally said. "But if Morgan won't take him, *you* gotta row him back, yeah?"

We had a deal, and within five minutes Taylor and I were in the rowboat, enjoying a row to the flagship. When we got there, we climbed aboard using a long ladder hooked over the gunwale. Once on deck, another man told us to wait and we cheekily told him the idea suited us fine.

Morgan came up a minute later, a look of business about him. His boots struck hard as he came toward us. "Mr. Wand," he barked. "Where have you been, man? I thought I told you you were on my ship."

"My mistake, captain! Must've swum to the wrong one. Won't happen again!"

"Who is this?"

"We came over from England together. Name's Taylor Land."

"I see. Welcome aboard."

He walked off and that was it: everyone went back to mopping or mending sails or whatever it was they were doing before we'd come. Taylor and I'd brought our scrub brushes and so we got to work on a part of the deck behind the forecastle, which we picked for its being out of view. That way, few noticed when we spent most of the day leaning against the gunwale, smoking cheroots and talking.

"So," Taylor asked me. "What's with you and Morgan?"

"Nothing."

"Dunno if I believe that."

"He's a man likes a game of chess now and again."

Taylor grinned. "If I know you, Benny, and I think I do, you've got something up your sleeve."

"Just my arm."

"Well, keep it that way. You don't mess about with his lot. And don't be going posh on me, neither."

"If only that was an option," I joked, and though Taylor laughed, it was the sort of laugh you give when you don't find something that funny.

THAT NIGHT, THERE was another dinner of mutton and potatoes, both boiled some days earlier and looking wrinkled and grey. Again we were limited to two jiggers of wine, a ration that caused grumbling and complaints about boredom and not knowing what the hell we were doing out here. Shortly after a blazing sundown, I was standing and looking out over inky water when someone tapped my shoulder. I turned. It was some blighter with a clean shirt and an air about him.

"This way."

"What?"

"This way. The captain wants a game, don't he?"

He turned and I followed, the two of us descending into an immense hold filled with hammocks. At the far end of the hold was a door. When the messenger boy knocked, Morgan opened.

"Ah, Mr. Wand." He stepped aside and motioned me in.

The room was cozy: a bed, a dresser, and a table with maps spread out. There were chairs on either side of the table. A small board with roughly carved men was on top of the maps.

"Have a seat," Morgan said. "Those bloody Frenchmen. They said they'd meet us in Port Royal, and then they sent word saying they'd be here two days ago. *They* were supposed to be waiting for *us*, the laggards. There's nothing worse for morale than sitting around doing nothing, am I right, Mr. Wand?"

"If you say so."

"I do. I'm also going out of my mind with boredom, and none of the captains can muster near the game you can. You're a godsend, Mr. Wand. You really are. Please. You're white."

I opened with pawn off to the left of the board, a way of freeing up my king-side bishop. He moved a pawn to the centre, and in those first two moves we'd both declared our strategies: he'd try to take the centre board from the start whereas I'd seize it all sneaky-like during the mid-game.

After thirty moves or so I was in trouble, my head-music turning to squonks and screeches; perhaps my attention was elsewhere, or maybe Morgan was playing harder than usual. Either way, it was like having a cold bucket of water dumped over my head: though we were even in material, was no denying his position was better and if he continued pressing and didn't do anything rash, it'd be me who crumbled and not him. My heart picked up a little. My vision sharpened, the details on the pieces leaping out at me.

"For Christ's sakes," Morgan said with a grin. "Is this going to take all night?"

It'd been minutes since I'd moved last and I was still staring at the board, trying to figure a way to right the noises in my head and seeing none. Morgan lit a cheroot and puffed fragrant smoke, and as he drummed his fingers on the table an idea did come. I knew Morgan, or leastways I knew the way he played the game. I'd take advantage of *him*, and forget what was happening in the actual game. Finally, I moved.

Morgan groaned — "About time, Mr. Wand" — and turned the screws a little tighter. So what did I do? I frustrated him. I vexed him. I started making moves with no obvious purpose except to waste time. I gave up trying to gain advantage on the board, instead looking for a way inside his head. This was another way chess was like life: most of it happened between the ears and not in reality, and if you couldn't see that, there was no hope for you. I kept backing up and springing sideways and then locking into a shell, my strategy not to win but avoid losing. I moved the same knight six times in a row and at no time did that knight threaten Morgan or seek position or do anything beyond exercising my fingers. I took my time about it, too, waiting a minute or two, thinking hard, before each seemingly pointless move.

Morgan did exactly what he was supposed to do. He grew impatient. I could see it in his lean suntanned face: he knew he was winning, though he couldn't actually *win*. By the same token, I'd never seen him play so carefully and I wondered whether those times I'd told him not to act rashly had sunk in. We passed the half-hour mark. At no point did I know whether my plan would work until he launched a parry would've toppled most players, but not me. The counter didn't kill him, but the game did shift in my direction and after twenty moves more he sat back in his chair looking deflated.

"I should have taken that one, by gum."

"Maybe."

"You're a wily one, Mr. Wand."

"Only on the board. Every other way I'm a dunce."

He chuckled, and took a long puff on his cheroot. "You sell yourself short," he said, and I brightened at the thought.

With a face full of blue-grey smoke, he looked me straight in the eye. Again, it was that feeling like he could see inside me, and me hoping he saw something he liked. What he said next was neither question nor statement but something in between: "You grew up wanting, didn't you?"

"I'm sorry?"

"Poor. You were poor as a boy."

"Not a pot to piss in. I know it shows. I'm sorry."

"It's nothing to be ashamed of. Some consider a man's background to be a measure of his worth, but I'm not one of them. Myself, I'm from a Welsh military family. I don't fool myself, Mr. Wand. Were it not for my father and uncles, I'd have never gained a Letter of Marque from the King. It's a rigged system back home, and you don't have to grow up poor to see it. What church did you attend?"

"I didn't. I'm not a godly man."

"Most aren't. At least you admit it. I myself find it a comfort. It can come in handy in a tight squeeze."

"I suppose."

"But not for you."

"Makes no sense to me."

"So you're a rationalist."

"Dunno what that means."

"It means, Mr. Wand, that everything you do is governed by reason."

I snorted. "I doubt that's the case, captain."

Morgan exhaled blue smoke. "Who taught you to play chess?"

"My granddad. He was pub champ. He passed on when I was six."

"You're a far sight better than some pub champ, Mr. Wand. What age did you start spotting him pieces?"

"Can't say. He was pretty good."

"But not like you."

"I suppose not."

"So you've the gift."

"Some have said so, though I wouldn't call it that."

"And your father? Did he play?"

I chuckled at the thought of it.

"I see," Morgan said, like he was trying to put together all the clues I'd given him.

Inside, I swelled. Again, it was that interest of his.

"What landed you in Port Royal?"

"A poor loser. Friends in the right places, he had. Trumped-up charges did follow."

Morgan nodded, as if it was a story he'd heard before. "I assure you that no one will hold your station against you here. Not in the Brethren of the Coast. Here, the only thing I care about is a man's ability. Do you know what a meritocracy is?"

"Merry ... uh ... how's that?"

"Meritocracy. It describes any system whereby a man's advancement is based solely on merit. Not family, not money, *merit*. It's the reason I'm tearing apart the Spanish. The best men rise to the top, if you can believe it. It's revolutionary. The enemy could learn a thing or two from us."

Morgan paused. His face changed. "Mr. Wand," he finally said. "Have you heard of a city called Portobello?"

"No, sir."

"It's a way station. On the coastal Main."

"What's there?"

"A roundhouse. Filled with gold and topped with soldiers."

"How many soldiers we talking about?"

"I don't have a figure." He shrugged and took a few hard puffs. He looked down and for a few seconds it was like his mind had gone elsewhere. Then his eyes flitted back up. "Though if I had to wager, there'll be a fair sight more than in Villahermosa."

"So that's it, then? Next target is Portobello? Why you tellin' me this, captain?"

"Please, Mr. Wand, it's no secret." He pointed to the ceiling with his cheroot. "Or at least it isn't any longer. In fact, by the time you go back up on deck, I think you'll find there'll be a rumour going around."

"Yeah?"

"Oh my yes." He gave me a sly grin. "It seems that some of the other captains have been blabbing."

THIRTEEN

THE NEW DAY meant hardtack and chicory coffee, no more rashers or fresh eggs, our disappointment lessened by two French sloops moored at the end of the inlet, their shapes hazy in the mist.

We were still chewing when we pulled anchor and sailed past the moored sloops, the men on board all waving. When the original five ships reached open water, the Frenchies pulled anchor and did their best to keep up. Morgan now had a decision to make. He could travel west, snaking down the Mosquito Coast before reaching the target. This would mean a two- or three-week sail, the advantage we'd have lots of nooks and inlets to hide in should hostile ships arise. The other option was to sail directly across the Caribbean Sea, a much faster route, but we'd be in plain view the whole time and easy prey for any warship on the prowl. The winds were blowing strong and, surprise bloody surprise, Morgan chose the more daring of the two.

It was a fine day for travel, the wind whipping so hard we had to yell to hear each other. Behind each ship were two or three long canoes attached to a line; even with the drag they caused, we skimmed the wave tops, moving at a fierce clip. We skipped lunch and raced on. When news spread that Morgan had decided to take Portobello—a city with an actual gold storage—there was excited talk and grinning. Around mid-afternoon, just as the sun was falling from the sky's bleary midpoint, the weather changed. One minute the wind was chill and dry; the next it turned warm and soupy, like it was weighted with manure. We were completely becalmed, going nowhere, stuck as a donkey in mud.

Morgan came on deck and marched from stern to bow, finding a hundred and one things needed doing, from ripped sails to cannons flaking with rust to ropes looking frayed and weak and in need of repair. Suddenly we were all too busy to study the horizon, looking for Spanish warships while growing ill with worry. A rowboat arrived with the other captains and they all climbed aboard using a dropped rope ladder. Morgan greeted them. They all went below to have a palaver, and twenty minutes later the captains returned to their own ships. For the next five hours we busied ourselves with one useless task after another while waiting for the Spanish to show up and riddle us with cannonballs. The skies turned orange and then purple and then they were an inky black.

The winds began to rustle in the middle of the night. We travelled south for several days and then the wind died a second time, though by this point we could see a hazy green line in the distance. After a bit the wind stirred, and over the next couple of days we limped toward that chalky green line. We reached the coast just before nightfall, and though we were all exhausted, Morgan ordered the navigators to

take us west along the coastline, being careful to avoid reef
and rocks and jutting points of land. Again, I don't know
how they did it, short of seeing like bats.

Morning rose and we moored in a tiny inlet. It was the
first time we'd felt safe or even somewhat close to it in a
week and so we all napped, pretty much dropping where
we stood. Two hours later, a first mate went around, kicking us in the boot soles and telling us to liven ourselves.

Across from the boats was a wall of jungle broken by a
spindly river. We started manning the canoes, though this
time we left a small crew with each ship, Morgan telling
them to moor offshore where they couldn't be attacked from
land. We pushed off. The canoes were slowed by low water
and driftwood blockades, meaning we were constantly getting out and, knee deep in brackish water, pulling the canoes
over sandbanks. We struggled for hours until we reached
a fork in the river, one way streaming up and to the right,
the other up and to the left. We were two hundred, more
or less. "Let's split up," Morgan announced. "If the Spanish
have rovers, it'll confound them. Make them think we're
half our real number."

Morris, Freeman, and Jackman led a party to the left,
Morgan and Marteen taking their crews to the right, with
the Frenchies split between two parties. We trudged on, saying bugger all, fear creeping in. As we got deeper into the
jungle, the canopy above us thickened and the light weak-
ened, turning everything dark green. The river turned to
creek and then the creek became so shallow we all had to get
out and slosh through murky shin-deep water, dragging the
bloody canoes behind us. After an hour we reached another
split in the creek.

"Any feeling?" asked Marteen.

"We stay right," said Morgan.

When we reached the next fork, we had three tines to choose from instead of two, one going left and one going right and the other heading straight ahead after a bit of a squiggle. "Look," Morgan said while pointing. Those of us who were close turned and saw a giant tree root that looked exactly like a mermaid with a flattened head. There were even two knots of wood making a pair of decent-sized breasts. Course, this inspired the usual vulgar comments, *nice knockers* and the like, though any laughter was cut short by Morgan picking right again. When we reached the next fork, he acted like it wasn't even there and went right again. After this fork we walked for a long time, the jungle growing thicker and thicker until the branches from either side touched over the creek, which was no longer wider than a foot or so, everyone keeping his mouth shut for it was obvious we were lost and the less said about it the better. When we reached yet another fork, we all spotted an immense tree root that looked exactly like a mermaid with a flat top for a head. The only difference was that this time she was on our left instead of our right.

Morgan stood staring at it, his eyes like cinders. Sweat dripped into my eyes and made them sting. We heard twigs breaking and branches snapping and low mumbling voices; we all went for our weapons just as John Morris stepped out of the woods, his men behind him. Though I'd never liked the bastard, it didn't change the fact I was happy to see him, even with him looking face-scratched and scowly.

"You lost?" he asked, and when Morgan didn't answer, you could hear the groans.

"I've something for that," Morris said, at which point he turned and whistled and a pair of ugly freebooters stepped through the jungle. Between them they held a Spanish soldier.

Morgan's face lit up. "My word! Where did you find him?"

"He was out having a stroll."

"Have you interrogated him?"

"Thought I'd let you have the pleasure, Henry..."

Morgan stepped up to the man. He was a runty little scout, maybe eighteen years of age, with a flat nose and beady little scorn-filled eyes. All forehead and big ears he was, and I knew he was the sort to watch out for, little pug-men who made up for their size by being as snotty as possible.

"You will lead us to Portobello now," said Morgan.

"No," grunted the Spaniard, though we didn't know was he saying no to Morgan's command or *no, I don't understand what you're bloody saying.*

"You..." said Morgan in a loud voice. "... *usted* ... will take us..." Here he held out his palm and made walking motions with his second and third fingers. "... to Portobello!" He then picked a direction and pointed, though nobody knew whether this was the actual direction of Portobello save the captured Spaniard.

Morgan looked down. The scout struggled against the big men holding him in place. "No," he grunted, to which Morgan again stated, "You will lead us to Portobello or suffer the consequences, man!"

The prisoner screwed up his little face and hurled a gob of spit at Morgan; it landed in Morgan's hair, where it hung like a dripping of bat shit.

Morgan breathed deeply, pulling a handkerchief out of a pocket and wiping away the spittum. He turned away, as if to have another of his famous thinks, when he heard the sentry chuckle. In that instant Morgan backhanded him hard, the slap like a pistol crack. With one side of his face bright pink, the Spaniard starting kicking and howling and yelling, "No no no no no!"

John Morris went up to Morgan, his smirk saying what was on offer. Morgan looked at the crazed little scout, and then he looked around the jungle, as if giving it one more chance to reveal where in the hell we were.

"Jesus Christ, Henry," Morris snapped. "The little prick's got it coming."

Morgan took a deep breath. A drop of sweat fell from the tip of his nose.

Then, he nodded.

THE TWO GIANTS holding the Spaniard dragged him toward the mermaid stump and threw him over it, the two men holding him down with all their might while the captive kept up a constant stream of shrieking Castilian babble peppered with English swear words. To keep him still, another of Morris's men stepped up and grabbed the Spaniard's arm; in a second it was held out and flattened against the stump top. While that was happening, Morris seized a machete and showed it to the runt.

"Right," he said. "First one hand... one *mano*... yeah? Then the other *mano*, *el otro* fuckin' *mano*, yeah? Then a foot, then the other foot... the other, er, *pee-ay*... you got it, *hombre*? *Comprende*?"

He held the machete high. Those who looked on jeered and pointed. Someone pulled the Spaniard's sleeve up to give Morris clear aim, and that's when things quieted. Even the Spaniard chose that moment to shut up, his face dripping snot and drool and what all else.

"*Uno* . . ." Morris yelled. "*Dos* . . ."

"Hokay!" shouted the Spaniard. "Hokay hokay *está bien!*"

Inside, I grinned; Morris had hesitated just long enough while counting to let the scout imagine a life spent handless and footless, and in my experience it's the imagination that's a man's fiercest enemy. Well played, I thought, for the stocky runt was leading us through the jungle, looking shaky and like the fight had gone out of him. Morgan went up to Morris and cupped his shoulder with his hand and said, "Good work, John, good work . . ."

After another hour, we stopped at a large glade. Beyond the glade was a thin fringe of forest and past that a huge stone building. It looked halfway between a castle and a roundhouse, and was near as big as bloody St. Paul's, a shock of a thing to see in the middle of nowhere. We all gawked up at it, wondering how we were going to get in, seeing as several hundred soldiers were milling about on top, each one dressed in a scarlet jerkin and peaked helmet and looking directly at us. At ground level was a tiny metal-strapped door that would've looked more at home on a small house. Circling the top of the castle was a stone battlement with a ten-foot gap above the castle entrance. Already, the soldiers were lighting bonfires beneath two huge iron cauldrons hung on winches, and it didn't take a mind reader to know what was *in* those cauldrons.

Morgan and Morris stood side by side, necks craned, eyes narrowed. Morgan spoke, his voice low: "They know we're here."

"Oh, they do," agreed Morris. "Oh, they fuckin' *do*. If there was one scout in them woods, there had to've been others."

"Send an advance team, and have them report back."

The rest of us retreated, the lot of us breaking camp on the edge of the glade, no worry about fires or cooking smells seeing as the enemy knew we were there and why. While drinking a mug of bitter tea, I heard a single gunshot, and I knew Morris had taken care of the scout once and for all. I was near Morgan and I could see he heard it too: he stopped and looked over his shoulder, and in that moment he grinned ever so slightly — you could still see where his hair had been dampened by Spanish gob. Though I chuckled at the sheer deservedness of it all, it was the sort of laugh gives you a discomfort you can't quite put a finger on.

Two hours went by before the leader of the reconnoitring party returned. He was a mid-sized fellow, with long hair and a scar around the mouth. Morgan waved the man forward. "I take it the town's empty?"

"Yes, captain."

Morgan looked at Morris and the other captains.

"Run off for help," said Morris. "While the gold's locked up tight in the roundhouse."

"Looks that way," said Morgan.

"What's the plan?" asked Jackman.

"Simple," said Morgan. "We get inside."

"We ram it?" asked Marteen, the words funny with his Dutch accent.

"We do."

Morris went off to assign men to axe the biggest tree they could find and then shear its limbs.

"Captain?" It was the advance team leader.

"What is it?" answered Morgan.

"There were a few priests hiding in the church, refusing to quit it, like."

"How many?"

"Eight or nine."

"You've locked them in there?"

"We have."

"Good man."

We waited. I could practically hear a clock, ticking away somewhere, reminding us our time was limited. When the battering ram was finally ready, two hours had gone by. At least they'd done a good job—it was twenty feet long and two feet in circumference and looked like it meant business. Morgan assigned a dozen huge men to hoist the thing to the edge of the forest; Taylor was one of them, and he picked up his section with a look saying he was determined to bash in that bloody door. Course, by then every man in the glade was on his feet, Morgan ordering them to follow along behind.

We crept through the thicker woods separating the glade from the clearing where the castle stood. This was tricky; the path was narrow and the ram kept getting caught on little trees and saplings. After ten minutes or so we reached a small part in the forest wall, Morgan telling Taylor and the others to put the ram down and rest their arms for a minute. Atop the castle, the Spaniards were rustling and pointing down at us and yelling. From up there they must've seen the rustle in the woods and maybe even the tip of the ram.

Morgan waited five anxious minutes, and then nodded. The men picked the ram back up.

Morgan raised his left arm.

"One … two … THREE …" and the twelve men erupted from the forest, whooping and wailing and hollering, running as fast as they were able, and up above, the Spanish all started firing with their useless old guns, muskets and arquebuses that didn't shoot straight if at all, while Taylor and the others ran full force at the castle door, gaining speed as they reached their stride. When they struck, it was the sound of a boulder dropped from great height. The door neither buckled nor groaned nor so much as budged, meaning the men lost their grip and kept going, running atop one another as they carried into the castle wall, and now that they were all bunched up and not moving, the Spaniards leaned over the castle wall and fired straight down. Even with useless firearms they couldn't miss, and there were cries as the men below were struck.

"RETREAT," Morgan yelled. "BLOODY RETREAT!" and the clump rose up, ten of them instead of twelve, Taylor still moving, thank fuck. They reached the safety of forest and we all stepped back under cover of trees and shrub, Morgan and his captains looking aggrieved. Another two men were injured, and held bleeding body parts while groaning. Taylor was no different; bent over, he was, holding himself and breathing hard. "It's my back," he said between groans. "That bloody ram weighed a ton. Didn't realize it at the time, the blood was up and I must not've noticed, can't believe that door didn't budge, bloody ram must've weighed a ton, Christ Benny, my back's yowling…"

The sun was starting to dip and turn a burnt orange. Morgan took a look around at the sad state of us, his men either hurting or suffering from the exhaustion caused by spending all day lost in hostile jungle.

"Gentlemen," he finally announced. "We've had a long day and it's time we all slept. We'll all be able to think clearer come morning."

With that permission, I suddenly felt so tired I thought my legs might give way. After stretching out next to a dwindling fire, I looked up at a million silver-light stars and a second later I was done for.

FOURTEEN

I CAME AWAKE IN a chilly pre-dawn. Already, fires were stoked, chicory coffee boiled, and chunks of boucan ready for the taking. Time passed, and it was an uncomfortable time indeed, for we all knew if Morgan didn't figure a way into that storehouse soon, we'd have to either run off or welcome the Spanish army.

I had another cup of shite coffee and another chunk of salty boucan when I noticed the captains were talking to Morgan, Morris waving around a burlap bag like it was a prize at a county fair. I didn't even need to wander close, for it was clear it was the captains against Morgan, just like in Villahermosa, with the captains trying to persuade him of something while Morgan was shaking his head and saying, "No no no no…" Freeman, Jackman, and Marteen looked fiercely annoyed, with their hands on their hips and their faces taken over by scowls, while Morris was gesturing with the bag and saying something in a low hiss. Morris stopped talking and the other captains all chimed in, waving hands and pointing fingers and Morgan just shaking his head, that same word coming out of his mouth, *no no no no no*, and that's when he looked over and his eyes fell on none other than me.

Though the other captains were still yammering, you could tell Morgan was no longer listening, for he'd fixed me with that same gaze he'd given me back in his mansion, when it was like he was appraising me for some job I didn't yet know about. He grabbed the burlap bag out of Morris's hand and left the other captains in mid-rant.

He came over. "Wand," he said.

"Sir."

"Let me show you something," and he led me away from the campsite. We stood out of sight in the woods. He reached into the sack and pulled out a wooden vise, a pair of screw-turned handles on either side. "This is a woolder, Mr. Wand. Captain Morris wants to use it on those priests within earshot of the castle. He says there's nothing like the scream of a man losing his eyes, and that they'll open the castle doors if only to make it stop."

"I see."

"He says if it doesn't work, we can drag the hostages onto the field and cut them limb from limb. Then maybe the soldiers atop the roundhouse will think twice about keeping us out."

Morgan was speaking slowly, choosing his words carefully. "What do you think?"

"What do I think? It's hardly . . ."

"Mr. Wand. You will answer the question."

"If you saw us doin' the likes of that, would *you* let us in?"

"Listen closely, Mr. Wand. I've got two hundred men counting on booty. I've got a castle locked up tighter than a drum. I've got the Spanish army on the way. I've got the King of England expecting me to appropriate the contents of that particular roundhouse. I could torture and kill those priests and still not get in and then we'd be out of time. If you've any suggestions, now might be the time to share them."

My head emptied. I blinked like a fool.

"Think, man! Pretend it's a game of chess and not real life. Just do what you do. We need a strategy."

There it was again. *We.* I could offer a thousand explanations why this word had such an effect on me, and not one of them would account for it on its own. My chest filled. My mind restarted, so eager was I to please Morgan, only now it was going too fast to be of bloody use, so to make sense of my thoughts I breathed regular, just like my poor ol' granddad always told me to do when I got rattled. Don't think, he'd say. When you think, all you do is dwell upon things you know, in this case that rock-solid roundhouse and the vats of boiling oil and the Spanish army racing toward us. *Think*, and you'll just dwell on facts getting in the way of an answer. If you're going to be imaginative, you have to imagine — so that's what I did. I narrowed my eyes and forgot everything I knew so I could find out things I didn't.

When the idea came, it was so horrible and wonderful I had trouble finding words for it. I was shaking and I hoped it didn't show. Without talking, the idea just grew bigger and bigger until there was no way I could ignore it.

"Mr. Wand. You look like you've seen a ghost."

"There's a way."

"Yes?"

"There's a..." I took a deep breath, tossing the idea about, looking at it from every direction. "Yes... there's a way."

"Well, out with it."

I looked straight into those blue-grey eyes. "We build a scaling ladder. Out of branches and vines. Won't have any trouble finding the materials, like."

"A scaling ladder? Might I remind you the enemy has cauldrons of boiling oil. Who am I to send up first? Who will have the privilege of that particular task?!"

"We send the priests. We use them as a human shield."

"May I remind you, Mr. Wand, that I am under strict orders to spare any and all civilians. Those orders do not include scalding men of the cloth to death. Have you ever seen a man doused with boiling oil? It's not an appetizing spectacle, I'll assure you."

"But that's just it! The enemy won't pour the oil. They'd still have to fight us, so why bother? With the priests guarding us, there'd be no *point* in dumping the oil. Either way, they'd have to do battle, so why kill their own?"

"So with the priests in advance, they'll let us up to do battle."

"They will, yeah."

"That's your opinion, is it?"

"It is," I told him, though something was nagging at me, something that hurt my temples and stomach but I couldn't put a name to.

"Or *maybe*," Morgan said, "you just want to see some priests boiled."

"It won't happen."

There was a long freighted pause. Morgan just looked at me, weighing his options.

"Well in that case," he finally said, "we'd best build ourselves a ladder."

WE WENT BACK to the glade and rounded up every axe, blade, and long knife amongst us. Twenty men went out to cut down heavy tree limbs, their instructions to find ones at least ten feet in length and as big as a man's fist around. Another twenty men were sent into the woods, where they'd find vines strong enough to support a man's weight. Everyone else was given some useless campsite chore, tending to the fire or oiling flintlocks or even cleaning boots — anything to keep minds off what was coming up.

Two hours later, Morgan was looking over a pile of thick branches stripped and cleaned and ready to go. The men who'd taken them down stood in a row, awaiting approval. They didn't get any Morgan looking around and barking, "Where in the devil are the vines?"

It was a good question: no one had seen or heard the men for two hours, it being a real fear they'd gotten themselves lost or taken by Spanish scouts. Morgan stood staring at the woods, as if doing so might cause them to appear. Then he grumbled something and assembled a group to fetch the priests locked in the town church. They went off and returned with the prisoners, all of them dressed in clerical garb and bowl haircuts, seven of them older and two of them young, each of them shaky and on the verge of tears. Morgan had them sit in a circle in the middle of the glade so that they all faced outwards. Then he told them to sit on their hands and if they moved off those hands by God he'd use them all for target practice.

They looked up at him, chins trembling, not understanding.

"Sit on your hands!" he yelled, and when they still didn't understand, we all yelled the same and a few of us demonstrated what they were supposed to do. Finally, they whipped their hands under their arses and sat there, chins low, whimpering. One of the younger ones—he couldn't have been more than eighteen—was crying and it was John Morris who walked up to him and slapped him hard, the young man's face turning the red of an apple, though he quit his snivelling.

When the first of the vine cutters finally came back, he was carrying a half-dozen thick vines. The same could be said for the other nine, who stepped out one by one as well, each one beaming like he'd already stormed the castle. We went to work. The idea was to build five lattices, each ten feet by ten feet, and then place them on top of one another with four or five feet of overlap; when bound together, we reckoned it'd be the height we needed. Each of the captains built his own grid of branches, and when they were done, those with a knowledge of knot tying went to work binding them together. When that was all done, we placed the first on top of the second and secured the two together. We worked most of that afternoon, for it was a job and a half, making all those knots and deciding which branch went where.

And then we were done. The priests looked on, bald spots gleaming. Morgan placed a line of strong men at one edge of the ladder, and when he gave a *heave-ho*, they lifted it to their shoulders, grunting loudly as they did so. Some others rushed over to take the sides and others made sure the base wouldn't slip. Then the men holding the ladder all walked forward, their hands moving down the rungs until the ladder stood at full height. It was a magnificent thing, not wavering nor bending nor showing signs of wanting to buckle.

It was late afternoon and Morgan had to decide whether to launch the assault that day or the next morning. He had a consult with his captains that lasted for a minute: their decision was we'd use whatever daylight was left to practise, for a botched assault would eat up valuable time. Morgan assigned a team of large men to be the ladder carriers. After explaining what he expected, he gave them a count of three, at which point they picked up the ladder and jogged across the glade. Upon reaching the jungle wall, they planted the legs of the ladder and pushed it skyward, and it all worked like it had to. With the scaling ladder mounted against the forest wall, John Morris' assembled a team to widen the path separating the glade from the castle. This took little time, seeing as the path was already well formed.

After filling our nervous stomachs with boucan and burnt coffee, we all flopped down where we wanted and stared up at a full-moon sky. Sentries were assigned to take watch, though we hardly needed them — fear and greed and excitement and glory-lust made everything look twinkling. We were a field full of men awake, our thoughts a high-pitched whine.

Daylight took forever to come. Though it was a cool night, I was sweating with the nervousness of it all, and that sweat stayed on my skin and caused me to shiver slightly. Finally, the evening sky shifted from pitch to a soft lavender. As soon as one man stirred and rose to his feet, the rest of us did the same. There was no stretching or yawning or any of the things a man does after a night of rest; nor did anyone bother whispering or keeping quiet. The soldiers atop that tower knew we were going to try a castle mount next morning, and we knew damn well they knew. I couldn't spot Morgan, though his captains were walking up and down, getting us into order. First they went to the Spanish fathers and kicked them on the soles of their slippers. The priests were marched to the edge of the glen, at the mouth of the path leading to the castle.

Behind the priests went the ladder-men, who picked up the scaling ladder and took their place. Behind them was most everyone else, though to show a keenness for the fight there was a lot of jostling and shoving to get farther up the line. This stopped only when John Morris hissed, "Stop it, you bastards, it'll all be the same when we get there."

I felt a meaty hand on my shoulder.

I turned and it was Morgan, taking me to the back of the line where Jackman and Marteen were waiting. Captains Morris and Freeman were at the front. For the longest time we stood there, nobody speaking, Morris and Freeman sorting out something with the priests. From far off I could hear Spanish voices and it was obvious the soldiers atop the castle were awake and watching as we formed ourselves. I looked up through a break in the woods and they were stoking the fires beneath oil-filled cauldrons.

We marched through the forest toward the castle. A few times the line stopped when the scaling ladder snagged on something; men with hand axes ran to the spot and started swinging and soon we were on the move again, the only sound our boots brushing against mulchy forest floor. There was a heavy scent in the air, a mix of mushrooms and armpit sweat and flowers opening for the day.

We stopped when Captains Morris and Freeman reached the far end of the forest. Thirty yards in front of them was the roundhouse. The sky overhead had turned a pale yellow, the tip of an orange ball showing itself atop far-off trees.

Again the wait felt like forever. The nature of time changed, stretched by serious thoughts, and then the men in front were running and yelling, their voices and foot stomps an explosion. I watched them take off in front of me, two by two by two, and then it was my turn and I was hollering and carrying on and following that enormous ladder onto the battlefield. The soldiers atop the castle started firing with their shitey guns and if they hit one or two of us it was by accident, though I did see one luckless bugger grab a bloom of red on his shoulder and yell *ah fuck* before scampering in an L shape toward the castle wall, and then I saw a second privateer stop and fall dead, a Spanish pellet having found the top of his head. There was the smell of gunpowder and burning wood and blood.

It was a dewy morning, the base of the ladder sticking hard in the soft ground. The ladder-men pushed it up against the castle wall in just two or three seconds, the soldiers on top yelling and hollering and firing downward, so we all regrouped and clung to the base of the castle where we were partially hid. There was a lull. We breathed hard and listened to Spanish words being shouted from above, though after a bit they shut it and all was tense and quiet and gloomy, our hearts beating like clubs on a drum stretched tight. Morris was now moving up and down, grabbing the priests and collecting them at the base of the ladder. Meanwhile, the soldiers looked down and if they hadn't put two plus two together before, they got it now, for they all started yelling down at us, and though I couldn't understand

Spanish, I could hear the word *no* being yelled over and over. Most likely they were threatening us, for they stoked the fires as hot as they could get them and were rocking the cauldrons on their hinges as a way of showing their general intent.

Morris walked up to the oldest priest, a doddering old fucker who didn't look fit enough to climb the ladder but by virtue of his age was no doubt their leader. Morris pointed to the ladder and gave the old bugger a shove and any idiot could see what he had to do. The old man shook his head defiantly and without a moment's thought or hesitation Morris pulled his flintlock and discharged it. There was a spray of blood and bone and what little was in my stomach splashed up and caused a burning. Morris turned to the second priest and he mounted the ladder without a second's hesitation, as did the second and third and fourth. The ladder was big enough for four men across, and so there were two rows of priests slowly moving up the ladder and then a row of Morgan's men behind and another row behind them. Soon the ladder was covered with bodies climbing up toward the break in the castle wall, and at no time did the ladder bend or bow.

It was all going according to plan, or at least it was until I looked up and saw the look on the faces of the Spanish soldiers. It was then I realized where I'd gone wrong. They weren't men but boys, eighteen or nineteen at most. Likely this was a part-time job for them, a way to make a little dosh in an outpost protected by jungle. No doubt they'd been told they'd never see action, oh no, just days of sunshine and cards and having laughs and won't the girls love how they look in their uniforms? And yet here they were, facing the one and only Henry Morgan, the man who took Villahermosa, and what I hadn't figured was they would panic. What I hadn't figured was they'd lose their heads. What I never figured was they'd scream and shout while our men kept climbing and climbing, or that they'd upend those cauldrons and the oil would come splashing down like some evil scorching waterfall. I was on the ground looking up when the oil hit the first row. It poured onto the priests' heads and shoulders and when it did, it melted the skin right off, leaving naked skulls affixed with remnants of ears and nose and lips, the eyes liquefying and running down bone like a spill of thick cream. The poor bastards didn't even have time to scream—they just fell off the ladder clutching at their horrible selves. They died curled up like babies. Desperate to stop us, the boy-soldiers tipped the second cauldron and the same thing happened, the oil burning off flesh and hair and clothing alike, though the second row of priests were a little farther away and they lived long enough to release a sickening high-pitched scream, at least one tearing at hot oil-soaked clothing, his skin coming away in sheets, leaving him a squirming mass of black muscle and bone, his eye sockets empty and cast upward in absolute agony.

I watched all this. I was the cause of all this. I thought I'd figured a way the oil would be spared, and instead my clever plan had come to *this*. Through stinging eyes, I saw the first of Morgan's men launch themselves up and over the castle rampart and start killing like butchers slaughtering hogs for market. That's when I noticed something at the far edge of my vision, and it bothered me even more than what I'd done to them old idiot priests.

It was Morgan. It was Morgan looking up. It was Morgan watching the mad killing under way.

It was Morgan's lean face and the satisfaction written on it.

FIFTEEN

W E RAISED ANCHOR at dusk, the sky a purplish blur, the holds so filled with swag we had to sleep on deck if we wished to sleep at all. Crossing open water was out of the question. With the fleet so burdened, we couldn't have outrun a floating washtub, never mind a Spanish warship with vengeance in its sails. Instead, we travelled northwest along the Mosquito Coast, our plan to hop east from the tip of the Yucatán to the western shore of Cuba and then limp from one protected cove to the next until we reached Jamaica. What should've been a week across open water turned into weeks of dangerous shoreline hugging, the ships taking on water with the slightest wave or roll. Most was done under darkness, Morgan's navigators relying on memory and stars and a sixth sense to keep us off the reefs.

Rations were a problem. Each morning, after dropping anchor, hunting parties would go ashore to roust up pigs and berries in dawn light; sometimes they were successful and sometimes they came back with nothing. We'd spend all day trying to rest, though it was tricky in bright sun, with or without a nagging stomach. At night we'd be off, our boats fat and slow.

For the first day or two, I saw little of Morgan. He mostly kept to his quarters or I'd catch glimpses of him moving about the deck, giving orders or inspecting the ship or staring out over open waters. Sometime during the third day, late afternoon I believe it was, I was on deck having a chat with Taylor when another of the scrub boys came up.

"Wand," he said. "You're needed, like. Down below."

Taylor gave me a raised eyebrow, his way of saying *well well well inn't we coming up in the world?* I shrugged my shoulders and went below deck, stepping my way around sacks filled with gold coins, nuggets, bars, bullion, and what all else. I knocked lightly.

"Yes?" I heard, and when I stepped inside, Morgan looked up from a small table piled high with maps and documents. On top of these papers was his chessboard, all set and ready to be played. There was a narrow bed next to a small dresser, a few leather-bound books and a glass of water on top. The room creaked with each rise and fall of the ocean.

Morgan smiled, long enough I began to feel awkward. Finally, he brought his hands together four times, Henry Morgan himself giving me a short volley of applause.

The feeling? Like rushing through air, it was. Like taking flight.

"Congratulations, Mr. Wand. Your plan with the scaling ladder. That was quite a move. I'll admit I was stuck. I am grateful."

"I was thinking I'd buggered it."

"There were unseen consequences. Yet we saved a lot of lives on *our* side. Plus we struck hard at the Spanish and that will benefit countless lives when we finally unshackle the New World from Spanish control. That's the way you have to think of it, Mr. Wand. A man needs to know that, ultimately, he's serving the greater good. But Jesus! What we did there!"

His eyes were sparkling.

"Please, please, sit..."

I took the chair on the other side of the table.

"So," Morgan said. "You've proved yourself."

"I'm sorry?"

"First Villahermosa, now Portobello... Listen to me, Mr. Wand. There are a lot of men who can put together a decent game of chess. Applying those tactics away from the board—well. That's another thing altogether. I want you to know something, Mr. Wand. I have plans for you. I'm not quite sure what they are yet, but I need you to know one thing: your role in the taking of Portobello will not be overlooked. I'm mulling over ways to recompense you, above and beyond your share of this mission's swag, but you have my assurance—it's coming. It is coming indeed. You are a good man, Mr. Wand."

"Thank you," I managed.

"You look rattled, Mr. Wand. Is anything the matter?"

"I've not heard those words before, captain."

"What? That you're a good man?"

"Yes."

"That's because most people are idiots. Most people don't understand they have eyes in their head for a reason. Now, what's say we have a game or two? Anything to kill this stultifying boredom, what?"

"Now you're talking," I said, and with my blood up I ran at Morgan full force, if only to show him that everything he thought about me was true. As I hammered away, he kept shaking his head and muttering little phrases of astonishment, like he couldn't believe what he was seeing. After resigning three times, he threw up his hands.

"You're unstoppable, Mr. Wand."

"Just having a good game."

"Well, I'm warning you now—I'll not be put off. One day I *will* find a way to beat you. I swear on my grave I'll take you one of these days."

"I'm sure you will."

"Oh, I will all right. Now, go have some dinner, Mr. Wand. We've another long night of travel ahead of us..."

We both stood. At the door, he held out his hand; for some reason I'd never noticed how fine it was, like something a sculptor or artist might have.

"Once again... thank you for Portobello."

"You're welcome, captain," and when he closed the door behind me I couldn't wipe the stupid grin off me, no matter how much it hurt my face to wear the corners of my mouth up so high.

AFTER A DIFFICULT sail up the Mosquito Coast, we finally reached the south shore of Cuba, which was littered with tiny islands known as the South Cays. Two days after that, the spotters hollered Jamaica was just off in the distance. A cheer went up and we voyaged under full sail, none of us scared of Spanish warships for we were in waters belonging to *us*. Of course, this didn't make sense: Jamaica or no Jamaica, we couldn't have fought them off, but such is the feeling brought by the idea of home.

Meanwhile, the swag had been counted and divvied, a single share of the gold worth seventy-five thousand quid. Back in Port Royal, a typical sod was earning two hundred a year, maybe three if the boss was your father-in-law, and how those poor bastards would survive once the new economy kicked in was anybody's guess. Mostly, I supposed, they wouldn't.

We dropped sail and anchored. After rowing to shore, we marched up from the docks, pant legs wet, sleeves dotted with blood, purchase stuffed into every manner of bag and sack. Our hearts thrummed with the pleasure of it all. Some piled their riches onto carts or barrows or anything else with wheels and a flat surface. Others, being of a size to do it, threw bags of loot over their shoulders and, walking like stooped old women, struggled forward.

I had four bags of gold coins. I dragged them behind me, leaving trails in the pink coral dust. Every few minutes I had to stop and have a rest, so I'd take the opportunity to look about and get my bearings and boot any wigglies snouting at my ankles. All around, slaves were pulling on ropes as thick as a strong man's wrist, hoisting up hogsheads and crates and bundles the size of small houses. Up above, men were leaning out of high warehouse windows, ready to snag the hoisted cargo and swing it inside. Already, wagons were leaving the warehouses for shops in the town centre, wagons groaning with pimento, ginger, cinnamon, cowhide, fustic, cochineal, tortoiseshell, silk, and logwood.

I dragged my burden far enough I stood in the shadow cast by the shops and houses lining High Street. I was panting hard, shirt soaked through with sweat, so I stopped and had another rest. Everywhere was bustle, commerce, excitement, vermin. Taverns that hadn't seen the light of day in weeks were getting swept and spit-shined and aired out. Good-Time Ladies were throwing open second-storey jalousies, breasts plumping out of corsets, calling *this way, gents, if it's the time of your life yer after!* Shills were already taking to the streets, directing us toward saloon doors not seen used in a month. Passing the Bear Garden, I fought the very real and pressing impulse to step inside and have myself a quick one and warn Tessie to have a nap for I'd be needing the full fury of her attentions. But no. Filled with direction and purpose I was. I dragged my bags of cob past the Bear Garden and every other grog shop on the strip until I reached Rodge's Lodges. I pushed open the door with my back and dragged my loot inside, where I found Rodge at his desk, having a cup of tea with, of all things, a bright yellow lemon.

"Well, look what the cat dragged in," he said.

"Where'd you get the lemon, Rodge?"

"The market. But who cares. Jesus, Benny... Portobello? What a coup! That Morgan must have stones the size of cantaloupe. Next it'll be bloody Cartagena! You'll be needing your old room, I take it?"

"If it'd be convenient. Course, if it isn't, I could always take my ill-begotten gains and go elsewhere."

"No need. I've kept it just the way you left it... In fact I turned away a few for I knew you'd be needin' it. Speaking of ill-begotten gains, what you planning to do with *that*?" He was pointing a finger at my gold-filled sacks.

It was a fair question and one I hadn't considered until that moment. While there was a bank or two on the mainland, I likened bankers to schoolteachers and factory owners and religious bastards and everyone else back home whose job it was to remind you of your own inferiority. "It's what my room's for, yeah?"

Rodge narrowed an eye. "You leave that in your room and it might decide to take a walk, if you catch my meaning. I can't account for every footpad and cutpurse decides to wander through my hallways."

"True."

"Come with me, Benny. I've an idea."

He took two of the bags from me and together we hauled them toward the back of the house where there was a rickety door slanting a little bit to the right, a curious fact seeing as the rest of the house slanted slightly to the left. Rodge fumbled for a key. It took him a half minute of jiggling to trip the rusted lock and open the door to pitch-black. There came the smell of damp rot and ammonia.

"Bugger," said Rodge.

He trundled off, returning a minute or two later with a candle. On the top step he lit it with a match, the dungeon caught in a warm orange glow. We dragged the bags down groaning wood steps. The air bore the cold clamminess of a grave and every time we turned around, our faces would snare in spiderweb. Sputtering, we'd pick the strands from our mouths.

Rodge walked about the cellar, his feet kicking up dust. There was little in the room, some wrecked furniture and an old tricycle and, in the corner, a mounding of potatoes sprouting eyes and giving off a weak vinegar scent. Rodge walked toward it, and when I failed to do the same, he turned and said, "You comin', then?"

Next to the mound was a shovel used for stoking a coal furnace—it was blackened from years of said use. Rodge picked it up and ladled some potatoes around my feet. He did this a few dozen times, his belly jiggling, and when he finished I could see what he'd been aiming for: the potatoes were hiding an old wooden crate. Rodge lifted the lid, a puff of dust coming with it. This time there was the smell of wood gone soft with flood water and termites.

Rodge gestured at my loot with his thumb. "You can put *that* in *there*, you can. It'll just fit. The cellar door will stay locked. Every time I let you in, a farthing goes onto your bill. It's a banking fee, like. In return, I'll guarantee it won't go wandering."

"I thought banks were supposed to pay you."

"Not in Port Royal, Sonny Jim. Not in a place like this."

I ASKED RODGE to draw me a bath. He nodded, saying he'd have the girls do it so long as another bob or two added to my bill wasn't out of the question.

Ten minutes later, I was sitting in Rodge's tub room, dressed only in underpants that'd seen better days, the rest taken off to a laundry so they'd be done by the time I was fit to get dressed again. A pair of twelve-year-olds were coming back and forth with pails of heated water. Each time they came, they kept their heads down, me doing my part by keeping a towel over my lap. When the tub was filled, I climbed in and sank to my chin. It was hot enough I turned red as a mongrel's nose, and was glad for it; all that steam slowed my heart and stilled my thoughts and opened my pores, releasing weeks of dirt and sweat and grubby old skin. I scrubbed hard, happy with the feel of it and happy to be me; after ten minutes the water was floating with ash-grey murk. Every five minutes or so one of the girls would knock and shyly enter with a new bucket. When I was clean, I got out and towelled off and dressed in newly laundered scrubs.

In short order I bought three pairs of breeches, three linen shirts, new boots, a bandana or two, and for special occasions a jerkin made of something called damask. As I was shopping, a kid no more than six years of age followed me about, face grubby and nose dripping and hair full of pink Port Royal sand. Though he never got close enough to say hello, he never left my sight neither, and in this way he reminded me of myself when I was a lad, all alone and needing attention though afraid to ask for it. After a bit it got ridiculous—those large crusted eyes, watching my every move, so I thought what the hell and bought a wooden child's game from one of the vendors, a sort of cup on a tapered handle and attached to the handle was a string with a little ball tied to it. I presented it to the boy. At first he wouldn't take it, just stood there looking up at me, like he mistrusted the very thing he most wanted. Again, he reminded me of me.

"Go on," I kept saying, until he finally reached out with a shaky little hand and took it. He was just standing there, looking at it like it was too good to be true, when a dozen other laneway children appeared, all of them pulling at my clothes while pleading, "Please, buy me a toy" or "Please, can I have some coins?" This went on and on until I slapped a particularly annoying little gremlin across the cheek and told them all to bugger off. They all scattered except for the kid I'd given the game to. Course, someone had taken it off him, and he was just standing there looking like he'd expected nothing less. He turned and walked off, head hung, and I decided I needed to see Tessie.

I went back to Rodge's and took off the clothes I'd worn during Portobello; even though they were clean, they were threadbare and spotted with little rips and tears. Holding my old slops at arm's length, like they were full of the plague, I walked naked to my window and tossed them into the lane beside the pen holding Katy and Mr. Pete. They grunted, and a legless ragman came scurrying along on a cart on wheels; he picked up the clothes and scurried off, his hands pushing against the packed-sand laneway. I dressed in my new clothes and felt clean and ready, and so I trundled down Rodge's stairway and into streets thronged with vendors and drunkards and homeless children and trollops too homely to gain work in one of the houses. More than once I was elbowed hard by the tough little Creole grandmothers who were everywhere in Port Royal, looking half African and half Chinese and half pissed at the world.

Already, the Bear Garden was full of carousers, desperate to squander their Portobello dosh, and I had to push my way through a throng of men, all talking loudly while gesturing with tankard or calabash. I passed Suzie's pit, where she was sitting on her haunches for lobbed sardines, and reached the bar. David Walsh was slinging a frothy warm ale he scooped straight from an open barrel, the beer floating with dropped thatch and plaster flakes. After serving a few thirsty blokes, he spotted me and his face lit up.

"Benny Wand!" he shouted. "What's your pleasure?"

"Only the finest," I shouted, so he poured me a suicidal measure of rumbullion. I took a long burning draft, the alcohol firebombing my brain and making me feel giddy and warm. "Tessie working tonight?" I hollered over the crowd.

"She is," he said. "But I'm warning ya, Ben, it's a busy night, it is."

I went upstairs and was directed to a bench where two other scarpy-looking buzzards were waiting. I nodded my hellos and sat, thinking business is business, when Tessie poked her head out of her room and beamed. "Benny Wand!" she exclaimed. "Back from Portobello, I take it?"

"In the flesh."

"There's a bit of a wait," she said.

"So I've noticed."

"You don't have to wait here," she said. "Go back on down, I'll have someone fetch you when the time comes."

So I did, Tessie pointing at the skinny fucker next to me who leapt up like a schoolboy let out for summer. Downstairs, I headed for the bear pit, where I watched Suzie ride around on a little bicycle with streamers hanging from the handlebars. It was all funny as hell, and before I knew it a little Creole woman with a missing ear was standing before me, saying, "Yoos is next there, mister, you sure some is..."

So I went upstairs and barged into Tessie's room, where I did throw myself upon her, showering her with kisses to the neck and shoulder and belly and legs and breast. The only place I didn't land my lips was upon hers, rules being rules and if you didn't respect them there were big men on staff who'd let you know the error of your ways. Throughout, Tessie laughed and giggled and squealed, "You're in a good mood, you is, Mr. Wand," and before we knew it we was through and I was staring at that awkward moment when there was nothing for it but getting dressed and buggering off so the next man could have his go.

"Let me stay till morning," I said.

"You kidding me? You seen the lineup. It's my night of nights. You lot just took Portobello!"

"What'll you make with them lot out there?"

"Why . . . it'll be a two hundred if it's a penny."

"I'll give you a thousand."

"Are you mad, Benny Wand?"

"Mad as they come."

She stood there considering. Her face soured. "If it's a sweetheart you're after, you won't find one in me."

"I know."

She relaxed. Still naked, she stuck her head out her doorway and announced, "Right. You and you and you, piss off. Yeah, that's right, down the hall's the place for you, ol' Buttock-Clench'll sew you up right."

She came back in. She sat beside me. Her hands were little, like they belonged on someone else. "Who *are* you, Benny Wand?" she asked.

"I'm a Brethren of the Coast. I'm one of Henry Morgan's, and don't you forget it."

"You'll have another go, I take it?"

"To tell the truth, I'm all in."

"Jesus, you're an odd one."

She lied beside me and that's the way we stayed, staring up at the knotholed ceiling, listening to the barrage of noise coming from downstairs. The poor girl must've been done for: already her chest was rising and falling all regular-like. I drifted off right after, my thoughts turning all wavy and odd, and the next thing I knew I was at my granddad's wake, walking up the middle of the pub where we was having it, a six-year-old boy in scuffed shoes and an ache in his heart he swore might kill him. Off to one side, my father was pulling on a bottle while blubbering *he was a good man he was, too good for this world, in the end it was this bastard world what got him, don't you forget what the world'll do to you my son, don't you forget this world is always out to get ya* and that's when I reached the casket and looked in. I gasped. It wasn't Granddad in the box. It was that old priest, the one John Morris shot for not going up the ladder, just lying there with a pellet hole in the middle of his smoking forehead.

The old bugger opened his milky eyes and I sat straight up, rib cage heaving. There was light poking through the threadbare curtains. Tessie put her hand on my shoulder. "Sorry," I croaked. "Didn't mean to scare."

"What happened?"

"Had a dream. 'Bout someone got killed in Portobello."

"Someone, or someone in particular?"

"Just some Spaniard had it coming. Means nothing to me."

Tessie's face was aged by daylight and smudged makeup: I'd never noticed she had lines coming out the corners of her eyes. "You sure you're cut out for this line of work?" she asked. "Not everyone is, you know. Walsh, for example. After his mission with Penn and Venables, he settled down and got a job here."

"Course I am."

"You look a little peaked is why I ask."

"Believe me," I told her, "I've had nightmares all my life. Ones a lot worse than this."

"Don't we all. You should see me when I have mine.

Screaming with the fright of it. Thrashing around like a madwoman."

"It's the price we pay for living, inn't it?"

"Oh, it is, Benny Wand."

My mouth was dry. My head ached. I yearned for the high mood I had last night.

"Benny? It's morning and a deal's a deal."

"Right," I said, and with her back to the sun-smeared window I got dressed and walked into streets filled with peddlers and washerwomen and rooting wigglies and grimy-faced children, and I kept picturing that head-shot priest, taking the place of my granddad in the saddest memory I had.

That's when I passed a little place called the Fox and Fanny. A barman was inside, cleaning up from the night before. I knuckled the window. When he heard, he looked up and yelled, "We're closed."

I wouldn't have it, though—I reached into my pocket, and as coins spilled from my palm I hollered, "Any chance you'd consider opening early?"

Which, of course, he would.

Sixteen

WITH NOTHING BETTER to do, I went on the bottle—up all night, barely eating, sick till mid-afternoon, believe you me, I wasn't the only one. It was what you did if you were a Brethren come into money. Practically expected, it was.

On the eighth day, I came awake shaky and cold. Like I'd done so many times before, I swore off bibbing forever. I stayed in my room or walked the beaches, though it wasn't long before another problem reared its ugly face. Morgan wasn't calling for me, and with the money I'd given Tessie she'd decided to take some time off, though where she'd gone was a mystery. Even Taylor had decamped, on some hunting expedition in the interior, intent on bagging a few wild boar with some natives acting as guides. The truth was, I didn't know what to do with myself. One morning, without really thinking, I dressed in my cleanest shirt and breeches and walked to the tip of the causeway. Here, buggy men for hire took people to St. Jago. I hired one and he dropped me in the middle of Jamaica's capital.

As I walked through the streets, I kept noticing things you'd never see in Port Royal, like doors left half open or children with clean faces or animals who clearly belonged to someone. Walking beside one house, I peered in through an open window and saw somebody's cook making eggs — she was plump and kerchiefed and the colour of caramel. Her backside shook as she worked. I moved on. I walked around for an hour. A woman tipped her hat at me and said, "Good day, sir," and all I could think was, what's so wrong with all of this, then? What's so wrong with living normal? "Good day," I said, and it was shortly after that I hired a driver to take me back across the causeway, those speckled fish arcing higher and looking even more like rainbows than normal.

I walked in the door and found Rodge at his post.

"Well well well," he said. "I'm glad you're here."

"What? First of the week already?"

"I didn't meant that. This came for you this morning."

The envelope was the size of a deck of cards, made from thick white paper, and closed with a red wax blob. I slipped in a thumbnail and popped off the seal. Inside was a small card with writing on it. I turned it over and over in my hands, admiring it's soft, starchy feel. Then I gave it back to Rodge. "What's it say?"

He read it over. You could see his lips moving, and his eyes were going over the same parts more than once. Finally, he looked up at me. "Jesus, Benny, you're goin' to a party."

"Whose?"

"Morgan's," he said. "It's at Henry Morgan's place in the hills."

"Rodge, you're jokin'."

"Some sort of celebration for Portobello, maybe?"

"Dunno."

"Well, whatever it is, Benny Wand, you're on the bloody list."

SO THAT WAS it, then, a real chance to get in with the island posh. Up and away, I was, the sky the limit. My only fear was I'd bugger it, offending people with my look and talk and manner. The next morning I asked around and was told there were several men's clothiers along High Street. I headed off, my pockets brimming with gold coins that, thanks to Rodge's banking system, smelled like potatoes turning to seed. I picked the first one I came to. It was panelled with nice dark wood, the salesman looking chummy and rich. I took a deep breath and went in and right off I had a laugh to myself: his posh accent was theatre pure and simple. He was one of *me*, acting outside his station, which I guess was why his shop was on the Port Royal side of the causeway. This calmed me down, for when you think about it, we all keep our real selves hidden in one way or another. In return I let him earn his keep, going on about this collar versus that collar, this sleeve versus that sleeve, this hem versus that poncey-looking hem, all in a Queen's English that dipped from time to time, revealing him as just another East End piker.

Finally, he ran out of steam and I told him the details didn't matter so long as I could pass for civilized by the time we was through.

"That, sir," he said, "is well within the range of possibility."

He picked out a white linen shirt with a ruffled collar. I put it on.

"Bloody hell," I told him. "I feel like a right fop."

"Far from it, sir! That collar is the height of fashion back in England!"

I bought it, as well as a doublet I could've swore didn't fit right, it was so wide around the waist and arms, but again he assured me this was the way they were doing it back home. He then gave me breeches with a long row of buttons running up the calf, which I found difficult to fasten and unfasten though he told me I'd get the hang of it soon enough. Next were lace stockings, which were supposedly all the rage, as were the buckled shoes to go with them.

"There," he said as I stood before a mirror. "You look like quite the gentleman."

"You takin' the piss?"

"Oh my goodness no."

"You sure?"

"You look quite handsome, sir."

I took the lot.

THERE WERE A few more things to do. I had my hair cut, and I visited that doddering old man to deal with the wiry black beard I'd grown during Portobello. This time I told him just to trim it instead of take it right off, seeing as I wanted something to hide the pocks on my cheek.

"Righto," he said, his shaky hands steadying the moment he started scissoring.

That Saturday, I stepped out of Rodge's Lodges at precisely four o'clock, feeling like an imposter and a fool besides. The carriage Morgan sent was no horse and trap manned by a stubby-armed man. This was good enough for the Queen herself, with doors and a roof and a platform where the driver sat. Speaking of the driver, he was dressed like a squire, with stockings and felt breeches and a red velvet jerkin. When he saw me, he jumped down and tipped his chin, throwing in a "Mr. Wand" for good measure.

He opened the door and I stepped inside, trying not to grin too much at the ridiculousness of it all—me, Benny Wand, a gin-house board player and a son of the gutter, dressed like the very thing I'd always despised. (Worse things, I reckoned, have happened.) The driver clicked his teeth and we were off, rumbling over pink sandy Port Royal streets, and then we were on the causeway, the waters fountaining with mad speckled fish.

It was quiet and comfortable in the carriage, my backside resting upon padded leather seats instead of hard wood. With a breeze funnelling through the opened windows, I was even cool, something you couldn't say all that often in Jamaica. Once we reached the mainland, we turned right, skirting the town and climbing over mountain foothills toward Morgan's plantation. Blimey, was my thought when we got there, for there had to be two dozen carriages, a goodly portion of which were works of art, hand carved with polished brass and in some cases pulling a team of horses instead of a single mare. I watched town burghers and their powdered wives climb from their carriages, and it seemed to me this lot did everything slowly, like being in a hurry was a sign you weren't posh nor rich enough. I was making a note not to move too rapidly when some tosser wearing a wig and face powder pranced up and opened my carriage door.

"Welcome to Jegorand," he said with a precious little bow.

He moved to the next carriage, though not before giving a sweep of his hand, which indicated I was free to walk up to the house. The mansion's huge doors were propped wide open and I entered a front hall filled with Morgan's guests, all greeting each other like they were long-lost relatives. I moved off to one side and after a bit I walked down the hallway leading to the huge room where Morgan and I played chess. Wide-eyed, I was. Unlike before, when the place had been near empty, there were sofas and chairs and tables everywhere the eye cared to land. There was art too, statues of men and women carved from ivory, their lack of clothing making me think of a high-class brothel I once patronized in Manchester (though I had the feeling this wasn't the impression Mrs. Morgan was aiming for). The walls were covered with huge dark paintings of people in broad-brimmed hats and collars the size of wagon wheels. Right gloomy they looked, and I had to wonder whether they were family.

Then another doorman welcomed us to the Great Room. It'd been finished as well, Morgan's six full shares of plunder going toward chandeliers and crystal vases and Arabian carpets. The wooden floors had been torn out and replaced by marble. The wall space between the windows sported paintings too, though these weren't of people. Instead, they were scenes out of the Bible, mostly. Christ laying his hands on some poor poxy bugger dressed in tatters. David holding Goliath's blood-dripping noggin by the hair. The Virgin Mary kneeling and praying, the heavens shining a bright light on her upward-tilting face. All of it fiction, though I had to admit as stories went it was pretty good, which I suppose was why so many people believed it to be true — like every good lie, it was all in the details.

I couldn't spot Morgan, though I could see a few of his captains. Jackman was over in one corner, in a crowd with Freeman and some others. John Morris was over by one of the high-arched windows, holding court with some blowsy old dowagers. No doubt he was entertaining them with tales of conquest, the contents of his crystal glass spilling whenever he swept his hand. If Marteen was in the room, I couldn't see him: a rumour said he'd buggered off back to the Low Country seeing as Holland and England were mad at each other again.

A servant dressed better than I came up and offered a glass of something with bubbles. I accepted, not sure whether to sip it or knock it back, though when I looked around I gathered it was strictly a sipping crowd. I had myself a taste, my pledge to quit drinking suddenly a pledge no more. After a bit I started moving around the big room, just for something to do. I'd completed one lap when I heard a voice I knew.

"Mr. Wand."

I turned and there he was, though with the way he was dressed—i.e., wig and face powder and fluffy French cuffs—I could've mistaken him for nobility, which I supposed was the point. Beside him was a jowly little man in a cloak with a single eyebrow across the width of his ruddy forehead. His cheeks were bright red and I had the feeling he was well in his cups.

"Mr. Wand. May I present Mr. Edward Bottlesworth, governor of the fine island of Jamaica. Edward, this is Mr. Benjamin Wand."

Hoping for the best, I thrust my hand out and was relieved when Bottlesworth gave it a manly squeeze. I'd no sooner shaken his chubby mitt than his heavy-lidded eyes opened somewhat, his face a sudden pink question mark.

"Wait a blasted minute! You're the chess player!"

I answered by smiling.

"Henry's told me all about you. He says you're a hell of a boardsman. The best he's ever seen."

"I do my best."

"Hah! Don't be so modest, man. His nibs here says you could beat him blindfolded, and he's a demon himself."

"Captain Morgan is exaggerating."

"The devil I am," said Morgan. "You should see this man play. Slippery as a fish. Born to the board, he was. He could play before he could speak."

Bottlesworth stepped toward me, as if about to share something he didn't want Morgan to hear. "Listen," he said, his voice dropping so low it was barely a voice anymore, more like the rumble you feel when a storm is on its way. "Maybe you and I could get together. Give me a few pointers. I'd love to give Henry a run for his money, what with the way he's been playing of late."

"Course, sir."

"And none of this 'sir' nonsense. The name's Edward."

To which I thought: *well, sod me.*

Bottlesworth spotted someone on the other side of the room who needed talking to, Lord Something-or-other I think he said, though with the hum of the room bouncing off the new marble floors I couldn't say for sure. I glanced at Morgan. There was a new seriousness in his eyes. He stepped toward me, taking my elbow hard, and I thought maybe I'd buggered it with the governor. Though he was holding a glass of the bubbly drink, his breath smelled of rum. "Listen, Wand," he said in a low voice. "There's something I want to talk to you about. Later on. It's important."

"Course," I said. "Anything."

"Good," and he let go of my elbow and strolled off toward some other people he had to greet, turning all smiles and graciousness again. Just then, I heard a light tinkling. A servant in doublet and hose stood in the doorway. In his right hand was a little bell, which he stopped ringing once we all looked over.

"Ladies and gentlemen, please follow me."

Everyone started nattering on again as we herded ourselves back along the hallway with the paintings of Morgan's relatives. We passed the manor entrance and the huge staircase leading upstairs, and after that we were in a room at the far end of the hall, in a part of the house I'd never seen. It was big as the room at the other end of the house, and festooned with an equal number of chandeliers and paintings and candelabras and mirrors, though stretched through its centre was the largest table I'd ever seen. The length of a small sloop it was, and probably as heavy.

Morgan's guests rotated around the table, eyeballs keened, the wives saying how lovely everything was and the men all saying *my word, there must be good money in privateering!* At each chair was enough china and silverware to sink a ship, and on top of all that were little cards with names on them. I froze, thinking the jig was up, and I had the urge to walk back outside, find the man who'd brought me here, and tell him my evening was over. Instead, I hovered, milling about, pretending to be fascinated by one of the side-wall paintings, acting like I was a dealer of art and artifacts when of course I was just a dumb freebooter who couldn't read his own name. What followed was minute after minute of torture, the guests talking and talking and taking their time sitting, as if having an appetite was a crime if you were wealthy. Finally, and I do mean finally, they got themselves settled and with a breath of relief I took the one chair not spoken for. To my right was an enormous woman with billowy sleeves and a painted-on mole. To my left was her opposite, a woman thin as a yardstick with teeth so bucked her lips had trouble covering them when she closed her mouth. They were both nice enough, and during the soup (a watery broth with bits of oxtail floating about) I learned they were both married to sugar men with plantations in the vicinity. I listened politely, asking questions when I thought a question was needed, though I was half listening at best, seeing as they were both so bloody dull.

"And what do *you* do, Mr. Wand?"

That brought me round. It was the fat one who'd asked, her jowls all wobbly when she turned her head toward me. I wasn't sure how to answer, having no idea how much Morgan's guests knew about what had or hadn't gone on in Portobello. "I work with Mr. Morgan," was my tactful stab at an answer.

"So you're a privateer!" said the skinny one, a bony hand on her even bonier chest.

"I am at that."

"Well, that's marvellous!" said the fat one. "I tell you, we all think the world of Mr. Morgan. I doubt very much that England would be able to hold on to Jamaica without his noble efforts. Truly, truly heroic."

"Quite right," said the skinny one. "I tell you, I feel perfectly safe living here. Don't you, Cornelia?"

"Oh I do, Priscilla. I do *indeed*."

"You just watch. It won't be long before control of the Caribbean shifts in favour of the British, wouldn't you say, Mr. Wand?"

"We're doin' our best," I said with a chuckle, the two laughing even though what I'd said wasn't particularly funny. Still, there were worse ways to spend an evening, feeding on nice soup and good wine and compliments. After a bit my tablemates started talking to some old gas-bag sitting across from us, who was going on and on about trade rights and sovereignty and other yawn-inducing bollocks. Though I wasn't particularly listening, I still noticed the conversation wasn't far off the one I'd just been a part of, people just complimenting and arse-licking each other. Everyone has a game, in other words, and I was figuring out theirs, so every time I was asked something I just gleamed like a polished knob and said something like, "That's a beautiful brooch you're wearing, Mrs. So-and-so," or "Mr. Morgan has spoken *so* favourably of your presence on the island, Mr. What's-your-name," even though I had no idea who I was talking to and couldn't give a toss even if I had.

A salad came, some sort of fancy lettuce with a whole prawn, antennae and all, propped up in the middle of it, staring at me like it was right put out. Though I was happy with the prawn, I was brought up to believe that eating raw fruits and veg was a sure way of getting sick. Still, no one else seemed to be concerned, so I gave it a go, thinking it wasn't all bad, the prawn tasting as if it'd been scurrying about just minutes earlier. Next came a fish—you ate it with a funny little knife—and after that there was beef with all the trimmings, including Yorkshire pud as light and fluffy as any I'd ever had back in England.

There was wine too, and I'm not talking about the lantern fluid poured in Port Royal. First there was a white one and then with the beef a purple claret. Even better, I only had to have a sip or two before a waiter would freshen my glass. Just kept coming and coming, it did. By the time the main course was over, the other guests were laughing and talking loudly and looking like they were right off their faces. My gaze drifted toward the very end of the table, and that's when I noticed something odd. Morgan was leaning back in his chair, his meal mostly uneaten before him, the mildest look of... of... what *was* that in his eyes? I kept taking little glances at the man, trying to figure out what it was without being obvious about it. After a few more peeks I decided it was boredom or mild contempt or maybe even both, all of which made me wonder why he was having this party in the first place. About halfway down one side of the table sat his wife, Elizabeth, who was lovely and lively and not sober herself. Was he hosting this night for her? It could be, though Morgan had never struck me as a man motivated by the wishes of others, unless of course that other was the King.

Dessert was a shaking white blobby thing that tasted like sugary foam; I didn't have much, preferring the sweet wine served with it. With dinner over, another little bell started ringing, and the same servant who'd told us dinner was served now told us there were cigars and brandy for the men and would we care to follow. All the gents stood, so I followed their example, traipsing herd-like back to the big room at the other end of the house. There was a fire burning in the grate even though it was hot as always that night. We were all given snifters, and a minute later I found myself standing next to a statue of some luckless woman without arms. Morgan was across the room, talking to a pair of burghers, though I could tell he wasn't really concentrating on the conversation. His sharp grey eyes kept flitting about, like he was looking for some excuse to leave. He found it when he spotted me — he came over and we both stood on the sidelines, backs to the walls. I made sure to stand tall.

"Reminds me of the parties my parents took me to when I was little," he finally said. "Everyone trying to impress everyone else. Talking about their last fox hunt or trip to the Continent. My brothers and I, scrubbed red behind the ears, noses tickled with powder. Once, I addressed some duke's wife by the wrong name and the next day I was switched till my backside was black and blue all over. Oh no, I didn't like these parties much then, and I can't say I like them much more now. I hope you're surviving."

"Can't complain about the bevvies."

Morgan drained his glass, and it occurred to me he was swaying a little. This surprised me, for I'd never pegged him as a drinker. "Come on," he said. "Let's get you out of here."

He turned and walked off, and when I hesitated, he turned to look at me, his expression asking was I coming or was I just going to stand there like a dolt. I followed. Morgan's buckled shoes strode hard against the polished floorboards. Past the staircase we reached a doorway leading off the main hallway. Morgan opened it and motioned I should pass. "Go on," he said. "Pleasures await."

I looked down at a winding staircase leading into darkness. There was a ledge with an oil lamp on it; Morgan lit it with a match, the glow on the stairs soft and warm, each step creaking beneath my weight. To be truthful, I was feeling a little nervous, for stepping down into darkness reminded me of the holding cell where they put me following my arrest back in London Town.

By about the sixth step I cheered, though: we were entering a cellar filled with rack after rack of wine. There was cobwebs and dust and cool moist air. Morgan lit a second lamp and placed it on an overturned barrel with a pair of glasses waiting on it. They were both clean, and no doubt placed within the last hour or so.

"What's your pleasure, Wand?" he asked. "Cognac? Port?"

"Can't say I'm fussed."

Morgan turned, trailing a finger over the bottles. "Hmmmm... where's the blasted... oh right, here we are."

He pulled out a bottle of ruby and held it before his eyes, admiring it like it was a woman. He poured two glasses and we drank. It was so good I felt guilty using it up. Morgan drained his glass and I did the same. He poured two more measures.

"Damned wonderful, this stuff."

"You're right there, captain."

"It's the least I can do for subjecting you to that lot." He glanced above us. "The landed gentry. If only they knew what it takes to make this island safe for them, they'd run back to England screaming. They've no idea what goes on. Not the foggiest. By the way. In recognition of services rendered, the British government has made me an admiral."

"I'm impressed."

"It's just a word. It means little. The King *is* happy,

though. I will say that. It seems that there's money coming our way from England, Mr. Wand. More men, more guns, a new ship. Oh, the King's chuffed, all right. He wants us to strike hard at the Spanish Empire, and he doesn't care how rich or powerful we get in the process. He thinks with a few more Portobellos the Spanish grip on the Caribbean will crumble. He might just be right."

"Glad you're impressing someone, admiral."

Morgan took a hard swallow of port. "I asked you here tonight for a reason, Mr. Wand. I wanted that lot to meet you. You know — get used to your face."

"Why?"

His eyes drifted off, like he was seeing something not in the cellar.

"Mr. Wand. I want to ask you something. At Villahermosa, when we came upon the butchered guards, our means of conveyance gone, what would you have done were you in charge?"

I could've told him the truth: that I'd have been too panicked to come up with my own name let alone a decent plan. Instead, I shrugged, trying to look unbothered by the memory. "I suppose ... I suppose I'd have gone searching for a fishing village, sticking to the coast, of course. If we'd found one, I'd have stolen some vessels. If there was time, I'd have gone back to get the swag. If not, I'd have made for Port Royal."

"And if we hadn't found a village?"

"We'd have been dead men, all of us. Your plan was better."

"I'm not sure about that. Another half-hour and darkness would have fallen and then we'd have suffered the same fate as the men guarding the boats."

"It was a close shave. I'll grant you that."

"So who had the better plan, Mr. Wand?"

"Impossible to say. You'd have to know things you can't know."

Morgan stared at his glass. "Mr. Wand, I have a proposition for you. I was wondering whether you would be available to offer me, er, strategic advice should I ask for it in the future."

I gulped.

He gestured toward my chest. "When I was watching our forces climb that scaling ladder, it came to me. With my leadership, and your cleverness, and the, er, *pluck* of John Morris... the King has a point. Perhaps we *can* take any city on the Spanish Main. Or Cuba, for that matter. We'll rewrite history, Mr. Wand. It won't be easy, but if you believe we're serving a higher good, we can do it. I know God's a sticking point for you. Just think about what is right. I need you to *believe* our cause is just. Can you at least have faith in that?"

"I can," I choked, and I was even telling the truth, for at that moment, in that musty room filled with bottles, Henry Morgan could've asked me to follow him into an inferno and I'd have offered to go first.

He poured two more glasses. He picked his up and admired the way it looked in the lamplight, like a magic elixir or some such. "Tell me something, Mr. Wand," he said. "When this is all over, what will you do?"

I blinked. "When what's all over?"

"When the Spanish stronghold in the New World has ended, when there's no more call for privateering, when England's taken its rightful place in the New World... what will you *do*?"

"I hadn't thought of it, admiral."

"What do you mean, you hadn't thought of it? You're a chess player, man! You *do* need an endgame, don't you? We *will* win one day, you know." He swallowed his drink.

I felt right stupid, or leastways I did until an idea popped into my head. I wasn't sure whether that idea had been there for a while and I was just now noticing it, or whether I'd conjured it so Morgan wouldn't think me a dunderhead.

"I was thinking... I'd like to open a tobacco shop."

"Go on."

"It seems to me every sod walking around Port Royal smokes something: a pipe, cheroots, cigars, and that doesn't even take into consideration them that chew or sniff. But the only place to buy tobacco, if you don't want to go into St. Jago, is from market vendors, yeah? Half the time it's old and soggy, and half the time they're selling so-called Cuban tobacco that really came from some shite plantation here in Jamaica. I figure a good and honest tobacconist, willing to sell people a fair pipeful for a fair price, would do wonders for Port Royal."

I couldn't believe the words coming out my mouth: all this talk about providing a fair product for a fair price when all I'd done my whole life was swindle people out of their money.

"The only problem is, prices are getting right stupid in Port Royal now that the gentry are coming over from England and buying like mad buggers and driving the prices sky-high—"

"Mr. Wand," he interrupted. "I will soon be launching another expedition. If you accept this new role—if you become my military adviser—you'll merit three full shares rather than the half you were getting as a scrub boy."

When I said nothing—couldn't speak—he went on, "Do you understand what I'm saying, Mr. Wand? With what you make on our next raid, you'll earn enough to buy a dozen tobacco shops."

WE BOTTOMED UP and went back to the Great Room, where Morgan's wife came running, her cheeks blazing. "Henry!" she hissed. "Where have you *been*!? The guests have been asking after you all night!"

He dead-eyed her. This stopped her in mid-sentence, Morgan's delectable wife snorting and then picking up her skirt and charging off. I could see there was a group of people clumped at the front door, all chatting nicely on their way out.

"Come," Morgan said. "I'll show you out."

He found another hallway that let out to the side of the house. We stepped into a hot humid night alive with crickets. "Look up," he said.

There were so many stars they bled into each other, the sky a wash of glittering milk.

"I admire men like you, Mr. Wand."

"What kind is that?"

"Men who can lay their eyes on a sight like that and still feel there's no God. It must take a degree of bravery, believing your only reward is your time alive. By the way, as part of your new job, I'll be sending for you from time to time. Our games... they relax me. Consider it part of your duty."

We stood gazing out over St. Jago and Port Royal. From up here, the torches lighting the streets looked like flaring match heads. Morgan held his hands behind his back. Either the view or the night air or his wife's harangue seemed to have sobered him up, for he wasn't flushed or wavering like he was before (though this could've been the darkness hiding it).

"Good night, Mr. Wand." He reached out his hand and I shook it.

"Good night, admiral. I won't let you down."

"I know," he said, before turning and striding off.

SEVENTEEN

I SAW MORGAN TWICE over the next week and a half. Each time, he wanted to talk about chess and only chess, asking me dozens of questions about strategy I knew bugger all about — as I've said, he came from a military family, and it'd been a rule the boys had to learn the game whether they wanted to or not. So he knew things I didn't, things published in books or taught by instructors that didn't help one whit. I showed him what I could, making something up if I didn't know for sure. The truth was, the last thing he needed was more knowledge — it seemed to me it was getting in his way, confusing him with things he thought he should be doing. It was the music he needed, both the good kind and the squonking awful kind, and sod me if I knew how to give it to him. So I showed him little puzzles my granddad gave me when I was still learning, and I was all the time telling him to be patient, to develop his pieces until they were right the way he wanted them. Each time, I was there three or four hours, and each time I left he was in good cheer, slapping me on the back and telling me I was welcome any time and if he sent his driver would I grace him with a game or two?

"Course," I'd always say, feeling ten feet tall. "Course."

SO IT WAS *me*, Benny Wand, Benny The Boy Wonder, Benny The Magic Wand, call me what you will, but was no denying I was also *Mister* Benjamin Wand, military adviser to none other than Henry Morgan, conqueror of Villahermosa and the scourge of Portobello. The strange thing was, I didn't have to trick Morgan into giving me the job. It wasn't something gained through slipperiness or guile or hitting a man in the head. Somehow, I'd just been myself and Morgan's offer came nonetheless, all of which got me to thinking I should be that way more often.

At night, there was bibbing with Taylor, who'd returned from his hunting trip minus the little finger on his right hand—as the whispered story went, he'd gotten too close to a boar in need of a little sustenance. It must've given the big man a hell of a fright, though, for he didn't like to talk about it; instead, he let me have it about my new friends. "Wha'?" he'd say with a pointed grin. "Still time for us lowly buggers?" To show that I did, I'd buy round after round— "Here ya go, drink up drink up!"—Taylor saying there were advantages knowing a man so well acquainted.

Later, with just enough of the drink to make me zestful, I visited Tessie, who'd returned to the Bear Garden after her lengthy and mysterious absence. It turns out she'd taken the money I'd given her and spent it on a medical procedure in St. Jago.

"Look," she said, opening her mouth wide.

"Blimey," I said, for the two halves of her tongue had been sewed up with thick black thread; it looked like a worm was wriggling its way to the back of her mouth. "Blimey," I said a second time, inspecting every nook and cranny. "That hurt?"

"Nope. They gave me three Chinaman pipefuls and the room filled with a pine-tar scent and the next thing I knew, my head was in clouds. Bloody hurt *after*, though. Ten minutes of sewing followed by three weeks of swelling and eating nothing but tomato soup. It was all worth it, though. Means I'm normal now." She looked around her little room, and you could practically hear the thoughts running through her head: *maybe one day I'll be good for something else.*

"Tessie?"

"Yeah, Benny?"

"Give us a kiss with that mouth of yours?"

"What you think, Benny? I'm your childhood sweetheart? Bloody hell, you know the rules."

I sulked for two seconds. "What about them other things you could do with that tongue of yours?"

"Ah well. In that department it's business as usual."

IN OTHER WORDS, it was a high time I was having. Good job, roof over my head, a girl with the normal allotment of tongues, all of it mine. I did have one problem: most nights I was visited by that nightmare, the one I'm at my granddad's funeral and I walk down the pub aisle and open the casket and it's that priest John Morris executed at Portobello. Other times it'd be one of those traders we'd chopped up in Villahermosa, and once it was that mouthy little scout we captured in the jungle. Yet one thing always remained the same: each time, it was that sad knowing on the dead man's face that made me bolt straight up with a gasp. Then I'd come to fully, and the dream would drift away to wherever spent dreams drift away *to*, and I'd remind myself how good it felt to walk down the street and have a complete stranger point and say, "You see that ugly sod over there? The one with the chewed-up skin? In tight with Henry Morgan, he is..."

One afternoon I was coming back from a pint when I saw Morgan's stubby-armed driver, waiting for me. I walked up grinning.

The ride was the same as usual, the driver not talking except to snarl orders at his horse. Elizabeth Morgan answered when I rapped with that huge King's-head knocker.

"Mr. Wand!" she said. "So lovely to see you. Come in, come in. He's in the Great Room. Please, do come in."

I thanked her and entered, though not before knocking off any dirt I might've collected on my boots.

"Please," she said. "Go on in." She lowered her voice. "But I have to tell you, he's in a bit of a mood. " She giggled, like you do when you want people to think you're having a joke when really you aren't. I nodded and gave a little bow and walked down the hallway, past all those portraits and paintings and fancy gilt mirrors. He was sitting at the little table where we played chess. A cheroot smouldered away in his mouth, and there was a glass of something amber and delicious-looking in front of him.

"Mr. Wand," he said without rising. "I haven't seen you for a time."

"That's true."

"I've been busy, but believe me when I say I've missed my lessons. Please. Have a seat." The board was in front of him. "Brandy?" he offered.

"Wouldn't say no."

A servant appeared with a tray and two glasses. I took one and had a sip. Lovely stuff, it was. Morgan downed his and asked for two more, and when they arrived, he sipped his second rather than throw it back. He looked up, like he'd noticed something on the ceiling. "Look at this place, Wand. Not bad for a Welsh boy."

"A right beauty, it is."

"You could have one too. Just play your cards right."

"I'm trying."

"I'm warning you, though. It doesn't come without a cost." He waved his hand in front of his face, like he was motioning away a bug and not his strange mood. "Don't mind me. A fellow gets a bit of cabin fever, trapped here all day and night. You wouldn't believe the meetings I have to go to up here. Bureaucrats, landed gentry, the *bourgeoisie*. They all have to put their two cents' worth in. And the captains! They're the worst of the lot, always telling me what I should and should not do." He lit a safety match and held it to the tip of his cheroot. He took a few heavy puffs. "I've a few things to tell you. And before you comment, keep in mind that none of it is of my making."

"Understood," I said, a pride swelling inside.

"In a few days' time an immense man-of-war called the *Uxbridge* will pull into the harbour. It'll be the new Brethren flagship. Designed from the start for sea battle. Twenty-six cannons, seventy-two feet long, it'll take 125 men. All for our use."

"Bloody hell."

"That's the good news."

"And the bad?"

"His Majesty has issued our marching orders. He sent them via Bottlesworth, who reluctantly passed them on to yours truly."

"Reluctantly?"

Morgan took a few smoky pulls. "It's Panama, Mr. Wand."

The blood drained from my face. I could feel it rush away, leaving my skin cold. A mangled horn played somewhere. "You're not serious?"

"I am."

"It's the third-biggest city in the New World."

"Yes, Mr. Wand. I know that."

"You ask me here to find out what I think?"

"In a way, yes."

"It's madness."

"Is it?"

"Can I speak my mind?"

"You must."

"You're Henry Morgan. You've a way of doing things— you attack cities defended *only* by long jungle walks. It's your strategy, and it hasn't failed you yet. Panama is defended by both jungle *and* an army. This time, the enemy won't have to run to alert the Spanish forces. They'll already be there, and we'll *still* have a jungle trek to repel us. If you're going to pick a defended city, at least pick one on the coast. It's a shite idea, pure and simple. No other word for it."

Morgan took a deep breath. He leaned forward. His eyes looked bloodshot. "Let me tell you something. I grew up in a little village on the coast. When I was six, my father decided it was time I learned to swim. So he marched me down to the town jetty, ordered my clothes off, and threw me in. He damn near drowned me in the process."

"I'm not following."

"I was terrified. You've not seen the Welsh coastline, but it's not a thing to be trifled with. Rocks everywhere, huge waves, cold. *Good* swimmers give it a miss. I survived, though I had cuts and bruises where I was tossed into boulders. Plus I was sick with the grippe for a week. He said he knew I had it in me."

"But—"

"Could it be the throne sees things in us we can't see ourselves? It's all well and good to say they're cushy bastards in London, all pampered and fat, no idea what we're up against and so forth. But on the other hand, we *are* at war with the Spanish, and sending us on a suicide mission would scarcely help. If we got trounced, the Brethren of the Coast would be no more, and then what? There'd be nothing to stop the Spanish from taking back Jamaica. Do you think the King would risk that if he didn't think we could do it?"

"Dunno. There's no telling how stupid people can be."

Morgan smirked. "Then again, maybe His Majesty *has* gone soft in the head. Isolated, out of touch, deluded. So which one is it? Advise me, Mr. Wand. Earn your shares. Is it a suicide mission or a high compliment or both?"

"It's the first. It just is."

Morgan took the news like he wasn't surprised. "You're probably right," he said. "We'll just have to do our best. I expect you'll be put to the test, Wand."

He stood and lumbered out and left me alone in that hot

cavern of a room. When it was clear he was done with me, no chess nor lessons that day, I found the driver outside, smoking a cheroot. The afternoon was a hot one with rain on the way, the clouds grey wool.

Two days after that, the biggest ship I'd ever seen moored in Port Royal harbour.

Two days after *that*, I was on it.

Eighteen

E WERE SEVEN vessels, all pulling empty canoes
on lengths of twined rope. Our number was
250, maybe 300, the most men Morgan ever had under his
command, but little compared with the army waiting in
Panama. We all knew this, and there was little of the back
slapping and grog toasting that went with the beginning of
an expedition. Still, none of us was being forced.

An hour after setting off, the winds turned to a whistling screech. I'd never seen trades blow so hard—the hull
groaned and the sails stretched so taut I feared for the
seams. Our faces went raw and our lips turned leathery
and they started to peel. With the wind, the sea came alive
too, though we were moving at such a clip we skimmed
the wave peaks instead of pounding against them. Behind
the *Uxbridge*, two foamy white lines were split by a length
of black calm.

The sky was an angry mauve and, not long after, an endless black sheet with a million blinking lights. The moon was
nearly full, navigating child's play. Gazing behind us, I could

see the outlines of the other ships as we raced toward our first stop, the shelter off Île de Vache. After a time, the winds dropped to a respectable breeze. While the other boats kept going more or less in a straight line, the *Uxbridge* faltered, bobbing in the waves and refusing to stay on course. There was a lot of yelling and rough language, and when the other captains realized something was wrong, they had no course but to drop anchor. They were tiny specks on the horizon, and it took our ship another three or four hours to catch up, by which point it was pitch-black, so we dropped anchor as well and called it a night. One by one, the men moved toward the hold. No one had slept for the past day and with the dying breezes came a weariness of the body. It hit me as quickly as the change in the weather, eyes burning and limbs aching, and all I wanted to do was go to my hammock and close my eyes to the world. Yet as I was heading below, a scrub boy came up and told me I had to go see Morgan in his cabin. I told the lad I was on my way.

I walked past row upon row of hammocks filled with rank unshaven men, all looking bothered by the shite progress we'd made that day. At the bow was a door leading to Morgan's quarters. I knocked and when told to come in, I did. The room was larger than the one he had on the *Pearle*, large enough that in the middle was a meeting table. Captains Morris, Freeman, and Jackman were there as well as some of the Frenchie captains I didn't know. There was also a man named Higgins who was head of rigging for the flagship. To a one, they all looked at me through narrowed eyes, as if to say *what's that scrub boy doing here?*

"I believe you all know Mr. Wand," said Morgan, and there were a few grunted hellos.

When the shock of my being there wore off, Higgins started complaining he had no idea how to sail a boat so huge. "I've never 'ad nuffink this size, Mr. Morgan. It's a mystery to me. Like sailing a bathtub the size of an island, it is."

This sparked a long debate, the captains going on about mainsail-this and aftsail-that and what about the bloody trades this time of year? And the whole time I could only wonder what I was doing there. Morgan settled it by saying we'd camp a few days at Île de Vache, where Higgins and his charges could take the *Uxbridge* out for a bit of practice.

"So it's settled," he said. "Thank you for coming, gentlemen. I'll wish you all a good night, now."

I found a spare hammock beside Taylor. I lied down, and was about to joke bleakly about invading the third-biggest city in the Americas with a ship no one knew how to sail when he rolled over, his broad back facing me, pretending to sleep.

THE NEW DAY arose pink and hazy and hot. As the sun burnt off the ocean mist, we could see the outline of Île de Vache, none of us realizing how close we'd been. The sun was still climbing when we sailed into one of the island's many inlets. Every ship anchored, the privateers rowing or swimming to shore depending on preference. The only exception was Higgins's men, who took the *Uxbridge* back out to sea; with nothing to do, we all stood on the beachhead and laughed while the bloody thing slogged its way over flat clear waters. With what was left of the day, a few men armed with muskets and daggers trudged into the woods and shot a couple of boars. We roasted the pigs over an open fire, their mouths stuffed with a furry, fist-sized fruit no one knew the name of but that grew everywhere on the island. We camped on the beach, the fleet more or less hidden, the flagship still out to sea somewhere.

This went on for three days, during which time I saw little of Morgan. Midway through the fourth day, a few men with keen vision started hollering they could see the *Uxbridge* coming back. Sure enough, a dark speck turned into a small boat and then a huge one and we could tell by the way Higgins was storming toward the island he and his men had made good use of the delay. The next morning, we pulled anchor and headed north to Cuba, where we poked around the South Cays, this time practising the big ship's manoeuvring when it was laden with men. That night, Morgan called another meeting, though this time Higgins wasn't there. This one, I gathered, had to do with navigation. Morgan had old Spanish maps, old British maps, old Dutch maps, and even a tattered Portuguese relic. All were different in various ways, our job to figure the ways they were the same. Under flickering low kerosene flames, we all agreed the city of Panama was on the far side of an isthmus some ninety miles wide, and the only way to travel from the north side to the south side was using a craggy little river called the Chagres.

There was the usual banter about whether to canoe in via the Chagres or try to surprise them with another exhausting jungle walk. "Gentlemen," Morgan said. "There's no point in trying to surprise them. The army is already there. They can fight us soon as they see us. There's no advantage to surprise, so we might as well avoid the hardships of a trek, are we agreed?"

"Agreed," said the others, the Frenchie captains murmuring *we we we*.

In the morning, we sailed across open water to the coast of Campeche. Here we camped a few days with some rancid half savages who cut down the logwood trees used for making red and brown dyes in the New World. We gave them some copper pots in return for boucan, turtle meat, and a brown unleavened bread they made in the heat of the sand. It was a zesty time, the logwood cutters crazy mad bastards, every last one of them. A few even decided to throw in their lot and join us, logwooding a job guaranteed to shorten your life with all the diseases lurking in the bogs where logwood liked to grow. Most stayed, though. In that strange English of theirs, they told us if there was one good thing about a logwood glade, it was that it couldn't spring a hole and sink into the ocean.

The following day, we finally left for a three-day voyage along the coast, hugging tight to inlets and coves just so we wouldn't give ourselves away until we had to. We travelled at night—had to—and like so many of the sailors I spent my time craned over the gunwale, mesmerized by the way the starlight glinted off ink-black waters. This was something known to every sailor: there's a drug in them waters, particularly at night, when there's quiet and nothing to do and the mind's gone all swimmy and blank. Anything can happen and one night it did, my leaning over the gunwale and looking at glistening black when the boiled heads of those Spanish priests in Portobello floated to the surface, their mouths still gaping, their eye sockets empty, their ears hanging off in stringy tatters. I leapt away from the gunwale, heart pounding, though when I inched forward they were gone, a trick of light and water and the shame living deep inside me.

We moored in a reefy cove, hid from any ships passing by. That night Morgan held his last meeting with his captains and me. Mostly we talked about inventory: how many guns, sabres, pikes, and cudgels we had, how much food we were carrying, exactly how many men we had compared to them. Course, it was all guesswork, each captain giving his estimates, and because they couldn't agree, a tone crept in the room — the captains were nervous, that much was obvious, and they showed it by being snippy with each other. When a slight argument broke out over how many canoes we'd brought along, Morgan spoke up in that smooth encouraging voice of his.

"Gentlemen," he started. "I know what each and every one of you is thinking. That we've lost our minds taking on the Spanish army in Panama." He paused, looking from one solemn face to another. "And yes, it will be a difficult task, one that surely will test our mettle and then some. But I can tell you one thing, my Brethren. We have an advantage. When we come across the city of Panama, we will fight for our own enrichment, whereas the Spanish will be fighting under orders. Who, do you think, will be stronger? More emboldened? Those men fighting for riches they can *keep*, or those men fighting for riches that'll just go on some ship bound for Spain?" I looked about. John Morris was grinning. "We saw it in Villahermosa and we saw it in Portobello, and I swear to you, gentlemen, we'll see it again in Panama. Yes, they'll outman us, but when they see us coming, an army with conquest in its soul, do you really think they'll fight as we will? I tell you, gentlemen, the Spanish dominance of the New World is coming to an end. Their empire is exhausted, bloated, antique. You've all seen the state of their guns, the rips in their uniforms. You all saw the children who were guarding the storehouse at Portobello. When we take Panama, it'll be the final nail in the Spanish coffin. *We* will rescue the whole of the New World from Castilian rule!"

Morris said, "Bloody right!" and then the other captains started gobbling about how they couldn't wait, how the moment was theirs and the only thing to do was seize it.

"Gentlemen," Morgan said. "We have a long day tomorrow. I suggest you get some rest."

There was a round of *hear! hear!*s and then we all turned and headed for the doorway.

"Mr. Wand," Morgan said. "Please, stay behind. I need a word."

The captains left, though not before John Morris gave me a right look. Morgan walked up, close enough I could see grey pouches beneath his eyes.

"What are you always telling me, Mr. Wand? About the board, I mean."

"Develop your pieces. Bide your time."

"So have we done that? Are we equipped to take Panama? What is your position, Mr. Wand? And please do remember that, in real life, courage and faith count as much as, if not more, than strategy."

I looked at Morgan's face. Though my brain knew we weren't in any way ready to sack that damned city, my heart was saying we'd somehow find a way.

"We're ready, admiral. That's my position. Now, we're ready."

NINETEEN

THE NEXT DAY, we moored in the mouth of the Chagres and started loading the canoes. Morgan left behind a small crew of expert sailors and told them to take the ships far enough away they could avoid any Spanish treachery, but to remain close enough to pick us up when we returned. He assigned another team to grease the muskets and pistols, gather them in oilcloth, and set them in the canoes. Then came fireballs and pikes and machetes and bag after bag of provisions. The rest of us waited, swatting at insects and wrinkling our noses at the rotting quagmire stench: the Chagres was narrow and shallow, more a muddy trickle than a true river.

With the canoes packed, a bunch of men climbed in and discovered we had a problem, the canoes sinking so low the bottoms scraped the river bottom. As they climbed out, Morgan came up to me. His voice was a gurgle, like it hadn't been used much that day: "The canoes are too laden."

"I can see that."

"We can't do without our weapons, Mr. Wand."

"Then we've a problem, yeah?"

"My plan is to leave most of the provisions behind, and depend on Indian villages along the way."

"What if there're no villages?"

"The better maps show there are."

"Which ones were the better ones again?"

Morgan took a deep breath. "If there is one thing I know, we aren't going to find any guns in that jungle. Food, maybe, but weapons? Not a chance."

"Then it sounds like you've your answer."

We unpacked crate after crate of boucan and dried beeve until the canoes didn't scrape bottom. We set off. By the end of that day, the Chagres narrowed to the width of a creek and, food or no food, the canoes bottomed out once again, so there was nothing for it but getting out and pulling the canoes up the river while we all sloshed along like pigs through mire. When it was too dark to see, we found a dry riverbank and camped best we could, some of the men sleeping on wet sand and some in the canoes, muskets and pikes and flintlocks piled around them. We woke the next morning and ate the last of the victuals and set off.

Without Indians to guide us, we kept taking false tributaries, which would snake around for ages before turning into full-blown swamp. We'd retrace our steps and take another guess at the true run of the Chagres, Morgan's face grim with frustration and memories of getting lost on the way to Portobello. After four or five hours, the men began to grumble they were hungry and hot. If Morgan heard any of this, or felt any need for food himself, he didn't show it. The captains followed suit and more than once that bastard Morris turned and yelled for us to keep up, what did we think this was, a sodding picnic? The men complied, not because they were easily cowed but because they all knew if they picked up their feet they'd come across a food source quicker.

And then another false creek masking as river.

And then a man got bit by something and started howling and fell in the water. An instant later he was a mushy pink fountain and we all watched the crocodile that got him, breathing over a huge lump that, one minute earlier, had been the poor bastard's leg.

And then one sorry bastard went all feverish and delirious, maybe with something he got earlier or maybe with something picked up on the river. Either way, we had to stop and lay him on top of a heap of muskets. He was moaning for some woman he knew named Abigail and through it all our desire for a meal in no way lessened.

Just before the next bend, we spotted a break in the foliage and from it wisps of grey-blue smoke — there were even a few Indian canoes dragged up onto the bank. Tasting lunch, we hurried toward the settlement, everyone chattering about how much they were looking forward to a chew of boucan or turtle gut or maybe that funny Indian bread made in hot sand, though as we neared I began to wonder why we weren't hearing the usual noises heard from an Indian settlement. There were no babies mewling or pigs grunting or dogs barking or mothers yelling at their children in a language of strange grunts and clicks. All we could hear was the crackle of low smouldering fires, and as we neared we saw why.

There were seven or eight log dwellings and to a one they'd been torched. Everything was covered in cinder.

Most of the Indians had run off, though a few weren't so lucky: they lay strewn about the campsite, charred and still burning slowly, and it was the smoke their bodies gave off that we'd mistaken for cooking flames.

So that's their play, I thought. Starve us out. Eliminate allies and take away our food source at the same time. Good on them, I thought, their scouts must've been watching from the moment we landed. It was a move we couldn't counter, so I went to find Morgan and discuss ways to return to the coast in one piece. That's when I saw that he and the captains were sloshing in a direction that'd only take them deeper into the jungle.

"Morgan!" I bellowed.

When he didn't stop, I yelled again. This time he turned, eyes filled with impatience. I struggled for breath as I sloshed toward him.

"I guarantee they'll have burnt every bloody village along the way, so even if we don't starve, we'll be too weak to fight. We have to turn around. Regroup. Rethink. Solve our food problem."

Captain Freeman spoke up. "Henry. I hate to admit it, but your scrub boy's got a point."

"Mr. Wand is his name," Morgan said calmly. "And he needs to learn to take chances."

WE KEPT MOVING, and spent that night in the second Indian village we came to, this one as covered with cinder and ash as the first, though at least it was free of bodies; the natives must've kenned what was coming and fled, the smell of smoke at their backs. We slept on a wide mucky shore, or at least we tried to. The ground was moist and our stomachs complained loudly and the air was so damp it was an effort to draw breath. Plus we knew the enemy was hidden somewhere in the forest and if anything'll ward off sleep it's knowing you're being watched.

We did without breakfast save for some crayfish plucked from the river. This barely helped, crayfish being bony little fuckers with barely a thimble of meat on them. We set off, the men grumbling and taking turns pulling the canoes. After that it was one foot in front of the other, legs weak, mind flitting, stomach in knots. Moving right slowly, we were. Our feet had gone clumsy, like they weren't attached proper to our feet. Men started slipping on the mucky bottom and falling, a bother as there was no way clothes would ever, ever dry in the damp jungle air. After a time, Morgan fell in beside me.

"What do you think?" he asked. His face, normally a rich colour, looked pale. Sweat dripped off him.

"They're waiting till we're faint with hunger and then they'll attack."

"Yes. I believe so as well."

A few minutes later, Morgan stopped the column and assigned a party to go up ahead and try to flush out the enemy. "Now, the rest of you! Let them know where we are. Make some noise. The sooner we draw those bastards into battle, the sooner we can seize their rations."

I swear it was the first moment I ever heard something other than sanity come from Henry Morgan, for in the middle of that cursed jungle, his men weak with hunger, the enemy all round, he started singing, at the top of his lungs, *ho ho ho and a bottle of rum*. At first he was alone, but so his actions didn't seem lunatic his captains started singing *forty men and a dead man's chest*, though their voices weren't as loud nor enthused as their leader's. The rank and file joined in as well, and there was still less enthusiasm in their voices. After a verse or two the song petered out, and then even Morgan stopped singing, a weariness on his face I'd not seen previous.

We spent that night in a damp clearing, nothing but worried thoughts to nourish us. The sun came up broiling. The jungle steamed. We walked on rubbery legs. We came upon another torched settlement, the bodies of undeserving Indians no longer making an impression, for all we could think of was *food, food, food*. Someone found a pile of leather sacks untouched by fire, so we knifed them into thin ribbons and for lunch we boiled them till they were soft (or at least softer than when we'd found them). We choked them down in small awful bites, and trudged off with our stomachs hurting.

After a bit we came to a full-fledged town, this one a little trading post with Spanish-style houses. Though it wasn't burnt, it was empty. The men ran into the few houses in the place and started looking. A few seconds after that, a Frenchie with a dazed look came running out, gnawing on a loaf of bread. In his other hand was a wheel of cheese with a few bites missing as well. "Food!" he hollered. "FOOD!"

This set the rest of the men to running, though before they could reach the cottage Morgan extracted his flintlock and fired a shot into the air. Everyone stopped.

"Wand!" he yelled.

"I'm here."

"I suppose the food's poisoned?"

"It will be, yeah."

Morgan took two or three shaky breaths. We stayed put and watched the Frenchman who'd eaten the bread and cheese. After fifteen minutes or so, when he was still on his feet, the men started to grumble, saying maybe Morgan was wrong and do we or do we *not* get to eat? These complaints petered when the poor Gallic bastard began to convulse, eyes bulging from his head, green foam appearing at the corners of his mouth. With nothing to be done, we moved on, the man groaning and clutching at himself and uttering prayers.

We had barely enough strength to lift our feet above water. Later that afternoon, one of Jackman's men tore a frond from a tree lining the riverbank and started gnawing it. "Tastes like cake!" he yelled, and though we all knew he was delirious, we all started grabbing fronds ourselves. Though they were bitter as life itself, at least it got the mouth working and in this there was the mildest of relief. We walked more. Time stopped working like it should. A single minute would refuse to pass and then it'd vanish altogether and you'd find yourself marching through jungle, knee-high in water, and not understanding where you were or why you were pulling a canoe filled with guns until the grim truth of it all came rushing back. Men began to faint. Mostly they were the biggest amongst us. When this happened, we piled the casualties atop the canoes, lassoing them in so they wouldn't fall off, and kept going. Taylor was the third to drop.

"Where am I, Benny?"

"You're in Port Royal," I said as I piled him on lumpy hard grease cloth. "You're in your favourite bar, with your favourite girl. You're 'aving the time of your life, you is."

"Jesus, Benny... I don't think so..."

At the next burnt-out village, someone wandered into the woods to have a shite and while doing so came across sacks of chicken feed partially covered by dug-up mulch. Our feeling was the Indians must've hid it from the Spanish so it likely hadn't been tampered with. Still, there wasn't much, and Morgan ordered we feed it to the weakest amongst us, Taylor included. This got them back on their feet, though just.

We kept going. Night fell and we had no idea where we were and how far Panama was or if we'd all be slaughtered in our sleep. When the order to make camp came, we stepped into jungle and found spots to curl up in. Sometime in the middle of the next day the river petered out altogether, turning into a skinny moist trail. Short of dragging the canoes over dry land, our only option was to tie them off, grab our weapons, and keep going. We staggered along, barely enough strength to stay upright and yet we toted muskets and fire pots and pikes and what all else. At least our feet were out of water. I looked at the man next to me. His face was sunken and his arse all but gone and I knew I looked the same.

Morgan found me and fell in step. He stopped walking and so every other bastard stopped walking too. They were all looking at us.

"We're close," Morgan said. His face had disappeared; something bony and eye-sunken was in its place. He was breathing hard, sweat dripping off his chin. His breath stank.

"If you say so," I said. In the last clearing I'd spotted woodsmoke in the distance, so maybe he was right. I didn't care. I was so weak it was hard to think. Morgan had the same problem, his thoughts coming in little trickles instead of a stream.

"This path will lead to the city."

"Likely, yeah."

"We are too weak to fight, Wand."

I ordered my mind to work. It wouldn't. It couldn't. We had nothing, there was nothing, my head couldn't make sense of anything. I was feeling hot and weak and ready to go limp.

"Remember the Spanish map?" Morgan asked.

"A little."

"It showed a big... a big ranch off to the west... to the west of the city."

"I don't remember."

I couldn't breathe, could barely talk. I closed my eyes. I'd had our next move in my head and now it was gone. We were all close to dropping and that's all I knew. Angry colours danced. Morgan just stood there, hand against a tree, having a hard time catching his breath. His head was low and he was panting. Mostly he looked like he couldn't believe the decision he'd come to: the only thing we had with a hint of safety was the bloody path and we were going to quit that and wander west into thick woods. Without looking up, he turned and staggered into the depth of the jungle, no footprint nor stream to follow, the jungle so thick overhead we couldn't even follow the sun's passage.

Every step was a battle against vines and branches and shrub. We were soon lost and maybe moving in circles; I was so weak I kept forgetting why we were doing this and then it'd come back to me, we were looking to steal food and get the army moving again. There was nothing to do but step over fallen men and keep going. We were all in an ugly trance. The legs moved but the mind was blank. It was hard to say if it was morning or afternoon or night: the eyes were playing tricks and I swear I saw wood nymphs, sinister little grey things in the corner of my vision, though every time I looked straight at them, they'd scatter. We kept moving. I was in Port Royal kissing a woman with a split tongue and then I was back in that infernal jungle trudging trudging trudging and then I was watching burned priests falling from a ladder. My legs stopped hurting, feeling more like they were made of air. Then my vision went: everything looked like I was peering through a tunnel and still we kept hacking our way through jungle, no path nor clearing nor nothing. I forgot my name for a moment, and when it came back to me I felt so grateful my eyes welled and I wanted to shout it to the next bloke — *Benny! The name's Benny!* — though I was too weak so I didn't, all I could do was put one foot in front of the other, and then the earth fell away and when I caught myself I was a boy and Mum had me set up in a corner of a grog shop in Birmingham.

It was a sewer of a place, reeking of sweat and old food, the ceiling low and letting in drafts. Course, she was shilling away, the fat under her arms slopping about, *step on up step on up, take on Benny The Boy Wonder, you there sir, surely you could beat a nine-year-old boy!* and the next thing I know she was pulling me aside and saying *see that rum bastard over there? wants to bet a hundred quid he does!* I looked over and it turned out the man was a priest and so I was scared. A hundred quid was ten times more than I'd ever played for, and besides, wouldn't he have God on his side? I asked Mum how we'd cover such a wager and she told me that's why I'd better see to it I won. So I played the father. And he was good. Said he'd been playing since he was two years old, and meanwhile he was wearing the collar and looking at me with a vile glare, the kind a cat gets when it's cornered a mouse. In other words I was rattled, and at first I didn't play my best. I got out of it by thinking what'd happen if I lost a hundred quid—me and my brothers and sisters, there was five of us by then, eating out of rubbish bins, and it was this thought made me hunker down. I steeled myself, in other words. Reminded myself I was Benny The Boy Wonder and who cared if I was nine years old or ninety? Collar or no collar, I was going to show the punter a thing or two, so I came on full force and sure enough he made a slight error and I took the game with a pawn advancement. He smashed a huge red swollen long-fingernail hand on the table. Pieces flew and a chair fell, but at least he paid up. Mum came over all grinning. She sat her fat backside down and told me I'd done good. I told her I was scared I'd lose the hundred pounds and this made her cackle like a stuck hen. She leaned toward me. Her breath was tobacco, sweat, and gin. *Oh, he didn't want no hundred quid. He wanted you, you little tosser! Imagine! A man of the cloth an' all!* She cackled even harder, slapping her knee and offering to buy drinks for everyone within earshot, and I looked at her like I could kill her. *Wha'?* she said. *Why the look? I knew you'd take him...* and then, from the corner of that miserable place, that wretched scum-dwelling drinking hole, I heard a cow mooing.

I stopped, thinking maybe my senses were playing tricks, for where was Mum and the grog shop and that diddling lizard-skinned priest? I looked around and saw what it

was, we were back in the jungle, and judging from the faces
about me I wasn't the only one who heard a moo. Somehow
we picked up our feet. After a bit we reached a fence with a
semi-cleared field on the other side. We crossed and walked
on and soon we were in pasture, and standing in that pasture were a few dozen cows, all chewing cud and regard-
ing us with dumb curiosity. No one cheered nor clapped nor
nothing. We just set upon them, hacking them into gobbets
which we cooked over high fires, the outsides blackened and
the insides barely cooked. Morgan marched about, grinning, as if he'd just enjoyed a nice walk in Hyde Park, saying, "Go easy, you blackguards, or it'll all come up!" Mostly
we ignored him. Our stomachs filled and a few puked, but
mostly it was a matter of our will coming back like a tor-
rent. With this was a fury — what those Spanish bastards
had put us through. What those Spanish cunts had *done* to
us. Strength rushed into our arms and legs and hearts and
brains and soon we were as good as new, with a fair bit of
anger thrown in as well. We were armed and strong and
bitter. We were frightful mad fuckers and they better stay
clear. We was deranged wilful bastards and scary as hell. A
few headed back into the woods and found men who'd fallen
along the way, and they dragged them back and soon they
were fed and thirsting not for water but for blood-soaked
vengeance.

That night, we slept where we dropped.

At dawn, we woke vicious.

Twenty

W E MARCHED BACK through dense jungle and found the dried creek bed we'd left a day earlier. Here we turned right and marched to the edge of the jungle and waited for orders.

Morgan sent a few men into the trees. They came down with branch scrapes on their faces, though they all agreed Panama was a few miles off and beyond that a blue bank of ocean. We trudged through light woods dotted with streams. Around noon the trail opened at the top of a plateau. Down below was a green plain about a mile wide and a mile deep and beyond that was the city.

Course, they were waiting for us, fifteen hundred or more Spaniards on horseback, all in rows. Morgan took this in, jaws gnashing. Beyond the enemy was the city, which looked like Portobello though bigger: it had the same square with a church and lanes leading away, the only difference being there was a square beyond that and another square beyond that as well. My eyes roamed, looking for weakness, and I knew Morgan was doing the same.

"Wand," he said while pointing. "Do you see it?"

"The hill? Yeah, I do."

Though the Spaniards had covered the right and centre of the plain, off to one side was a large rise where their horsemen were fewer. Separating this hill from the rest of the plain was a dip in the land; if we stormed that hill via that dip, we might draw the enemy to engage us there. And once they were there, it wasn't hard to imagine all those Spanish horses gumming up and being more hindrance than help. On foot, we'd move easier than them, and if enough of our number weren't felled, we might even take the hill. From there we could storm the city, flintlocks blazing, murder in our souls, the best part being our plan just might work.

Morgan talked to his captains. In short order, word went round that the hill was the target and we'd all take it via the fall of land in front of it. We waited another hour for word to travel until finally the captains settled the men and a quiet fell over us and you didn't need to be a genius to figure this was our time. Across the battlefield the enemy sensed it as well, for they'd all aimed their guns, and their horses were beginning to jostle and champ, and they were thrusting pikes and cudgels into the air while yelling. Spoiling for action, they were, and still we wouldn't give it to them: we made them wait another hour or so, just the two sides staring across a void, making each other think, which is a trial for those who've made the decision to engage. All that stoppered zeal: it cramps the muscles and weakens the blood and tightens the lungs.

There was never any signal. Or if there was, I never heard or saw it. All I know is one moment we were at the edge of the woods, blood turned to lava, and the next we were running and yelling like madmen. As we stormed the plain, the men kept up the hollering, though it quickly started to feel like wasted effort, for the enemy wasn't taking the bait, the lot of us running and firing pistols and shrieking like madmen and still they did nothing. We slowed to a march. We headed toward the hill. Our hearts thundered and our breath came in great heaving storms and we were all of us wondering if they were just going to let us walk in like unruly house guests. A few hundred feet from that hill, the enemy still hadn't moved — and that's when it happened, one of those things you don't believe is possible, so you test your eyes by waving a hand in front of them and when both eyes pass, you're forced to figure they're giving you the real story.

A hundred bulls stampeded toward us, tongues lolling and heads lowered, and only then did those bloody Spaniards come at us, the bulls like a giant shield. How they'd kept the bulls from view or how they'd released them so sudden like, I'll never know. I can only tell you those bulls were supposed to send us scrambling with fear. Instead, we set our flintlocks to blazing and then the bulls panicked and started careening in every direction and getting in the way of the Spanish gunners. Though a few of us fell, it was again a matter of us having modern pistols and them having old arquebuses and fowling pieces, and with the bulls running amok, we took one after another after another, the field a haze of powder smoke and falling Spaniards and stampeding bulls.

We kept on toward the hill. The Spanish soldiers came out to engage us right where we wanted them, their horses bound by the rise on either side, and so they went crashing toward the middle, where they began to collide with one another and rear with the shock of it all. Of course, we opened fire and then men and horses were falling beside downed bulls, and soon the ravine was a carpet of fallen bodies, groans coming in English and Spanish and moos and low frantic whinnies. We made the hilltop. Here we stopped to powder our weapons and then we stormed down the other side of the hill, still firing at everything that moved, be it bull or horse or anyone wearing a pointy Montero hat. We hit the city walls. I won't say we hadn't lost a man, but compared with the enemy, we were intact and strong. Here we met our biggest challenge, for they'd set up a row of sharpshooters, but what they hadn't counted on was us not giving a toss, not when it meant riches and glory and vengeance. We didn't slow. The first up and over the walls mostly fell to Spanish pellets, but the bastards had to reload and soon we were in amongst them, lost in that city of wood houses, fighting over narrow streets amongst fleeing women and children, and that's when we smelled smoke.

There was a pause as we all looked for fire. It got worse, the air turning black. We coughed and sputtered and rubbed our eyes, and then flames started licking the sides of the houses and it was plain they'd set their own city ablaze. In the same way they'd deprived us of food, they were now taking away our plunder — there was nothing for it but falling back and watching it burn. Soon the city was a mountain of flame.

The assault had taken an hour. Throughout, I'd hung back with Morgan. Though I'd fired my French musket again and again, it was difficult to say whether I'd taken my first life amidst all that smoke and flame and howling wounded animals. The city was getting hotter and hotter, and we kept moving back farther and farther upon the plain, mindful of fallen bulls and wounded screaming horses and limp dead men. Along the way, I spotted Taylor, face stained with cinder, running away from the heat with the rest of us. About halfway through the field we all stopped, there being enough churned earth to halt the advance of the blaze. Morgan, meanwhile, was pacing back and forth, face dripping soot, nose tip burnt, eyebrows gone, pounding a fist into his palm. "Can you imagine!" he ranted. "Running bulls at a foe! Torching their own city! Who'd have thought they'd be so utterly spineless!"

We supped on burnt animal parts we dragged off the field, little bits of burning floating thatch landing on our food. If we slept at all, it was the sleep of men who knew they'd been rooked proper.

TWENTY-ONE

B Y THE NEXT morning, the city had mostly burned itself out, though there were still a row of houses around the square that were well blackened though for some reason still standing. We started moving through the smouldering rubble, a thankless task for it was all of it gone. Plate, gold, coins—it must've slipped out on ships while the city burned. Still we looked. Even the household swag was mostly burnt, though we did find the odd half-melted candelabra or spittoon. It was hot stupid work. There were no bodies caught in the fire, and this showed that every man, woman, and child in Panama knew the plan all along was to set the city ablaze if it came to that. I suppose our reputation was too frightening, something that'd always helped us in the past but this time didn't.

Morgan, reckoning there were townsfolk hiding in the woods, picked a group of fleet men and sent them out, their orders to find anyone who could be questioned and bring them back still breathing. The rest of us had to keep searching for loot, though we were getting little more than singed fingers for our troubles. By mid-afternoon, heat from the sun had risen as well, and all the ash in the air started to stick to the sweat on our bodies. We were starting to look like ghosts, our faces white-blue. One by one Morgan's men brought in escapees found in the forest, their hands bound behind their backs. Though a few struggled, most marched forward, eyes wet and looking at the ground beneath their feet. If they tripped or fell, they were yanked upward by their elbows and told to get on with it. Anyone who struggled or hesitated took a musket breech to the head. There were women and children too, though packing them into the town church wasn't an option seeing as little of it was still standing, just a stone altar surrounded by charred smoking ruins.

This went on all day. A miserable bunch of shackled Spaniards they were, so exhausted and scared it was all they could do to stay on their feet. Some had head wounds. There were fifty, maybe sixty of them. Morgan paced in front of them, hands behind his back. At every man he stopped and stared, venom in his eyes. Midway down the line he paused before an eight-year-old boy who stood before him trembling.

"Go!" he ordered. "*Vaya!*"

The kid glanced up and instead of running off, he moved closer to his mother, wrapping a shaking arm around her waist. She was sobbing and begging Morgan for something in Spanish, my guess to spare her boy. Morgan grabbed the lad by the shoulder and pulled him away from his bawling mother. Then he kicked him in the seat of the pants and pointed in the direction of the forests siding the city. This propelled the boy two or three yards, though he managed to stay on his feet. "*Vaya!*" Morgan yelled again. "*Vaya, vaya,*

vaya!" though the kid just stood there, shaking and looking back at his weeping mother. This time Morgan took
three lengthy strides and kicked the boy as hard as he was
able; first the boy fell and then he was scrambling hurt on
the bloodied cobblestone, and still, still, he wouldn't bugger off like Morgan wanted. His mother stopped crying and
yelled words that must've been frightening to the boy, for
there were tears streaming down his cheeks even though
he didn't seem to be crying. A second after that and he ran
like wolves were nipping at his heels.

Morgan went to the four or five other kids in the line and
sent them off as well. He continued his pacing, muttering
at his own bad luck, at one point stopping before a beautiful Spanish woman who'd clearly been the wife of some
wealthy merchant. She had olive skin and big eyes and a
figure grown shapely to the point of sin. More to the point,
she had a necklace with a ruby the size of a plum; Morgan
lifted it and then looked at his captains with a face saying
*you see? you see? of course there's bloody swag, and it's all hid-
den in those woods...* He dropped the jewel and moved on.
Black hair stuck to his stubbly face. His hands were balled
tightly to his sides, and when he'd finished inspecting the
prisoners, he moved to the middle of the line and turned
his back to them. He just stood there, no plan coming, heat
and exhaustion and frustration and bitterness having robbed
him of his greatest talent.

He lifted his head and called for Morris. His second-in-
command marched up and said, "You know what's needed."

Morgan said nothing. Just kept looking ahead.

"Henry," Morris said again. "You *know* there's swag hidden in those woods. Only one way to find out where it is."

Still Morgan didn't move; he just stood there looking forward. His breath was coming in short little bursts. His face was like chalk. Seconds passed by, Morgan looking almost mournful.

"For Christ's sake," Morris charged. "Give the bloody *order.*"

"There's women," Morgan finally murmured.

"And there's men," growled Morris. "We'll start with them."

WITH THE DECISION made, John Morris went through the ranks, picking men trained in the sort of work at hand. They weren't the biggest nor the fiercest nor the dirtiest amongst us; it was a blackness of the heart they had, their difference hidden till you saw them get to it. Morris split these men into groups of four and five. Each group led away a begging and pleading Spaniard toward the homes around the city's smoking main plaza. The rest of Morgan's men went dispatched to the plain with Jackman and Freeman.

This left Morgan and me, alone before a burnt-out city.

"The swag's gone," I told him.

"Perhaps."

"There's not a boat in sight, every house burnt, this is pointless. It all went out the back door. They can't give up hidden loot, for there's none to be had."

"Perhaps."

"Torture those Spaniards if you want, but it won't get us anywhere. That's my advice."

"I don't recall asking for your advice, Wand."

"If I was you—"

"Well you aren't!" Morgan turned, venom in his eyes. "You are not *me*, Wand, and for that you should be grateful."

I heard moans drifting over the charred ruined black city. I walked toward the town's main square, Morgan not calling out nor asking where I was going. I came to the first house, the window boxes sooty and the shutters burnt right off. I stopped for just a moment. I knew when I swung open that door whatever I saw would stay with me for the rest of my life. I opened it anyway, as there's something about horror that's hard to look away from.

A Spaniard, maybe forty years of age, was lying naked on a browned kitchen table. Four of Morris's men were holding him down, and he was squirming and fighting and begging. Morris had raised a fire in the grate and was slowly rotating a metal rod over blue-hot flames. He pulled it out, the tip glowing bright orange, and he turned and stepped up to the man and pressed it hard against his naked thigh. His screams were so high they weren't screams at all, just rushing air, the room filling with stench. Morris took away the rod and the poor bastard was shaking and sweating and all he could do was feverishly insist in bad English there was no swag, it went out on ships when the bulls were released, *pleeze pleeze pleeze I beg you no again.* Course, there was more screaming and more of that sickly burning smell, his back arched, his eyes bulging, the tendons in his neck strained tight.

I backed out on hollow legs. Morgan had gone off, maybe to one of the other houses; I was relieved, for I didn't want him to see what I was about to do. Face burning, I slunk off to the campsite. Once I reached it, I kept going, following the path back into the forest, feeling weak of will and courage and smarts and what all else made me a

Brethren. Still I kept going, focusing on my feet moving beneath me. Soon I was far enough away I could no longer hear the screams of men and, yes, women. There was only birdsong and rustling wind and the churr of winged insects. After a bit I found the dried-up creek bed and I followed it along, lost in bleak thought, until I reached a clearing and heard a rustle and looked up. A Spanish soldier was sitting on his helmet, staring into woods, eyes filled with the things I'd just run from.

He leapt to his feet and yelled something in Spanish and I knew he was a deserter just like me. There our sameness ended. He was tall and strong-jawed and clean-shaven and all of eighteen. With just a few years on him, I was homely and pockmarked and grown old.

His every movement slowed. Everything turned gradual, like it was muddled in jelly. He reached for his rubbish old matchlock. It took an eternity for him to aim. Fear inched across his young face when his taper went out and the thing refused to fire and then there was nothing to do but die. His arms hung at his sides. Turtle-paced, I levelled my flintlock and aimed at his chest, the boy giving me a look saying *just do it, just get it over with*.

I tried to squeeze the trigger and nothing happened, my finger not behaving. The barrel wavered and my hand shook and the Spaniard watched it all, not understanding. That's when a voice came from somewhere. It was deep and bellowing, and though it sounded a bit like my own, it was also a world apart. I looked around, trying to figure where it was coming from, thinking I'd gone off my nut.

Let 'im go, it said.

What?

Let 'im go, it said again, and this time a relief did come over me.

I waved the tip of my gun. The Spaniard hesitated, thinking I was a coward and I'd shoot him in the back once he moved. His hands inched into the air. "Piss off!" I yelled, wagging the barrel again. Again he wouldn't move. "PISS OFF!" I hollered. "BUGGER OFF!!"

This he understood, and I listened to his feet scurry and crunch against the jungle floor. I was shaking, not because I was alone and who knew how many other Spanish deserters were running around the jungle, pistols at the ready. Oh no. I was shaking because the *one* thing I was sure about in life — that we're born alone and die alone and there's nothing to guide us ever — had gone away, leaving something more complicated in its place.

I WALKED THE two miles or so to where we'd slaughtered all that beeve. The forest was hot and buggy and I swore if I ever saw another mosquito it'd be too soon. My plan was to rest and eat charred meat. Yet I wasn't hungry and all those butchered animals lying about made me think of all the dead horses and bulls and men I'd just left behind. I packed some up and kept going; I'd decided I was going to make it to the Chagres and follow it all the way back to the sea, where I'd report on what'd happened. I sweated and mumbled like a madman, for every time I closed my eyes I was hearing the voice that'd stopped me from killing that Spanish kid.

I reached the point where the path filled with water and became a river again. I gave a shudder, for the boats were gone and was no way out but to swim. Then I realized the water had risen and I wasn't where I thought I was. After sloshing another mile or so downriver, I found the canoes where we'd tied them off. I loosened one and climbed in.

With the water up and flowing to sea, it was short work going back, a six-hour paddle instead of wandering famished for days. I never worried about getting lost, for I kept passing the same burnt-out villages we'd passed on the way in. At one, I spotted a few vine-skirted Indians, poking through the coal-black remains, hunting for pots or bowls or anything that might've survived the burning. Seeing me in English clothes, they just stared, not knowing whether to kill me or flee from me, so instead they did nothing.

It was dark by the time I reached the mouth of the Chagres. The fleet would've been moored well out and I had a decision to make. I could've signalled them with fire, though I had no matches and had never mastered the trick of making a spark with a block of wood and a sharpened spool. Plus there was no telling who or what was out there. So in the end I decided I'd let my presence be unknown, leastways until morning, when I could see what I was dealing with.

So I camped for the night. It was a ghoulish feeling, being out there all by myself, wondering what Morgan would do when he caught up with me. My fear didn't last long, though. I was exhausted and, minutes after curling up in the sand, sleep came over me, and I awoke feeling like the night had passed in a blink. I chewed some boucan and looked for the fleet. The sun had to rise fully before I spotted them, looking like shadows, well out on the horizon. I jumped and whooped and hollered. After a while I was spotted, a trio of strong-backed men rowed out to meet me.

"Where the fuck're the others?" one asked.

"They're comin'."

"How was it?"

"We cocked it. The swag slipped out to sea while they torched the place."

"*Who* torched it?"

"They did."

"Wha'? Their own town?"

"Their own town."

"And there's no swag?"

"They're all back there looking for scraps, but I'm telling you it's bugger all."

I climbed in and was rowed back to the *Uxbridge*. Word went round and everyone turned gloomy and treated me like I was the cause of it. A day later, the rest of the Brethren returned to the shore empty-handed. We set sail immediately, everyone hacking and coughing and choking up sputum.

During the journey home, Morgan didn't speak to me. I didn't take this personal, for he kept holed up in his cabin, coming out only to bark the odd order. We stopped at Île de Vache, our usual place for counting swag, though this time there was none to be counted. We stayed there for two days, licking our wounds and getting our body weight to where it should've been. Then we made the short sail to Port Royal. It was an easy jaunt weather-wise, though we all felt stupid and blue. As we came upon the city, the island constabulary was on the docks, truncheons in hand, though what they were doing there was anybody's guess. The *Uxbridge* was the first to drop sail. Morgan climbed in a rowboat with a few privateers and was ushered to shore. I was watching from on deck and this was what I saw:

Morgan's men docking.

Morgan striding up the pier.

Police grabbing Morgan and slapping him in manacles, Morgan bellowing, "How dare you? What's the meaning of this?! Damn you, let me be!" at the top of his smoke-ravaged lungs.

TWENTY-TWO

As MORGAN WAS taken off the jetty, his men watched from the bay, all of us wondering why the Hero of the New World and the Bludgeoner of the Spanish would suddenly be a wanted man. It was a thing made no sense, so most of us just stood there blinking. After a stunned silence a hubbub arose, every bastard giving his two cents, some saying Morgan must've had it off with the wrong man's wife or maybe he owed the wrong man money or maybe he'd cheated the wrong man in a business deal. Though these were typical ways of destroying yourself, none seemed to fit with the man I knew.

It was an agony waiting for a rowboat, so some of the men who could swim threw themselves in warm blue water. No such luck for me, so it was another hour before I finally set foot on Port Royal proper. While there were a few desperate vendors about, it was nothing like the buying and selling frenzy after our first two missions; I suppose it had to do with each and every man stepping off Morgan's ships having an air of defeat about them. It was on our faces, in the way we moved, in the slump of our shoulders. I slunk through the streets, and as I did I pined for clamour and risen voices and what all else.

At Rodge's, I called my landlord's name, thinking if anyone would know what'd happened, it'd be him. He came from upstairs. "Jesus Christ," he piped. "Keep your voice down! You're not the only lodger here!"

"They've taken Morgan off, Rodge."

"I see," he said, like it was obvious it was going to happen. Without answering, he invited me into the breakfast room, where we sat. "Cup of tea?" he asked, and I yelped, "Forget the sodding tea. What's goin' on, then?"

He leaned in like he was about to confess. "First off," he said, "tell me what happened in Panama."

"Disaster. Complete disaster. The swag got out and they torched the place."

"Torched it?"

"As in burnt it to the ground."

"Well, it all makes sense, then, though I tell you I wouldn't want to be Morgan."

"Start making sense, Rodge."

He stood and walked toward one corner where there was a pile of inky broadsheets. He rifled through them, finally saying, "Right . . . 'ere it is." Then he came over and dropped it on the table. "I read this about a week after you was gone."

"What's it say?"

"We been talking to the Spanish, Benny."

"We? We who?"

"The British, like. Our government. Our bloody King."

"What you saying?"

"Peace, Benny. Seems we're fighting with the Dutch again and we needed some new friends."

Rodge was right. It was all making sense, but in a dark and twisted way. The city of Panama was gone from the world and no one but us would believe they'd done it to themselves. If King Charles the Second was really making nice with Spain, someone would have to take the fall. "So they're pegging it on Morgan."

"On Bottlesworth as well. They took him away too. The job of governor's available if you're interested."

"It isn't fair."

"It's the way it is."

I could feel myself quicken, like they'd done it to me. "It isn't *fair*."

"Look who believes in fair all of a sudden."

"Bloody hell."

"There was really no swag?"

"Not a penny."

"Everyone suffers when that happens, yeah?"

"Morgan'll hang for this," I said as my anger turned to dull sadness. Despite what he might or might not've done in Panama, he was still the man who had me to his home, gave me the finest in cigars and wine and other sustenances, and told me I had a talent that would make other men sick with envy.

Rodge fetched two glasses and gave us both a pour. We toasted Henry Morgan and drank a bit more and mostly I sat there feeling like I'd lost someone close. After a bit I went up to my room and had a lie-down. When I got up, there was still daylight, and for a moment I had that panic you get when you don't know where you are or why. I pulled my boots on and made my way back down to the basement to check under the pile of potatoes Rodge called the Bank.

Though it wasn't empty, it was getting there.

I FIGURED THERE was only one way to spend what I had left, so off to the Bear Garden I headed. It was mostly empty, and whatever men were at the few tables all glanced up when they heard my footfalls. David Walsh was at the bar along with Suzie, who was now trained to sit on a low stool and occupy herself by chewing on an old slipper.

"Benny," said Walsh.

I sat a few stools away from the bear. Walsh gave me a rum, which I drank slowly for I was rationing myself.

"So. Benny. You've any plans now that Morgan is no more?"

I shrugged. It couldn't be. Morgan was a man who didn't just go under.

"Seriously, what you going to do?"

"First off, I'm going to see Tessie."

"Well, she'll be glad to see ya."

I drained my rum and left a coin on the table. Walsh nodded and Suzie made a low grunting noise that made her sound like she didn't approve. I went upstairs and was glad to see there was no one before me. I tapped on Tessie's door.

"Who is it?"

"It's Benny Wand."

The door flew open and there she was. "Well, what do ya know?"

"How's the tongue?"

"You want to see?"

"I do."

She stepped up and opened her mouth; the black worm thread was gone, and in its place an off-white scar you'd only notice if you were searching.

"It looks good."

"Can't say it's done much for business. Seems my customers preferred me the old way. I'm glad to see you inn't one of them. Now. What's your poison?"

"Would the usual be too much of a bother?"

"Well," she said with a grin. "I'll try to fit you in."

WE BOTH LAY looking up. She was in no rush and that was nice.

"Benny?"

"Yeah."

"I've a question."

"Let's have it."

"You ever thought of leaving Port Royal?"

"What you mean?"

"Think of it. What's the purpose of Port Royal? To protect Jamaica against the Spanish. But now we're not fighting the Spanish no more, so what's the point of it? Now we're just another wicked city."

"So?"

"So the world will only tolerate wickedness if it has a point."

"What you saying?"

"Oh, I dunno. I'm just talking. I reckon I've had it with this place." She turned to look at me. "You know my own mum put me out on the street when I was twelve? Said was no other way I'd ever make money with my mouth the way it was. Can you believe that bollocks?"

"I can, yeah."

"I could move to St. Jago except there're too many men over there who know me—you wouldn't believe the types come through that door. Family men, burghers, pillars of the community. Oh no, they'd find a way to make my life difficult, and if they didn't, their wives sure would. Don't know if you heard, but the British settled some island called Eleuthera, and I figure I could go there. I just don't see much future in Port Royal, Benny. It'll turn into a place unwelcoming to the likes of us. Either that, or one of them tremblers will hit hard and knock the whole town into the ocean. Oh no, it's better I be off, and find a life somewhere else. There's only one problem..."

"Which is?"

"Same problem as always. A new start takes money, and with the Panama failing and Morgan put away, I don't see how I'm going to earn it."

Every time I heard the name Morgan, my throat clamped, like he was a loss to get over. No doubt he was chained shivering to a stone wall, eating bowls of watery gruel, kicking away rats. Or he'd been neck-strung by now and was dead in the ground for treason, the news still fighting its way across the ocean.

"But what about you, Benny? What you going to do?"

"Seems everyone's asking me that today."

"Well, what's the answer?"

"Only one thing *to* do," I told her, and the following afternoon I found myself a used board with its men in a trinket shop. That evening I went out, the scratched-up board beneath one arm. It was a poor feeling—one moment I was one of Morgan's inner circle, a needed man on the rise, and the next I was a boardsman again, stumbling from one grog shop to the next.

At least there was one good thing about all the money settling across the bay in St. Jago: the punters had no trouble crossing the causeway to Port Royal for a bit of lowly fun. Since they all fancied themselves gentlemen, they all reckoned they were good at chess, which they'd played around roaring fires back in London, drinking claret and smoking cigars. My first mark was a dumpy blighter, all good manners and nice clothes and the scent of smoked cheese. He opened. I'd seen six-year-olds play better. I dropped two or three games, no easy feat seeing how shite he was—pretending I'd had a little too much rumbullion was part of the show. After my fourth razor-slim loss I acted frustrated, which he saw; he suggested we make things a tad more interesting. I won the next game so narrowly he asked for double or nothing, and so I won by a shave once more. He was on the verge of asking for another game when he looked up at me. His face turned red, and the blubber beneath his chin wobbled.

"I see," he said.

"Wha'? I got lucky, squire..."

I treated three others just like him, though I threw to some bristly fucker with a moustache so big it looked like an opened umbrella. He left boasting at the top of his bleaty lungs, never imagining I'd lost on purpose so word would get round I was beatable.

That night I could've done better and I could've done worse, but at least I left with a few cob in my pocket.

TWENTY-THREE

MONTHS PASSED. THE New Year came and went. I was doing neither well nor poorly, though it all felt like I was doing nothing but let time slip through my fingers. Port Royal wasn't itself and neither was I — the swag we'd taken in Villahermosa and Portobello had showed me I'd never make any real money playing the board, that I was as much a sucker as those I was robbing. You could even say I was *worse*, for I was doing it to myself. Yet I was without a plan, buying a tobacco shop as likely as my flying to the moon. It was a hard way to be, especially when you're bred to be a schemer. Mostly, I was drinking and fretting, for the two go together like steak and kidney.

One night I was having a break at a place called the Bat and Belfry, nursing a bitter, when Taylor walked in. He sat. He didn't look cheerful, but then again most didn't in those days. "Stand you a drink," I offered.

"Sure, yeah."

We sat sipping.

"Benny," he said after a bit. "There's a rumour going round."

"There usually is."

"This one's about Morgan." Taylor shifted his pink eyes in every direction. "There're blokes who think there *was* purchase to be had in Panama. There're blokes who think it wasn't all burnt to cinders, who think there's a nice package waiting for Morgan if and when he returns. There's more'n just a few, Benny."

"Well, that's bollocks and you know it. You saw what they done to that city. Left it in bloody cinders! Plus it's my guess Morgan is hung by now, so it really doesn't matter."

He gave me a look. "If you say so, Benny."

"Think, Taylor. We was near 'im twenty-four hours of the day. So was Morris and Jackman and Freeman and every other bastard. Pretty hard to imagine Morgan buggering off with a chest filled with loot."

"There's an awful lot of talk for something that can't be."

"There's also a lot of stupid people out there."

We sat in silence for a few moments, both of us wondering where the ease we once had around each other went to.

"Can I ask you something, Taylor?"

"You can."

"Your swag must be running low, yeah?"

"All but spent."

"What'll you do when it's totally gone?"

He answered in a low voice. "There're others now. Others who don't care about Letters of Marque and what the British government says you can or can't do. Real pirates, like. Maybe I'll join up with one of them. You?"

"It's this till I think of something better," I said with a

nod to the board. "I've had it with privateerin' or piracy or whatever it's to be called now. I'm not cut out for it, if you want to know the truth."

Taylor drank up. "I'm not sure I am either. I've bad dreams, cities burning and what all else. Still, what other choice do I have? I'll be seein' you, Benny Wand."

A LITTLE WHILE later, a buttery whale sauntered up and asked was it true I was the man to beat. I told him I was *a* man to beat, and if that's what he was looking for I'd happily oblige. He beached himself. He wasn't even half bad, though he had high-and-mighty opinions about Port Royal — "It's time we did away with all these cutthroats and bully-ruffins and made this a proper place to live, wouldn't you say so, sir?" Naturally, comments like his brought out a cunning in me — "Oh yes, oh yes, I agree totally, it's nice havin' a game with a man of similar beliefs it is." Strung him along nicely I did, giving him a win here, a draw there, narrowly taking a few myself so as not to overdo it, convincing him any difference in our skill level was so trifling as to not really be there.

We were at it for two hours and that's when I told him others were waiting so one more game and if you wanted to make it interesting this was the time. Even though a quick turn of the head would've revealed no one was waiting, he agreed — over the years I've learned if a fish is in the boat, it's because it wants to be.

"Shall we say... one hundred pounds?"

I faked being fearful. "A hundred? Hell's bells, mister, I dunno... I lose and it's the poorhouse for the likes of me."

"But you said you wanted to make it interesting, man!"

I walked home whistling. It was three o'clock in the morning, my usual knock-off time. The moonlight speckled off the coral in the sand. It was quiet and peaceful out, strange for High Street, but there it was: Port Royal was a changed place, rich burghers thriving on plantation money while the privateers who'd built the place wondered how they were going to have their next meal. Still, I was in an all-right mood, a rare occurrence of late, so I walked slowly, enjoying the cool air. I reached the Lodges and walked up to my floor, only to find a rummy old sod lurking in the hall. He had a nose the size of a squash, and the flesh beneath his eyes was sunken and grey. He tilted his head toward me and asked: "You're the bloke down the hall?"

"I is."

"The one plays the board, yeah?"

"I dabble."

"Tell me..." His voice was croaky and old, and his hands quivered. "You play backgammon?"

"I know the rules."

The old codger grinned. "Fancy a game then?"

My first reaction was to say *what...now?* but something in the trials etched into his face stopped me. "If it's a quick one."

His name was Gerald. I followed him into a room filthy with dust and food-crusted plates. As with all the rooms in Rodge's Lodges, there was a little table over by the window. We played game after game, Gerald offering me mugs of warm ale and, when we got peckish, ends of thick bread with broken-off hunks of a sharp cheddar he kept wrapped in paper. "I'm 'avin' me a fine time," he kept saying. "A fine time indeed. Thanks for the game, I know it's a comedown for a man like you, so thanks, mate, thanks for spending some time with an old buzzard." There was pickle too, the black and smeary kind, and I admit after a mug or two he'd managed to make me feel right welcome. I even liked playing a game with luck to it instead of nothing but skill. A nice change of pace it was.

"Lookin' at the likes of you makes me think of my first-born," Gerald said while shuffling the deck. "He had the same beard over ground-up skin. Sorry if I've offended."

I grinned. "You haven't. I knows what I look like."

"Went off to sea, my boy did. They all did back then. Never heard from 'im again. Either the ship went down or he's living the good life in the South Seas. Drinking coconut milk on an island somewhere. Wouldn't that be something? Course, he'd 'ave no way of findin' me or me findin' him. Doesn't stop me from wondering, though. That was over thirty years ago. He was my first-born, so you wonder. Looked just like you! What I'd give to just see what he looked like now, assuming he's still alive and kicking, oh yes, I tell you what I wouldn't give to see my boy again."

Gerald had stopped shuffling and was staring off into middle space, his saggy jowls trembling. Just as quickly he snapped out of it and said, "But best not to dwell on the past. Can drive a man mad, can't it?"

"It'll do that, yeah."

We had another game. I asked him more than once if he was feeling tired and he kept telling me no, he was an old man and prone to being awake at odd hours and asleep at even odder ones. After a time the darkness outside his little window began to lighten and turn lavender, and I could hear the muffled sounds of Port Royal coming alive: hens squawking and carts rambling and charwomen yelling at one another in rough cockney.

"Looks like we've been at it all night," I said.

"Looks like we 'ave."

"I'd like to thank you for a grand time," and the thing was I meant it, even though it was just backgammon and not a single coin had changed hands. "Gerald," I told him. "I'm ever around, and you want to play backgammon, you just come and knock, though next time I'll bring the cheese and pickle. We've a deal or what?"

"Oh, we do, Benny Wand. We do indeed!"

It was about eight o'clock in the morning. My head felt thick and the light bothered my eyes, but for some reason I didn't feel like sleeping. I went back out and found an open tavern and ordered a dram of breakfast whisky. Just then a boy entered the tavern. A real ragamuffin he was, his clothes ill-fitting and his face streaked with dirt. If he'd had a chess-board beneath his arm instead of morning papers, he'd have been a walking memory of me.

I waved him over. "Up and at it early, isn't you, Sonny Jim?"

"The early bird, squire."

"Well, don't keep me in suspense. How much for the day's news?"

"Tuppence, sir."

I handed him the money and when he went to give me the paper I stopped him. "I've been up all night carousing, like, and my eyes are tired, so give me the gist of it."

"What you mean 'give'?"

"Just tell me."

"Why . . . it's Henry Morgan, sir."

My heart stopped. So that was it, then. The man and his myth, no more. I felt a dull welling pity, one I doubt I'd feel for my own dad were I to hear he'd topped it. For some reason I started thinking about Villahermosa, how when everyone else wanted to go back to the city and spread terror, Morgan walked over to the water's edge like he had all the time in the world to ponder.

"They've done away with 'im, then..."

The boy blinked. Looked at me like I was daft.

"Why no, sir. He's on his way back to Port Royal."

TWENTY-FOUR

I RAN BACK HOME and thrust the paper at Rodge. His eyes flitted over the words, and as they did I never felt so frustrated or embarrassed I couldn't read. Like a bloody idiot I was, just standing there, tapping my feet and fuming, thinking how everyone used to say school was a place for proper children and not thieving little runts like myself.

Finally, Rodge looked up and explained. It seemed one Henry Morgan had been named the new governor of Jamaica. It seemed he'd be arriving shortly after a lengthy "respite" in London Town. It also seemed that, as a brave defender of British holdings in the New World, there was no doubt he'd continue to perform great deeds for the fledgling island of Jamaica.

"That don't make sense," I said.

"Didn't write it, did I?"

I went upstairs. Even though I'd been up all night, I had trouble falling asleep, not from drink but from my own confusion. I drifted off and woke up tired; I had a cheap dinner of kipper and eggs and went back to bed. When I woke the next morning, everything had changed—the town, the people, the scent of the air even (though this last one could've been my imagination). Though no one had yet laid eyes on Morgan—or leastways none I'd talked to—they all believed he was back for one reason and that reason was to go raiding. And if *that* was the case, it'd be a short time before Port Royal was awash with swag once again. Men who were holding on to their last farthings no longer gave a toss, the grog shops filling. The music of fiddles and washboards spilled onto the streets, there being something about a melody makes a man want to order another tankard, if only to have something to wave about in the air.

And the talk! The giddy speculation! Morgan had set his sights on Havana! On Santiago! On Cartagena ! I heard one lout swear Morgan was going to steal a flotilla of galleons and take them all the way to El Dorado and pilfer Spanish gold at its source. The town was beside itself, the streets running with merriment and vomit. Cutthroats and pad men descended on Port Royal like ants on spilled sugar. Morgan was coming back! He *was* back, if not in body then in spirit! Nothing but nothing could stop Port Royal now, not the bloody King, not the Spanish, not the rich wankers filling St. Jago across the bay. Oh no, with Morgan at the helm it'd be the Port Royal of old, home to hellions, Creoles, and the demented.

One night, around three in the morning, I was walking home along High Street. I was tired and the streets were full of drunkards, all making enough noise to damage the ears, so I cut over to Queen Street where it was mostly houses and the crowds were smaller, just a few men lolling home with an arm over the shoulders of whatever lovely they'd found themselves that night.

Someone called, "Oi."

Though the bloke was right behind me, I figured he must be addressing someone else for his voice was loud, as if trying to attract the attention of someone farther away.

"*Oi!*" he said again, this time with a charge in his tone, and I knew he was talking to me. If I wasn't mistaken, he wasn't alone: I could hear another set of lungs, breathing hot air.

I don't even recall being clubbed. All I know is I turned and saw two bullies, both grinning fierce. I woke up a few minutes later looking up at two of everything, an immense welt on the back of my head. Naturally, my pockets were relieved of that night's board money, though thank God it'd been an average night and not a good one. My plan was I'd get up and find some huge bastards I knew, killers from my Morgan days, and hire them to put this right. The first problem was I couldn't remember what my attackers looked like. The second was any huge bastards I might hire could very well be the ones that'd done it.

I sat up slowly and held my throbbing head and worked my way to my feet. There were others about and none of them thought to help me out, the exception being a beggar with one arm who pointed along the lane and said, "They went thataways." He then held that same hand out for a tip; I told him to bugger off, I'd had every pence to my name taken. "Ah, right," he said. "Sorry."

I lumbered home and went to sleep. I'd heard tales of hard men who'd taken raps to the head and then died in the middle of the night, so I was pleased to see morning, even if there was still an agony in the back of my head and my vision was still a little blurry. I groaned and touched my noggin and decided to stay in bed that day; with my vision bollocks, I felt sick to my stomach, too. I was in bed all that day and the next and the one after that. Thank God Rodge was around to bring me soup and tell me not to worry, if anyone had a hard skull it was me.

The following night, I ran into Taylor at the Bear Garden, which was now officially just the Garden seeing as Suzie had eaten a bad plate of kippers and passed on. My guess is I was looking pale and unsteady and a little thin.

"Jesus," Taylor said. "What happened?"

"You need any work?"

"What's this about?"

"Be here at three in the morning."

"Here?"

"Here."

"What for?"

"Just do it. It's business, like."

Six hours later, Taylor appeared just as he was supposed to. I took him to a corner of the tavern and asked if he'd walk home with me. "With a big bugger like you, the cutpurses'll think twice, yeah? I'll make it worth your while." Ten minutes later we were back at Rodge's and I was peeling a few quid off my earnings to give him. "Wasn't too hard, wha'?"

"Can't say it was."

"It'll be like that from now on. Each night we'll rendezvous at three at the Garden. You'll be an escort, like."

"All right."

We stood looking at one another, like there was something unspoken between us.

"By the way," he finally said. "You seen him yet?"

"Morgan, you mean?"

"Got off a sloop loaded with ale casks and cotton barrels earlier today. No fuss. No fanfare."

"This another rumour?"

"I was *there*, Benny. Trying to get work. Saw him with my own two eyes."

"You sound serious."

"That's 'cause I am."

"How'd he look?"

Taylor paused. "To tell the truth," he said, "he's looked better."

A FEW DAYS passed. Instead of staying cooped up in his mansion, Morgan was supposedly in town every night, doing the rounds, for what reason I didn't know, but there it was. The man was on the prowl or leastways that's what everyone kept telling me. The strange thing was I kept missing him. One night I wandered into the Cat and Fiddle, board under my arm, and the barkeep told me I should've been by the night before: "Henry Morgan himself was 'ere! Buying drinks, holding court, keeping merry. Oh, you missed a high time, you did. You missed a high time indeed!" Later that night, when I saw Taylor, he told me he'd seen Morgan at the Crown and Anchor, so full of Kill Devil he could scarcely stand: "I never knew he was such a character, like."

The next afternoon, I bought a bunch of plantain at the market, the warty old vendor saying Henry Morgan himself had been shopping there the previous afternoon. "Not only that, he gave me a tenner — a whole tenner! — for a melon what was far from perfect. 'Keep the change,' he said. Just like that. 'It's for you, madame...' Why, I never..."

This went on for days, my missing Morgan by a day or an hour and in some cases ten minutes. Late one night, feeling peckish, I popped in to one of my favourite eateries, just a little place where a man could get himself a plate of hot food and a glass of stout. As a bonus it was off High Street, so the prices were lower and you could hear yourself think. I ordered bangers and brown gravy from the big-hipped matron.

"By the way," she said. "You wouldn't believe who was just here."

"Not bloody Morgan."

"'Ow'd you know?!" she crowed. "Look... there's his dirty plate and mug right there. He left not two minutes ago."

I hopped up and ran into the street and there was no sign of him. I went back to my seat and waved over the matron. "Look here," I said. "You sure it was him?"

"It was! Look what he give me..." She reached into the trough of her skirt and pulled out a misshapen piece of eight. "He said it was a bit of genuine Portobello swag. Said I should keep it, what with it being a good luck charm an' all. Ha! If this is worth 'alf of what I think it's worth, I'm spending it before prices go back up!"

I ate up and decided I'd finish at the Garden. So far it'd been a slow night and I wasn't sure I was going to need Taylor's services. That was the problem with our arrangement: on nights I did well, he was worth the expense, but on nights I didn't, it was money flying out my pocket. I arrived in a mood bothered by heavy thoughts, and went over to say hello to David Walsh, who was polishing glasses at the bar. The Garden had come up a bit since Suzie's demise. Walsh looked dapper, wearing fine cloth breeches and a clean linen shirt. Instead of an old plank stretched across puncheons, the owner, an old woman named Agnes, had invested in a dark mahogany bar that would've looked at home in a real English porter house. Suzie's old home, the bear pit, was now a stage used for dance spectacles.

Walsh looked up and told me someone had been in there asking for me. I nodded; probably some punter wanting a go.

"It happens."

"It was Henry Morgan. Said it was important."

I stayed put, again to no avail, and went home feeling sour. The next afternoon I was trying my luck at a place called the Black Dog, which was lively and dark and invented for mischief. I planted myself in a corner, ale glass in hand, board on view, eyeing every chancer who happened along. After a while I grew bored, and I started to think I'd try someplace else or maybe give it a rest till after dinner. Just as I was about to rise, the Dog's heavy wood door opened with a loud groan. Sunlight cleaved the place like a hatchet. I turned and had a look.

I grinned. Couldn't help it.

It was him.

I'D EXPECTED MORGAN to look half starved, what with him being in the Tower and all, but instead the opposite was true. He'd somehow gained twenty pounds or so; the flesh padding his jaw wobbled a tad as he came my way. He was dressed like aristocracy, in a wide-rimmed hat, satin doublet, high laced collar, and stockings. The only differ-ence between him and the posh classes was a wig—he wasn't wearing one—and the general state of his clothes, which were wrinkled and worn thin in spots. He was also wearing a patch over his right eye, not unlike so many of the privateers he'd once commanded.

He reached the table. I took his outstretched hand, and he said, "So *there* you are! I was beginning to think our paths would never cross again. Where the devil have you been hiding?"

"I was about to ask you the same."

He sat in a rickety wooden chair. Once landed, he rotated his shoulders and gestured with a forefinger. The waiter responded right off.

"Two whiskies," said Morgan. "And some dinner, if you would. Whatever you have will be fine." He looked at me and grinned. "What do you think of the outfit? It comes with the territory, I'm afraid."

"You're the new governor, I hear."

"In the flesh."

So many questions were running through my head, I couldn't land on a particular one to ask him. After a bit, my being so tongue-tied was like a question in itself.

"Go ahead," he said. "Ask me what happened. Everyone else has since I've been back. You might as well hear it from the man himself."

"All right. What happened?"

"I was in the Tower for two weeks. Another two would have finished me off." He tapped the side of his noggin. "It's funny what putting a man in chains can do. The thoughts it'll put in his head. But then. Well. The public was against them jailing *me*, the great vanquisher of the Spanish. The great defender of British honour in the New World. I tell you, Wand. Things are *not* going well back home. The Dutch and all that business. And don't get me started on the French—they seem to be up to their old tricks as well—and as far as this détente with the Spanish? We'll see, is all I can say. Oh no, it seems I was the only hero they had over there. A symbol, in a place gone to pot. They *had* to let me out..."

He dropped a palm against the table just as the barkeep deposited two whiskies. Morgan downed his and ordered two more.

"Sounds like you was lucky," I said.

"Lucky! You must be joking! Eight *months* I was in London, waiting for my sedition trial. In the meantime, let's just say the upper classes like to have a little spice at their parties. A man who can tell a story. A man who can entertain."

It was hard to picture him dining at the finest restaurants, eating with the posh, giving brash accounts of Villahermosa and Portobello and the burning of Panama. "So you lived it up."

"Singing for my supper, I suppose you could call it. Turning public opinion. Getting them on my side. Growing fat as a sow, I'm afraid." He slapped his belly. "It's a full-time job, believe you me. I couldn't wait to get back to Port Royal. Over there they haven't a clue, Wand. They don't understand what the likes of you and me had to do to keep the money flowing. They've no bloody idea how much hand-dirtying goes on, and I wasn't going to be the one to tell them." He leaned closer. "You should have heard me on trial. It was the only way I could save myself. The way I described it, Portobello was a garden party, Panama a friendly drop-in. They love hearing that, you know. They love hearing that what we're doing is noble and just. They love hearing us Brits never had to stoop so *low*."

"So they let you off."

"Indeed they did. Of course, there was a condition. There always is, you know. Backroom meetings, secret agreements, et cetera et cetera. It's the way of the world, Wand. No such thing as pure justice. Maybe one day I'll tell you about it, but for now I won't bore you. Nevertheless, here I am, your new governor, a little worse for wear but still a going concern."

"Congratulations."

Morgan held up a hand. "Please. Don't. As I say, the job comes with certain unpleasantries. But a man does what a man has to do. *You* should know that, of all people. You learned that lesson in Portobello, with those Spanish priests, didn't you?"

The barkeep placed two plates of roast beeve with potatoes in front of us. Morgan looked up and said, "Bring us some claret, there's a good man." He looked back at me and winked. "Only thing the French are good for, wouldn't you say?"

Morgan ate wolfishly, like he hadn't had a meal in days. Every few bites he'd wash it all down with a swallow of wine so big I could hear the whoosh of liquid down his throat. I was surprised—between the two of us, I'd always thought it was me had a weakness for drink.

I ate quickly to keep up, though not so quickly I couldn't enjoy the taste of the meat, which was cooked well-through and delicious. The potatoes came with sliced onion and I liked that as well. By the time I'd had my supper and a glass of strong wine, some of the old feelings for the man were coming back, Panama or no Panama.

"So," said Morgan, dabbing his mouth. "I see you've got the board. I've been waiting a long time for this. Tell you what—I'll take white this time."

He lit a good cigar and handed me one, which I lit as well. Delicious, it was, like every smoke I'd ever had from the man. We played. For the first twenty or thirty moves I felt the excitement any player feels when the game looks like it might prove to be a good one. Shortly into the mid-game, however, his position faltered, and it wasn't long before you only had to look at the board to see who was going to win and who wasn't.

He sat back. There was a sheen of perspiration in the wrinkle of skin beneath his eyes. "You caught me at the wrong time of day. But I want to play more. I've missed your lessons more than you know, Wand. In the Tower, I used to imagine ways of beating you, and I swear to you one day I will. I've new strategies, locked up in here." He tapped the side of his head. "One day I'll give you a real drubbing, and that's a promise. But not tonight. I've had a dram or two. Perhaps tomorrow? I could send a horse and buggy. I hear you're in the same place. Say around one?"

"Course," I said with a grin "It'd be my honour."

TWENTY-FIVE

THE NEXT DAY, a heavy knocking came to my door. It was just noon, and I figured it was Rodge, wanting to know whether I was supping in or out that night. I opened the door and had a gulp.

It was John Morris.

"Let's go, Wand."

"You're the driver?"

"What of it?"

"I thought you was comin' at one."

"You're *due* at one. Now get moving."

He drove ferociously, taking risks on turns and narrow straights, whipping the horses till they were covered in froth. He didn't speak, though I could feel his bitterness at having to squire about the likes of me. We got there in less than a half-hour. As soon as I climbed down, Morris snapped the reins and was off, the wheels making a *clack clack clack* against the rocky lane. It was a windy day, my hair swirling in the air. I walked toward the house and rapped on the doors.

Morgan himself answered. He was dressed in breeches and a cotton shirt and those big black boots he always wore during his expeditions. I noticed his hands had a slight shake to them.

"Well, look who it is! Benjamin Wand himself. Come, come. I've been waiting all morning. Finally I couldn't stand it and I sent Morris a little early. My apologies! Come in, come in."

We walked along the marble hallway and as we did, I tried not to notice the mess. A tray of filthy dishes, buzzing with flies, was on a mahogany sideboard. A toppled champagne bottle rested on the floor beneath one of Morgan's Biblical paintings. The whole place had a stale odour about it, the kind you get when no one's opened a door for a while.

We made it to the Great Room, where Morgan's ivory chess set was on its usual little table by the window.

"Fancy a sherry?"

"Wouldn't say no."

He filled two small glasses from a decanter. When he handed me mine, I saw it was smudged with thumbprints. We sat at the board. "Please," he said. "Excuse the mess. Elizabeth is at the other plantation. She's taken the staff with her, and when it comes to domestic chores I admit I'm next to useless. It's just me here, all by my lonesome, if you can believe that. It wasn't long ago that would have been unthinkable, eh Wand? What with all the escaped slaves running around? They'd have crawled through a window in the middle of the night and cut my throat. Or some long-lost Spaniard, dying for revenge, would've burst through the door. In some ways I miss those days, when danger was well and truly in the air."

"Er... you've another plantation?"

"You haven't heard? I bought it when I was in London. It's out by Port Antonio. Huge. Sugar. That's about all I know."

"What, you haven't seen it?"

"I *have* been busy, you know. No rest for the wicked, as they say, and that includes the governor of Jamaica. Now play."

Sober, Morgan was every bit the player he was before, and all his thinking in the Tower hadn't hurt him either. Somewhere around the forty-fifth move he sacrificed a knight to open a file on my king. A right bold move it was, and it put me in a scramble; for a couple of moves the game could've gone either way.

"Bugger! One day I *will* beat you, Wand. You'll see. In the meantime, I think I'll have a dram to help with the heartache."

We played three more games, Morgan downing sherry throughout. As the shake went out of his hands, the skill went out of the game. By the fourth, he was in trouble right off. "Clearly it isn't my day. What say we head into town for lunch?"

Without waiting for my answer, he was on his feet, marching through his empty house. He disappeared for a few minutes, and when he returned, he was wearing his nobleman's clothes. "Oh I *know*," he said. "Appearances, and all that."

I followed him outside, squinting away the sunlight.

"Now," said Morgan. "What's that Morris done with himself?

He looked around a little more and then gave me a

grin, saying he'd drive us himself. We climbed in. Morgan smacked the horse's haunch with a crop. We took off, Morgan whooping as he stung the nag again and again. If John Morris had driven fast, then Morgan was on the edge of lunacy, particularly where the path strayed close to the mountain's edge. Even with a drop that'd kill us five times over, he neither slowed nor seemed to notice. All I could do was breathe deep and wonder why he'd take such risks when there was nothing to be gained — it didn't seem like the Morgan I knew.

Meanwhile, he nattered on, and it occurred to me maybe those drinks he'd had with me weren't the first of the day. "Listen, Wand," he yelled over the wind. "Things got a little hot in Panama. Ha, that's funny... I mean, things became a little *charged* in Panama, people desperate, things said that shouldn't have been said, bad decisions all round. I can't say my memory of it's all that clear, so anything I might've said to you and what you might've said to me... well. Let's put it behind us. Let's let bygones be bygones. You know, be gentlemen about it."

"Course, governor."

"Call me Henry, for goodness' sake! My being governor... it's a game you definitely do *not* have to play. You're my chief military strategist, and don't you forget it."

We stopped in front of a place on York Street I didn't know called the Country Glen. With the leather chairs and white linen I felt out of place. Full of landed gentry, it was. I didn't know such a place existed in Port Royal, for it had all the earmarks of a place across the causeway in St. Jago. While we waited for our food, men kept coming over to introduce themselves to Morgan and telling him if he ever needed any help with this matter or that matter, they were at his beck and call. Each time, he'd ask the man to repeat his name before shaking his hand and then turning back toward me.

The food came. Morgan adjusted his eye patch, which had a habit of tilting to one side. Then he tucked into a bloody steak sided with potatoes and greens, pausing only to swallow red wine. Within minutes his meal was gone, his chin stained dark with gravy. He wiped his mouth and stood. "I've got some people to see in town, Wand. Morris will pick you up same time tomorrow, is that all right?"

Before I could answer, he lurched toward the doorway and stepped into daylight. The proprietor came over to collect the dishes and when he stood there, hovering, it made me think Morgan hadn't remembered to pay. I had a bit of a panic, for a meal like the one we'd just had, washed down with a bottle and a half of claret, would cost me a night's winnings and then some. "What's the tally?" I asked, feeling ill.

The owner wore a huge squirrel's tail of a moustache. "None," he said. "We've an agreement, the govnah 'n me."

EACH DAY AROUND one, Morris arrived glowering and took me to Morgan's mansion. We'd have a few games while drinking port or sherry or whisky or a combination of the three. Some days he played well, and some days his mind just wasn't on the board. On such days I got the impression something was troubling him, something far more important than his mid-game. "Bloody hell," he'd say while adjusting his eye patch. "I'm having one of my days, Wand. I'm sorry about this. I don't understand what has come over me..."

The calibre of his play wasn't the only thing that changed from visit to visit. Some days, he'd talk like his tongue was on fire. "Can you believe," he said one afternoon, "that we made peace with the Spanish? Can you believe that? Stupid. *Stupid.* They're Spaniards, for Christ's sake, and not to be trusted. You mark my words. Any day now we'll wake up and those Iberian barbarians will be running through the streets of Port Royal, killing all the men and having their way with the women, all in the name of taking the island back for the King of Spain. And what can I do about it? What can I, the governor of Jamaica no less, *do* about it? Nothing, if you want to know the real truth. My hands are tied. I've no moves, no options, other than wait for it to happen. In fact, you should see what they *want* me to do. Were it up to the King, I'd be inviting the Spanish around for tea parties. It makes no sense, Wand. I tell you, it makes no bloody sense!"

Other days he'd say nothing, minutes and minutes passing before he'd finally move a piece. During such times I could hear birds outside and the rustle of his boots on the floor and that was about it. One afternoon he popped out of just such a funk, his good eye squinting. He took a long swallow of sherry and said, "So what do you think, Wand?"

"Mostly I try not to."

"I mean it. What do you think about what they're saying?"

"What you mean?"

"About Panama, Wand. What else?"

"About you... about you getting away with a bit of swag, you mean?"

"That's the one. Do you believe it?"

"The city burnt to the bloody ground. Nothing left but ash and ruin. We all watched. Was no way there was any treasure *to* steal."

Morgan leaned back in his chair. He lit a cheroot and took a few puffs and watched blue-grey smoke spiral off the end. "Well, you would be wrong, my friend. Do you remember that Spanish woman? The one in the red dress?"

I nodded.

"You remember that huge ruby she wore around her throat? The way the sun gleamed off it?"

"I do."

"Do you remember the way it matched her dress?"

"Course."

"After you left, she and I . . . well. We had a little meeting."

He winked in a way that bothered me. He then reached a hand into his jerkin. Upon pulling it back out, he opened it before me, the skin of his palms cracked and leathery. In the centre was a jewel the size of a baby's fist. The light twinkling off it was a glorious red. "You are looking at the entirety of the Panama purchase," he said, his voice gone hollow. "What was I supposed to do? Smash it into bits so we could share it? I'll never part with it, even though it's worth a fortune, you know." He slipped it back into his breast pocket, where it made the slightest bulge. "I always have it on my person, Wand. Always. It's a reminder of what men will do to one another, given half the chance. It's a totem, nothing more."

"How many know 'bout this?"

"You do and I do. That's all. You're the only one I trust."

Inside, I swelled, for I did believe he was telling the truth.

"Now play," he said. "Do your worst, Wand. Do your bloody worst."

USUALLY, MORGAN CAME back down to Port Royal with me. Sometimes we supped together; other times he complained of stomach pains or a lack of appetite. On such nights he'd be off, saying he had business to attend to. As far as I could tell, his business was bibbing hard in a half-dozen taverns and grog houses each night until Morris drove him back to his mansion. Morgan was gaining a reputation as a man you wanted to know, if only because no one paid for drinks when the governor was about. When it came to his weight and his new-found taste for drink, many believed his time spent in the Tower had done something to him, and it depended on your point of view whether that something was good or was bad.

Nights, I played the board in town: despite Morgan's promise to pay me for all the games I gave him, no money ever exchanged hands, my payment more in the form of free meals and drinks. Still, I had rent to pay, the problem being that word was getting out about me; some were even calling me Magic Wand, despite it being a name I'd left back in London. This hurt my business. Unlike cribbage or backgammon (and there was no shortage of men hustling those games as well) there was no element of chance in chess, and so nothing to make the punters think they might get lucky and beat someone better than they were. I was working harder and harder to make less and less. I stopped using Taylor as a bodyguard, explaining there was no point. Though I'd occasionally land a game with a belly-stuffed landowner, the line "Fancy a go, squire?" no longer worked the way it had before. If they did take me on, they'd wager a pittance, saying, "Oh, I've heard about you, sir. I have most assuredly heard about *you*." Mostly, they were willing to lose a few coins just to see what it was like to be trounced by someone who actually knew and understood the game. Curiosity matches, I called them, and they were barely worth my time.

One time, I faced a skinny pale-skinned blighter with enough money to buy half of Port Royal if he'd a mind to. He was a pretty good player, so I'd suckered him in with a different ploy: I won the first two games but only just, victory so close each time he could smell it. Then I let him win the third game. I made it close and exciting. He was all thrilled by the thought he might be getting a bead on me, and that's when I suggested we up the wager, separate the men from the boys, see what's what, put our money where our mouths were . . . I had a dozen lines and I picked all of the better ones.

He stood, grinning, smug all over. "Not tonight. As it happens, a little bird warned me about you, sir."

He winked and moved off, an hour's labour come to bugger all, yours truly just sitting there thinking *what little bird? what's he on about?*

I STARTED OFFERING two-to-one odds, and three-to-one odds, and four-to-one odds; this meant the games I lost for show cut into the bottom line way more than they should. Or I spotted pieces: a knight, a bishop and two pawns, sometimes a rook or, if my opponent looked particularly dozy, a queen. I played games so low on men the most I could hope for was a draw. As another attraction, I started playing blindfolded. Though this helped at first, soon I was drawing more onlookers than go-ers. It went this way: After sitting alone in front of my board, watching betting types squander money on obvious fleeces like three-card monte and the shell game, I'd curse the stupidity of the average bloke and try my luck at another location. Sometimes this helped and other times it didn't. Throughout, I'd drum my fingers, chin in hand, eyes stinging with woodsmoke. So I'd move on again. Soon, I spent more of my nights rambling than I did playing the board, and in this way I started to resemble a certain Jamaican governor with a drink in his meaty gloved hand.

Now I saw Morgan everywhere, both in taverns and on the street, where more often than not he'd tip his hat at me and keep going, as though I was a friend of a friend's friend and not the bastard who'd been in his Great Room three hours earlier, playing his board and drinking his brandy and still wishing for a lifestyle like his.

Or I'd be sitting in the corner of an alehouse, hoping some pisser might forget who I was and have a go, when Morgan would saunter in, all smiles, sidling up to the bar and offering to buy whoever was there a free draft. Soon there'd be a crowd around him, Morgan entertaining with tales of pillage and adventure, the point of his story always the same: without the privateers to defend Jamaica, the island would be just another Spanish stronghold and the King was a fool to sign the treaty. After "buying" a few drinks and telling a few stories and getting a rouse out of his audience, he'd often take a few steps back and turn broody.

His eyes would narrow and shift from side to side, as if he was in the place only to keep tabs on who was there and who wasn't. This unnerved me, for at such times he looked like an imposter, a gritty stranger dressed to look like Henry Morgan at a masquerade party. Within the hour he would drink up and be gone to the next place, where he'd do likewise. After a bit I began to understand why he described his nighttime roving as "work" — it really did seem that way if you noticed the ceaseless trolling of his eyes.

One afternoon, John Morris delivered me to Morgan's door, though not before warning me I'd be unlikely to get much of a game that day. I found Morgan lolling in his chair, in no shape to stand never mind plot a decent strategy. He'd gained even more weight since his return, and he did not look well: his hands were pink and slightly bloated, as if someone had pumped them with air.

"I should go," I said.

"No!" he blurted. "Sit."

Morgan stared straight through me, and I don't mind saying it made me feel right awkward seeing him this way. But then, as if someone had thrown a switch inside him, his eyes focused and he sat up.

"May I confess something?" he asked.

"Course."

"I am *bored*, Wand. Don't you miss it? The adventure?"

"Sometimes," I lied.

"Of course you do. It's no way to live, dry-docked, put out to pasture, old age your biggest fear, nothing to do but decide what to have for your supper! It's a woman's life. No way for military men like ourselves to live, now, is it? You know what I was thinking the other day? No, course not, how could you? Well, I'll tell you. I was thinking about that time we got lost in Portobello. When I was a lad, my uncles would take me blindfolded out in the woods and then set me free, miles from the forest edge. Their fathers done it to them, and their grandfathers done it to their fathers. It's a military tradition, so you wouldn't panic when you lost your bearings in thick woods. Sometimes it'd take me hours to find my way out. One time I had to stay the night, and climb a tree in the morning to see where I was. But no matter how long I was gone, they wouldn't come looking for me. They said it would defeat the purpose of the exercise. Jesus, it'd scare me, but I'm glad they did it. If I'd panicked every time we got lost on expedition, we wouldn't have accomplished all that we did, am I right, Wand? Jesus, how I miss being put to the test."

He leaned close to me, as if about to confess something. "In fact, you know what I should do? *I* should get the old gang together."

TWENTY-SIX

OVER THE NEXT week or two, I saw Morgan a half-dozen times, off in the corner of a usual haunt, tankard or calabash in hand, gut now in danger of drooping over his waistband, whispering in the ear of some laggard I recognized from the raids. What he whispered was a mystery, until one night in the Three Crowns. I was nursing a dram over my unused board while cursing every cheap bastard in the place, along with all the stresses life can and will heap on a man.

Morgan came in and one glance told me he'd had more than a few. He came over, toppling a chair on the way. He leaned his pink hands on my table. "Wand," he said in a low voice. "It's *on.*"

"What's that, then?"

"There'll be a wagon, waiting just beyond Gallow's Point, near the causeway, at half five on Saturday. Be on it or I'll take it personally. Just don't tell anybody. We wouldn't want any bruised feelings, now, would we?"

Over the next few days it wasn't hard to figure who was

and who wasn't invited to Morgan's little get-together. If I saw one of his men looking cheerful instead of put upon, I knew he was on the invite list. The next time I saw Taylor, a Wednesday it was, he leaned over his pint and asked, "Benny, you goin'?" After playing dumb for a few minutes, I told him I was, and on the Saturday in question the two of us walked down together. When we got to the causeway, there were thirty or forty others, each of whom I knew by either his face or what was wrong with him: that bloke with no fingers on his left hand, that bastard with just one ear, that crusty sod with a dent in his forehead. Mostly we stood around bored, wondering whether Morgan's invitation was or was not a windup. We grew hot and restless, and I heard at least one skunky blighter say was no way the governor of Jamaica would have the likes of *us* to his mansion.

As soon as he said this, we all heard the drum of hooves and the grind of wheels on coarse sand. We looked over and saw John Morris coming toward us on a large open-air wagon pulled by a pair of horses. When he reached the Port Royal end of the causeway, we all backed away so he could turn the thing around. "Let's go, ya scabby bastards," he shouted when he was done, and so we all jumped on. There were whoops and howls, and after a few minutes of bumping along the causeway I started to feel an excitement myself. What with my dosh running low, and my board earning me less and less each night, a good night out was going to be a dose of medicine I sorely needed.

At St. Jago, we turned and began our climb up the mountain. It was a huge wagon with only two horses, so Morris had to whip them again and again to keep us climbing. The group went quiet when we reached the ridge overlooking a rocky cove several hundred feet below, though we all whooped and laughed and whistled once we'd cleared the danger. We arrived to find Morgan standing outside his mansion, waving his thick arms.

"Good evening, gentlemen," he called. "I hope you're all ready for a high time indeed!"

A cheer went up as we leapt over the wagon sides, the exception being a few men with peg legs who had to work their way off slowly. As we filed into the house, Morgan shook all our hands, and when it came to me he added a slap on the shoulder and said, "Happy you could make it, Wand. It'd wouldn't be the same without you."

Someone had cleaned the place up—there were no dirty plates or toppled bottles on the floors. Still, it had none of the woman's touch it'd had before; there was still a smell in the air, of loneliness and unwashed socks, and I had to wonder whether Morgan's wife was really tending to another plantation or whether something had happened between the two of them. I will say this, though: on his dining room table was every food a bored ex-privateer would ever want, from goose to chicken to beeve to lamb to every vegetable you'd ever seen or wished to see, all wafting steam like it'd just come out of some great brick fire-heated oven. Servants with dark skin and white shirts stood in the doorway, and I could only imagine there were more working away in the kitchen.

On the sideboards were butts of rum and whisky, along with casks of lager and ale and stout. In the middle of one surface was a barrel of wine with a spigot; already the guests were lining up for the privilege of having the spray hit full force upon the tonsils. Taylor was gleeful, no other word would describe it, his eyes wide and his grin a wonder.

"Where to start?" he yelled in my ear. "Where to bloody *start*?!"

Before I could answer, he was off, waiting his turn at the barrel spigot, looking like a child queuing for giveaway candy. Morgan was striding up and down the room yelling, "Have anything you want! And by the way, that's wormwood wine not regular wine so boys be careful! Eat up! Eat up!"

He found me standing off by myself. He was winded, and his face was flushed. "I'm glad I could do this for them. They deserve it after the miseries of Panama."

"Well put."

"When I think of the parties I used to have up here. Every stuffed shirt and pompous arse in all of Jamaica. It made my head throb if you must know." He spread his arms out like he was a king looking over his land from a castle window. "Now I'm the governor I can do what I want, at least until they throw me out of the job. These men, Wand. These unwashed *villains*. They're my people, whether I like it or not."

He moved off and I gulped two big glasses of wormwood wine, which was different from other drink: it had a way of making things look shiny and super-real instead of dull and fuzzy. I had a glass or two more, thinking *sod it, you only live once*. After a bit my insides started to feel light and when I waved my hands in front of my eyes I saw a bouquet of fingertips moving through space. "Now eat up, mateys!" Morgan was still bellowing. "It'll all go to waste if you don't!"

We turned on the table like buzzards on a kill. I had my fill, though I asked myself if there was a way I could take some of the meat back to Rodge's, seeing as my diet was turning to porridge and potatoes and suet pudding. A musical group arrived—hornpipe, fiddle, drum, and a lanky fair singer with a loutish mind. With his lads playing along, the singer gave us tavern ditties and sea shanties, though when it came to the popular songs of the day he tampered with the words. "Man Is for the Woman Made" was lowered to "With a Woman a Man Was Laid," and "Alas I Love a Lass" became "I Lost Myself in Her Ass." His renditions caused peals of raw laughter which spurred the musicians to play louder, and soon everyone was linking arms and singing along, and a fair bit of the night was spent this way. Meanwhile I kept slurping wormwood wine, and soon I was having a vacation from being the man called Benny Wand. Englishman, chess player, privateer, brother—one by one these titles floated out of me, and I can tell you it was scary and invigorating, but mostly I was just happy to be a member of Morgan's fold once more.

Around eleven o'clock, the weapons started coming out. It had to happen, as these were men who lived by their pistols and with a belly full of spirits their thoughts turned to their proudest possessions. Soon the singing was replaced by hollered boasts along the lines of *look at this one!* and *I bought this li'l beauty from a dealer in Barbados!* and, from one nasty looker with an egg-sized goitre clinging to his neck, *I took out the eye of a Spaniard with this wee gem!* He was holding up the most beautiful flintlock I'd ever seen, with a carved wooden handle and ivory inlays running up and down the barrel. It was hard to know what to look at, his beautiful-looking gun or that sickening glob attached to the side of him.

Either way, his claim of shooting out a Spaniard's eye was met with belly laughs and mocking howls, one mouthy bastard yelling, "Yeah, but you was aiming for his backside you was!"

Everyone laughed again except for the owner of the story, who suddenly looked put out, and I could see it was rum and pride mixing together to make poison. "I'm telling you I could blow the nose off a parrot from a half mile with this bastard."

Again there was laughter and someone called out, "Tell us another one, you blithering arse bandit."

"It's fuckin' true!" said the man, who was growing red in the face. "I could take the cock off a monkey, the feathers off a crow, the tail off a bloody bull..."

There followed a mad back and forth between the boastful man and the rest of the crowd until Morgan himself stepped in. Everyone quieted. It was something about Morgan's expression.

"Then prove it," he said.

Goitre-neck eyed Morgan. He puffed out his chest. He really was an ugly little goon, and with all that wormwood wine in my blood, his lump was reflecting light like it was the source of a diabolical rainbow. "My name," he hissed, "is Jacob Long, and I'm the best shot in all the Caribbean."

"And *my* name is Henry Morgan, and I believe you are full of gob shite, sir."

The musicians looked on. There was a wiggly in the corner, feasting on a turkey wing. Everything was quiet now.

"Tell you what," said Morgan. "I'll make you a wager." He took an avocado from the sideboard. After taking ten long steps away from the group, he removed his felt and feathered hat and placed the fruit upon the tip of his head. "Imagine this was your Spaniard's eye. If you hit it, I will make it worth your while. If you kill me, you'll swing. Now take your aim."

A look of determination crossed Long's face. It was madness, this, for even if Long *was* the shot he said he was, he'd been into the grog and this was no time to put his talents to the test. Morgan grinned, adding to the dare. Long raised his weapon. After aiming for a second or two, he squeezed the trigger and the flint sparked powder and that lonesome avocado erupted in a shower of pulpy green. There was a burn in the air and I thought Morgan might draw his pistol and fire upon the man for taking such a risk, challenge or no challenge. Instead, he brushed fruity guts off his shoulders, still looking as solemn as I'd ever seen him. Then he leaned back and let out a laugh you could've heard back in Port Royal. He marched up to Long and clapped him on either shoulder and bellowed, "You nervy bastard! I said I would make it worth your while and now I *will!*"

Morgan placed two fingers between his teeth and whistled. Appearing in the doorway of the big room was none other than No-Conscience Nan, the most famous whore in all of Port Royal. She was grinning as she walked up to Long and slipped a hand through his arm. "Let's see what you can do with your other pistol, eh matey?" and the others all roared. Next thing I knew, the room was full of girls brought in from town, Morgan throwing up his arms and yelling, "In fact, I'm going to make it worth everybody's while! Go ahead, gents, it's on me!"

The room was swimming and I felt like I'd stepped into a dream, for the colour of Morgan's jerkin was slipping into the air, and his voice sounded hollow. Stumbling through the room, I spotted someone in the corner and I stopped. The breath was out of me. My knees wobbled. I didn't believe in ghosts, so what I saw couldn't be. Yet he was there, frail as a baby bird, face coated in grey stubble, shuffling toward me, all grinny and old and *him*.

He rested tiny blue-veined hands on my shoulders and, in a tiny voice, said, "'Allo there, Benny."

All around us, men were yelling and howling and acting like maddened animals, but it was like the two of us had stepped into a noiseless bubble.

"Granddad?" I peeped.

"Ay, you're a big boy, inn't ya now? All grown? Tell me — what you done with your life? Something worth telling, I hope. What you done with it, my boy?"

"Granddad," I peeped again, eyes filling. "I can't believe it's you."

"Well, who else would it be?" and I laughed and hiccuped at the same time, making a sound was nothing but longing. Then I held him. Squeezed his tiny body. All bone and sinew it was, his shirt smelling like cheroot smoke and ash. I wouldn't let go. I must have squeezed a little too hard, for he started to wheeze and still I couldn't stop, all I wanted was to keep him where he was, right next to me, where he could never escape again. Spindly hands crept up between us and gave me a little shove, and when I pulled back I died a little, for it was some old geezer with a dustpan, probably hired to keep things in order.

He looked at me, stunned. His lower jaw wobbled. "Right off your face, you is," he said, and I was about to say sorry when a strong hand came down hard on my shoulder from behind. It was like being sucked through a tube, though it was a tube made of time and light and wishing for things.

I turned and there was John Morris. "You're coming with me."

"What? But I—"

"Night's over, scrub boy. It's the wormwood playing tricks, is all. Nothing's real."

He marched me outside and put me in a small buggy driven by a Creole, the driver's skin a gold-tinged black. Then he turned and walked off.

"Morris!" I called out. "Why you doin' this?"

Morris gave me a look. The trees behind him were swaying sentries. "Morgan's orders," he answered.

"But *why*?"

"No idea," he snarled. "Though I do know one thing: you'll thank me come morning."

TWENTY-SEVEN

T HE STREETS WERE dark and empty, and my feet scuffled as I made my way back to Rodge's. I went up the stairs and sat on my bed feeling alone, though I could hear an old man's voice whispering somewhere far off. Like a soft gurgle it was, not getting louder but not going away neither. The floor was a light/dark pattern. I felt like I was coming apart, like I was in two different places at once, like the whole world was a chessboard and I was nothing but a useless last-rank pawn. They call it falling into the chess zone, when everything turns to black and white squares in a man's head, and was no way on earth I was crawling out alone.

Desperate, I crept down the hall and knocked on the door at the end. Gerald opened and took one look at me.

"You all right, my son?"

I suppose I wasn't, for he stepped forward and led me shaking to his chair. "Uh-oh," he said, "looks like you been into the wormwood, oh I know I know, some like it, but it's not for those what're half mad already. It's not for the likes of us, inn't that right? Here, I'll fetch you some tea, inn't no problem on earth a nice cup won't help with, yeah?"

He left his little room. As I sat there with my loosening mind, I heard him tromp through the house, his gait echoing off old walls and floors. I don't know how he did it, maybe he roused Rodge or maybe he just invaded the kitchen himself, but he came back with two steaming mugs, one of which he set down before me.

I took a sip.

"Now," said Gerald. "You fancy a game of backgammon?"

"Don't know if I'll be much good."

"Oh, you will. Smart young feller like you. Go on, go on, roll the dice and let's see what becomes of it..."

My first move was double sixes. "Whoo-hoo," said Gerald. "There you go. See, you are a lucky man. Tonight's your night, a blind man could see that."

We played game after game until the walls stopped breathing and I was in my right mind again. I yawned, an ache coming over me.

"Had enough?"

"Yeah," I said, and after thanking him I went back to my room. Whether I slept or not that night I can't say, except that time must've gone by somehow and then it was light out and I was on my side, lying in the same clothes I'd worn the night before, so I reckoned I did have a wink or two though it sure didn't feel like it. My head throbbed and my hands felt shaky like they had no strength. Worse was the feeling I'd lost my mind the night before and hadn't quite got it back; I was still thinking in an odd way, some things making no sense whereas other things were adding up clearer than ever.

I stood and felt shaky. Down the street, I went into a little store selling provisions. I was about to buy a cheroot and a roll when I overheard two middle-aged biddies having a conversation. "You 'eard about last night?" said the one.

"What about it?" said the other.

"Why Gracie, it's all over town!"

"What is?"

"*Well*. It seems Henry Morgan invited his old lot up to his mansion for a party. When it was late and they was all sleeping and too full of grog to muster a fight, the Port Royal police came and arrested every single one of 'em."

"Really?"

"That's what I heard, Gracie. That's what I heard..."

I stood for a moment, heart pounding. So that's what Morgan was saving me from when he had Morris take me out. For a moment I even felt grateful, though I had to wonder why he'd invited me in the first place.

That's when I thought about who else'd been at the party. I dropped my bread, the store owner yelling, "Oi! What you doin'?" as I took off running. After charging along Queen Street, I made a quick right at the market, where I nearly overturned a cart of beeve hearts sitting in the sun, so red and new and dripping they were practically still beating. Then I rushed along High Street, where a crone swung a cane at me and yelled, "Slow down! Ol' people are about, you speedy prick!"

I got to the jail breathing hard. It was manned by an immense bald man with sledgehammers for fists and dark pouches beneath his eyes. He lowered his jowly face at me. He was unshaven and had a smoky reek about him.

"Some arrests," I managed. "Last night... a load of 'em... they here?"

"Bugger off." His voice was the grinding of ox-cart wheels.

"I gotta see one of the prisoners. It's life or death, like."

He did nothing; it was like I'd fucked off already. I reached into my pocket and grabbed a few gold coins, which he took without thanking me or showing any surprise. Then he unlocked the wrought iron gates and took me into a dingy hallway. Our footsteps echoed, the damp seeping into my flesh and making me feel clammy. We reached another heavy wooden door. It opened upon stone steps heading downward. We both stared into pitch-black while the poor bastards in the hold started yelling and pleading they were innocent and how they needed to be let out. There was a kerosene lamp hanging at the top of these stairs and the jailer lit it, the steps now a bronze glow. We started to march down and I had memories of my nights spent in lock-up before they shipped me off to the New World. A fear grew in me. I was a privateer myself, or leastways had been, and who was to say the ghoul with the giant hands wasn't going to throw me in the pen as well, and then brag to his pub mates about how easy he'd snatched another and even got paid by the dumb bastard he'd done it to.

We reached bottom and moved along to a huge pair of cages, one on either side of a pathway, filled with ex-Brethren I recognized from last night. The jailer looked at me like I better make this quick, and as I walked up and down the aisle, hands reached toward me, hands accompanied by panicked voices saying *help me fer fuck's sake help me I'll give you anything you want just help me* . . . I ignored these cries and pleas and begging, and that's when I spotted a shock of red hair in the back of one of the pens.

"Taylor!"

He yelled something I couldn't hear over the clamour. Then he fought his way to the front of the cage, which took a few minutes seeing as the men were packed in tight as herrings in a jar. He pushed his face into a space between bars. He'd been clobbered, one eye blackened and one cheek bruised, his nose looking all swollen and crusted. Still, the bugger smiled. "By God, Benny, you're a sight for sore eyes you is."

"I'm gettin' you out."

"That'd be right appreciated."

"I'll go and see Morgan now and tell 'im if he ever wants to have a game of chess again, you'd better see daylight by the end of the day."

"Thank fuck, Benny. There's talk the hangmen might be busy come next morning."

I was going to ask Taylor if there was anything I could bring him, but I didn't have a chance: the jailer rose to his bread-loaf feet and grunted my time was up. I flashed Taylor a look saying everything would be okay or at least close to it. Then I marched back up the thirty or forty steps to the earth's crust and burst squinting into bright bright sun.

AT THE END of the causeway were cart men for hire. I ran up to one and said I needed to go to the plantation belonging to Henry Morgan. Beyond us came the splash splash splash of leaping speckled fish.

"Wha'? The gov'nah?" He was old and he shook.

"Yeah."

"Well... it'll be a full quid, tha'."

We set out on a tottering old donkey cart, moving at little more than the pace of a grown man walking. "I'll give
you another quid," I told him, "if you use the whip."

"You're an impatient bugger, you are," he said before
snapping his donkey's ear. This sped the animal for a brief
period only, and when we next slowed I reminded him I
was paying extra and he snapped the doddering old animal
again. Still, it took us an hour to reach where we were going,
my stomach filled with bile and dread instead of the excitement I used to have when visiting Morgan. I paid the man
and told him to wait and then I rushed into Morgan's home,
there being no need to knock for those towering front doors
were wide open, geckos and forest mice and who knew what
manner of jungle cat prowling in and out. A parrot was flying around squawking in the entrance room.

"Henry Morgan!" I yelled, and when I heard nothing,
I bellowed, "HENRY MORGAN!" as loud as I was able.

Again I heard the squawking parrot and cicada hum and
that was it. Figuring he was still asleep, I ran up the marble
staircase to the second floor and threw open a few doors;
each empty bedroom was littered with spent bottles and
spilled food and grunting rat-faced wigglies. I spotted a door
at the very end of the hallway and I guessed it to be his, for
the room inside would have a view of Port Royal and the
ocean beyond it. I rapped my knuckles against the door and
when there was no answer I pushed it open.

Bloody hell.

Morgan was lying bloated and asleep. There was a naked
native girl on either side of him, and when I say "girl" I'm not
using the word fancifully, for they both had teacup breasts
and hips better suited to a boy. They screamed when they

saw me and pulled sheets over themselves. "Out!" I ordered, though they wouldn't move for fear of me. I rolled my eyes and walked toward the window. This gave them room to race out, little feet skittering along the floor.

Morgan was still lying naked and as white as a beached whale. I might have even thought him dead were he not making a noise somewhere between a snore and choked breathing. There was a half-smoked cheroot on the mattress and a brown singe around it. A flagon rested on the table next to his bed and out of anger I squirted whatever amber-coloured liquor was in it onto his belly.

Morgan came awake sputtering. He opened the eye not covered by a patch. "Jesus, Wand. You gave me a start!"

"You know why I'm here."

"Give us a minute."

I went back downstairs, and as Morgan dressed, I took in the carnage of the night before. Turkey carcasses and hacked-apart roasts littered the floor, buzzing black clouds above them. Broken glass and shattered china were everywhere. Furniture was overturned and curtains torn and all that fine French plasterwork was now jiggered with pistol fire.

Morgan appeared in the doorway, dressed in that ridiculous gentleman's outfit of his, though his jerkin was messed and his boots badly scuffed. His white hairless belly oozed out of his breeches. It jiggled as he came toward me. His cheeks were run through with thin red veins. For the first time I noticed that his nose, always so lean and aristocratic, was starting to swell and look pitted, and I couldn't help but think of the drunk judge who'd exiled me to Jamaica.

What've you done to yourself? I wanted to yell at him. What have you bloody *done*?

Instead, he spoke first. It was always that way. "Sit down, Wand. Before you say something you shouldn't."

We were in the chairs next to the fireplace, the ones we always took when playing chess. The board itself had been flung over to the corner, lying next to what looked like a bloodied shirt. As Morgan lit a cheroot, I looked around the room and spotted a knight over by the hearth, a rook by the window, pawns here and there. Pitiful it was, this disregard for a board so beautiful. He exhaled a deep blue-grey spume in my direction.

"Go ahead, Wand. Judge me. It helps. It means there's still some good left in this world of ours."

"Fine. Done. I'm judging. Now tell me what you done it for."

Morgan's face went slack, like it had no blood nor muscle in it. For a second or two he stayed that way, not moving, till he finally put the cheroot in his mouth and had himself another heavy puff. His features went all smoky for a moment. "Would you like to know why they didn't hang me in London? I'm talking about the *real* reason and not all that bollocks in the papers."

"Tell me."

"Look at this island, Wand. Just look at it. Crawling with men who'll turn to piracy soon as their money runs out. They knew it back home. They aren't stupid, or at least they aren't all of the time. They needed someone to stop English piracy from fracturing the treaty with the Spanish. Now whom were they going to get to do that, eh Wand? Some administrator? Some magistrate? Some aristocrat with a law degree? Or would it be a man like me? If you were them, what would *you* have done?"

"So you cut a deal."

"I didn't want to. Oh, I assure you of that. I'd have stayed in London. I'd have stayed in the Tower, eating bowls of gruel. I'm a man of loyalty, Wand. Of honour. Or leastways I used to be. Oh, they've taken all that away from me. Now I'm whatever they need me to be."

I felt my righteousness falter, like it was being poked apart with a stick. Still, I held on to my anger, telling myself what he done last night was an outrage, deal or no deal. But then Morgan leaned forward, his unshaven face within a foot of mine. "Would you like to know how they changed my mind?"

I didn't answer. He gave me a grin was nothing but sinister. Then he flipped his patch.

The hole was run through with red and blue scarring, its surface crusty and hard, like oatmeal left out too long. I struggled to stay calm, but inside I was shrieking. "The other eye would've popped in a second. I tell you, Wand, it teaches a man about himself, facing a lifetime of blindness. I'd have murdered my own mother if it'd meant saving my vision."

He sank back in his chair. His good eye half closed and he gestured at me with the fingers holding his cheroot. He replaced his eye patch. "So tell me, Wand. What do you do when the men you're fighting for are worse than the men you're fighting against? Hmmmm? They've got me, is the long and the short of it. I'm a pawn, not a governor. The only way out is the grave."

Seconds went by. The house was silent. I thought of that stunt with the avocado. When I finally spoke, my voice was robbed of its fury. "One of the men arrested last night is a friend of mine. I'd like you to release him."

"All right."

"If you don't, we'll never play…"

"Oh, don't be so dramatic, Wand. It doesn't suit you. Of course I'll let him go. Just because I'm a traitor doesn't mean I don't value your friendship. What is the name?"

"Taylor Land."

"I don't know him."

"Yes you do. Red hair. Size of an ox. Gets on with everybody."

Morgan nodded. What this meant I couldn't say. He arched his left eyebrow and asked, "You know what they'll do for last night's arrests? They'll knight me. You just wait. That's the world we live in, Wand. They will *reward* me. If there's a God above, I bet He's having Himself a good cry over the way things work down here."

"I'll be the first to call you sir. Just let Taylor go."

"Of course," he said, at which point he stood and left the room.

TWENTY-EIGHT

THAT NIGHT I stayed in, tired of Port Royal and the board and what'd become of Henry Morgan, the man who'd once looked at me hard and seen something others couldn't. Feeling no appetite, I skipped dinner and was about to take to my bed when a light knocking came to the door. I opened it and there was Taylor, looking pale and worked-over and smaller than usual.

He came in and accepted a mug of dark tea. We chit-chatted a few minutes, mostly about the cool of the evening. The small talk over, Taylor started to look fidgety and uncomfortable, his thick freckled fingers gnashing in his lap.

"Benny, I'll admit it. I'm out of dosh. One step away from sleeping at Turtle Crawles."

"You're not alone."

"I figured I'd join up with one of them foreign pirates, but after last night, I dunno."

"I know."

"It's Morgan. He's got eyes and ears everywhere, working for him, like. I always had my suspicions about him, but

I never thought him capable of this."

"He's been through some things."

"You mean being woolded an' all?"

"So you know."

"Everyone knows. It don't excuse what he done." Taylor caught his breath. "Thanks for getting me out," he said. "Another night in that dungeon, I'd have lost my mind."

I looked at the sadness in Taylor's face and didn't have the heart to tell him he'd probably lost a little of it already, that after a time in lock-up a man takes on a tiredness never goes away. He stood. I showed him out and told him not to worry, things have a way of working themselves out. He looked at me like he knew I was just saying that, which of course I was.

I took off my clothes. My knees creaked. I climbed into bed and though I was tired, it wasn't a comfortable or pleasing sort of tiredness. My bones ached and my eyes hurt and my imagination ran like a beheaded chicken. I lay looking up at darkness, thoughts spooling, and as always my problems turned into men on a chessboard, each one looking up and begging me to reveal the solution they were hiding. This went on for a few minutes and that's when a picture popped up. It just hovered there, whether in my mind's eye or in the dark of the room or maybe it was caused by whatever of that demon wormwood was still in my system. No matter how many times I blinked, it wouldn't go away. It just hung there, refusing to go away, all shimmery and ghost-like, a plan taking shape before me.

It was that ruby, that deep red beautiful jewel, and with this vision came Morgan's words, which I could hear as clearly as the first time.

I always have it on my person, Wand.
Always.

SOON THE GROG shops started closing, the hotels and boarding houses looking bereft. To make matters worse, the feeling was that Turtle Crawles would be too much of a temptation for Morgan. All those privateers, camped in one place, living on tortoise flesh and plaintain—he could've taken them all in an afternoon. So instead, the old Brethren disappeared into the hills, hunting wild boar and taking native women as their own. Others fled the island on makeshift watercraft, their aim Tortuga or Île de Vache, where they could camp on a beach and eat turtle till their stomachs swelled. Others just made do, the way people have always done when their backs are against it.

Through it all, there was only one kind of talk in the city: who was thinking of leaving and who was actually doing it. One sky-hot day, I was sitting on a bench in the town square, which was normally filled with market stalls but had dwindled to just a few vendors hawking meat and cassava, the rest of the plaza covered with garbage and rooting wigglies and lolling bibbers. After a bit, a pair of rough-looking men sat on the bench one over and started talking. With only my own thoughts to occupy me, I gave a listen.

"There's a sloop," one of them said.

"Where?"

"One of the coves west of St. Jago."

Silence. Mulling. "You goin'?"

"Dunno. You?"

Later that day, I took a mule cart to the mainland. The

driver was a boy, no more than ten or eleven, and he spoke half Creole and half English and half something else altogether. On the way, we started chatting, not easy given the way he spoke, though if I understood correctly he'd seen the boat himself from where he lived in the hills. I asked him to take me, and we clopped along to a small jungle-covered mountain at the far end of Jamaica's capital. He stopped and pointed up.

"Go dere," he said. "And you gon see dat der boat."

I wished I could afford a bigger tip, seeing as he was dressed in rags, his shirt so big he might've been sharing it with an older brother. There was a well-trodden path, the boy again pointing.

"You can't be lost-gettin', so long's you go up on the way up and down on the way down."

I set off. It wasn't long before my shirt soaked through, so I stopped and drank water and ate fruit for a bit of energy. An hour later I reached a spot cleared by machete. For the first time I could see the whole of Jamaica, north south east and west, the island a blanket of lumpy green reaching toward blue in every direction. Sure enough, about a half mile west was a small cove protected by cliff and black rock. Anchored there was the sloop. As far as I could tell, it wasn't fitted for pirating, so I figured the boat's owner had other designs. Most likely he'd heard about the mess Port Royal was in and for a fee was taking people away.

That night, I saw Taylor. He came to my room, Rodge letting him into the house without telling me. A rucksack was weighing down one shoulder.

"For fuck's sake," I said.

"Nice to see you too."

"You're taking that boat."

"I am."

"Where to?"

"Eleuthera. An island a little ways from here. Newly taken by—"

"—the British, I know. It's a long way, is it?"

"I'd reckon. It's costing me every penny I have, and even then the captain's doin' it for next to nothing."

"Who is he?"

"Don't know. Haven't seen him yet. He's got blokes on the street, though, selling reservations to men with a keen desire to leave. All on the hush-hush, like."

"When's it go?"

"In two hours."

"That's ten o'clock at night, Taylor."

"It's safer that way."

"What'll you do there?"

"That's the part I haven't figured, though I was think-ing it was high time I took on a trade. Offer myself up as an apprentice. Make an honest man of myself. You should come. If you don't have the money, they're taking a bit now and you can pay the rest later, once you're on your feet, like."

I shook my head; something about it didn't feel right. "Can I come see you off?"

When we hit the street, he turned away from the cause-way. I looked at him, confused, until he told me there was another way. We trudged toward Port Royal's northwest tip, well beyond Turtle Crawles, to a rickety little-used dock where we found a group of men milling about and looking nervous. After a bit, a powerful brute with gold hoops in his ears rowed up and a few of the men boarded. "The cove's just a few over," Taylor explained.

Twenty minutes later, the rower came back for another lot. There was torchlight sparking off water, faces lit orange like ghouls. I could smell woodsmoke and spilled grog.

"Goodbye, Benny Wand. Wish me luck."

"Send us a note, yeah?"

"What? You readin' now?"

"Stranger things've happened, you red-headed bastard."

He snorted and then he was wading through warm water and stepping into the rowboat. He didn't look back or wave, and as I watched him meld with the moonless night I knew I'd never lay eyes on him again.

THOUGH THERE WERE still a few privateers left in Port Royal, the population was changing. Most town folk were now the type who went to church and had regular jobs and stayed in at night. I hadn't even realized they were such a number: but there they were, in the streets, in the marketplace, talking to one another like they owned the place. Port Royal's taverns, having sat empty for the past few weeks, began to close entirely. The Jamaican Arms was the first to go. Then it was the Cat and Fiddle, which was followed by the Sign of Bacchus and the Green Dragon. And then one day I was walking down the street and there was David Walsh himself, nailing planks over the doors of the former Bear Garden.

"Things'll get better," I offered.

"No. They won't. Those days're gone, Benny. The wickedest city on earth is wicked no more. Might as well face it."

"At least Suzie isn't around to see it."

"Probably rolling in her grave."

I had a panicked thought. "Walsh," I said. "What about the ladies?"

"Agnes put them out. Some was crying."

"But where they gone to?"

"Who knows. I know there's a home run by Christian women, out at the end of Lime Street, that took a bunch of 'em in. But I'm not sure."

There was nothing left to say and I walked on, head lost to worry. I went back to Rodge's and had a lie-down while I still could. I'd just woken when my landlord came to the door.

"That bloke's down below for you," he said.

"Which one?"

"The hard bastard."

Sure enough, it was Morris.

"Let's go," he said. "Morgan wants a game, yeah?" He saw me hesitating. I both did and didn't want to go, if that made any sense. "Wand. It's not an invitation."

It probably took our normal time to reach Morgan's plantation, though on that day it felt longer, for my thoughts were dark and I was feeling betrayed and this made time pass slowly. The day was broiling and my face was beet red with sun and my own angry blood. When I couldn't stand it any longer, I turned to Morris. "That's why you're his driver, yeah? 'Cause of what he's got on you?"

Morris stared straight ahead, jaw muscles gnashing between red leathery skin. Instead of him answering, I talked more. "Wish I'd been on that boat left north harbour the other night. The one bound for Eleuthera. Wish I'd been on the damn thing."

"You sure about that?"

It startled me, his voice. "About what?"

"Wishing you were on that ship."

There was some sort of hawk rotating above us and it let out a squawk that sounded more like a moan than any sound a bird had the right to make.

"Think about it," Morris went on. "A fellow no one knows, showing up in the middle of the night, offering to squire away any privateer with a few pence to rub together. Rather convenient, yeah? I wouldn't be surprised if that particular ship captain had been hired by Morgan, and that particular ship was now swimming with Davy Jones."

I felt throat-punched. No matter what'd happened to Morgan, he wouldn't do that. It wasn't possible.

Morris was never a man for words and now he wouldn't shut up. "You ever heard of a captain who took partial payment? Now me, I'd have waited till the north side of Hispaniola, out of sight and out of mind, and that's where I'd have scuttled it, in the middle of the night, when everyone was sleeping. Make my getaway in a canoe or some such." Morris turned and looked at me. "Imagine you was Morgan. Imagine you had his job. Sinking a boat's a hell of a plan. One fell swoop, just like his bloody party. He would've liked the simplicity of it."

"You know this or you guessing?"

"Dunno. You're the chess player. You tell me."

That feeling. Like your world's lost. Like up's down and down's up, and the one thing you always knew—that you've a cleverness about you—turns out to be dead wrong. I felt shaky and weak and like I couldn't trust the earth to catch me when I next stepped down on it. I wanted to go back and sleep and maybe I'd waken back in London. Maybe I'd come to in drizzly dark alleys I knew as a boy, all of Port Royal a dream.

THE JUNGLE TURNED hotter as we climbed, the air so damp it muddied the skin. We reached the pathway to Morgan's plantation, Morris pulling hard on the reins just as a harried-looking middle-aged man came rushing from the mansion, his hair loose and a flush on his cheeks. He jumped into a buggy of his own and yelled something harsh to his animal.

Morris looked at me and shrugged and then buggered off somewhere.

I entered the house just in time to hear bellowing come from the main room. Quickening my step, I rushed into the Great Room and found Morgan, face up on a lounge, holding his stomach, face beet red and swollen.

"It's about time," he said while struggling to catch his breath. "Did you meet Sloane?"

"Sloane?"

"The doctor from town. He says I've the dropsy. He says the only thing for it is to give up the drink, the bloody fool."

"You don't believe him?"

"It's probably a plot. I've enemies everywhere. It's what happens. Then again, they say he's the best in Port Royal. Still, you never know how they're going to get you. You taught me that, didn't you, Wand? A player can't be too careful, and all that? Let's have a game. What do you say? I could use a little distraction."

Morgan's board was across the room on a sideboard bathed in sunlight. I fetched it. The pieces lost during

Morgan's party had been replaced by cheap imitations. The board was now mismatched, half the pieces marble and half the pieces roughly carved wood. All in all, the board was sickly as its owner.

I set it on the little table next to him and pulled up a chair. As always, he insisted I play white. His swollen fingers trembled when he moved his first pawn. After twenty moves he blundered stupidly. "I'm out of practice, Wand. It's a damn shame. But I tell you, the day will come when you bow down, just like the Spanish did. Now move."

This time, after a dozen moves or so, he grew winded and lied back on his divan. He'd broken into a light sweat, and his hands were shaking so badly he couldn't move the pieces. He closed his eyes and breathed deeply, though it seemed like even breathing was tiring him.

"Morris!" he hollered, and within the minute John Morris was in the room with a bottle of expensive brandy and two glasses. He poured one for each of us and left the bottle. Morgan reached out and, with shaky hands, downed his in a gulp. "So much for doctor's orders," he said, and with hands a little steadier he poured himself another measure, this one filling three-quarters of the tumbler; it took three or four swallows to get it down the hatch. Colour returned to his face, and his hands steadied. "Ahhh, the elixir of life, eh Wand? That's why I know Sloane's after me. The only time the throbbing in my limbs and stomach goes away is after a dram or two. And he says that's the *cause* of it? Nonsense, if you ask me. He's probably an assassin. There're lots who'd like to see the likes of me dead."

He set up the pieces. "Go," he said, and though his moves were more assured, I was playing full force just to show him.

"Blast!" he roared. "I thought I had you, Wand. But I promise you, one day I really will beat you."

"No you won't. You're not good enough."

"What's crawled up your snout?"

"Nothing. I'm tired."

"You've never once fooled me with a lie, Wand. Out with it."

"There's talk you scuttled a ship filled with your men."

"What ship?"

"It left a week ago, bound for Eleuthera."

"Jesus, Wand. It's them plotting against me, telling lies! I'd also remind you I've no men anymore. It's just me. Now play."

I crushed him again, in fact I relished doing so, and by the time we set up the pieces for the following game, he was lost to drink. "Must be getting old," he said while offering a handshake. His fingers and palm were both cold.

"I'm off," I told him.

"No, Wand. You're not."

I looked at him blankly and that's when everything about him changed. He slumped, and held out his palms.

"Don't go," he pleaded. "I'm alone here, Wand."

"You got Morris."

"He hates me. He hates everyone. I don't trust him." He pointed a wavering finger at my chest. "You're the only one I can turn my back on. You're the only one I can lower my guard around."

"I've got to work."

"Come now, Wand. I'm not stupid. We all know they're on to you in Port Royal. Magic Wand, I dare say? Best boardsman in Jamaica, if not the Caribbean? Everyone knows.

Everyone. That's the problem with your profession, eh Wand? Soon as you get a glowing reputation, it puts you out of work."

He reached into his pocket and pulled out a quid and plunked it on the table between us. "Who's your best customer, Wand? Who's the only one stupid enough to take you on? Oh no, your race is run. Port Royal's a different place now. Oh no, Wand. The safest place for you is right here" — he pointed toward the floorboards — "next to your old sea captain. There's no telling what trouble a pair of old buccaneers such as ourselves might get up to, wouldn't you say?"

He leaned close. I smelled brandy and unwashed teeth. He brought a meaty purplish hand down on my knee. "Tell the truth, Wand. You miss it, yeah? Course you do. We had ourselves a time, didn't we?"

Morgan struggled to his feet, an exercise that took a minute and much grunting, his feet so swollen they no longer seemed to take direction from the rest of him. He stumbled out of the room. I heard boots clap against stairs. I was still sitting there, wondering what I was supposed to bloody do, when I heard a female voice, a gruff bellow and a hand slapping flesh. They weren't sounds for another's ears, so I went outside and looked over miles of Jamaican jungle; after two years on the island, I'd yet to learn the name of a single bird or a single tree or any single thing outside a tavern. Bred for swindling and swill I was, though I wasn't even sure this was true anymore. I dug a cheroot out of my breeches pocket. I sat and smoked and waited until the sounds coming out of Morgan's bedroom window stopped and all was quiet again.

Morris came around the corner of the house and told me

it was time to go. We had a wordless ride back, Morris not talking until I was stepping out of the buggy.

"Be ready tomorrow."

"I don't think so. I've had it."

He stared forward, no expression. "Wand," he finally said. "Face it. You and me, we're the same."

"And how's that, Morris?"

"He owns us both, now."

TWENTY-NINE

THE NEXT DAY, Morgan fired his doctor, calling him a charlatan and a fool and a free man only because the Port Royal jail was full. With no authority to curtail him, the governor started drinking the moment he woke in the morning; by the time Morris delivered me, he'd be up and about, shakes gone, though he still complained of swollen feet, flaring joints, belly wind, and despicable thoughts. ("They've made me a ghoul, Wand, no two ways about it.") Either we'd play a game or I'd give him chess puzzles. Sometimes Morgan could solve them, though mostly he couldn't—he'd react in one of two ways when I showed him the answer. One was he'd bellow with laughter, holding his stomach and saying he could've had a fortnight and still not have seen the bloody answer. The other was he'd turn foul and broody, like failing the puzzle was the worst thing that ever happened to him. One time, about a week after Taylor left, he looked at me, eyes marked by red lines and patches of sickly pale yellow. His voice sounded like it'd been trampled by horses.

"A year ago, I'd have seen the answer in a minute."

"I doubt that."

"You're a liar!" He slammed his fist on the board, scattering pieces. I flinched and he looked at me through bleary eyes. "Get out of here. Leave me be."

I paused for just a second, and then I left the room, wondering what I was supposed to do. That's when I heard giggling coming from upstairs. I couldn't stop my curiosity, so I snuck up the staircase to the second floor. I crept toward the source of the noise, getting close enough I could hear gibberish. I was outside the door, listening to high-pitched yammering, when the door opened and I was caught out.

There were five of them, all bronze-skinned and small and so pretty it hurt to look. They stopped giggling and fixed a bead on me, though after a bit of girlish blinking they all went back to what they were doing. Yet the one who'd caught me just stood there, looking up, eyes black, lips like slices of ripe tomato. Her thin cotton smock clung to the rise and fall of her young body. I couldn't look away, and maybe this caused her to reach out and wrap twiggy black fingers around my wrist.

"Me go wit you."

I shook my head but didn't move.

"Me go wit you," she repeated, so I broke her wrist hold and marched off, face burning, wishing I'd never been sent to this cursed island. I marched down the stairs and found John Morris smoking outside.

"I've had it."

He looked at me up and down, his way of reminding me it was up to Morgan to say when I did or did not venture back down the mountain. After a bit he motioned toward his trap and somehow I knew it was up to me to follow. Halfway down, I couldn't resist. "Those Indian girls. They ever go home?"

"That's a good one. They just keep showing up. Half my job is shooing away their relatives. Go *home*? Bloody hell, Wand. They get three square meals and a sound roof. Couldn't get rid of them if we tried."

He dropped me off. Rodge's Lodges was like a morgue; if I wasn't the only guest, it certainly felt like it. I grabbed my board and found a pub still operating on High Street— the ones that hadn't gone out of business now had irregular schedules, opening and closing when the mood struck. I took up a corner and waited as usual. It was the same old story, not a punter to be had and no money to be made. I ordered a pint, feeling guilty for spending the coins. I drank it slowly. I didn't feel like going home, so I kept on the move. For a while I even set up my board in the town squares, in view of the church I'd looted all that time ago, hoping upon hope someone might happen by and feel lucky enough to take me on.

There was no such luck, leastways not that day.

SIX HOURS LATER, Morris came for me. When we reached Morgan's mansion, we heard rattling and moaning and some fool chanting in a hellfire rumble. Inside, we found Morgan on his best felt divan, holding his stomach and groaning. An immense Indian, dressed in a loincloth and a chicken-foot necklace, was prancing about with a thicket of smouldering herbs. His eyes and mouth were ringed with charcoal, and there were discs inserted in his drooping earlobes. Whatever language he was moaning in wasn't English or Spanish or even patois but something more ancient. After twenty minutes of low grunting, his thicket burnt down to nothing and he looked at it confused, like it was a timepiece that'd wound itself down. He shrugged and skulked out.

Morgan opened his blood-red eyes and noticed me. "Come here!" he blurted. His mouth looked parched and he was holding his badly inflated stomach. "The madman in his lair, what?"

"Who was that?"

"An Arawak man. A spirit doctor. Better than those Port Royal quacks. Now help me up."

He reached a hand toward me, seizing me with fat sausage fingers. I leaned back, craning him to his feet. He waved me away with a grunt and tottered off, the back of his shirt hanging out of his breeches. I walked off and Morgan seemed not to care or notice, for that was the ruined state he was in. With nothing to do, I walked the property. There was a blue sky and a blazing sun overhead and I could smell something roasting. I turned the corner of his big house and there I saw a family of natives, roasting a goat over low white embers: no doubt they were related to one of the girls in Morgan's bedchamber. They looked at me with sad eyes and said nothing as I walked past them. At the very back of the house I saw other families, and that included squalling babies right the way to thin-armed grandmothers. They were all sitting around little fires, waiting for something to happen; each one had shiny black hair grown long at the back and short at the front. Some had built lean-tos like the ones we'd built on Turtle Crawles. As I walked past them, I could feel their eyes on me, like they were sizing me up for dinner. I came back round the front of the house and there was Morgan, stretching his back, looking put off.

"Where'd you go?"

"Had a walkabout."

"Well hurry up. Don't doddle."

We went inside and sat at the little table in his Great Room, his board set up and waiting. "You take white," he said, and I opened. After a dozen shite moves he was in trouble. The game ended so quickly it might as well not've happened. He glared at the board. Slumped in his chair he was, looking worn and old. I'd never seen a man so morose.

"What will it be, then, Wand?"

I said nothing.

"How's history going to remember me? Will I be the man who liberated the Caribbean from the Spanish? Could be, you know. That would be fair, though when has the world ever been fair? Everything's changed now, you know. People trade with anyone. People worship who and what they like. People earn a quid and they get to keep it instead of sending it off to the King of Spain. It's a different world out there, and it's all thanks to me. The Spanish would've never struck a compromise if they hadn't been scared of me." He waved a hand in the air. It was swollen and pink and looked nothing like the hand of a feared man. "Or will I be the madman who used priests as a shield against boiling oil? Who wiped Panama from the face of the earth? Who kept a harem of native girls? What do you reckon, Wand? For those offences a man could spend his eternity in hell."

He looked down and belched quietly, his body quaking.

"Governor," I finally said. "Why do you have me here every day?"

"I told you, Wand. You're all I have left."

"I don't believe you."

"You don't have to."

"There's Morris."

"I told you. The bastard hates me."

"What about—"

"The town burghers? In their eyes I'm no better than a lowly pirate. Everyone else sees me as a traitor. I can't say I even blame them. You've never seen a man more alone, Wand."

He lit a cheroot. His hands were shaky and when he sucked on the tip to ignite it, his lips sounded dry. He sat smoking and looking through me. "And what about you, Wand? What will be thought of *you* when you're gone? What will *your* legacy be? Of course, you don't care, do you? You've no soul to suffer for the sins you committed while alive. You're lucky, I suppose. You've nothing to atone *with*. I tell you, Wand, I'm beginning to see the wisdom in your way of thinking."

He coughed and sputtered. I didn't tell him I was feeling different about such things of late. While I still figured heaven and hell were gob shite, lately I'd begun to think maybe there was something inside us, something that, when it wakes up, makes you feel like you belong more than anything else. It was my only explanation for what spoke up in that Portobello jungle, that voice telling me not to kill the Spanish deserter. While it'd startled me, there's no denying a comfort had come with it, though as soon I tried to understand it, or figure where it was coming from, the feeling vanished.

I looked over at Morgan, thinking was no way I was going to explain any of this, when I saw that his eyes were closed, and he was making a sound halfway between snorting and breathing.

It was my chance. Finally, he'd fallen asleep in my presence. I rose slowly to my feet. I stepped around the little table separating the two of us and stood hovering over Morgan. I waited a few seconds, wondering whether my shadow would wake him. It didn't. His timid half snore turned to the sound of wood being sawed; with each exhale, the skin swaddling the underside of his jaw jiggled. My trembling hand reached toward the lapel of his jerkin, a mere inch or two from the inner pocket where he kept that ruby. The way I reckoned, there was no way he could report something missing if that thing didn't exist.

I heard footsteps. It was Morris, standing in the doorway, eyes narrowed.

"What you doin', Wand?"

"Er... loosening the governor's clothing, like. It sounded like he was breathing a little queer."

It was a terrible answer, though I could've done worse. I made a fuss of adjusting Morgan's yellowed collar while Morris gave me a look saying he had his eyes on me. "Enough," he said. "I'm taking you back."

"Right," I said, and I rode back to Port Royal with the feeling I no longer had the luxury of time.

THIRTY

SHORTLY AFTER THAT, I started having trouble sleeping. I spent my nights awake, staring at the ceiling, feeling like a weight was on my chest, making it difficult to breathe. If I did manage to fall asleep, I'd dream I was in some cube and the door was closing and if I failed to make it out in time I'd be locked in forever, doomed to expire slowly from lack of food or water or what have you. Still asleep, I'd bolt out of bed, racing for the door, only to come awake in the middle of my room, feet cold, heart pounding, struggling to catch my breath. Coming apart at the seams, I was, bothered by visions both hellacious and divine, like the night I'd had all that wormwood wine and only Gerald saved me from going off my nut.

One afternoon, I was sitting in Rodge's lunchroom, drinking bitter black tea, my head a shaky fog. Rodge came in. He sat opposite. He looked like a man at a funeral. Even with my being so distracted, I knew what he was about to say.

"Benny, I'm sorry."

"You been more than fair, Rodge."

"It's come to the point it's cheaper for me to just close up."

"If I was you, I'd do the same."

"Take a few days."

That afternoon, I took to the streets of Port Royal. Though prices had dropped in the past few months, they were still higher than what I could afford. Finally, I knocked on the door of a home on Queen Street. A hag answered. She had a dishtowel on her shoulder.

"You've a room?"

She shrugged and motioned I should come. I followed her up a dark cobwebby staircase and down a damp hall smelling of turnip. She opened the door on a single room. I had to swallow, for the sight was chilling, the room filled with little wooden dolls, of the sort girls play with. And when I say filled, I mean *filled*: every inch of surface space, bed and floor and dresser, was covered with pinafore-wearing figurines. Each doll was facing the window, like it was watching for something.

"Feller lived here before just up and disappeared. After not seein' 'im for three weeks, I opened up and this is what I saw. Didn't surprise me none. Crazy as a wounded badger, he was. You clean this mess up, I'll lop off first month, yeah?"

"Yeah," I said, and with a tiredness in my bones I spent the rest of that afternoon throwing dolls in an old jute sack. It was disgusting work, for some of them were sticky and some were covered with thick red splotches I could only think was blood. I filled two huge sacks and left them on the street for the urchins to pick apart. With an achy heart I gave the new place a sweep and collected what clothes I had from Rodge's. He caught up to me just as I was dragging my trunk onto the street.

"Benny," he called, and said nothing. Just held his hand out and I shook it and that was it; I turned and walked off, no words to the effect I'd be back for we both knew that was my intention. The question was whether it'd happen or not.

THAT NIGHT, I went out, board in hand, finger-crossed, determined. At one of the few beer halls still open, I made enough for a beef tongue sandwich though what I would've given for a libation to go with it. I got frustrated around one in the morning and left. The street was quiet and empty. Moon glinted off the sand-covered lane. I moved along, feeling wary without Taylor. Only the odd drunkard and desperate trollop was out, both with the same sad aim, *have you a few pence for me sir?* and I couldn't help but wonder if I'd come across poor Tessie, selling her wares in the gutter.

About ten minutes from home, a figure came from one of the little closes that criss-crossed the lane. He walked toward me, head down. Luckily, he had nothing of the cutpurse or footpad about him—he was one of the town's new lot, a burgher come from London, you could tell in the cut of his jerkin and the polish of the buckle on his shoes. I knew the type, of course. A fine upstanding citizen by day, a rover of knocking-shops and gambling dens by night. My line of work depended on them needing to lose a little dosh once in a while, if only to feel they were being punished for what they got up to.

He looked up, and I swear I knew him from somewhere.

"Good evening," he said, and I gave him a head nod though as I did I was picturing every lowly place in Port Royal, trying to figure how I knew him. Then it came to me. I whipped around and yelled, "Oi!"

He stopped and turned. I walked up to him and had a good long look at his face and I knew I was right.

"Yes?" he said. "May I help you?"

"I know you..."

"And I know you, sir. You're the chess player." He was starting to look a little nervous, like maybe playing the board was the least of what I got up to.

"You remember when we played!?" I blurted. "You said a 'little bird' told you I was a man not to wager with."

"Yes, that's correct."

"Who *was* that little bird, then?" I took a step forward, closing the distance between us, making him smell my breath and beard. The truth was I had the odour of the poor, and that's a smell scared his type half to death. He took a half step back. He was breathing hard. The scars on my cheeks helped too.

"Why... it was Mr. Morgan."

"You tellin' me the truth, mister?"

"Of course I am. Right from the beginning he was telling everyone in town to keep away from the likes of you. It took us a while to see he was right."

I was trembling, both with rage and from the utter confusion of it all. I grabbed the man by his shirt front and lifted my free hand, ready to give him a right pummelling, when I realized I had the wrong man in my clutches. *He* wasn't the man who'd arrested all my friends. *He* wasn't the man who'd sabotaged my livelihood. *He* wasn't the man who let those poor old idiot priests go up that ladder, even though he knew full well what would happen.

I dropped the posh bastard, and told him to bugger off. I was so confused I could barely breathe. If Morgan had wanted to ruin me, why not have me arrested with the others that night at his mansion? Why put the knife in so *slowly?*

I started walking, shoulders hunched and head reeling, when I turned a corner and there, in the middle of the street, was a broken bottle, just the stem and a body of shards. It was a common-enough sight in a place like Port Royal, but it took me right back to a laneway in Manchester. Years ago, this was, Manchester the gloomiest dampest town we'd lived in yet. My parents were drinking more than ever, Ma a mad flailing battleaxe and my dad always in some corner, snivelling at how the world was a terrible place and *why go on oh why why go on?* until she'd yell at him to put a cork in it. Though I was playing the board—*come one come all and try yer luck with Benny The Boy Wonder!*—I'd not yet figured the hustle of it and was making next to nothing. You feel stupid and cold, not having enough to eat. The mind goes weak and convinces you you deserve it.

At least we weren't alone. A good half the kids in the city were too skinny; I once saw this gent walking down the street, eating a nice-looking apple, with two or three kids following along behind so they could fight over the core when he was done. It was the sort of image stays trapped in the mind, forming your impression of the sort of place the world is.

There was this one grocer the older kids always stole from. They chose him 'cause he was a bibber through and through, and usually too in his cups to give chase. Still, he did come after kids, so you had to be of a certain age, ten or eleven, to outrun him. Like I say, I was no more than seven or eight, but I'd watched the other kids nick all those lovely apples and potatoes and turnips. This would make him furious, but he always had a stagger to him so he'd rarely catch his prey (though if he did by God you were boxed soundly about the ear).

One day the temptation proved too much. The grocer was on his stool, bottle in hand, half dozing. I walked by the shopfront two or three times, which was a right stupid thing to do for it probably tipped him off, but I was not yet practised in the art of foolery. On my third pass I nicked a wobble of cheap meat. Headcheese or some such. For one second I looked at it drooling, thinking how food was like gold when you're starving. But I'd awoken the lion — the tottery bastard leapt up and took chase. I'd never run faster, had no idea my legs could carry me that quick, yet I was little and the grocer was gaining ground while yelling, *I'll fuckin' kill ya, I catch you and I'll fuckin' kill ya*, while waving the bottle he was drinking from. Panicked, I was, everything a blur. If I didn't run faster, I'd be a dead boy, pure and simple, so I accelerated around a corner into a brick-wall lane and it was a matter of my body going faster than my legs could handle. I went down like a sack of cabbage and then he was on me, pulling me to my feet by my hair. I was crying, both from being caught and at the frustration of being so needy. The grocer yelled he'd had it and was going to give me a lesson I'd never bloody forget. He broke the bottle on the wall next to him, and till this day I know he was just trying to put the scare in me and that's what would've happened except he was drunk. He was waving the broken end in my face, just to terrorize me like, when something caused him to lose his balance and pitch forward, and that's how I got stuck.

I screamed and soaked my pants and my cheek burned and that's how I got these marks poking out over my beard. It wasn't the pox or a bad case of spots like most think; it was a drunk grocer, who gasped when he seen what he'd done. As I rolled at his feet, weeping and holding my face, he started saying, *my God my God my God I didn't mean it boy*, and it was him scooped me up in his arms and carried me home and explained to my ma what'd happened and she was of the opinion I had it coming. The next thing you knew, the two of them were having a drink together, the grocer pleading, *I'm not a bad man, I'm not, everyone thinks I is, but I inn't*, while my ma kept nodding and saying, *'course you inn't now pour me another ya clumsy bastard . . .*

And it was like my scarring happened just five minutes earlier, not to a little boy on the run in Manchester but to an ex-privateer living in the wickedest city on earth, and there was something about that memory being so clear and so close that made me go to my fetid and awful boarding-house room and open the trunk I'd moved over from Rodge's. I pulled out old socks and skivvies and breeches until I saw my French flintlock on the bottom.

I dug it out, and the following night, when I headed out with the board tucked under my arm, I had my flintlock tucked inside my waistcoat pocket, keeping me safe from the spectres of my past. But first I decided to pop by my old boarding house, and see whether Rodge or maybe Gerald wanted to keep me company. When I got there, the door was locked and it was dark inside. I tapped on the window, hard enough the pane rattled, thinking maybe Rodge had run out of candles. It was foolish thinking. He'd closed up once and for all, and though I wasn't worried about him—no doubt he had some money socked away somewhere—I fretted over poor Gerald, for where was an old codger like him supposed to go in a place like Port Royal? A place where only the rich or the larcenous survived, and him being neither? I pounded on the door and called both their names—"Rodge! Gerald!"—and listened. There was nothing. I stepped back and called, "Gerald! You there? You there, Gerald?!"

It was just me, wishing I could hide in a week's worth of sleep. Instead, I found a little place called the Hook 'N Ladder which was still open despite everything. There I nursed a pint while taking dirty looks from the bar owner. I was down to my last few coins, and the only plan I had— nicking Morgan's jewel without swinging for it—was the sort of strategy you cling to rather than believe in fully. My head ached with worry. I ordered another pint and downed this one quickly. They say whatever doesn't kill you makes you stronger, only I reckoned the opposite to be true— I'd been without food or shelter more times than I could remember, and every time it was worse than the time before because you know how it's going to feel come day three or four.

"Oi," called the man behind the bar. He was a roly-poly sort, with mutton chops and suspenders. "You drinkin' or just sittin'?"

"I'm doing neither, though thanks for askin'."

I got up and figured sod it, I've had it for the night if not forever. I went back to my sordid little room, sighing when I stepped inside; cobwebs still spanned the corners, and there was the same dull settled-in mustard smell. I lied on my bed. The mattress was thin and made of straw; the bed frame creaked every time I rolled over. At Rodge's, I had a bit of a cross-breeze, but here the air just squatted like an overweight bully, refusing to budge, and I wondered if that was the reason Port Royal was so lost—it was the heat, simmering people's minds, rupturing the way they think. No wonder we were all so mad. It was our awful childhoods mixed with relentless heat and rumbullion. A recipe for corrupt thinking if ever there was one.

I was awake for hours that night, head aching, feeling low, sweat rising on my chest and the backs of my knees. Finally, my thoughts started to curl and turn in on themselves, and I started dreaming I was locked in that little cube again, only some giant hand was giving the cube a good shake, and I was banging my head on the ceiling, thinking I was done for.

This woke me, and I saw my plate and spoon were falling off their shelf. The pitcher I kept on the windowsill crashed to the floor, water and bits of white clay everywhere. Dust sifted from the beams and cries came from down the hall, a madwoman shrieking, "They're here! They're here!"

Another trembler it was, though this one was way worse, the ground rumbling like it was hungry for food. As the walls shook, I thought maybe I'd *be* that food, the shaking getting worse and worse until there was a mighty crack, like the house was being ripped from the earth below. It tilted just enough I fell and tumbled along the messed wooden floor.

And then it stopped. It'd lasted for a half minute and now there was nothing. All of Port Royal was drummed into silence; the madwoman next door turned mute. After a minute or so I heard risen voices and wailing and the cries of animals. These started to build and soon it was all I heard, the town going into noisy shock, all together and all at once. I got up and pulled back a torn soiled curtain and peered out. Carts were overturned and people were running in every direction and directly beneath the window a horse was struggling to find its feet though it was injured and needed to be put down. I put on breeches and a shirt coated with splinters. In case there was looting, I took my flintlock too, tucking it in my waistband.

Pandemonium, it was. The streets full of debris. Children wailing. People all rushing in the same direction, so I followed and soon discovered why. A house off High Street had collapsed and people were pulling off fallen beams to try to get at the poor bastards trapped inside. A middle-aged woman in a streaked apron was screaming there was a family in there, a nice family, *we have to help the nice family inside!* I joined the search, though little was to be done with there being so many helpers already. I was readying to leave when there came a scream so loud everyone stopped yelling and shouting and hollering directions. It was a woman, holding a crushed baby, the tot no bigger than some of the dolls I'd found in my new lodgings. She just looked at it and screamed, over and over, and a little bit of me died seeing that sight as well.

Debris was everywhere, not a house in sight without damage. Crones walked around dazed and asking if anybody had fresh water. I stumbled through it all. You couldn't do otherwise with all the shite in the streets. There were fallen trees and battered people calling for help. There were more collapsed roofs, more ruin, more chaos. On Lime Street, just opposite Turtle Crawles, I came across another tumbled-over house. Thinking I heard muffled voices, I waded in, pulling on beams and planks and smashed-apart boards. There were little things lying broken everywhere, like splintered wood toys or a fractured basin or a torn woman's slipper. Soon the voices were clear, and I knew the family living here had rushed to their root cellar where they were trapped and calling, *we're here, we're here, please help us!* I stepped out and hollered and people came running. We dug the family out and even though their house was gone, they were wearing big smiles for they'd been given their lives back. That's when I noticed something: the man of the family was one of Morgan's privateers from Portobello. He looked at me and recognized me and the funny thing was, we both pretended to be strangers, as if ashamed of something we couldn't name.

I moved on. There were places where laneways had buckled and come apart, leaving holes big enough to swallow a man, so I had to be careful. Air was getting to buried embers and causing little flames to leap to life: people were calling for water and running back and forth with buckets in their hands.

I went back down High Street. A bloke came up and asked could I help water an alehouse that'd caught fire. When I got there, I saw it was pointless, the thing had mostly burned itself away, the fire about to go out seeing as it had nothing left to burn. Still, there was no telling the owner his business was gone, and I joined a bucket brigade, the water pulled from a nearby well and handed from man to man until we tossed it on the blaze. "It's working! It's working!" yelled the owner, though the fire was only dying down since there was less and less for it to burn. We didn't stop until the tavern was nothing but cinders and charred beams and a stone-wall foundation. The owner couldn't see it, his own eyes wouldn't let him, and the saddest thing was his own relief, for he was doing a little jig and yelping, "We did it! We saved it! Thank yoos all so much, I couldn't have done it alone..."

I moved on. More panic, more cracked roadways, more loosened animals, more children crying. I passed the Port Royal jail and the thought did sicken me, how the poor souls locked up below would've been shook like beans in a tin, though at least the jail hadn't collapsed atop them. I helped an old man to his feet and I helped another woman chase a pig who'd gotten loose, not an easy task but at least the pig was overfed and ready for slaughter so he was easier to corner. It felt good, being useful, and that's when a voice called out my name. I shook it off, thinking it my battered imagination, when it came again, though louder.

I looked up and there was John Morris, at the mouth of the causeway, riding toward me.

"Wand!" he yelled again as he pulled up.

"Bloody hell, Morris, what you want?"

"Get in."

"Not today."

"Yes, today."

I was about to tell him this was one time Morgan wouldn't get what he wanted when I had a feeling like when you sense the board's about to turn, and the only thing you don't know is in what direction.

The causeway was full of cracks and sinkholes and there was water rushing over it, leaving behind hundreds (if not thousands) of those speckled flying fish, who all flopped around trying to get back to water. When there was a pothole, we had to slow and in some cases get out of the trap while Morris led the horses through it or around it.

St. Jago had been hit too, though not as hard as Port Royal. Parts of houses had fallen, though at least they'd stayed standing. The streets were a disaster, though. Every twenty feet or so we had to clear the road of fallen wood or flung shingles or the like. As we moved away from the town, the roads weren't any better; there were fallen coconuts and splintered branches and birds dropped dead from shock. As we kept going, there was less and less damage, though when we got to the stretch where the road clung to the very side of the mountain, we came across a crevice about a foot wide. "Jesus," said Morris.

"Take me back."

"Bollocks."

To our left was the mountain wall and to our right a drop to a rocky bay: was no way the trap was going to cross, so walking was our only choice. Morris took a rope and hobbled the horse just to be safe. The sun was hot and straight up in the sky and before long we were both panting and wet. The road switched back up the mountainside and it occurred to me we had no food nor water of any kind. "You thirsty?" I said.

"Don't think about it," and we kept on, moving one foot after the other, until we came to a small path that cut straight up the jungle.

Morris stopped. "We can switchback our way for the next two hours. Or we can take this path straight up and be there quicker."

"How much quicker?"

"Dunno."

For the first twenty feet or so it was flat, the path narrow and hot and buggy, and I couldn't help but think of the jungle marches we'd taken with Morgan. Then there was a wall of green, the path going straight up over roots and tree stumps and gaps in the forest floor. We started to climb, our hands on the earth in front of us, looking for things to grab on to and pull us up. It was hard work. Soon my lungs were so full of hot jungle air it was like I'd swallowed a sponge. Morris must've felt the same way, for he stopped and took deep sucking breaths and then he went on. After another ten minutes we stopped and rested, our faces and lower backs and armpits soaked through.

Though I expected Morris to move off, he didn't. He was still taking huge racking lungfuls and I could see he was in trouble, that all those nights spent in Port Royal grog shops had hurt him. The sweat dripped into my eyes and all around us birds squawked and you could hear snakes slithering about, disturbing leaves and twigs and what all else. Finally, we moved on, though five minutes later Morris stopped again, the break in the forest just up ahead. After a bit we found a final burst of energy and then we were up, the path ending on a long wide lawn grown over with weeds. Morgan's mansion stood on the other side and we walked toward it, Morris still panting and looking ill, and when we made it to the front entrance he just pointed at it. I stopped and watched as he walked off, hands on his waist, moving slowly.

The air was still as still gets. I noticed that someone had bashed away the King's-head knocker, badly splintering the wood behind it. The damaged door swung open and Morgan was there, a fat man in a sorry wig. He eyed my condition: clothes stained, hair glued to my forehead, bugs in my eyelashes. "What happened to you?"

"The road was a wreck. We walked."

He ignored me. He turned to his mansion. "It's held up, more or less. You want to see something, Wand? Walk this way..." and he took me along the same path I'd followed around the outside of the house the last time I was here. He breathed hard and raspy, like a dog on a hot day, practically panting with effort. As he rounded the corner of the house, he stopped.

"Look," he said. The lawn backing his house was covered with Indians, all cooking or tending to little ones or washing clothes in metal basins or, in the case of the men, just sitting there looking. "They've been showing up all day. I think the trembler has driven them out of their villages. Look at them, Wand. Helpless. Pathetic. The once-mighty Arawak, beaten up by the Spanish and the English. Even the escaped slaves living in the interior, those blasted Maroons, are letting them have it. It happens, you know. You put people to the test over and over and over, and one day the muster goes out of them. But I tell you something." He grinned. "When they all showed up from Hispaniola three hundred years ago, they didn't think twice about slaughtering the natives that were already here, now, did they? It's the way of the world, Wand, and there's nothing anyone can do about it."

He eyed me. If he'd been drinking, it didn't show: his eyes were a piercing cool grey, the eyes of the man I'd first met all that time ago.

"My knighthood's come through, Wand."

I was speechless.

"The decree's been writ. If I was in England, there'd be a ceremony. Here, no one likes me enough to throw a party."

"Congratulations," I said with a bitterness in my voice.

If he noticed, he didn't show it. Instead, he turned and looked out toward water. "I've accomplished everything I ever wanted to accomplish, Wand. Everything I've ever dreamed. Look at me, Wand. Look at the *sight* of me. I'm what they reward you for."

I said nothing.

He turned back toward me and grinned sickly. "You and I are going to have a game, Wand. I'm feeling strong today. This is it. I'm sure of it. It's this bloody trembler. It's brought out the might in me."

We went to his Great Room. He sat in his chair. A few of the windows had shattered, glass shards everywhere. A loose cat picked among them, looking for food. The board was set up. As always, he said, "You take white."

I moved. I didn't care. Inside, I was screaming with whatever it is makes your hands shake and your stomach feel funny and your nose run like a spigot. We didn't speak. Morgan poured himself a drink from the bottle sitting on the little table. When he offered me one, I nodded. We drank and played chess and I can't say I really cared whether I won or lost, so I played like a runty beginner. Morgan was just as bad. He could've taken the first game, though he blundered around the fortieth move.

"Goddamnit," he roared. "Where was my head at?"

"Attached to your shoulders," I grumbled as he set up the pieces again.

The second game was a repeat of the first, Morgan

opening with a king-side gambit, an aggressive opening though littered with ways it can go wrong. If he was aiming for surprise, it failed miserably. From the second move on, he was down a piece and I wouldn't let him get the position he wanted in return. He could've given up right then and there, but he didn't, we kept on playing, me tired and fed up and not caring, Morgan too lost to whatever sickness had seized him since he'd come back from London. A pair of tossers we were, pissing at the nature of the game. I hated him and I hated all the blunders I'd made with my life, for again it was my past melding with my present and making me feel crazy.

Morgan looked at the board and realized he was done.

"Again," he said.

"No."

"What do you mean, no?"

"I'm a boardsman, Morgan. It's how I make my living now. You want to play me, we play for money."

He eyed me, grinning. "So that's how it is, eh Wand? A little bit of money? No time for a game with an old friend? All right, you rummy bastard. Here." He reached into his pocket and pulled out ten quid and slapped it on the little table between us. "There," he grunted. "Can you match it?"

"Don't need to."

"You lose and there'll be consequences."

"I won't."

"It's your move," and I opened once more with the Spanish opening, just to get under his skin. With money on the table, we both settled down and started playing for real, Morgan holding on for longer than I thought him capable of, though after a time he faltered, just as I knew he would:

he got all clumped up in the corner, his men cramped and useless, a knight exchange opening up a hole in his wall and then he was clobbered.

I reached for the money and he brought his hand down hard on mine.

"Double or nothing."

"Let me see the dosh."

"What is your problem today, Wand? Money, money, money. You're like a Port Royal whore. You're like that Two-Tongue Tessie of yours, only I hear she's not so quirkily endowed these days."

Inside, I burned. He reached into his pocket and plunked down the same number of pounds again. He opened with his queen-side knight. I yawned to show what I thought of it.

Morgan smirked and said, "Just you wait, Wand. Just you bloody wait."

I moved and he moved, repeat repeat repeat, and I was barely paying attention until the moment I was. Morgan was trying something different: instead of flying pieces at me, he'd gone into a defensive shell, moving two pieces forward and one back, trying to wear me down.

"Remember doing this to me?" he said with a mocking grin. "Annoying, isn't it?"

"If I got somewhere to be, I don't know about it."

We kept playing. I felt hot and sooty, and the things in the room — table, chairs, fireplace — went gauzy, and I feared they'd turn to phantom chess pieces. My breath was coming in short sharp bursts, followed by seconds when I couldn't think at all. Suffocating, I was, and somewhere around the fiftieth move or so I made the stupidest blunder I'd made in years, my ears filling with the sound of crashing plates. Two moves after that, Morgan opened a file on my queen, my only option to hang a rook to stop it from happening. At the time I was up two pawns, so with my rook gone I'd be down three points, and with my position what it was, it didn't look good. But first Morgan had to see it. He reached for a pawn and I stopped worrying. He'd choose some stupid stalling horse-shite, for that's what his game was going to be, strategy and wisdom being close cousins: given half a chance, they can blinker a man instead of guide him. Morgan was just about to touch his pawn when his fingers stopped in mid-air—they were fat and greasy with whatever he'd had for lunch. They just hovered, trembling, wanting for drink. He lowered his hand and grinned at me. He chuckled, and gobbled my rook.

"Didn't I say I'd beat you one of these days?"

"You haven't won yet."

"Look at the board, Wand. Look at what you've left me."

The only thing left was bluster. "It's a trap. You're just not good enough to see it."

"That so?"

"It is."

"You sure, Wand?"

"I bloody am."

"In that case, let's make this interesting. It's what you boardsmen dream of, yeah? Making things interesting? Landing a whale like me? Well, here's your chance..."

He reached into the inner pocket of his jerkin and pulled out the noblewoman's ruby. He placed it on the table, where it sparkled blood-red. He regarded me coldly. "You could start your shop with the likes of that."

"Maybe," I said, trying to sound calm though he was telling the truth.

"The question is, what'll you put up on your end?"

"I don't need an end."

"Look at your position, Wand. You *need* an end."

I thought hard and eyed the bastard. "I win, you give me the jewel. You win, I surrender. You throw me in the Port Royal jail with all the other privateers down there. With all the other men who used to serve you well. You can tell the King you've captured your former military adviser, the man who brought down Portobello and Panama. They'd love you for that, yeah? They'd make *you* king for that."

He grinned sickly. "I don't need a chess game to have you arrested."

"Not if you want a clear conscience."

"Oh, I'll never have a clear conscience again, Wand. And neither will you, I can promise you that. What if we draw?"

"I win the bet. I'm risking more and you've the advantage. You want to keep your ruby, you have to defeat me."

"You end up in that jail, Wand, and I won't stop them feeding you to the gibbet."

"I know it."

He moved and I gave up my rook and that was that.

"Wait," I said. "This'll be the last game I play with the ruddy likes of you, so let's have a toast, yeah?"

"Fine."

I took the bottle and poured two tall glasses of brandy and offered him one. "To your health."

"To yours."

We lifted our glasses, Morgan downing his while I just let the liquid touch my lips. When we put our glasses back down, mine was full—it was my way of saying he'd get every trick I knew thrown at him.

"You're a coward, Wand. I saw the way you ran off in Panama, like a frightened girl. Now play."

I moved, my only intent to blockade his most advanced pawn, a strategy that wouldn't work in the long run but would frustrate Morgan in the meantime.

"Typical," he said with a dark chuckle.

"What?"

"I figured you'd do something spineless like that. I've news for you, Benny Wand. I've all day. I've the rest of my life. You won't wear me down this time."

"We'll see."

"That we bloody will," and he advanced a pawn himself and I did feel a chill, for it was his best move and I'd hoped he'd start leaping at me like a jaguar tracking a kill. No such luck. Suddenly he was the most careful man in the world, a man who didn't know the meaning of risk or gamble. Ten moves went by, fifteen, twenty. Instead of attacking, he positioned his pieces, not winning any material but gradually aiding his position. Another ten moves went by, and I felt a panic creep in. Breathe, I told myself, fuckin' breathe, though it was difficult, for I was picturing myself squeezed into that hot airless jail, just like my nightmare it'd be, except with the gibbet waiting. The more this picture kept popping into my head, the less I could think straight, so I forced myself to go elsewhere, back to London a long time ago, back to Sunday mornings, and rashers and eggs, and everything my granddad taught me. *Imagine, my good boy, imagine* and that's when I saw the answer.

Morgan had learned *my* game. He'd learned how to defend against it and only it. What he didn't know was his own game. He didn't know how to deal with rashness, with boldness, with impatience. Maybe he didn't know how to deal with the likes of bloody *him*. My queen came barging out of her hold; I put Morgan in check, which made him chortle, for on the surface it was a useless move except it stopped him from slowly tightening the noose. He blocked. I checked with a bishop, lessening my own defence slightly but sod it. He blocked. I checked with my queen again, and he offered a swap that I avoided by checking with my bishop again. He moved his king once more and I checked again with my queen and this went on, move after move, *check check check*, playing like I was Morgan, and I could tell he was puzzled, for why would I do this if not for good reason? He was taking longer and longer while I played quicker and quicker just to throw him off, and that's when he finally made a weak move or two: I could fork his bishop and a pawn with my knight. His obvious move would be giving up the pawn. If he *did* this, though, it left the way for a perpetual check with my queen, and I'd draw the game. Yet if he gave me his bishop, we'd be even in points, and though a better player could still challenge me on position, that player wasn't Henry Morgan.

He thought. He was breathing hard through a plugged nose. He moved his hand and it hung in the air and then he took it back. He sat staring at that board like it held the secret of life. He leaned forward like there was something new there, like there *had* to be a way. When he saw there wasn't, he leaned back in his chair looking bitter.

"So it's a draw, is it? A poor way to end things if you ask me."

"I saw it when you couldn't. Now give me the ruby."

"No."

"What you mean, no?"

"I mean just that, you homely bastard. *No.*" He put it back in his chest pocket. "This match is over. Null and void, Wand. It never happened. A draw means nothing."

"So you're a welcher."

"Looks that way."

"I can't stand a welcher."

"Oh please. Get off your high horse. Think of what we did in Panama. Think of what *you* did to those priests in Portobello. We're barbarians, Wand. Lowest of the low. You think welching bothers me?"

His grin was back and it turned my blood to hot lava. It wasn't my brain in control anymore, but twisted guts and hatred. I watched myself pull my flintlock and point it at Morgan's chest. "I want that jewel."

"Ha! Don't make me sodding laugh, Wand."

My hand was shaking.

"Oh for the love of Christ. Put it down. You haven't the stones."

"So help me God, I'll do it."

"Oh, so it's God now, is it? I thought He didn't exist." Morgan's face tightened, all amusement gone. "Face it, Wand. You could no more kill me than fly to the moon."

The barrel wavered, like a spastic was holding it.

"You know what, Wand? I've grown tired of you. In the morning you'll be arrested on my orders. Sedition. Abandoning your post. Anything I can think of and more. It's the gibbet for the likes of you."

Sweating all over, I was. Like the whole room had gone damp.

"I'll get you out of the way, just like I got that big ape friend of yours. The one with the red hair and a moron's grin."

"Stop talking!"

"What? You didn't think I was telling the truth about that ship reaching Eleuthera, did you? Ha! The only place it went was the bottom of the sea."

The barrel was shaking and I waited for that voice to pipe up, the one I heard when I came across that Spanish sentry outside Panama. I gave it a moment, and then another. Nothing. All I could do was yell, "SHUT IT!"

"Oh, and by the way? My next order of business? I'll go to that cesspool of a city you live in and see if I can't find a whore with a nice deformity. To tell the truth, I'm getting sick of these native girls, and freak trollops always seemed to treat you right."

"DO NOT!"

"Oh yes. I'll enjoy watching you swing, Wand."

"NO! YOU'RE LYING!"

He leaned closer toward me. "Oh, but I will. You know what the real truth is? I never much liked you, Wand. You're a bit of a useless—"

The room was burnt powder and blood. Morgan reached for his gut wound, a pond of oozing blue-green pulp, and when he touched himself, it was the noise of a hand sinking in a bowl of noodles. He pulled his fingers away and a patch of jerkin came with it, and then his insides came spilling out onto his lap, the sound unspeakable. He tried to talk, but it came out garbled. He tried again and failed once more, and then he motioned me closer. I leaned in close, his hot breath on my ear. I wasn't scared, for he was beyond movement, and if I wanted anything, it was to hear the great Henry Morgan's last words.

"*Wand,*" he rasped. "*I told you I'd beat you one day.*"

His chin lowered, as if weighted. His chest was rising and falling slowly, though otherwise he was still. He looked up at me, eyes softened, and I swear he turned into the Henry Morgan I'd first met, the one who'd peered inside me and saw something good. My bones ached and I hated myself. His gaze was far away, now, and he no longer saw me. He took another deep breath and his face drained of fight and ambition and knowledge, and in that moment I could imagine how he must have looked as a boy. He took another breath, this one more shallow, and then he stirred slightly, propelled by a final impulse to stay alive. He stilled and sunk deeper into his chair, and for the first time ever I watched Henry Morgan surrender. His muscles relaxed, and his bones went loose with acceptance. He sunk deeper still. A weak smile crossed his face, and I could tell that his vision was filling with things that'd pleased him in life, like walks in woods and warm toast and the sound of lambs bleating. I could see everything he saw, for there was a tiny theatre, flaring in his eyes. He took another breath and his left hand quivered slightly. I'd never seen anyone look so defeated, though in this defeat there was a letting go. His eyes filled with tears of release. I reached out and put my hand on his, and found his skin was turning clammy. His last breath was a gurgle. The room filled with the smell of piss and shite. His eyes were still open, though the little play in them was done, the stage covered with ash-coloured curtains.

All was silent. No insects or birds or wind, just quiet. I pocketed the jewel. I had to. Then, from somewhere far off, there came an icy howling, a wailing over what I just done.

THIRTY-ONE

THOSE WORDS. THOSE bloody last words.

I told you I'd beat you one day.

They hung in the room's fouled air. I closed my eyes and breathed steady and struggled to understand. How could he say that? *I* was the winner and not him. That certainty was a mountain, and it was all I could see. So I banished it. *You're nothing,* I told it. *You're a mirage, a delusion, a foothill at best,* until it started to fade from a deep slate to a light film.

Which I could see right through. My bones turned cold, but there it was, refusing to go away, that bastard called the truth. We'd been playing a game all along, Morgan and I, ever since he got back from London, only I'd been too thick to realize it. I was his endgame. I was his escape. He knew the trap he was in and the beast he'd become—*there's nothing for it but the grave, Wand*—and so he strung me along. He stole my livelihood, he murdered my friends, he showed me a fat sparkling reward—he did everything but put the gun in my hand. He was right. He *made* me kill him, and by doing so had trounced me. Worse, he'd done it where it mattered, in real life and not some pointless board game.

And then John Morris was there. Behind him stood a dozen shirtless natives, all with the same slack-jawed expression, like they couldn't believe what was before them. If Morris was shocked or surprised, he didn't show it. "Get him out of here," he said blankly.

I did nothing.

"*Wand*," Morris said a little louder. "Get him *out* of here."

When I still didn't move, he walked over to the hot and still-dripping corpse, the Indians parting to let him through. He took Morgan's hands and pulled Morgan out of the chair and he started to drag him across the floor. "Take his feet," he snapped, and we half carried and half dragged Morgan out of the house. At one point his fingers slipped from Morris's grip and Morgan's head struck the stoop with a thud. Morris rested, hands on his knees, suffering. We picked Morgan up again and dragged him toward the jungle edge.

"I'll get shovels," Morris said. He left me in a little clearing where the ground was soft and it'd be easy to bury a man. I watched as Morgan's squatters started packing up and leaving for the interior of the island. It was the right move. Sooner or later, someone would figure Sir Henry Morgan was dead and they'd be the most convenient to blame.

Morris appeared with two shovels, one a real one and one little, like the type you'd use for scuttling coal. I got the shite one and we went to it. We dug and we dug, though after a bit Morris got winded again and he gave me the good shovel. When I was about three feet down, we dragged Morgan over and dropped him in on his back, face up, eyes open, feet splayed, looking no more at peace dead than he did alive. Morris helped me heap earth back in the grave. We tamped it down and covered it with vines and dropped fronds and any other rubbish we could find on top so it looked like unbothered jungle floor.

We were both sweaty and bug-bit. I looked at John Morris and he peered at me, breathing hard. He was free now too.

The two of us clambered back down the mountain, half hiking and half sliding to the roadway below. We walked along till we came to the wagon. Morris clicked his teeth and we went back to Port Royal saying nothing. Near the end of the ride I asked what I had to ask.

"You gonna tell?"

It took him seconds to answer. "Not unless you make me."

I got out, and looked at him. Though he was a cruel man, I don't believe I once caught him uttering a lie, and that made him a rare thing. I held out my hand and he looked at it like it was meat gone off. Without a word, he sped off. I knew it'd be the last time I ever saw him and I can't say I was sorry.

AFTER A SLEEPLESS night, I took the ruby into St. Jago and sold it to one of the gem dealers who'd opened up over the course of Morgan's raids. As I suspected, there were no questions asked and none answered: he wanted the jewel and where I got it mattered not a whit to a man such as him. When he made his first offer, I dead-eyed him and proudly said I was one of Henry Morgan's Brethren of the Coast, and if he wanted to live to see his next customer he better reconsider his price. He doubled it and I took it, though we both knew it was still on the low end.

Then came the hard part. I walked all over Port Royal, stepping over debris, skirting holes in the laneways, asking the "right" sort of people if they knew of anyone with a boat who could take a man off the island. This wasn't easy, for the "right" sort of people were no longer in the bars or squalid hotels or camping on Turtle Crawles. Instead, they were hiding in lonely little alleys messed with fallen wood. They were in the backrooms of stores that'd closed down, the locks damaged in the trembler. Or I'd spot them, standing in clumps, in corners of the unlit market. One such group told me they knew a man who knew a man who knew a bloody man, and *that* man, it seemed, conducted business out by the unused north docks. I headed there and, sure enough, came across some unkempt bastards who looked the part.

One of them had a missing ear and he was the one looked up. "What you want?"

"I'm a man looking for passage."

They all went stony, not a word among them. This way I knew.

"You won't find one 'ere."

"I heard different."

"You heard wrong."

"I've money." I pulled a few pounds out of my pocket and pledged there was more where that came from.

"There better be more than that," he said, and then he gave me some details—there was a ship and it left for Eleuthera the following night. "Best be there," he said.

"I will."

"Any other questions?"

"There is. You got room for one more besides me?"

"There's no discount rate."

"Don't want one."

"In that case, yeah. But you listen to me. I don't exist, yeah? For that matter, you don't exist and neither does your friend. You get me? And one other thing: payment in full the moment we shove off. This ain't one of Morgan's death ships."

ON LIME STREET, I dodged potholes and stray dogs and ruptured houses and Chinaman shills and jackfruit stalls and low-burning fires and dirty-faced children and men with blank dusty faces and grunting fierce-mouthed wigglies and old Creole women with handcarts and saws, who were cutting up fallen wood so they could sell it later for fuel. As I went farther along, the houses thinned, for the north end of the island was low and often moist with dank salty water. The house had lace curtains and a picture of Jesus in the window. It'd been mostly untouched by the trembler—the stoop sagged a bit, and there was a single pane of broken glass in one of the upstairs windows—and I knew the women who ran the home figured it was God's protection that'd shielded them. Next to the door was a plaque, and though the written word was a mystery I knew it was announcing the place as a Home for Fallen Women.

I climbed the steps and knocked on the door. A nun answered. She had dark dug-in lines spanning from her eyes and mouth. It's what the Jamaican sun did to white English faces—it scarred them, surely as any dagger.

"May I help you?" she asked.

"Yes," I said in my most polite voice. "I believe a friend of mine is staying here. May I speak with her?"

"What is her name, young man?"

"It's Tessie, sister."

"No one by that name lives here," she said, and closed the door.

I stood for a moment, thinking how stupid I was. Of course Tessie wasn't her real name. I knocked again. The sister opened the door a second time.

"I'm sorry, sister. But I might have her name wrong."

"You're her friend and you don't know her name?"

She had me there. All I could do was motion toward my mouth and say, "She has a, mmmm, that is to say, she *had* a bit of a..."

"It's Theresa you're looking for."

Theresa.

"Is she here?"

The sister eyed me impatiently. I swore I could hear her black pointy boots tapping the stoop boards.

"We don't allow gentlemen callers."

I just looked at her, thinking there was only one thing made the world do your bidding, so I reached into my pocket and pulled out a few notes and held them out. She looked at my outstretched hand but didn't take the money.

"What is your name, young man?"

"Benjamin Wand."

"Let me tell you something, Mr. Wand. Here I have shelter, nourishment, and God's love. I want for nothing else. Please put your money away."

I felt ashamed, like I'd offered her a fistful of ox droppings. Maybe she saw my face redden, or maybe she detected a sadness in the slump of my shoulders. Either way, she softened. "Wait here. I shall ask Theresa to come down."

A second later, Tessie came to the door. She stepped onto the stoop. She was wearing a plain grey cotton dress. She was plumper and her eyes were brighter and it occurred to me they were treating her right.

"Benny," she said. "What's happened to you? You're all shaky and thin, like. Course, who am I to talk? How do you like my new frock? Lovely, isn't it? Bloody potato sack with arms. It seems I'm a fallen woman, now."

"It happens to the best of us."

"See, that's what I always liked about you, Benny Wand. Quick with a consoling word, you is."

I took a deep breath. "I'm leaving for Eleuthera tomorrow."

"So you've come for a goodbye, then? I'm afraid I'm out to pasture..."

"No. I want you to come. You can have that new life."

Her eyes widened. She wiped the underside of her nose. It was like she couldn't understand what I was asking, so I pulled out a wad of money from my pocket and showed her. "I soaked a rich bastard in St. Jago. This dosh is my ticket out of here and it could be yours too. Just meet me at the docks on the northwest corner of the island. Tomorrow at midnight."

She still didn't speak, unless a quivering lip is talking. She looked down and she looked up and that's when she said it.

"I don't love you, Benny Wand."

"I know."

"It isn't you. It's the way I am. No one ever showed me how."

"I won't blame you for it, if that's your worry."

She just stood there looking at me, like I was someone she'd never seen before. Then she sighed and tilted herself forward, her forehead thudding against my chest. It was funny, that. I'd been punched there and clubbed there and one frightful East Ender with an ugly imagination once smashed me there with a hot iron. Yet none of it made as much impact as Tessie's little head tap.

Yeah, she was saying.

I'll come.

THAT NIGHT, WITH everything taken care of, and sleep out of the question, I finally had time to puzzle over why Morgan had done it. If he'd wanted to die, why not just do it by his own hand? If anyone had the nerve, it was a man such as him. I struggled with the answer. This time, it wasn't a matter of having to see around an obstacle. This time, there was nothing there, my mind gone blank and dark and silent. It was a matter of creation and not imagination, and it finally came to me in the wee hours, not all at once but in little pieces that slowly, by sunrise, formed a whole.

From our first meeting, Morgan had reckoned me for what I was, a menace to no one but myself. Was probably one of those things the whole world saw and I myself was blind to. By tricking me into killing him, he proved that anyone can be turned into a killer. By goading me into doing away with him, he showed that anyone can know an animal's fury, if only for a few seconds, and it didn't matter if you were a London street urchin or the son of a Welsh army officer. By shooting Henry Morgan, I absolved him. I let him off the hook. I showed him how circumstance was to blame for his ruination and not *him* — this must've been a comfort during those last few breaths. He was a God-fearing man, in his own way, and damnation was on his mind. Far from killing Henry Morgan, I saved him. I *saved* the poor bastard, or leastways that's what I believed.

This calmed me, enough that I finally fell asleep. I woke at midday, roused by the heat of the room. My impulse was to find Rodge and Gerald and David Walsh and say goodbye. I didn't, though; I didn't want the whole world to know I was running out in case Morgan's body was found and people started to put together two and two. There's a big difference, mind you, between what you tell yourself and what's the truth, and in my case I was an Englishman whether I liked it or not, the emotion involved with parting not to my liking.

Instead, I spent that day doing what I always did. I ate beans on toast in a grubby alehouse (the only difference was my pockets were stuffed with money). After, I hunkered down with my chessboard, and opposed some tiresome grunt who played about as well as a tree stump. I can't say why, exactly, but I let him win, just so he'd have something to tell his mates. On the way out, I tossed my board in a trash bin and vowed I was done with it.

After that, it was a matter of putting my few things in a bag and then thinking *sod it, I'll go with nothing, just the way I came,* the one exception being my weapon — with the money I was carrying, was a good chance it'd come in handy. Then there was nothing but the wait. I sat on my squeaking lousy mustard-scent bed, chin in hand, thinking about the things Morgan told me about his childhood — his father tossing him off the Welsh shoreline and losing him in forests and caning him for being less than polite at a party. All of it must've spawned a bleakness deep inside him, and though Morgan was a man who could beat the Spanish army and overcome the King of England, the one thing he couldn't defeat was his own swelling rot. In that way, he was just like everyone else: what's inside us is inside us, good or bad, and there's sod all you can do about it.

I decided to get out. The next thing I knew, I was standing on the beach at Turtle Crawles, breathing cool salty air, wondering. The place was deserted save for a few turtles and some native boys, who with the falling light were coming down from the coconut trees at the top of the beach. From the town proper came the sound of hammering and sawing, the repairs now fiercely under way. As usual, there were birds cawing and the sound of waves licking the beach.

The sun began to dip, changing from bright white to marigold to pale orange to a burst of fiery red. It ended too quickly — it always did — and I was left thinking about the first time I ever saw the sun fall over Caribbean waters. I was standing in more or less the same spot, dressed in threadbare slops, an exiled prisoner guarding his eyes against the brilliance of it all. Mostly, I remembered how much that first sunset hurt me. It hurt because my head was already pounding from drink. It hurt because it was so beautiful, and there's something about beauty causes a man to dwell upon large matters, like the things he hopes to do and the things he misses most and the things that make him *him*. But mostly, it hurt because it was a new day, and I was in a new land, and I was surrounded by new people, and I couldn't even guess at the things that would happen.

Epilogue

B ENJAMIN WAND DEPARTED the island of Jamaica on
August 4, 1688. His boat arrived unscathed at the
island of Eleuthera, in what later became known as the
Commonwealth of the Bahamas. Land registrar entries
show that, shortly after his arrival, Wand purchased a small
sugar plantation on the northern tip of the island. Records
also show he married a woman named Theresa McDonald,
with whom he'd reportedly travelled.

On June 7, 1692, a massive earthquake severed Port Royal
from the rest of the island of Jamaica, causing it to sink
into the ocean. The entire population of Port Royal, which
was still occasionally referred to as "the Wickedest City on
Earth," perished.

In 1698, following the success of several biographies chron-
icling the golden age of buccaneering in the West Indies,
Benjamin Wand lent his name to an autobiography entitled
A First-Hand Account of the Treacheries Committed by Sir Henry

Morgan in Villahermosa, Portobello and Panama. It was published by a small Nassau-based company called Broomfield and Sons; one of the few surviving copies, available for viewing in the archives of the British Library, was an invaluable aid in the writing of *The Man Who Saved Henry Morgan*.

Benjamin Wand died on February 6, 1730, somewhere around his seventy-fourth year. He left behind three daughters, seven grandchildren, two great-grandchildren, and a plantation that remained operational until the mid-1960s, when it was finally replaced by vacation properties.

Sir Henry Morgan died on August 2, 1688, at the age of fifty-three. He is still remembered as the great liberator of the New World, as well as a perpetrator of unconscionable acts during his campaigns in the Caribbean.

Owing to its suitability to the Internet, chess is now the most-played game on earth.

ROBERT HOUGH'S previous novels have been nominated for numerous awards, including the Commonwealth Writers' Prize, the International IMPAC Dublin Literary Award, the Trillium Book Award, and the Rogers Writers' Trust Fiction Prize. His most recent novel, *Dr. Brinkley's Tower*, was longlisted for the Scotiabank Giller Prize and was a finalist for the Governor General's Literary Award. He lives in Toronto with his wife and two daughters. Chess-wise, Hough is what is dismissively known as a "patzer." For more information, please visit www.roberthough.ca or @Robert_W_Hough.